MARKMAKER

MARKMAKER

MARY JESSICA WOODS

CHRISM
PRESS

This is a work of fiction. All characters and events portrayed in this novel are either fictitious or used fictitiously.

MARKMAKER

Chrism Press, a division of WhiteFire Publishing
13607 Bedford Rd NE
Cumberland, MD 21502

ISBNs:
978-1-941720-95-0 (paperback)
978-1-941720-96-7 (eBook)

To my fellow Troubleshooters:
Donan, Brandon, Andrew,
Maggie, and Anthony.
Honor with you, Watchmen.
~ MJW

Plant me a trallak tree, maker of dyes,
Harvest its black bark curling.
Mix me an ink that will sink in the skin,
All for my little soldier.
Kesh alah ke'la, kesh alah ke'la,
Ink for my little soldier.

Carve me a burrik tooth, maker of pens,
Grind out its gray edge gleaming.
Chisel a path for the ink to flow,
All for my little soldier.
Kesh alah ke'la, kesh alah ke'la,
Pens for my little soldier.

Paint me an honor-sign, maker of marks,
Seal its sigils shining,
Trace out a truth in violet and gold,
All for my little soldier.
Kesh alah ke'la, kesh alah ke'la,
Marks for my little soldier.

– Old Noxxiin Lullaby

CHAPTER ONE

My name is Mariikel. I am a son of Clan Serix. I am a markmaker, and a traitor to markmakers.

The workday is ending at Kilmaya's studio. Our final client, an apprentice deepcraft warrior, lies facedown on the cushioned bench as I trace the last of the verity lines on the back of his neck. Then I set aside my pen and brush the whole tattoo with sealing-glaze. The scarlet sigils, edged with silver, gleam against my client's jet-black skin. I am careful not to let my brush touch the deepcraft implant, the metallic disk set into his spine, just at the base of his neck. It is not activated, of course, but one can never be too cautious.

"This is a mark of truth. May you never mar or dishonor it." I replace the brush in the bottle and remove my artist's gloves.

The young man sits up, stiff from nearly an hour of lying on the bench. He blinks, his four eyes narrowing as he stretches. Then he stands and bows to me deeply, touching two fingers to his neck. "Thank you, markmaker. Honor with you."

I see him out into the front room, where Kilmaya, the head artist, stands conversing with an elderly but distinguished master deepcrafter—my client's witness. I hear the clack of polished wood as the man drops several coins into my teacher's hand. The two of them turn to us as we enter.

"Finished, Mariikel?" Kilmaya's mouth quirks in a smile. "You took your time."

"Only the time I needed. I would not want to rush a new *van'shor*'s mark."

"He is not a van'shor until tomorrow," the old deepcrafter says in a stern tone. But his eyes glint with pride as he regards his apprentice. "Here, Khalon. Put this on."

He hands a dark bundle to the younger man: a hooded cloak. Khalon slips it on, raising the hood to cover the new tattoo on the back of his neck. He may not show his van'shor symbols until the initiation ceremony tomorrow—

the bond-kindling—when I will finish his marks in the arena and he will use his deepcraft in public for the first time, with the whole ship watching.

Is he as nervous about it as I am? He does not appear anxious now—but then, Van'shorii never do. With the kind of power they wield, they have little to fear.

Kilmaya opens the door for our clients and bids them farewell. They step out into the corridor, and the door hums closed, leaving me and my teacher alone in the studio. I return to the back room and busy myself at the worktable. One by one I gather the tattooing pens—the broad-blade tip that fills swaths of color, the javelin tip for writing the sigils, and the tiny verity tip for the lines that guard against forgery. I pull the stained tips off their handles and drop them into a bowl of cleansing solution. Ink plumes up through the clear liquid—like smoke, or blood.

Kilmaya joins me in the workroom, wiping down the cushioned bench and capping the ink bottles on the table. Her upper eyes are slightly narrowed with weariness, and she flexes her hands—her fingers ache sometimes, especially at the end of a long festival day like today. But she moves around the table with the brisk energy of a woman half her age.

"Thank you, Mariikel." Her lower eyes gleam as she glances at me. "I'm sorry I had you cleaning pens for us both all day. You're past that now."

Smiling a little, I pick one of the tips out of the water. "The apprentices have earned a day at the games. It was good you let them go. I don't mind cleaning pens." With my dry hand, I touch two fingers to the mastery-mark on my brow. "I am still learning from you, teacher."

She laughs. "For how much longer, I wonder." Shutting three of her eyes, she regards me shrewdly with only one.

Kilmaya's hands may no longer be perfectly supple, but her vision is still keen. Sometimes I fear that she might see into my mind as easily as she can read the intricate marks on my skin. What would it do to her to know that her best student has broken the markmakers' oath, to obey the guild and to paint no falsehood in the flesh?

I dry the pen tips and slip them into the soft sheaths of my satchel.

"Taking your tools home again?" she asks.

I merely blink in affirmation as I add a bottle of sealing-glaze to my bag. "I need to practice for tomorrow."

"You're never satisfied, are you? Why don't you go to the arena? There are still a few events this evening. Go enjoy yourself."

I fasten the buckles of my satchel. "I'll be seeing enough of the arena tomorrow. I think I'll go home."

She smiles, then shakes her head. She pulls off her long markmaking gloves, lays them on the table, and flexes her slim black hands, wincing.

"*Hakk*, perhaps it's just as well. I've heard the sparring matches are decidedly less impressive this year—what with all our best warriors down on the planets. I suppose they're better off fighting with the half-sights instead of each other." After a pause, she adds, "How is your cousin, by the way? Isn't he a *hvoss'ka* now? Have you heard from him?"

I scoff quietly and sling the satchel over my shoulder. "You should ask my aunt. Askko doesn't write to me."

I walk out of the workroom towards the door. Kilmaya follows me, untying her ink-stained apron from her slender frame. "Don't stay up all night practicing. I'll need you here in the morning with fresh eyes and rested hands."

"I know." I tap the entry pad, and the door slides open. "I don't need much rest."

"You are single-minded." I wonder if she senses my preoccupation, my eagerness to leave.

"Honor with you, teacher."

"And with you, Mariikel." She hangs her apron on the wall, and I step out of the studio into Rixarii Street.

It is past the eighth hour, and the corridor lights have dimmed to an evening orange. The street of the markmakers, however, is still bustling. Many studios have their doors open, and clients and artists file in and out. Under the hallway's arching crossbeams, hung with Van'shorvanii banners, little knots of people gather around the athletes as they show off the new victory tattoos they earned at the games. Children dart past me, shouting, dressed in masks decorated with tufts of fur and feather. The air is heavy with the tang of fresh sealing-glaze and the muted sweet aroma of *kiili* oil. Yet neither the scents nor the happy commotion excite me. Where I am going tonight, there are no celebrations.

Weaving through the crowd, I leave the Serix studios behind and begin passing the workshops that belong to Clan Trev'ban. There are some athletes here, but not many. No self-respecting warrior goes to a Trev'ban studio if he can afford to get his marks from Clan Serix. We have trained the best artists and governed the guild for generations. Trev'ban artists serve the lower-ranking clans—only a handful of their markmakers are qualified to give tattoos for major festivals like Van'shorvanii.

The clients who still linger in the hallway have come here for more ordinary marks. Ahead of me, a married couple steps out of a Trev'ban studio; the mother carries a sleeping infant. Both parents are bright-eyed, and every now and again they look down to admire the new clan-mark on the baby's neck. The mother, too, wears a fresh tattoo on her upper arm. I read the sigils briefly as I slip past them. *Dakali-dek'ar*—the baby is her second child, a daughter.

At last I make my way to the end of Rixarii Street. Just before the sector gate, the corridor opens into a plaza surrounding a pillared, circular build-ing—the clan's ancestor shrine. The Serix symbol, painted in striking black against a silver background, adorns the shrine's doorway: a swooping crescent, like a dagger or a *burrik* tooth, embellished with intertwined sigils that mean "Truth in the Flesh."

I pause in front of the shrine, then reach up and touch the matching clan-mark on my neck. It is an old habit. I used to stop here often to visit my par-ents' ashes and to pray to my forebears. Now, though, the gesture is an empty ritual. I have failed my clan and betrayed my heritage of truth-painting. But no one knows that except me—and my ancestors.

I leave the shrine and pass through the Serix sector gate, coming out into a transport hub. The whirr and clank of the elevators echoes off the low ceiling, piercing the din of the festival throng. I duck my way through the crowd, past the street musicians playing a blood-tingling tune on their *raith'aal* pipes, past the pair of young laborers engaged in a playful brawl. A ragged ring of specta-tors surrounds the fighters, cheering and heckling them by turns.

Eventually I slip past the crush and into one of the descending elevators. As I enter, my eyes are drawn to the large gold-and-scarlet symbol painted on the back wall of the chamber: *Akkano'dath*, the name of our home, the great flagship of the Noxxiin Fleet. The sigil, like the ship, is ancient. Serix archi-vists still debate whether to translate the name as *akkano dath*—"ancestors' will"—or *akkano kodath*—"ancestors' peril." I suspect both interpretations might be equally appropriate.

As the elevator moves down through the levels of the ship, more people file in, pushing me towards the back. I find myself standing next to an older man, a mechanic from Clan Tizzan. The mastery-mark on his forehead tells me that he gained his profession many years ago, but he bears few tattoos of achievement; his arms are nearly bare. He glances at me once, and seeing my face, inclines his head in a submissive gesture.

"Markmaker." He tries to move deferentially aside, even though there is little room to do so.

My palms tingle with a surge of shame. I wish I were wearing my disguise already, but I cannot put it on yet—not here.

At the next stop, a pair of pilots, still wearing their battle helmets, saunter into the chamber. I am unsurprised to see the mark of the Ascendance printed on their helmets, the violet double-trident embellished with the sigils of the faction motto: *Noxxiin Aurorii Chi'ar*, Children of the Stars Rising. Kilmaya and I have had droves of clients asking to receive the tattoo of the ruling party, especially in the past year and a half, since the beginning of the war against the half-sights.

A rowdy group of warriors-in-training crowds into the elevator. "*Kol-dawra*'s on me tonight if Tobiax loses the match!" one declares.

"Tobiax won't even draw blood," someone scoffs. "Why don't you buy us drinks now and get it over with?"

Laughter ensues. Some of the young men are bare-chested, showing off their Ascendance marks, and some have fresh tattoos of adoption into Clan Trechik. It is so easy now to join a warrior clan. Kilmaya dislikes it; it is reckless, she says, for a clan to accept so many non-blood members all at once. But war calls, and battle-glory, and the chance to stand on the surface of a real planet, to breathe air that has not been recycled through the ship's filters for hundreds of years. I admit the attraction. It will be a long time before anyone who is not a soldier will have a chance to see a planet's surface.

The elevator has reached the arena level. The crowd files out—the warriors-in-training harassing the pilots for battle stories, the pilots pretending to ignore them but clearly enjoying themselves. By the time the doors close, the Tizzan mechanic and I are the only people left in the chamber. He glances at me again, and this time I avoid his gaze. Is he surprised that I have not followed the crowd?

I tell myself there is no way this old mechanic could guess where I am going. If I can keep my secret from my own family, I am safe from a stranger.

At last, the elevator stops at the atrium level, and I step out, glad to be alone.

A wash of moist air hits my face; I breathe in the scent of leaves and loam. Overhead, the long oval ceiling of the atrium hangs above the thickly forested walkways of the public garden. The droning of insects among the dim trees does not quite drown out the hum of the hidden vents, pumping the atrium's oxygen-rich air to other parts of the ship.

I pause and peer past the broad leaves of the stately *karu* trees, letting my gaze linger on the murals that adorn the ceiling—huge, faded paintings of landscapes and battle scenes bordered by sigils so ancient and complex that their meaning has been forgotten. When I was a child, I used to spend hours trying to decipher those beautiful, archaic marks. Serix artists painted them—my ancestors.

Lowering my eyes, I hurry through the gardens, glancing about to make sure I am not being followed. Fortunately, the walkways are deserted except for two or three wild *ech'taanin*—pale-furred, sinuous little creatures that dart back into the brush at the sight of me. But I encounter no fellow Noxxiin. Everyone is at the games tonight.

I slip into a grove of black-barked *trallak* trees, where the dark, triple-lobed leaves hang thick enough to hide me. I sit down in the soft loam and unstrap my sandals, then rummage in my satchel and take out a long-sleeved, hooded tunic—the kind that a laborer might wear while working in the ship's chilly maintenance shafts—and quickly change into it. Then I reach into my bag again for the most important part of my disguise.

My false skin is made from the same synthetic fabric as the markmaking gloves that I use in the studio—but the material serves equally well as a disguise. One by one, I pull on the mask, the elbow-length gloves, the long stockings that reach past my hocks and knees. The elastic material conforms perfectly to my face, hands, and bare feet. Besides my tattoos, I have to hide my pale gray skin; it is an uncommon color, too easy to identify. My false skin is an ordinary dull black adorned with a handful of unremarkable sigils. The idle passerby would take me for a low-ranking mechanic, like the man who stood next to me in the elevator.

My disguise complete, I put on my sandals, step out of the trees, and hurry over to the raised fountain in the center of the garden. The sound of rushing water fills the air; mist flecks my eyelids. As I approach a maintenance door in the side of the fountain, I activate the mark-scanner on the wall, which is meant to keep out everyone except authorized workers. But it is not designed to detect forgeries as good as mine. The scanner blinks its approval, and the door unlocks. I glance over my shoulder one last time, then slip inside.

The maintenance shaft is dim, lit only by a faint light-border along the wall. Somewhere down here there is a transport hub with elevators and vehicles that the workers use to haul supplies throughout the ship. But I am too likely to meet other laborers if I ride the elevators. So I take the long way. I walk.

The tunnels become narrower and more dingy. Gaps in the walls expose vents and pipes. I can hear the hiss of air and water and the thrum of gravity generators. The air grows dank and cold. When the light-border on the wall eventually gives out, I pull a lamp from my bag and continue.

Even before I begin to hear the Underbelly, I can smell it. A reek of decay mixed with the tang of rusting metal thickens the air around me. I round a final corner and stand in front of a dilapidated doorway that bears a crude depiction of a Noxxiin face: the four eyes black and staring, the mouth agape in a snarl, the skin stark white and devoid of marks. The face of the Deep Sleep—a fitting symbol to mark the barrier between the upper world and the realm of the exiles.

I shiver.

I have sometimes wondered why this door is not guarded or kept locked. Perhaps it is because, in truth, no physical barrier is needed. The inhabitants of the Underbelly know that escape is impossible—not because they cannot reach the upper levels, but because they would be helpless there. Everyone knows to shun a man with an exile-mark. No family would invite him into their house. No merchant would sell him food. No pilot would ferry him to another ship. He would be spat on, driven away like a sick animal. No one dares to help an outcast escape—for that, in itself, is a crime punishable by exile.

If the markmakers' guild knew what I have been doing here, I would be exiled fifty times over. But like a disease, this place has infected my brain and my bones. I cannot stop myself from coming.

I breathe deeply and lay my palm against the grimy painting, covering the savage face and the dead black eyes. I push through the creaking doorway and pass into the Underbelly.

I find myself on a long, dimly lit walkway above a vast network of piping. The choking stench of sewage fills my nostrils—all the waste of the ship's million or so inhabitants ends up here, eventually. The thought that all the water I drink also comes from this place, albeit after being purified, is enough to make me gag.

Holding my breath, I hurry forward until I reach an open hatch in the floor. A ladder descends from the hatch into the stinking darkness, and I step down onto the rungs. Whenever I make this journey, I always feel as if I am climbing down into Axdraa'dah, the pit of the Deep Sleep. I would pray to my ancestors for courage, but I do not think they would aid me. Not in this.

As I descend through the levels of the Underbelly, a vast network of platforms, walkways, and support beams opens around me. A hot wind from a vent tugs at my clothes; the roar of machinery becomes palpable. On the platforms below, in the uncertain red light of the forges and recycling vats, I catch glimpses of the exiles bent over their workstations. The shouting of a taskmaster echoes between the pillars.

All the clans depend upon the work that takes place here, in the bowels of the ship: the cleansing of our air and water, the recycling of scrap and refuse to conserve precious raw materials. The labor is filthy, backbreaking, and crucial for our survival, yet most of the people who work here do not even have the dignity of a clan name.

I continue to descend through the thrumming, windy space. I am halfway down another ladder when I hear someone below me clambering up the rungs. Before I can move, the laborer swings to the opposite side of the ladder and continues climbing. When he reaches my level, he glances at me, taking in my face, my hood, and my satchel. Then he pauses for an instant and inclines his head.

"*Rethurax.*"

He scrambles up the rungs and disappears.

Rethurax. Skin-changer. In the upper world, that word is a label of dishonor. It is strange to hear it spoken in a tone of gratitude. Still, I hate the name. I am not a mercenary. I do not counterfeit tattoos, and I never ask any payment for the marks I give to the exiles.

At long last, the ladders end. I set foot on the true floor of the Underbelly.

The roar of the machinery above has faded to a rumble at the edge of hearing. The air is cold, the floor slick with condensation under my feet. In the shadows between the support beams, scrap metal and tattered sheets mark off partitions—the houses of the unclanned.

Cries echo between the miserable shacks: an infant screaming, women quarrelling. A laborer shuffles through the alley, clutching his day's rations. At the base of a pillar nearby, a sick man sprawls, motionless. Two or three children—unmarked children, without so much as a clan tattoo—shriek and scramble through the squalor, chasing a mangy dog. I step aside to let them pass.

As I make my way through the maze of shacks, I reach a thick support pillar, larger than the others around it. In the nook of this buttress, I take off my satchel. My lamp I place on a ledge to illuminate my workspace. My pens and inks I set out on the floor. Then I sit, my legs crossed, my hood drawn up, and I wait.

After only a few minutes, two figures approach me. One seems to hang back, while the other urges her on. When they finally step into the circle of my light, I see they are both women. The older one wears the tattoo of a healer on her brow and a pale, faded exile-mark on her neck, which contains the sigils for poison and murder.

Mazatii. I recognize her, and trust her. She has brought people to me before.

The younger woman carries a fretting child in her arms—a tiny infant, only days old. She holds it awkwardly, blinking in the lamplight, her lips pulled back in a grimace. On her neck, the stark, white tendrils of the exile-mark display the sigil of a smuggler.

I wonder what she did. Nothing, perhaps. It is not unknown, especially since the Ascendance took power, for whole families to be outcast for the crime of a single member. This woman is younger than I am. I cannot imagine that she has committed any crime worthy of exile.

The old healer bows her head. "Honor with you, markmaker." She tugs her companion forward another step. "We ask for your service."

I look up at the younger woman. The dirt that clings to her face cannot hide the four sunken hollows of her eyes. She looks ill, exhausted. "I don't need anything," she says. But even her voice lacks strength. She does not try to free herself from Mazatii's grip.

"What is your name?" I pick up a pen and affix the javelin tip. I suspect what the requested mark will be.

"Lakkia," she whispers. In her rigid arms, the infant squirms and whimpers.

"How can I serve you, Lakkia?"

She does not respond. Squeezing her arm, Mazatii rasps, "She needs a clan-mark for her child."

"Are you her witness?"

"Yes. I helped to deliver him. By the blood of my ancestors, I swear he is truly her child."

"Very good. Please, sit." With the same formality that I would use towards a great athlete or a wealthy councilor, I gesture for them to sit on the grimy floor. Mazatii crouches down, and the young mother follows, still glassy-eyed and dazed. The baby—a tiny, maroon-skinned thing, wrapped in a dirty rag—winces at the light and wails.

I reach into my satchel and pull out a vial of sleeping-powder. "Give him this."

Lakkia does not seem to understand. "Here," says the healer. She takes the baby from the mother's arms, then accepts the powder and begins feeding it to him on her finger. The child sucks at it greedily. Lakkia stares at her hands.

"What is his name?" I ask.

For a moment, Lakkia does not answer. Then, in a barely audible mutter: "He doesn't have one."

"No?" I pause and send an inquiring glance towards Mazatii. She scowls, her upper eyes narrowing, but says nothing.

With a twinge in my belly, I begin to understand. "Well, no matter. I only need to know the clan name." I hesitate. "What is his father's clan?"

Lakkia's face contorts. She stares past me and does not speak.

"Markmaker," Mazatii breaks in. In her lap, the baby is already quieting. "She does not know."

It is the answer I suspected. I have heard it often since starting my work here. As I gaze at Lakkia's clenched jaw and trembling eyelids, I wonder whether she chose to give her body away—for an extra scrap of food, or a mouthful of clean water—or whether she was forced. My palms grow hot, and my fingers close tightly around my pen.

"I understand." I do not meet Lakkia's gaze, do not try to comfort her. A respectable markmaker would turn these women away. How can an artist inscribe the truth if the truth is unknowable?

But I am not a respectable markmaker.

"I will give him your clan-mark, then." In the lamplight, I glance at Lakkia's neck. Under the four swirling arms of the exile-mark, I can still read the clan tattoo. "You are Penthar."

Lakkia shudders. Something changes in her face—some spark of aware-

MARKMAKER

ness flaring up in her gaunt, rigid body. I have seen that expression before, the mingled anguish and astonishment. The exiles often stare at me that way when I address them by their clan. They are supposed to be clanless now; their ancestors will not help them or speak for them when they face the trials after death, the great battle before the Long Dream. They will meet the Deep Sleep alone. I am committing a crime every time I speak the exiles' ancestral names. Yet I speak their names regardless because it kindles light in their eyes.

I turn towards the child. My pen is ready, and I uncap my bottle of green ink. "Is he asleep?"

"Almost," Mazatii replies.

"Unwrap him for me."

The old woman pulls the rag away from the baby's neck. The infant stirs and moans, but his four lids are heavy now. The healer holds the thin, gangly body on her lap as I lean over and wipe the grime from the child's neck with a cloth. By the time I have finished, the baby is soundly asleep. Then, as I dip my pen into the ink, Lakkia stirs.

"I want to hold him," she whispers.

Without a word, Mazatii hands the sleeping child into the mother's arms. Then the older woman slumps as if relieved, her eyes closed, her thin shoulders quivering.

I position the baby's head so that the right side of his neck is exposed and well-lit. "Don't move him," I tell Lakkia.

She says nothing, but sits still and breathless, as if the smallest twitch of her body would shatter this moment.

I begin.

In the studio, on a busy day, Kilmaya usually makes me use a stencil when giving an infant its first tattoo. There are no special sigils to add to the clan symbol, and the pre-made pattern makes the process faster. But I have always resented using stencils. I do not need them; my memory is clear and my hand steady. Few things make me happier than to paint unhindered, on the fragile skin of a child, his or her first tattoo. Now, with each stroke of my pen, I murmur the lawful words of marking—the words I always speak over a newborn, whether in Kilmaya's studio or here, in the pit of the Underbelly.

"Son of Lakkia Penthar. You are born weak in body, feeble in mind, and bare of marks. By this ink, I commit you to your ancestors."

I complete the outline of the sigil and turn to replenish my ink. As I fill the pen, I can hear Lakkia's breath hissing through her teeth. Again I touch the tip to the baby's skin.

"Let this mark be for your pondering and striving. Let it guide your thinking and your walking. Let it be your pride when you are strong, and your chiding when you waver. Let it be your memory that you will never merit the gift of your blood and your breath. You owe your life to your forebears and to Ka the All-Watcher. By this mark, I bind you to this debt."

Lakkia trembles. Her movement disturbs my hand, but I pull away before it mars my final stroke. Rather than scold her, I take my time to change pens and prepare the verity tip. Only once do I glance up. Her eyes are squeezed shut, and grief spasms through her thin face. But she holds the child closer now, like a part of her own body—as if he had not been truly alive until this moment.

No doubt it is wrong of me to give her this false taste of hope. But it is all I can give.

When Lakkia has calmed a little, I add the verity lines between the swirling, vine-like sigils. Then, finally, I brush the whole tattoo with sealing-glaze. "This is a mark of truth. May you never mar or dishonor it."

I lift the brush. The new tattoo glows a vivid emerald on the baby's dark red skin. Lakkia reaches towards it as if she cannot believe it is real. Gently I pull her hand away.

"Leave it alone for a few hours." I wrap a soft bandage around the child's neck so that he will not touch the fresh mark when he wakes. Then I pick up my pen again. "It's your turn."

"My turn?" Lakkia's eyes widen, and her face freezes in terror.

"He is your son." Mazatii speaks sharply. "You must have a mark, too."

Lakkia shrinks away. "I don't want it. I don't want it." A keening cry bursts from her throat, and she bends over, weeping. The healer lays a hand on her shoulder.

I watch with pain swelling in my chest. Softly I say, "I'm not going to give you a shame-mark."

Lifting her head, the young woman chokes back her sobs. Her eyes glitter, large and dark with pain, and her mouth twists in a snarl. Bitterly, she cries, "Don't you want to paint the truth?"

The healer grips her shoulder. "*Kesh*, Lakkia."

Lakkia ignores her. "What are you doing here?" Her gaze is fixed on mine with a burning intensity. "What do you get out of this?"

In silence I regard her while ink drips slowly from my pen. It is not the first time an incredulous outcast has asked me such a question. But how can I answer? How can I explain to this woman what I hardly understand myself?

"Lakkia," the healer urges. "Let him do this. Who else will?"

The young woman glares at Mazatii, then at me. She bows her head, staring down at the sleeping infant in her lap. Then, without saying a word, she extends her left arm towards me.

She shivers a little as I pull back the sleeve, exposing her shoulder. Her upper arm is bare of tattoos. "Is this your firstborn?"

Her face contorts again. "Yes."

I guessed as much, but I had to ask. If she had borne any other children in the Underbelly, she would not have received marks for them. As I clean her dark skin with my cloth, grief and anger seize my throat.

My craft is so inadequate. I cannot change the past; I can only record it.

"Lakkia Penthar." I place my pen on the warm, smooth skin of her shoulder. "You have honored your ancestors by bringing this son into the world. Let this mark be your pride when you are near him, your memory when you are apart, and your consolation if he should die in honor." With a few slow, curving strokes, I draw the two intertwined symbols. *Dako-chi'ar*—firstborn son. "By this mark, I bind you to this child."

Lakkia weeps silently. I seal the tattoo, wrap a bandage around it, and pull her sleeve down to cover it. She clutches her own shoulder, as if at a wound. Then, after a moment, she gathers her baby into her arms and hugs him fiercely. The infant wakes with a muffled cry.

"Ancestors bless you, markmaker." Mazatii's voice cracks as she stands up and bows her head. "Thank you."

Lakkia rises with the older woman. Before she steps out of the lamplight, she turns an awestruck gaze on me. "You're not safe. You're in great danger, coming here."

I meet her eyes. The baby wails again in her arms. "Don't worry about me. Go home and name your child."

CHAPTER TWO

The evening passes. In twos and threes, the exiles come out of the darkness, and I give out marks until my fingers are stiff and my back aches. But I do not mind the discomfort. Instead I focus on the tattoos: a memory-mark for an old man whose son died falling from a ladder; honor-marks for a group of laborers who saved the life of an injured comrade; marriage-marks for a couple who have already had three children together but have never been united by law.

Many of the outcasts walk away weeping. Others cannot stop touching my hands and feet in their gratitude. The only reason I can keep my own composure is because they expect me, as a markmaker, to be impartial and detached. And it is just as well. If I allowed myself to share in the sorrow of these clanless people, I would exhaust myself.

At last my eyes grow strained and my stomach taut with hunger. It is time to leave. My aunt and uncle are accustomed to my irregular hours—even in my apprentice days, I frequently stayed late at Kilmaya's studio, practicing. But if I were to be out all night, they would probably send someone to look for me.

The mere thought of their concern fills me with guilt. If they knew where I go to practice my craft now, would they still acknowledge me as their adopted son?

Briefly I wipe down my pen tips and cap my inks. I settle my satchel over my shoulder and stand up with a grimace. Just as I am about to take down my lamp from the ledge, a lone figure stalks out of the shadows.

"Rethurax. Don't go yet."

I glance at his clan-mark. My breath hitches, and I clutch at the ledge.

The angular violet mark of Clan Tarriks is strangled by the ugly, swirling tendrils of exile. The mark that haunts both my waking thoughts and my nightmares.

The mark that I gave to Talorak.

I blink and collect myself. The tattoo is not the same, only similar. This man is not Talorak. He is a Tarriks soldier, certainly, but he is much younger than the old warrior I knew.

"I'm sorry." Turning away to hide my agitation, I take my lamp down from the ledge. "I must go. You are welcome to find me another day, if you come a little earlier."

"What I want you to do cannot be done in the open." His upper eyes narrow, and he clenches his hands. His clothes are relatively intact, not yet reduced to rags. I can tell—both from the health of his muscular body and the way that he looks me in the eye, without shame—that he has not been exiled long.

"What do you mean?"

The young outcast shoots a glance into the darkness, then draws nearer to me. "I've heard you can get people out of this filthy pit."

I inhale sharply. "No. Whoever told you that—"

"I've seen the marks you give. They're as good as real. You're no ordinary skin-changer."

"I'm not a skin-changer. I only paint the truth."

He laughs harshly. "What are you doing down here, then?"

I regard him in silence. The exiles call me skin-changer because it is the only word for an artist who works outside the law. But I have only ever given one tattoo that I considered false, and my blood still burns with shame at that memory. This outcast would not understand that. He only considers me a fellow criminal.

I bare my teeth, trying to look scornful. "You have no idea what you're asking for. It's too dangerous. And what would I get out of it?"

"You don't take payment," he retorts. "You never do."

I say nothing. The Tarriks exile glares at me, breathing heavily. When he shifts his stance, I find myself glancing down at his feet. The spurs protruding from his ankles are curved and sharp—far more deadly than my own short, blunted spurs. This man is a trained fighter from a renowned warrior clan; he could kill me with his bare hands and feet.

But the exile does not attack me. Instead he drops his eyes, and when he speaks, the words sound as if they have been wrenched from his body. "If you are asking for payment, rethurax—I have nothing."

"I don't need payment. It's you I'm thinking of. You don't want to do this."

"Yes." His tone is harsh, but I can see him trembling. "I do."

"You want to be mark-stripped?" My voice rises, cracking slightly. "You want to wear a lie for the rest of your life? Your ancestors—"

"My ancestors are dead. And if I stay here, I will die in disgrace and never see them. I will never enter the Long Dream. Rethurax—" He stares at me and takes a breath. "Markmaker. I've thought about this. I know what it means. But if I could only get out of this place—if I had a chance to live honorably—I could make up for the shame of a few false marks." He gives a short, bitter laugh. "Or at least I could try."

I should rebuke him for those words. I should tell him *no* and walk away. But I don't.

"I know it's dangerous," he resumes. "I'm not afraid. If they catch me before I get off the ship—so be it. But the world's not as small as it once was." His eyes glint. "The planets are within reach."

He says that word, *planets*, with the heartbreaking breathlessness of hope.

"I'll go where no one knows me," he says. "The marks will not matter. I'll even live among the half-sights, if I have to. They will not know the difference. Markmaker." His voice breaks. "Look around you. Do you *see* this place?"

"I've seen it." I turn away from him. My pulse hammers in my throat, and I am afraid—not of him, but of myself.

"I don't want to die like this. I want to live. Kin's heart—" Abruptly he reaches out and clutches my wrists. He sinks to his knees and presses his bowed head against my hands. "I beg you. Let me live."

I stand in his grip as if paralyzed. My eyes are drawn to his clan-mark again. And a voice speaks in the silence of my own mind.

If this were Talorak kneeling at your feet—would you refuse him?

I know the answer. But it terrifies me.

Roughly I pull my hands out of the warrior's grasp. Then I take my lamp and shine it close to his face. He winces at the sudden light but does not move. I study the tattoo on his neck. The sigils, nestled between the four sweeping arms of the exile-mark, tell me that he was cast out of Clan Tarriks barely a month ago on the charges of treason and unpardonable cowardice in battle.

"You have dishonored yourself. What makes you think you deserve a life on the planets?"

"It's a false charge," he replies. "A false mark."

"That is quite an accusation. Any good markmaker would contest a false charge." But I shake as I say it.

"My warband was raiding a half-sight station among the asteroids. We won easily—the half-sights weren't warriors. They barely had weapons between them for ten men. My *valk'taro*, my commander, told us to slaughter them anyway. Unarmed prisoners." He snarls. "A breach of the honor-code. I would not do it. And for this—for *this* I was branded a coward. I am already wearing a lie, markmaker."

I glare down at him, my teeth bared. But I feel like I am suffocating. "Why should I believe you?"

"I swear it." He presses two fingers against his clan-mark. "It's the truth."

For a moment I cannot say a word. His story is too much like Talorak's—
almost as if he were a younger version of that old warrior come to expose me
for the lie that I wrote on his skin.

Well. The soft voice echoes in my mind again. *Let this be your reparation.*

"It's…a slow process."

He stiffens. "You'll do it?"

"I have to think." I hardly know what I am saying. "I must study first."

He throws himself at my feet. I untangle myself and step away. "Not now.
I have to go."

"When will you come again?"

"Tomorrow—no." Tomorrow night I will be at the arena for the festival.
"Give me two days."

"Thank you… Thank you."

"Kesh. Go."

He stands up. His eyes fix on me with a strange, almost wild reverence.
"I'll be here." As if seized by sudden terror, he turns and darts back into the
shadows of the slum.

His footsteps fade. I exhale and turn off my lamp. In the darkness, I lean
against the pillar and place my hands over my eyes.

What have I done?

This is madness. Serving the exiles is bad enough, but their tattoos, if
illegal, are at least true. If I am caught, I will be banned from the studios and
most likely outcast from my clan. But to paint a false mark—a whole set of
false marks, to help a criminal escape his sentence—I could face execution for
that. Maybe even death by mark-stripping.

But the memory of Talorak and his unjust punishment torments me. I am
sick of doing no real good. I am sick of giving marks to children like Lakkia's,
knowing that despite everything I am risking, they will live and die here in
the filth of the Underbelly, and there will be no honor for them. If my marks
could change a man's fate—

In a daze, I stumble back through the labyrinth of pillars and shacks. I
reach the ladder and begin pulling myself up, hand over hand. As I climb, I
barely notice the hot and choking winds that buffet me, or the workers who
brush by me on the walkways. I am thinking. I am thinking what it will take
to create a new man out of nothing—nothing but ink and the skill of my
hands.

By the time I haul myself out of the Underbelly and make my way back
up the maintenance shafts, I have already begun crafting the Tarriks warrior's
new identity in my mind. Only then do I realize that I never asked for his
name.

I emerge at last from the maintenance door and step into the dark atrium.

Silence and the aroma of soil and sap envelop me—the gardens, at this late hour, are deserted. I duck into the trees, take off my disguise, and change back into my clean white tunic. Then I return to the fountain, sit on its edge, and rinse my gloves and mask from the dirt of the Underbelly. I wash my sandals, plunge my hands in the water and splash my face, scrubbing fiercely at the hollows of my eyes.

When I raise my head, still dripping, I watch the disturbed water settle until I can see the silvery image of my own face. Above me, reflected in the water, the ancient clan murals glow and flicker in the ripples.

Are my Serix ancestors, who made those paintings, watching me now from their place in the Long Dream? Where were they when I stood before Talorak with the order of exile in my hands and the Ascendance soldiers at my back, waiting with their blades and their hard, expectant eyes?

"What was I supposed to do?" I whisper it aloud. The water glistens darkly, lapping against the edge of the fountain. No one answers.

Let the ancestors judge which deed is worse; I have made my decision. For Talorak's sake, I will help this young exile.

I rise, strap on my sandals, and walk home.

CHAPTER THREE

I t is late when I return to the Serix sector, and the corridors are dim with the warm, orange glow of the night-lamps. Amber reflections gleam on the glossy leaves of the shrubs lining the walkway. The beauties of my home sector—the lush gardens, the decorated ceilings, the sigils of hospitality written over the door of each dwelling—are a welcome relief from the squalor of the Underbelly.

But the streets are not as quiet as I would like them to be. I almost forgot it was a festival night. Everyone has returned from the arenas, and now men and women linger in the plazas or in their own gardens, sharing drinks and discussing the athletes. I catch a word here and there as I pass.

"Perroth Tarriks won the burrik hunt again. I don't think it's fair—he's got no one to match him this year."

"Hakk, no one grudges an old champion another honor-mark. Though when he comes to my studio tomorrow, I don't know where I'm going to put it. He hardly has any bare skin left!"

Laughter echoes between the richly painted pillars. I walk quickly and do not meet anyone's gaze. All I want is to go home and sleep.

At last I reach Elantii Street and my aunt and uncle's house. I pass through the garden and step up to the door that bears Hakham and Chervani's marriage-mark. Even as I reach for the entry pad, I can hear loud, cheerful voices inside. I groan inwardly. My family does not usually stay up this late. Have they invited guests?

With a faint dread, I tap the entry pad, and the door slides open. As I step into the front room, the warm, floral scent of brewing *klasindi* tickles my nostrils.

"There you are at last!" Hakham's voice is boisterous. "Look, Mariikel. The Ascendance has left us a Van'shorvanii gift."

I blink, closing the door behind me. On the low half-circle of couches in the front room, my uncle sits across from a muscular young man in a military tunic. It takes me half a moment to recognize him—and then all my eyes widen in astonishment.

"Askko!"

My cousin rises with a grin. "Hello, little painter."

I am too amazed to reply. I haven't seen Askko in over a year. There are new honor-marks on the dark gray skin of his forearms, and the hvoss'ka tattoos on his shoulders are more elaborate. He is just as tall and imposing as I remember him, with his long, well-muscled legs and sharpened spurs. The military tunic he wears is open in the front, revealing the six-pointed, violet tattoo of the Ascendance on his chest.

Askko has always had the build of a warrior—an oddity in a clan of artists and record-keepers. When we were children, my uncle used to joke that I must be his true son and Askko the adopted one. Askko never appreciated that jest. Neither did I, because my cousin had a habit of knocking me down for it.

But there is no animosity in Askko's face now. He laughs as I continue to stare at him in shock. "Aren't you going to greet me?"

"I didn't know you were coming home," I stammer. "Honor with you."

He steps forward and grips both my forearms. "And with you, little painter."

I gasp involuntarily. Askko has always been stronger than me, but now his arms feel as hard and ropy as tree roots. His grin widens at my expression.

"It's called planet-strength."

"What?"

Askko lets go of me and reaches into a small pouch at his belt. Then he tosses a handful of a pale, grainy powder into my face. It fills my open mouth and stings my eyes. With a yell, I stagger backwards.

"It's sand!" Askko's shout is joyous. "From the islands of Kol'ihaz. Brother, I'm a planet-walker!"

I rub my eyes, coughing and spitting out the sharp grains. Both my uncle and cousin laugh. I wipe my face with one hand, then stare down at the tiny white particles that cling to my palm.

"Is it real?"

"Yes, it's real." Askko throws an arm around my shoulders. "All the warriors are bringing it home."

Too bewildered to be angry, I let him guide me to the couch, and we sit down, joining Hakham. I wince as I take off my satchel.

"Askko, are you throwing dirt all over my floor?" Chervani's clear, amused voice drifts in from the kitchen doorway.

"It's the soil of our ancestors, *nakki*. I'm blessing the house." Askko abruptly reaches for my satchel. "What's this? Are you still carrying around your work? We thought you were at the games."

I snatch the bag away from him and hug it to my chest. Startled, Askko frowns. Then he squints his lower eyes.

"All right, little painter. I won't break your pens."

I place the satchel between my feet. "I always have my work with me."

"You haven't changed much, then. That's a relief."

I sigh, but I am grateful that Askko did not take my reaction too seriously. If he were to find out what I have done tonight—but I refuse to think about that. I tilt my head and try to work a few stinging granules out from under one eyelid. As I do so, my glance falls on the low table in front of the couch.

On it, there is a gun. A small, compact one, not much longer than my own hand—but a real gun, nonetheless. In our house.

"What is that?"

"This?" Askko leans over and picks up the weapon in one smooth gesture. "This is what I carry instead of a pen. It's an Arroqi—the latest build. Do you like it?"

He tilts the handgun to one side, letting the light glint on the decorative sigils inscribed on the sleek barrel. From his glib tone and roguish expression, I can tell he is fully enjoying my unease. Even more disconcerting, Hakham is restraining a smile as well. I cannot fathom what my uncle would find amusing about his son bringing a firearm into a civilian area of the ship. Even the security guards who patrol the corridors are only allowed swords, daggers, and the spurs on their own feet.

I shift my seat, edging away. "Isn't that...?"

"Dangerous?" Askko laughs. "Only if it has bullets in it. Which it doesn't, at the moment."

The tension in my limbs eases a fraction. "I was going to say illegal."

"Not for hvoss'kan. One of our numerous privileges."

"Since when?" I see high-ranking warriors in the studio often enough; I have not noticed them carrying guns.

"I don't know. Recently? They are standard gear now on our battle fleets. They're not nearly as dangerous to carry inside the ships as they're made out to be—not if you're trained." He makes a show of pressing a mechanism, sliding open the gun's empty chamber, then closing it again with a sharp click. With a satisfied air, he places the weapon back on the table. "They are the tools of our trade. Why shouldn't we be allowed to carry them?"

Still I eye the firearm with distaste. Even when allowed, they have never been considered honorable. The only reason we use guns in the current war is because the half-sights carry them, too. The alien soldiers do not follow our ancient combat-codes. "I don't think it's quite the same."

Askko chuckles. "Well, I had to bring it this time. I was specifically told that I should wear mine for the honor-ceremony."

"Honor-ceremony? What for?"

My cousin blinks at me and then guffaws. He smacks my shoulder with the back of his hand, a blow that sends me reeling against the couch cushions. "What for? That's a fine welcome for a victorious warrior. What do you think I'm doing here in the first place?"

"Askko surprised us all." Hakham smiles. "His warband won an important battle on Kol'ihaz. The High Council wanted to honor them in a special ceremony."

Slowly I sit up, rubbing my shoulder. I am surprised both at the news and at the pride in my uncle's voice. Hakham is a record-keeper; he does not know anything of war. I remember his disappointment when Askko chose to join the military instead of finding a profession within Clan Serix. But now he sounds like a proud father from a warrior clan.

Because Askko has set foot on a planet now. Isn't that what we all want?

"Congratulations." I suppress a pang of envy. Brushing the last flecks of sand from my tunic, I say, "What's it like, then? Tell us about Kol'ihaz."

"I will try. But there are no words for it."

Askko's face is radiant. The light in his eyes and the reverence in his voice—he reminds me, suddenly, of the young Tarriks exile when he spoke of the planets.

"Wait," says Hakham. "Your mother wants to hear this. Chervani!"

"I'm coming," Chervani calls back from the kitchen. "I'm preparing the spoils of war."

I give Askko a mystified look. He smiles again.

"There were several half-sight farms on the island we captured. I brought back some of their fruit."

"We can eat it?" I exclaim.

"All of us soldiers did. Why not? The ancestors probably ate it. These *are* our home planets."

At last, Chervani emerges from the kitchen, balancing a loaded tray in her hands. She wears a deep red tunic hung with tassels, and the tattoos on her steel-gray skin gleam with the sheen of kiili oil. My aunt is no longer young, but she still knows how to look lovely on a festival day.

Behind her pads our old *dalrikhani* hound, Miika. Her black muzzle is flecked with gray, and her gait is shambling—but at the sight of Askko, she whines and trots forward, her long whip of a tail lashing back and forth. Askko catches the dog's head between his hands, fondling her pointed ears.

"Hakk, now, Miika! There's my brave one. I've missed you, too."

I get up, sidestepping my cousin and his overexcited war-hound. "Do you need help, nakki?" Chervani's tray is loaded with cups and a steaming jug of klasindi as well as round slices of an odd, sour-smelling fruit that I've never seen before.

"Sit down, dako," she says good-naturedly. I obey, and she sets the tray on the table in front of us. She hands out the cups and joins us on the couch. "Askko and his fellow hvoss'kan received special leave from their duties just so they could come back to the Fleet and get their honor-marks from Clan Serix." She, too, sounds proud.

Askko glances at me and inclines his head. "You'll do me the honor—won't you?"

I stare at him, slightly taken aback. My cousin has never requested a mark from me before. But then, I have only been a master artist for a little over a year, and he has often been away. "Of course. Whenever you like. I mean—as soon as the guild has approved the battle."

Askko looks pleased. "That won't take long." He strokes Miika's head as the dog settles at his feet. "They'll hold the hearing tomorrow."

"Tomorrow? So quickly?"

"Our commanders can only spare us for a few days. They need us back on Kol'ihaz as soon as possible." He hesitates. "There is so much work to be done on the island. I'm not allowed to talk about all of it. But if we're going to retake our home—well, we have much to learn."

Our home. I feel an odd touch of resentment at the way he says those words. The Fleet is our home—the seven remaining city-ships of the forty our ancestors built as a refuge from the half-sights and other alien invaders who devastated the Arovaan system, our native planets, a thousand years ago. At least, so the chronicles say. Most of our records from that era have been lost on board the many ships that did not survive. In the fragmented accounts we have left, it is often difficult to discern history from myth. All we know for certain is that the Noxxiin people have lived and died on these ships for generations. Planets or no planets, the Fleet is not a heritage to be discarded lightly. But I am not sure Askko feels that way.

Chervani pours drinks for us all, then settles back on the cushions. "Tell us about Kol'ihaz."

Cradling his cup in both hands, Askko inhales deeply. "Klasindi. We don't have *this* on Kol'ihaz."

My aunt and uncle laugh. I join in, trying to relax. But as Askko describes the wonders of the water-planet, Kol'ihaz, unhappiness steals over me again. The words that he uses—*sky, sunrise, ocean, storm*—sound archaic and exotic. The only place I have ever encountered such words was in the fragments of the ancestors' chronicles that I studied as a child. But Askko now uses these ancient terms with familiarity.

Hakham and Chervani are enthralled. Yet I find my mind drifting to the exiles and their children. I have never seen this thing that Askko calls a sunrise—and Lakkia's tiny son will never even see the ordinary daylights that brighten the corridors of the ship. He will die as he was born, in darkness.

Askko shoves me lightly, interrupting my brooding. "Hakka, Mariikel. Did you hear what I said? I'm going to take you swimming. In the ocean."

"What?" I sit up, blinking.

Askko breaks down laughing. My aunt and uncle look amused as well. Before I can respond, Hakham speaks up.

"How was the gravity? I've heard it's stronger down there than here on the ships. Did you have any trouble?"

"Trouble? No." Askko flicks his hand in a dismissive gesture. "Of course, we had to acclimate. But after that, it only made us stronger." He flashes another grin. "I feel like a giant now, here at home. I can move so *easily*. I'm afraid I'll break something!"

"Not in the house," Chervani smiles. "If you want to break something, go to the arenas."

"It's too bad you didn't come home a few days earlier," says Hakham. "You could have entered one of the festival competitions."

"That hardly would have been fair. For my opponents, that is." Askko's eyes glow with pleasure.

I stifle another surge of jealousy. My cousin has been trying for years to impress his father with his athletic prowess. Why should I grudge him his success now?

"Mariikel is in the festival, though," says Chervani. "Did we tell you that, Askko? He's been chosen as one of the artists for the bond-kindling."

"Hakka." Askko gives me a sidelong glance. "You've been doing well for yourself, little painter."

The reminder of the ceremony tomorrow makes me suddenly uncomfortable. "Kilmaya nominated me. If I'd known——"

"If the guild saw fit to select you, then you are perfectly qualified, Mariikel." Hakham sets his cup on the table. "You know the marks. There is nothing to be anxious about."

"Only the Van'shorii." Askko smirks. "Don't worry, they have good aim."

I scowl at him. He breaks into laughter again.

"That's enough, dako." Chervani's voice is severe, but her mouth twitches with restrained mirth. "It's a great honor. Don't tease him."

I take a sip of klasindi. I forgot how easily Askko can rile me with his taunts. But it is probably just as well if he believes I am afraid of the deepcrafters. It means I do not have to explain the real reason I dread the ceremony.

"Here," says Askko suddenly. "No one's tasted the fruit yet."

Chervani chuckles. "I think we're all afraid of it."

Askko reaches across the table, picks up one of the round slices, and pulls it in half. The wet, pink flesh tears apart, spraying juice across the table. "Try it, Mariikel." He holds out one half to me.

I take it gingerly, sniffing its sour aroma. Askko bites into his piece without hesitation, watching me with amusement. Finally, I place the fruit on my tongue, trying to imagine the blue expanse of sky under which it grew.

The taste of acid fills my mouth. I nearly choke, but I force myself to chew and swallow. Askko will mock me if I spit it out.

He grins as I drop the yellowish rind back onto the plate. "Well?"

"You ate that?" I manage.

"What can I say? We were hungry."

I swallow a mouthful of klasindi, attempting to wash down the aftertaste. But the sour fruit only spoils the drink's delicate flavors. "You soldiers can keep them. The spoils of war are too bitter for me."

"You'll be glad of them yet." Askko tries offering his rind to Miika; the old dog only whuffs at it, suspicious, before sinking to sleep at his feet again. "Food isn't the only thing that grows on the planets. You need ink, too, little painter."

"There's been talk about that at the trallak farms," says Chervani. "Some people are afraid that our trees won't grow well on the surface."

Askko scoffs. "I wouldn't worry. Didn't they come from these planets?" He nudges me. "What do you think, Mariikel? Come back to Kol'ihaz with me, and you can have your own studio with ink made from planet-grown trees."

I give him a wan smile. "I think Kilmaya might have something to say about that."

"Oh, she can't keep you forever. Besides, all the most honorable deeds are done on the planets now. You don't want to lose business, do you?"

"Certainly not." He is teasing me again. But it makes me wonder—what is my business? For when I entertain the idea of leaving the Fleet, the first thought that crosses my mind is, *Who will give marks to the exiles?*

Askko and Chervani are still talking, but I am no longer listening. I watch my cousin with a faint horror, noticing how his shoulder muscles ripple under his military tattoos.

What would you do to me, Askko, if you knew what I was?

All at once I feel ill. I tell myself it is the half-sight fruit, but I know better. Here I sit pretending to celebrate my cousin's victory, while in the back of my mind I plan out the false marks that I will give to the young Tarriks exile. Askko is the honorable one now. I have agreed to be a skin-changer—a painter of lies.

"Are you all right, Mariikel?" Chervani touches my arm. I look up. Askko and Hakham are talking now, and only my aunt has noticed my prolonged silence.

"I'm tired," I say truthfully. "There were so many clients today. And yesterday. The festival…"

"You've been working too hard again. You need rest for tomorrow." She squeezes my arm. "Askko will be home for a day or two. You'll have time to spend with each other. Go to bed."

I feel sick at heart, but I muster a grateful smile for Chervani. "I'll do that. Thank you, nakki."

As I rise, I apologize for my weariness and say goodnight to Askko and Hakham.

"See you at the festival tomorrow." Askko leans back, propping his feet on the low table. "That will be a first, won't it? I've never watched *you* in the arena before." He waves one foot at me, flaunting the curved, polished spine on his ankle. "Spurs sharp, little painter."

"It's good to have you both home. Both of you, bringing honor to the house." My uncle nods reverently towards the ceremonial sword hanging on the wall behind him—our family funeral-blade, inscribed with the names of our deceased kin. Then he turns back to me and Askko, his eyes glimmering. He stands and reaches out, placing a hand over the clan-mark on my neck. "Goodnight, dako. Ancestors keep you."

I flinch in surprise. Hakham almost never calls me son—I still address him as *na'thalo*, uncle, after all these years living under his roof.

"Ancestors keep you," I murmur. I draw Hakham's hand away from my neck. Then I pick up my satchel and take my leave. The bright, bitter scent of the alien fruit lingers in the air.

When I enter my own bedchamber, I am disconcerted to find Askko's gear—his travelling pack, armor, and blades of various sizes—lying in a pile on the floor. I did not even think about the fact that we will be sharing a room again for the next few days. He has already cleared my belongings out of his old bunk in the wall. But I am too tired to be annoyed.

I lock the door and take my hooded tunic from my bag. It still reeks of the Underbelly. I rinse it in the washbasin and hang it up in the very back of my closet, where Askko will not see it. Then I wipe down my satchel. Finally, when I can find nothing more to clean, I unlock the door, dim the lights, and stretch out on my bunk. At last my weary body has mercy on me, and I drift into the unquiet sleep of the guilty.

CHAPTER FOUR

The next morning, I awake to a cluttered and deserted room. Askko's bunk is empty. The only reason I can tell he came in at all is that his pack has been moved, and his belongings have been scattered even more widely across the floor.

One would think that military life would have taught my cousin some semblance of orderliness. Apparently those habits do not apply when he is at home.

I rise and begin picking my way across the room. My glance falls on Askko's bed. Among the pieces of armor and other warrior's gear is a heavy belt with a decorated holster that holds the Arroqi handgun. The grip is emblazoned with Askko's name-sigil and the glaring faction-mark of the Ascendance.

I stare at the weapon with a mixture of wonder and unease. Until yesterday, I had never seen a firearm up close before—they are not normally allowed in civilian areas of the ship, or in the combat arena. Bullets are just as likely to destroy some critical ship's component as they are to bring down one's enemy, and killing from afar is no way to fight a fellow Noxxiin. Except in the wars against the alien half-sights, firearms have always been *axariix*: coward's weapons. When did wearing them become a sign of honor?

I decide not to speculate further. Askko's business is his own, and I have enough to worry about today. I will spend this evening surrounded by deepcrafters, who are more lethal than any gun ever could be.

I dress quickly in my festival attire: a close-fitting black tunic, white belt, and black sandals with straps that lace up to my hocks. Then, after a moment of hesitation, I open the bottle of kiili oil that sits on my washbasin. I dislike wearing kiili, but if I am going to perform tonight in the public arena, I can hardly go without it. I use it sparingly, though; I have always found the smell suffocating. I pour a few drops of the clear, sweet-scented oil into my hands and begin rubbing it into my skin—first my arms and shoulders, then my face and neck. The oil makes my gray skin glisten with a smooth, silvery sheen, and deepens the colors of my tattoos.

When I finish, I step out of my room and head to the kitchen, expecting to find Askko bolting down his morning meal. Instead, only my aunt and uncle sit at our small dining table. A warm, spicy aroma fills the room, wafting from the jug and the platter of baked wafers on the table. Chervani has prepared something stronger than klasindi for this festive morning.

My aunt rises when she sees me. "There's our master artist. Good morning, Mariikel."

I cannot help relaxing at her smile. "Honor with you, nakki." I nod to my uncle. "Na'thalo."

Hakham blinks in greeting. "Honor with you."

Chervani takes down an empty cup and pours a steaming, amber-colored liquid from the jug. Bright-eyed, she hands the drink to me. "*Kazen val Van'shorii.*"

Honor to the deepcrafters. I accept the cup, drawing its pungent scent into my nostrils. Deepfire kol-dawra: the traditional drink of the festival, named, of course, for one of the foremost powers of the Van'shorii. The cider is made from sour *yekri* fruit laced with *alkani* spice and a generous splash of kol-dawra—a stronger beverage than I am used to, especially this early in the morning. But the first drink that passes my lips today must be dedicated to the deepcrafters and their ancestors. So I brace myself and take a sip.

The tang of the yekri fruit, the heat of the spice, and the burn of kol-dawra liquor flood my throat. I swallow, cough, and set down the cup with a gasp. "Kazen val Van'shorii."

Chervani laughs. "Awake now, are you? Sit down."

Gratefully, I take a seat across from my uncle. "Where's Askko?"

"Gone to the arena already. He said he didn't want to miss a day of training, even while on leave."

"Oh. Of course." I reach for the spiced wafers on the platter, wondering whether discipline is Askko's primary motivation. More than likely, he is taking the chance to show off in front of warriors who have not had the benefit of training in planet-gravity.

Chervani returns to her place at the table. "When do you have to be at the arena, Mariikel?"

"Not until sixth hour." I bite into the soft warmth of the wafer. The alkani flavor tingles on my tongue, but fortunately it is much subtler than in the drink. "I'm eager to have it over with. I prefer the studio."

"Well, *I* am looking forward to it," Chervani retorts. "I never get to see you work. Do it for me, if no one else."

A searing heat spreads through my chest. Possibly it is only the kol-dawra. I smile anyway. "I will do it for you, nakki."

I sip my pungent drink again. "Na'thalo—" I suppress a cough. "May I use your study this afternoon? I need to look at some honor-marks in the archives."

Hakham turns to me. "What for?"

"For Askko. I am doing his mark, too, remember? I want to study some examples."

"I thought you needed to prepare for the ceremony."

"I'm ready for tonight." That much is true, at least.

"Very well." Hakham waves a hand in assent.

"Thank you, na'thalo." I stare at the table. I haven't lied to him, exactly; I do plan to spend part of the time studying for Askko's mark. But I am also going to research the records of the young Tarriks exile—and I would much rather do that on my uncle's private display desk than on the public computers in the Serix record hall.

I grab a few more spiced wafers from the platter and stand up. "I should go. I'll see you both tonight."

"Don't forget we've invited Recordmaster Virik and his family over for supper," Chervani says. "So I don't want you disappearing after the ceremony. I know you."

If only you did. I ignore the ache in my chest and offer her another smile. "I'll be here, nakki."

Rixarii Street is already bustling with the day's festival crowd when I arrive at the studio. Kilmaya puts me to work at once, and I bury myself in it gratefully. The apprentices have returned from their day off; they resume their chores of pen-sharpening and ink-mixing, allowing me to focus on the clients and their tattoos. Clan-marks, marriage-marks, mastery-marks—all properly witnessed and perfectly legal.

And, of course, I give out the jagged, purple faction-mark of the Ascendance. During the midday lull, when Kilmaya asks me what colors of ink we need to order, I do not even have to go look. "Violet," I say dryly. "What else?"

Kilmaya squints. "What else, indeed?" She reads through messages on her datascroll, noting the afternoon appointments—she agreed to take my clients for the rest of the day, since I am leaving early for the festival. "You would think there's hardly anyone left by now who *doesn't* have a faction-mark. I don't know where they all come from."

"The Ascendance is doing good work for us." I say it more to soothe her than out of conviction. "Which reminds me, teacher." I slip off my gloves and pack them in my satchel. "Askko is home on leave to receive an honor-mark. He especially requested that I give it to him. I expect him to come in tomorrow, as soon as the guild approves the battle."

Kilmaya does not respond. "Is that all right?" I ask. "Can you spare me?"

She stares at her datascroll with a strange expression on her face. "What battle?"

"The recent one on Kol'ihaz. They took an island…"

Kilmaya blinks slowly at the screen. "Come read this."

I step over and take the device from her hands. The message she has open begins with a stylized violet-and-black trallak leaf, the official sigil of the markmaker guild:

> To the Artists of the Guild,
> The members of the guild council have not approved the Battle of Ariik Island, which took place on the nineteenth day of Peth'aal on the planet of Kol'ihaz. The Ascendance warband under the command of Pe'char Trechik failed to fight a worthy foe in the capture of this island, and thus the battle did not fulfill the conditions of the combat-code. Any warrior requesting an honor-mark to commemorate this battle is to be turned away without appeal. This is the order of the guild, and it is not to be trespassed.
> Mekkalluthak Serix, Guildmaster

I read the message twice in disbelief, but there is no mistaking it. Stunned, I hand the datascroll back to Kilmaya.

"Is that Askko's warband?" she demands.

"Yes." My eyes are still fixed on the guildmaster's name-sigil emblazoned on the screen. "When did you receive this?"

"Just now. They must have just finished the hearing."

"What do you think—I mean, do you suppose—"

"Do I suppose that Ascendance soldiers have fought a dishonorable battle?" Kilmaya finishes with a wry expression. "Oh, of course it is *possible*. It seems Mekkalluthak has not deigned to give us the details."

I lean back against the worktable. *Askko…what have you done?* But I push the thought away. I may not understand my cousin's military inclinations, but I know he is honest at heart. He would never ask for an honor-mark unless he truly deserved one. There must be some mistake.

"Can they do that? Disqualify an entire battle?"

"Yes…although it hasn't happened recently. The commanders are usually quite careful about these things. If there is any question about the battle meeting the honor-code, they will not even request a mark." She regards the message for a moment longer, and then her eyelids flicker in amusement. "Something has upset Mekkalluthak, that's certain. I haven't seen him write like this since the time Clan Tarriks adopted that half-sight—what was his name?"

"Toh Maas?"

"Hakk, yes."

She chuckles at the memory, although it was not a laughing matter at the time. It was eight years ago—I was still an apprentice, and the Fleet had only arrived in the Arovaan system a few months before—when Clan Tarriks announced they were adopting a half-sight into their ranks. Evidently this alien, Toh Maas, had saved the lives of a few high-ranking Tarriks warriors during a disastrous hunting expedition in the jungles of Kol'ihaz. Impressed by his courage, one commander offered to adopt him into the clan as long as he could pass the ritual combat trials—which Toh Maas did with ease.

That was how the Fleet's most prestigious warrior clan brought home a Peshyak, a half-sight, demanding that he be given the marks he'd earned. The request threw the guild into an uproar. Clan Tarriks insisted that he *had* passed the trial, and nowhere in their adoption law did it specify the recipient had to be Noxxiin. Besides that, granting the mark would send a message of friendship to the half-sight race. This, of course, was before the rise of the Ascendance, when the High Council was still open to negotiating for territory on the planets instead of waging war.

Kilmaya puts the datascroll down on the worktable, still smirking. "Toh Maas. I remember the speech Mekkalluthak made when the guild approved that mark. He was so furious. *We shall not ply our ancient craft on the sweating skin of a half-sight!* Oh, Kallu. Always eloquent. He wasn't guildmaster then, though—not much he could do about it."

"I remember the riots. When Clan Tarriks brought Toh Maas to the studios."

"Do you?" Kilmaya squints at me. "I distinctly remember telling you to stay home that day. So you *wouldn't* get trampled in the street."

"Askko convinced me to come." I smile too, despite myself. "We didn't want to miss our chance to see an alien."

I remember that day clearly—the mob jamming the narrow corridor of Rixarii Street and the escort of Tarriks warriors plowing their way through the crush, fighting off eager onlookers and angry dissenters alike. I was, in fact, nearly trampled in the violent crowd, until Askko helped me climb up onto one of the support beams that spanned the corridor ceiling. When the Tarriks guards at last passed under us, we glimpsed the alien: a swarthy, sandy-skinned creature, wearing strangely drab armor. His head was covered in dark, bristling hair, like a beast's, and out of this ferocious face glared two small eyes, dark in the middle and white in the corners.

Askko, I remember, gaped at the hair and the too-few eyes. But I was struck by something else: the sight of a strong, intelligent, confident being, whose skin was utterly devoid of marks. I pitied him. How this half-sight must have suffered! An accomplished warrior whose own people would give him no recognition! I was glad, for Toh Maas' sake, that he had become one of us.

"You were there?" Kilmaya exclaims. "You never told me that. Great Ka," she laughs, "you can keep a secret when you want to, quiet one."

My smile fades. If only that were the only secret I have kept from my teacher.

I turn back to the worktable and clear away the last of my tools. "Do you think there will be trouble over this ban?"

"Mark-bans always cause trouble." Kilmaya's face has turned pensive. "But I wonder if this one has less to do with the battle and more to do with the guild."

I blink in confusion. "What?"

My teacher turns and regards me frankly. "Mariikel, you are a fine artist. But your neglect of politics is becoming inexcusable."

I sigh. Kilmaya has been nagging me on this point ever since I gained my mastery-mark. Because I earned the highest possible ranking in my mastery-trial, I automatically received the right to vote during guild meetings—an uncommon honor for so young an artist. But I have never taken advantage of this privilege, mostly because I have little interest in attending the meetings in the first place. "What are you talking about?" I ask.

"If you had gone to even one assembly in the past few months, you would know. You remember Toh Maas because there was fighting in the streets. But there were no riots when Clan Serix lost its seat in the High Council two years ago."

"So?" I am not sure what her remark has to do with Askko's battle. "Not every clan is able to get on the High Council every year. There aren't enough seats."

"Not every clan is Clan Serix," Kilmaya retorts. "We have *always* had a voice there until this war began. Take a guess, quiet one. What does every member of the current High Council have that we do not?"

I frown, uncertain, until she taps two fingers on her chest, just below the hollow of her throat. "A faction-mark?"

"Indeed. Artists, guild councilors, record-keepers—no one who has a hand in the marks is allowed to join a faction. We must remain impartial, yes?"

"Of course. But the guild is not opposed to the Ascendance. They want to reach the planets, like everyone else."

"Certainly. We have not had a reason to oppose them...yet." Her mouth twitches in a mirthless little smile. "But neither can we give allegiance to them. Our guild is the only one Valo T'sarek cannot fill with his own pledged followers. A fact that irks him to no end, I would imagine."

I can feel my upper eyes tightening with impatience. I am already familiar with Kilmaya's reservations about High Councilor Valo; she grumbles about him often enough. I point at the datascroll on the table. "But what does all that have to do with this mark-ban?"

"A great deal, perhaps. Mekkalluthak has not cared for the way the Ascendance has taken hold of the clans these past few years. And he is not the only one. The guild may have decided it is time to remind the faction what it feels like to be refused."

"Are you saying they wrote this ban out of spite?" Horror fills me. For Askko to suffer an unjust humiliation merely because of resentment between councilors!

"Well, not spite alone." Kilmaya narrows three eyes in amusement. "I'm sure they disqualified the battle on some foundation. Still, this ban is a statement for the High Council. Why else would Mekkalluthak announce it now, right before the bond-kindling? What better time to remind Valo that even he and his deepcrafters depend on the guild for their marks?"

My gut tightens. As if I were not anxious enough already, now tonight's ceremony has become part of some political sparring match. I have no desire to play a part in councilors' quarrels.

All at once another, more alarming thought occurs to me. I clap a hand to my mouth.

"Askko. I was supposed to give him that mark. When he finds out..."

Kilmaya blinks. "Ah. I forgot your cousin was mixed up in all this. He's the hot-tempered one, isn't he?"

"Well..."

"If you find yourself threatened—" the sparkle has come back into her eye— "simply remind him whom you work for. He is Serix too, after all. He won't maim a student of mine, if he knows what's good for him."

CHAPTER FIVE

I leave the studio shortly after midday and head home through the crowded corridors. The halls are still noisy with street music and high-spirited chatter, but I discern a faint tension beneath the revelry. Markmakers stand in their studio doorways, reading their datascrolls and conversing in low tones. Every artist in Rixarii Street has received the news by now. I wonder how long it will take for the rest of the ship to hear about it, too. Yet despite Kilmaya's speculations, I am not worried about any trouble at the deepcraft ceremony tonight. I'm far more concerned about being confronted by my furious cousin.

When I reach the house, I open the door with some apprehension. My fears are unwarranted, however; the light-panels are dimmed and no one is home. My uncle and aunt are still at work—Hakham at the record hall and Chervani at the trallak farms—and Askko does not seem to be here, either. Only Miika, lying in the kitchen doorway, greets me with a cautious wave of her tail. The old hound lurches to her feet and pads across to me, ears pricked in a puzzled but happy expression. I never come home in the middle of the day.

"Hakka there, Miika." I kneel and run my hands down her lean black flanks and white belly. She pants open-mouthed, savoring the attention. I can still remember when my aunt and uncle gave her to Askko, many years ago—a purebred dalrikhani pup, from the same bloodline of war-hounds that are trained to hunt burriks with their masters in the combat arena. Perhaps Hakham and Chervani hoped that raising such an animal would satisfy Askko's childhood obsession with becoming a warrior. If that was their intention, it didn't work: as soon as he was of age, Askko received an adoption-mark from Clan Trechik and began his military training.

Now he fights battles with aliens on the surface of distant planets—battles that the guild refuses to acknowledge as honorable, though I do not know why. I have an uneasy feeling that I no longer know Askko as well as I thought. In the past, he shared all his combat stories eagerly. But now that I think of it, he did not even mention the half-sights in last night's conversation, or anything about his part in the capture of the island.

I rub Miika's chest, still mulling over the guild's message. *Failed to fight a worthy foe.* That can only mean one of two things: either Askko's warband fought a much weaker force than their own, or they took the island from unarmed civilians, and there was no real battle at all. Of course, such things happen in war—but soldiers are not supposed to receive honor-marks for such unequal conflicts.

Askko should know better than to request a tattoo that he did not merit. What has his time in the Ascendance done to him? I sigh. Miika tilts her head, studying me with her clear gold eyes.

"If only you could go to the planets with him," I tell her. "Maybe you would keep Askko out of trouble for us."

The old hound whips her tail back and forth at her master's name. But she has no answers for me. I rise and head down the hall towards my uncle's study, while Miika sprawls out again in the kitchen doorway.

It is tempting to pull out my datascroll and see if the guild has published a report with additional details about the battle. But I will hear more about the mark-ban soon enough. For now, I have more immediate problems—such as beginning my official career as a skin-changer.

I slip into the study, drop my satchel on the floor, and sit down before the broad screen of the display desk. I allow the device to scan the mastery-mark on my forehead. As an artist, I have access to all the guild's archives, which I normally use to study the work of other markmakers. But today I have a different purpose: I need to know the name of this Tarriks outcast. Since I remember the date on his exile-mark, it does not take long to find him. I open his full record, and immediately the screen fills with images and descriptions of tattoos.

My exile's name is Kophas. His record is typical for a Tarriks: he is the son of a long line of warriors, the victor of many hunts and arena battles, and, most recently, a soldier for the Ascendance. I scroll quickly through the images. All his marks were made by prestigious studios and respected artists. All his tattoos are honorable. He does not have a single shame-mark on his body.

Unease steals over me. Talorak's record, I remember, was also flawless.

At last, I arrive at the final image, the hideous tattoo of exile. I study the swirling, stark-white design: the double crossbar slashing the central line, the four arms reaching out like the tentacles of some ravenous water-creature. There is something primal and archaic in its fluid lines; it does not resemble the sharper, more angular sigils of the modern Noxxiin script. The exile-mark must be very ancient. I have painted it only once in my life, but those grasping, tendril-like lines are forever burned into my memory.

With a faint shiver, I turn my attention to the sigils written within the main mark, which indicate the wearer's crimes—treason and cowardice in battle. Underneath the image of the tattoo is a brief document: Kophas's official sentence from the Ascendance military court. It tells a terse story: that Kophas was part of a force attacking an asteroid mining station, and, when ordered to advance on the half-sight soldiers, he disobeyed, abandoned his post, and refused to return to it.

As I feared, there are no recordings of the trial itself. I glare at the screen in frustration. Ever since the war started, the Ascendance has become increasingly stingy about the amount of military information released to the public archives. I wonder if my uncle would be able to track down a transcript of the trial. Probably not. In any case, I can't ask him for such a favor; he would want to know why I need the information.

I lean back from the desk and rub my eyes. I'm not certain what to think. Aside from the exile-mark, Kophas's record is clean; there is no indication that he ever acted dishonorably before. It is his word against the word of the Ascendance: he is either a coward or a noble warrior who refused to slaughter unarmed enemies. In the darkness of my memory, I can still feel Kophas's vise-like grip and see the rage and desperation in his eyes. Perhaps I am thinking too much of Talorak—but I know which story I am more inclined to believe.

My gaze drifts to the time-sigil in the corner of my screen. It is half-past the fifth hour already; I need to head down to the arena. Now, though, I have even less heart for the initiation ceremony than before. The deepcrafter I mark tonight will most likely go on to fight for the Ascendance, and I am growing sick of serving the faction's ends. But for now, I have little choice.

With a few taps on the screen, I erase my search entries, close out the archives, and shut down the display desk. Then I take up my artist's satchel again and depart.

After a quarter-hour of walking and riding elevators through the transport hubs, I make my way to the lower entrance of the main combat arena. I find the place even more crowded than Rixarii Street. Pausing in the throng, I stand at the threshold of the warriors' preparation rooms, daunted by the clamor within the narrow tunnels: the shouting of excited athletes, the clatter of armor, the barking of war-hounds. The whole place reeks of animal musk and kiili oil.

I suppress a shudder and glance at the symbols decorating the wall above the door. Three sigils stand out, brilliant violet against the black lintel: *dethra*, worthy weapon; *kolar*, worthy opponent; *piitro*, worthy cause. These are the tenets of the combat-code, the three conditions of honorable battle, which every warrior knows by heart.

Or they should. Again I remember Askko and the mark-ban, and I feel ill at ease.

A passerby in the crowd clips my shoulder; I stumble forward. The man, an arena official in ceremonial armor, glances back at me with eyes narrowed in annoyance. But then he sees my face.

"Apologies, markmaker!" He bows, touching his clan-mark in a respectful salute. "Are you looking for the artists' room? It's by the Heartsblood Gate."

I mutter a word of thanks, telling him I know my way. Which is true—I came here a few days ago for a rehearsal. The halls were less chaotic then. I take a firmer grip on my satchel strap and step through the doorway.

The rooms underneath the arena are still a maze to me. I dodge through jostling groups of warriors clad in embellished armor, past the lithe dalrikhani hounds that yelp and strain at their leashes. Stern-faced trainers shout orders, adding to the din. Through the commotion, I can feel rather than hear the noise from the arena above our heads: a muted rumble, like a massive generator, and a steady throbbing as of distant drums.

Heartsblood Gate. Where is it? Reaching an intersection of two tunnels, I find my path blocked by several arena officials, who are holding back a small but eager crowd with the hafts of their javelins. Everyone seems to be looking at something in the hallway beyond. I slip through the crush, craning my neck, trying to see what is causing the delay.

A growl pierces the commotion—a rippling, guttural sound that stops me in my tracks. Past the row of officials, I catch a glimpse of brindled, gray-and-black fur. A different beast-odor wafts over me, sharp and unpleasant.

Burrik.

I freeze, hemmed in by the athletes around me who clamor for a view. I can see the creature now: the sinuous, muscled body, three times the size of a war-hound; the clawed feet; the heavy, tapering tail. Long horns spring from the slender, strangely graceful head, overshadowing four small and savage eyes. The burrik is restrained by a muzzle and several taut ropes held by armored handlers who are trying to lead the beast down the corridor.

I do not breathe. I have never been so close to a burrik before; I have only seen them in arena battles from the safety of the spectators' seats. Those taloned forefeet can rip open a Noxxiin's chest with a single swipe—another thing I have fortunately never seen.

This beast must be a part of the events later tonight. For the moment, though, it is clearly drugged—its movements are clumsy and its dark eyes glazed. Even so, it strains against its bonds so powerfully that it takes all three warriors to drag it down the hallway. The burrik rears once, snarling, pulling its handlers off balance. Shouts echo; claws screech against the tunnel floor.

Then a hand lands on my shoulder and grips me, hard.

I yell in surprise. Turning, I find myself face to face with a tall, bare-chested warrior wearing only a sparring kilt and leather spur-guards that encase his lower legs. The double trident of the Ascendance dominates the dark gray expanse of his chest.

"Little painter." Askko digs his fingers into my shoulder. His nostrils flare.

"Askko," I gasp. Behind me, the commotion subsides as the burrik handlers tow their charge further down the hall. "Deep Sleep, did you have to grab me like that? What are you doing?"

"We need to talk."

"I have a ceremony to get to. I need—"

"Now."

Before I can object, Askko propels me down the corridor back the way I came. I am too bewildered to struggle. He spots the open door of a small side armory and pushes me through it. A couple of arena apprentices sit at a table, polishing weapons. They startle at the sight of us.

"Out," Askko barks.

The apprentices take one look at the hvoss'ka tattoos on my cousin's shoulders and bolt from the room, barely even stopping to salute him. Askko hits the entry pad, and the door slides shut behind us. Then at last he lets go of me.

I stumble backwards, staring at Askko and holding one hand to my shoulder. He is much stronger than I remember; if he'd gripped me any harder, he might have cracked my collarbone. No warrior dares lay a rough hand on a markmaker, even in jest—no one except my own adopted brother, who still only sees me as his younger sibling and not as an artist of the law. Heat wells up in my chest. "What in Ka's name is wrong with you?"

"You know what's wrong." He stabs a finger at me. "You and your arrogant painter's guild—"

Axdraa'dah. He's heard about the mark-ban for his battle.

I sidle away, easing behind the table littered with oiling-cloths and elaborate daggers. I do not want to have this conversation now, but Askko has not given me much choice.

"Askko, I had nothing to do with that. How could I?"

He does not seem to hear me. Instead he paces the cramped room. "'Turned away without appeal.' Is that all they have to say, after everything we've done?" He turns and slams his fist on the table; blades jump and rattle. "They can't do this to us!"

Yes, they can. But I do not say this. My cousin looms over me now, and the ugly twist of his features sends a quaver down my spine. Askko has not tried to bully me for years—not since we were young boys—but I have not forgotten what his blows felt like. Yet I meet his gaze and say, "I wish there were something I could do."

"What do you mean? You're one of them!"

I lower myself onto one of the stools beside the table. "I'm a markmaker, not a councilor. I have to obey the guild."

"Oh, yes. And you are so dutiful, little painter." He sneers the name. "Aren't you glad the guild has *freed* you from the burden of honoring me?"

The words stab me in the belly. "Askko, I wanted to give you that mark. I didn't choose this ban." I draw in a slow breath. He is so angry—is it possible that the guild made an unjust decision? I recall what Kilmaya said this morning about political squabbles and the guildmaster's resentment of the Ascendance. "Can your commander submit a formal appeal? If there was some mistake..."

"We don't have time for a formal appeal. We need to get back to Kol'ihaz. Do you think we have nothing better to do than to listen to your councilors argue for days on end? They may have forgotten, but we are doing warriors' work out there. We are the ones dying to protect *them*. And yet they think nothing of making us a laughingstock."

I watch my cousin warily. The last thing I want to do is anger him further. "I haven't read a report of the hearing yet. Do you know why they declared the battle..."

"Dishonorable? Go on. You can say it."

I sigh. "What did the guild say?"

"They said it was *axkolar*. That we did not have a worthy enemy." He bares his teeth as though to spit in disdain. "As if they were there."

"I heard that much. But what did they mean?" I try to sound equitable even as my anxiety grows. "A worthy enemy must be a fighting force equal or greater in numbers—or at least greater in skill—"

"Don't recite the honor-code to me!" His face is livid. "What do you know about it? You've never even had blood on your spurs!"

I stare at him, stung. After a minute, I find my tongue, but it is a struggle to speak calmly. "Askko, I'm trying to help."

"You wouldn't understand. You think the whole world is as orderly as your pens and your stencils. If you would bother to wash the ink out of your eyes—"

"Askko!" I am used to his jeering, but even my patience has a limit. "This isn't about me; it's about the battle. Those half-sights on the island—were they soldiers, or were they farmers?"

He pauses, but his glare brims with scorn. "You think it's that simple, don't you? It's *war*, little painter. We must use whatever resources we can get."

"I understand that. Go on and take what you need. But if all you've done is raid a farm, don't expect the guild to give you an honor-mark!"

Askko's upper eyes narrow to slits. "Raid a farm?" His lips curl back from his teeth. He steps forward and leans both hands on the table. His broad, tattooed shoulders quiver. "I had a friend in another warband. A pilot. Do you want to know how he died?"

"Askko…"

"He wasn't shot down. It wasn't even a battle. His ship burned up in the atmosphere because he couldn't slow it down." The sinews stand out on Askko's neck as he leans over me, his nostrils wide. "The planet itself is our worst enemy. We have had to learn how to fly all over again. Kin's blood, we've had to learn how to *walk* again."

I gape at him. "What do you mean?"

"Do you know how many weeks we had to spend on the surface, camping on a bare strip of rock in the ocean, before we could even think about invading that island? Some of us could barely crawl off the transports when we first touched down. And that was after training in high-gravity chambers on the Fleet."

I gaze up at my cousin, disturbed. I have heard that the gravity on Kol'ihaz is stronger than we are accustomed to, but not that our warriors find it debilitating. "I thought you said the gravity was no trouble."

He glowers again. "Why do you think it has taken us two years to put troops on planet-soil in the first place? This is why we need the island so badly. We need places to train. To acclimate. We will never be able to land a major invasion otherwise."

I shake my head, trying to make sense of his tirade. He lied last night when Hakham asked him about the planet-gravity, or obscured the truth, at least. But why?

"Does the guild know this? Do they understand how difficult the gravity was?"

"I doubt they *understand*. But they have been told. They had to know the circumstances of the battle."

"Of course." My brow furrows. *The circumstances…* "Askko." I frown as I meet his gaze again. "What about the half-sights? Were they warriors or not?"

His face stills, and for a moment, his eyelids flicker involuntarily. Then he says, "Do you think they let us walk in without a fight? Good Noxxiin died taking that island. Don't you dare insult their memory."

"I'm not. I'm only asking—"

"A planet-born half-sight child can lift more weight than most trained

Noxxiin soldiers when they first reach the surface. Think about that, Mariikel—" He breaks off, breathing heavily. "Maybe they were not all warriors. But they certainly fought. I swear to you that we earned every inch of ground we claimed."

I stare up at him, wordless. What can I say? I have never felt the pull of planet-gravity; I do not know how crippling it is. Probably he is telling the truth—but that does not change the honor-code. All at once, I remember Kophas Tarriks, and a fear begins to take shape in my mind. Kophas said he was banished because he refused to kill unarmed opponents when he was ordered to do so. But my cousin...

What have you done, Askko? What did you do to those half-sights who were not warriors?

"Do you understand now?" Askko straightens. "The only way we are going to take the planets is if all the clans are united. That's the purpose of the Ascendance. We can't afford to fight among ourselves anymore. We can't afford this ban."

His words, for once, sound reasonable. But I find it hard to listen because I am staring at the faction-mark on my cousin's chest and wondering if he is a murderer.

"The purpose of Clan Serix is to safeguard the truth. Honor-marks are for conflicts between warriors. If that is not what happened—"

"The Deep Sleep take you, Mariikel!" His fist crashes down on the table again. "Haven't you heard anything I've been saying? This is the most important war we've waged in centuries!"

"War! Do you think of nothing else?"

"Do you want to die on this miserable ship?"

My chest tightens as if struck by a dagger. Slowly I rise from my seat, meeting him eye to eye. "Our ancestors died on this *miserable ship*. So did my parents, if you recall. I am not ashamed of them."

"Go on and join them, then!"

I do not reply. I only stare him down, my fingers gripping the edge of the table. Askko opens his mouth to shout again but says nothing. His rage falters, and his chest deflates.

In my anger, I can almost feel the memory-marks on my back tingling. I was so young when I received them that I have almost no recollection of my own parents' faces. But Askko has never allowed me to forget what I am.

"I didn't mean it, all right?" he exclaims—roughly, but with a note of genuine remorse. "I spoke without thinking. You've never been on the planets. I should not have expected you to understand."

Since that is probably the best apology I will get out of him, I relent.

Lowering my gaze, I run my fingers over one of the daggers on the table, tracing the sigils in the decorated hilt. "So. What are you going to do?"

"I don't know yet. But I don't think my commander will let us leave the ship without that honor-mark."

I keep my eyes fixed on the dagger-hilt. "Don't come to me for it."

"I won't. I would never ask you to defy your precious guild." He laughs, contemptuous. "It would probably kill you if you tried."

With that, he turns and exits the room. The door opens, letting in the hubbub of the corridor, and then shushes closed behind him. Slowly I sit down at the table again, feeling strangely numb.

Oh, Askko. I am made of sterner stuff than you know. I bury my head in my arms. Who am I to play the honorable markmaker? I have defied the guild more times than I can count, and I am about to do it again. It has not killed me yet. But it may well drive me mad.

CHAPTER SIX

When I finally find my way to the Heartsblood Gate, it is almost time for the ceremony to begin. My fellow markmakers—four of them, all wearing black tunics and long artist's gloves—are waiting by the steps. The great door into the arena is still shut; I am not too late.

I slip out of the traffic of the corridor and hurry towards the other artists. Whatever my cousin may have done on Kol'ihaz, I still have a duty to perform.

"There he is!" One of the markmakers, a middle-aged man with a sour expression, turns and spots me. "Great Ka, where have you been? We thought we'd have to process in without you."

"I'm very sorry." I halt in front of him, touching my brow in apology. "I got a bit lost."

The other artist narrows his eyes. "That's why you were to come early. This is Van'shorvanii, not an appointment in the studio. If you are not here when those doors open—"

"Well, he *is* here, Narrik, so kesh now." A female markmaker, frail and elderly but still bright-eyed, touches my arm. "I'm sure you got lost down here on your first time, too."

Narrik exhales, annoyed, but inclines his head. "Very well, Rinavi."

I send Rinavi a brief glance of gratitude. She is one of the oldest markmakers on Rixarii Street and a good friend of Kilmaya's; her studio stands directly across from my teacher's. Rinavi has known me since the first years of my apprenticeship and has always been kind to me. I am glad to have her by my side in this unfamiliar place.

Rinavi smiles and says in an undertone, "Don't mind him. He's only nervous—he doesn't care for it down here, either."

I grimace in agreement, then take off my satchel and rummage for my markmaking gloves. When I find them, Rinavi reaches out and grasps the strap of my bag. "Here, let me take that. We can leave it in the artists' room."

I tense, about to clutch the satchel to my chest—mainly because my Underbelly disguise is sitting in the bottom of this bag. But Rinavi is only trying to help. Blinking in confusion, I release my grip. "Thank you."

Rinavi disappears into a small side room with the bag, and I pull on my gloves. Then I smooth down the front of my tunic, trying to settle my nerves. The other markmakers acknowledge me with quiet nods. They are all Serix, of course; the guild would never select Trev'ban artists for an event as important as the bond-kindling. I do not know these other markmakers well, but at least we are clanmates. I feel a little less out of place among them.

I turn my attention to the closed door at the top of the short flight of steps. Heartsblood Gate—the main entrance to the great combat arena of the *Akkano'dath*. Countless generations of warriors, deepcrafters, and markmakers have passed through this door to honor the ancestors, to perform before the clans during our yearly festival. Beyond the door, I can hear the noise from the stands, a restless roar, and the thin, piercing skirl of raith'aal pipes.

I flex my fingers, feeling my palms tingle with anticipation. I shut my eyes. In the darkness of my own mind, I trace the shape of the van'shor tattoo, the mastery-mark that I am about to paint. Line by line I recall the sigil: the silvery half-circle breaking into three upreaching spirals, like three tongues of flame. I know the strokes almost unconsciously, like I know how to walk or run or breathe. The mark will be perfect. I have no doubt of that.

Why then am I so afraid?

Rinavi rejoins us just as an arena official in ceremonial armor approaches. The sigil on his breastplate designates him as the markmaker escort.

"Serixan." He touches his clan-mark. "All is ready for you. If you will follow me, please."

Without a word, we arrange ourselves as we rehearsed: Rinavi, the eldest, at the front of the line, and the rest of us following in order of age. I, of course, am youngest and last. The official climbs the stairs to lead us in. The great door releases a hiss, splits in the middle, and slides open. Blinding light and a blare of music spill into the stairwell. Then we mount the steps and enter the arena.

I shut my upper eyes. I feel I have stepped into an abyss of brightness and noise. The air seems to vibrate with the wailing of raith'aal pipes and the booming, heady pulse of drums. I breathe in the scents of dust and heat and the ever-present sweetness of kiili oil. Slowly, my vision adjusts; the arena shimmers into focus.

We stand at one end of an elongated oval ring. The white, synthetic sand that covers the floor blazes under the lights, stretching out in front of us for hundreds of feet. Above the arena walls rise the stands in dizzying tiers, teeming with dark heads and bright clothing. Highest of all hangs the great oval dome—the largest dome in the entire Fleet—glowing with a crystalline blue radiance.

This room is an absurd extravagance in a place where every square foot of living space is precious. The ancestors built this dome, they say, to remind them of the sky on their home planets. But Askko said the real sky on Kol'ihaz would dwarf this room—that he had looked out over miles and miles of sea and empty air, which ended only at the boundary-line that he called a *horizon*.

I cannot even imagine an open space that huge. The sight of the arena alone gives me vertigo. So I stare at the sandals of the markmaker in front of me and focus on walking. The synthetic sand is firm and springy under my steps—so smooth compared to the coarse, gritty grains that Askko brought home from the planets.

I have been in this room before, of course, but only as a spectator. Cautiously, I raise my eyes and scan the crowd. Hakham, Chervani, and Kilmaya are somewhere in those stands. Every one of the three thousand seats is filled tonight; the rest of the ship's inhabitants must be satisfied with viewing the events on their display desks or datascrolls at home. Hundreds of thousands of eyes will watch us wield our pens in the name of the law and the ancestors.

A coldness settles deep in my belly. *I should not be here.*

But there is no escape now. We cross the length of the arena at a solemn processional pace. At the opposite end of the room, a circular platform has been erected on the sand. Five chairs with slightly reclined backs—chairs of real, polished trallak wood, jet black and elaborately carved—stand beside small tables that hold our tattooing pens, bottles of ink and sealing-glaze, and other supplies. Beside the tables, clad in their distinctive silvery robes, are the deepcrafters.

There are ten of them on the platform: five master Van'shorii and their apprentices, the initiates who are about to receive their marks. The masters wear long robes, while the apprentices are clad more lightly in sparring kilts. Their bare arms and torsos glisten with oil under the glaring arena lights. All the initiates are from Clan T'sarek, as usual, and they look eerily alike: deep black skin; tall, muscular builds; broad faces with wide nostrils and square jaws.

If I did not know better, I might think they were blood siblings. But of course, most T'sarekan share a strong resemblance. They are seldom allowed to marry outside their own clan. Deepcrafters must keep their bloodlines pure, lest they lose the genetic traits that allow them to perform their art.

At last I pick out the initiate I have been assigned—Khalon. He stands beside his master, lithe and bare-chested, hands clasped behind his back. Here, the young man looks much more imposing than he did in my studio yesterday afternoon. He could probably throw Askko to the ground with little effort. I am not sure my cousin's new planet-strength is a match for generations of T'sarek breeding.

The artists in front of me split off from the procession line, mounting the platform to greet their respective clients and witnesses. I do the same. As I climb the steps, I inhale deeply, relax my shoulders, and try to stand tall.

You are a markmaker. You come bearing the authority of the guild, of Clan Serix, of truth in the flesh. Even deepcrafters must give deference to that.

That thought might be more heartening if I were not an oathbreaker, as well.

"Honor with you, markmaker." Khalon and his master speak in unison, touching their clan-marks in formal greeting.

"And with you." I almost bow, almost raise my hand to my own neck, but I stop myself just in time. In any other circumstances, it would be incredibly disrespectful to refrain from saluting a van'shor. But tonight, I must not make any gesture of submission. They are coming to me for my skill, my legal sanction. It is all part of the ceremony—or the farce, perhaps. Tonight, I may be the bearer of the markmaker guild's approval, but that does not change where the real power lies.

All the artists have greeted their charges. The pipes play a last, wild fanfare as everyone on the platform turns to face the nearby stands. We are near the arena wall, directly under the honor-seats for the clan leaders, important council members, and of course, the High Councilor and his family.

A few tiers up, I spot a vaguely familiar figure: a man about Kilmaya's age with a cool, imposing bearing that belies his rather slight frame. His white tunic and gold belt set off his dark violet skin, and on his brow gleam three separate mastery-marks: markmaker, guild councilor, guildmaster.

Mekkalluthak Serix. I know him, but not well—I have always found him intimidating. Naturally, as leader of Clan Serix and the head of the markmaker guild, Mekkalluthak has a place in the honor-seats. Yet it takes a bold man to show his face at a public festival only hours after denying a tattoo to the most powerful faction in the Fleet. But then, it would be a scandal for the guildmaster not to attend Van'shorvanii.

Another fanfare plays, and a cheer sweeps the crowd. A man in the front row of honor-seats rises and steps forward into a small balcony built into the arena wall. *Valo T'sarek.* A renowned van'shor, a founding member of the Ascendance, and High Councilor of the Noxxiin Fleet. Unlike Mekkalluthak, this man is tall and athletically built. The cut of his tunic reveals the Ascendance faction-mark, emblazoned like a battle flag on his broad chest.

An uneasy thrill goes through me. Will he say anything about the mark-ban? I glance up at Mekkalluthak again, but the guildmaster's face remains impassive.

Valo lifts his hands for silence. Slowly, the cheers of the assembly settle to a murmur. Then, in the quiet, the High Councilor begins: "Noxxiin Aurorii, Children of the Stars, my people—honor with you on this solemnity of Van'shorvanii!"

His words boom out over the arena, unnaturally loud and ringing. No doubt he is using deepcraft to enhance his voice. It is difficult to tell under the bright lights, but I think I can see the silver tattoos on his brow and cheekbones glowing faintly.

"On this first day of Akk'aal, in the nine hundred and sixty-fifth year of the Wandering, we come together in thanksgiving to our ancestors. In their wisdom, they have given us the precious gift of deepcraft and the guardianship of the Van'shorii Order. Today, on their festival, we bear witness to the initiates of the Deep, the newest wielders of the silver flame. By our marks, let us implore the blessing of our forebears."

Bowing his head, the High Councilor places one palm on the side of his neck, covering his clan-mark. A rustling of robes ensues as the whole crowd rises and imitates his posture of invocation. I feel a reflexive qualm as I raise my hand to my own neck. When was the last time I prayed sincerely to the ancestors? Not for many months—not since my first journey to the Underbelly.

"Honorable ones, we call on you. By the bonds of our clan-marks, hear us. Remember the children of your heart's blood, we who wander the stars. In ancient days, when you walked our home soil and stood under the light of our native sun, you endured much evil. Long did the clans suffer under the Sko'larik, the savage Devorak chieftains, who worshipped the beasts and ate the flesh of their own kind. In this time of blood and blasphemy, you, our ancestors, rose to the salvation of the Noxxiin people. You reached into the realm of the Deep and bound its power to your own bodies. Light and air, fire and stone—all matter you made subject to your wisdom and will."

The prayer goes on. I find my eyes drawn to Khalon and his master, standing in front of me. The metallic disks of their implants are clearly visible on the backs of their necks—the deepcraft bonds. The origin of the technology is obscure: the construction and operation of the bonds are among the Van'shorii's most jealously guarded secrets. I suppress a shiver. Deepcrafters may have been our saviors in some ancient, crueler time, but only a fool would be at ease among people who can spark fire out of thin air and mold matter with their minds.

"...having freed the clans from the sacrilege of the Devorak, you established the Van'shorii Order, leading your people back to the true worship of the ancestors." The High Councilor's voice rings out, clear and sonorous. "From that time, in all ages and trials, you have been our guardians. During the Thousand-Year War, when our home planets came under the scourge of the Three Races—the ruthless Syr, the foul Arik'nae, and the deceitful Peshyakin—the Van'shorii led our warriors into battle. And when, through treachery and dishonor, the Three brought desolation to our lands, the gift of deepcraft allowed us to build a refuge among the stars: our glorious Fleet."

I try not to fidget as the long invocation continues. I wonder how much of it the High Councilor himself believes. The Devorak chieftains and their cannibal warriors are the stuff of children's fables, and our records of the Thousand-Year War are only slightly more reliable. Two of our ancient alien opponents, the Syr and the Arik'nae, seem to have disappeared or died out in our centuries-long absence. Only the Peshyakin, the half-sights, remain. They are real enough, I suppose, since we are still fighting them.

Or slaughtering them. I can still hear Askko's words, see the flicker of hesitation in his eyes: *Maybe they were not all warriors, but...*

"...after generations of wandering the void, rebuilding our people's strength, we have returned at last to the planets of our birth. One final test awaits us: to take back by the strength of our heart's blood the land that was stolen from you, our forebears!"

The High Councilor's voice rises to a shout. The crowd responds with a surge of noise. My mouth tightens in a frown while Valo waits until the long cheer dies away.

"Tonight we ask your blessing on these initiates, who have chosen to pursue our most ancient and honorable of crafts..."

I feel a taut resentment in my gut. Markmaking is at least as old as deepcraft, if not older—and certainly no less honorable. I find it doubtful, too, that Khalon and his fellow apprentices truly chose this occupation. Only a small proportion of the Noxxiin population has the physical and genetic traits necessary to use a deepcraft bond. If a child is born compatible, he is usually apprenticed to the Van'shorii long before he is old enough to have any say in the matter.

The High Councilor is still extoling the virtues of the initiates. My gaze falls on two figures standing near Valo in the honor-seats: a middle-aged, female deepcrafter and a much younger woman, almost a girl, with a sullen expression. I recognize them both—Tekra T'sarek, the High Councilor's wife, and Shekali, their youngest daughter. Both of them come to Kilmaya's studio for marks; they are among her most prestigious clients.

Tekra listens to Valo with rapt attention. But Shekali does not even look at her father. She stares out across the arena, dull-eyed and despondent.

But of course. I remember something Kilmaya said: Shekali is the only one of the High Councilor's children who is not genetically fit for a deepcraft implant. This ceremony must remind her of everything she can never attain.

A pang of sympathy aches in my chest.

"...give them wisdom in the craft of the Deep, and the strength to overcome every enemy." The High Councilor is approaching the end of the prayer. "As they enter the great battle for the homeland, give them the courage to pursue every honorable deed—regardless of praise or acknowledgement."

My breath catches softly. *Regardless of acknowledgement?* That line does not belong in the invocation. There is no honor without acknowledgement, without the visible mark in the flesh required by the law...

Oh.

I sense a stir from the other artists on the platform. They have noticed the unusual words, too, and understood their meaning. I send a surreptitious glance towards Mekkalluthak, up in the honor-seats. His composed expression has hardened.

The moment passes; the rest of the crowd does not appear to react to the added line. But my fellow markmakers and I know that Valo T'sarek is speaking of the mark-ban. We know the veiled threat he just implied.

Do not cross the Ascendance, little painters.

I blink rapidly, dismissing the thought. The High Councilor cannot threaten Clan Serix in any serious way; the decisions of the guild do not come under his authority. Our Fleet, our law, our order of life—nothing could function without markmakers. Valo T'sarek knows that as well as anyone.

"Ancestors, look upon us now as we welcome these new guardians of our people. Let us stand witness to the truth in their flesh." The High Councilor lowers his hand from his neck, ending the prayer. He turns his gaze to the platform. "Witnesses, request the marks."

A booming drumroll plays, the crowd roars, and the deepcrafters and their apprentices turn away from the honor-seats to face their respective artists. Khalon's master bows to me deeply.

"Markmaker, I ask for the mastery-mark of deepcraft for my apprentice, Khalon T'sarek."

I lift my chin and adopt an expression I can only hope looks authoritative. "Do you swear, as his master and witness, that he has proven himself worthy of this mark?"

The older deepcrafter touches his neck. "By the blood of my ancestors, I swear it. He has suffered our trials and passed through. He is proven."

"Khalon T'sarek." I turn to the apprentice. "Is it your wish to join the Van'shorii as a master of deepcraft, to obey and serve the order with all the strength of your heart's blood?"

Khalon's eyelids flicker briefly, and a tremor runs through his body. "This is my wish, markmaker. I pledge my heart's blood to the Van'shorii and their law. May my ancestors turn me away, and may my eyes never see the Long Dream, if I break the ink-bond of this oath."

A chill grips me. I, too, swore an oath like that once.

May my ancestors turn me away...

I force myself to speak. "Then by the law of truth that binds me, I may serve you with honor." I nod towards the chair beside us.

The raith'aal pipes start a low drone as all the initiates take their seats. With a sense of relief, I tug at my gloves. At last, I can do what I came for. I reach for the ink bottle on the side table and pull out the stopper. The delicate, earthy scent of trallak extract tingles in my nostrils—familiar but tinged with a harsher, chemical edge. The dye used for Van'shorii marks is not like other inks; it is specially made to interact with deepcraft. When the implants are active, the ink will glow.

I have always thought the effect a little ostentatious, but it is not as if I have any choice in the matter. This is the ink the law prescribes. I take up the pen and make sure the tip is securely fastened. I dip it in the bottle and turn to the young warrior reclining in the chair. Then I lean over and touch the tip of my pen to his brow.

The mastery-mark itself is the work of a few minutes. I trace the sigils without hesitation, as if my pen is running along invisible grooves. It shocks me, almost, how mindless it is. I could be half-asleep, and my hand would still be able to perform the necessary motions, like a machine. I have striven for years for that kind of skill. Yet, in this moment, it gives me no sense of accomplishment.

I switch pen-tips and start on the verity lines. Khalon lies motionless, his eyes closed, but I can sense the coiled tension of his body. What is he feeling? He has been preparing for this day even longer than I have—since his early childhood. Is he praying to his Van'shorii ancestors right now? Does he fear the power that he has learned to channel in his mind and body? Or is he eager to unleash it upon the alien half-sights in the war for our stolen planets?

I complete the last flourish of silver ink and lift the pen. The new tattoo glistens flame-like on Khalon's black brow. Around me, the other artists are finishing their marks, too. I open the bottle of sealing-glaze and brush the clear liquid over my handiwork. The words of sealing rise to my lips automatically, a reflex rather than a thought: "This is a mark of truth..."

It is done. I put down my tools. The new deepcrafters rise from their seats to a great thundering of drums and applause.

"Kazen! Kazen! Kazen val Van'shorii!"

The initiates and their masters step off the platform down onto the sand. Deafened by the noise and feeling suddenly overwhelmed, I turn to follow. All at once I am desperate for a quiet room, darkness, and solitude—anywhere away from this arena and its unbearable lights.

A touch on my shoulder stops me. I look back, startled, at Rinavi. The older artist regards me with amusement.

"Not yet," she whispers.

Chagrined, I step back from the edge of the platform. How could I forget? We cannot leave our places until after the battle-dance.

Hoping no one else noticed my blunder, I join the other markmakers in the center of the platform. Down on the arena floor, each master van'shor stands behind his or her apprentice, resting a hand on the initiate's shoulder. Khalon's fists clench by his sides. For an instant, I can see his limbs trembling. Then the whole arena falls dark.

The spectators murmur in anticipation from the now-invisible stands. In the darkness, the drums begin playing a low, steady, blood-thrumming pulse.

A light appears out in the arena—a ghostly, silver-white luminescence, outlining the shape of a bond-tattoo. I know I am looking at the back of one of the initiates, whose deepcraft implant has just been kindled. But in the pitch dark, it looks as if the glowing sigils hover in midair, disconnected from any body.

One by one, more luminous tattoos appear as the master deepcrafters activate their students' bonds. Exactly how they do so is a secret of their craft—another reason for the darkness, no doubt. In a few moments, all five initiates are visible, faintly silhouetted by the glow of their marks. The throbbing of the drums reaches a feverish speed. The new deepcrafters lift their hands.

Five orbs of flame, searing white, spring into being. For a moment they hang suspended, casting stark shadows. Then they rocket towards the roof.

I look on, spellbound as always, though I have seen the same performance every year since I was a boy. I remember I was always terrified that the deep-fire bolts would rip through the dome, raining down shards of metal on the crowd below. But that has never happened. As I watch, the five orbs collide with each other, high above the stands but still well below the ceiling. A bloom of silvery flame—a cascade of sparks—then darkness again, and silence. A shout of awe wells up from the crowd.

Now the music resumes, and the arena lights come up again—only dimly, so that the Van'shorii's luminescent marks remain distinct. The master deep-crafters leave the initiates in the center of the arena and return to the mark-making platform. As they form a circle around the dais, the tattoos on their own faces begin to glow. Moving in unison, they raise their hands. I suck in a breath.

A sharp hum disturbs the air. Before our eyes, a transparent, dimly radiant barrier appears around the platform, enclosing us in a small dome. *Deepshields.* No flame or projectile can pierce the barrier as long as the deepcrafters maintain its energy. I should feel safe, but instead I only feel trapped.

I clench my teeth, trying to ignore the faint drone of the shield, swallowing the panic that rises in my throat.

Rinavi touches my shoulder again. "Watch the dance," she murmurs.

I attempt to obey. I look beyond the shield, out into the dim arena, where the new deepcrafters sway and stamp to the rhythm of the drums, moving in a slow circle out on the sand. The pattern of lights made by their luminous tattoos is mesmerizing. They duck and spin, striking combat stances as they follow the measure of the music. Every now and again they loose a fierce shout, a battlecry:

"*Kalimaa!*"

All at once, the music shifts; a single pipe plays a harsh wail of warning. The great gate at the far end of the arena splits open, and a swarm of warriors pours out. They wear extravagant costumes of feather and fur, with grotesque animal masks that cover their faces. The masks are embellished with a close mesh of decorative sigils painted in phosphorescent blue dye.

The Devorak. I cannot help the old thrill of mingled terror and excitement as I watch the costumed warriors enter the arena. Beast-worshippers, blood-drinkers—the ancient enemies of the Van'shorii. The myths say the Devorak had mystical tattoos that allowed them to transform into animals and gave them unnatural abilities in battle. But to gain these powers, they had to eat the flesh of their fellow Noxxiin.

Most of it is nonsense, of course. The Devorak, if they existed at all, were probably an obscure cult with a particularly savage way of honoring their animal deities. But it makes for a good story—and a good spectacle in the arena on Van'shorvanii.

The masked warriors, about twenty in all, charge towards the circle of deepcrafters, howling and shrieking as they brandish hatchets and javelins. The Van'shorii initiates turn to face them. With a yell, they summon their orbs of silver flame. Then they fire them over the heads of the Devorak.

The warriors fall to the sand, letting the deepfire bolts burst harmlessly in the air. But then they are on their feet again, whirling, stamping, and screaming, surrounding the deepcrafters on all sides.

The arena explodes into a frenzy of lights and movement. Warriors leap and tumble, lashing out with weapons and the spurs on their own bare feet. The deepcrafters respond with bolts of pale fire. But none of the blows land, and none of the flames hit their seeming targets. This is only a dance, after all.

The momentum of the mock battle is turning. One by one, the deepcrafters lay hold of the warriors' animal guises and tear them off, casting them to the sand. Unmasked, the warriors drop their weapons and flee, staggering out of the arena. In another few minutes, the ring is empty once more except for the initiates. The crowd roars, and the music swells.

My jaw clenches again. It is not over yet. And I have just remembered what is coming next.

The arena lights grow suddenly dimmer. A large gate in the right-hand wall rumbles open, revealing the black mouth of a tunnel. Out of the shadows springs a huge, horned, and luminous beast—a great burrik.

It must be the same creature I saw earlier. If it looked fierce then, it appears monstrous now. Every inch of its brindled fur drips with the same glowing blue paint that decorated the masks of the warriors. It tosses its slender, savage head, and lets loose a guttural howl.

The tumult of the spectators vibrates the air.

The burrik is meant to be a Devorak chieftain, transfigured into terrifying animal form. But this is no supernatural warrior. It is only a beast, covered with dye and drugged for the sake of the spectacle.

Dethra, kolar, piitro. Worthy weapon, worthy opponent, worthy cause. I cannot see how this encounter meets the laws of honorable combat. And yet the crowd will stand and cheer as the Van'shorii slaughter this half-crazed beast.

The burrik swings its glowing head, eyeing its opponents, as if unable to decide whether to fight or flee. Then all at once it wheels and springs towards the nearest initiate.

The creature's reflexes are terrifying, but the new van'shor's are faster. The half-sphere of a deepshield flashes into existence, blocking the burrik's way. The beast slams against the barrier and rebounds, sprawling on the sand. For a moment it lies dazed while the crowd screams approval. Then it lurches to its feet and charges again.

I lower my eyes. I do not want to watch this mockery of a hunt. When I was a child, it thrilled me to watch warriors who could bait and taunt a burrik with such ease. But now the sight only sickens me.

Another howl of rage echoes from the ring. Against my will, I glance up. The burrik stands in the middle of the arena, clawing at the sand, as if trying to lunge forward but held back by some unseen force. Four of the initiates crouch close to the ground, flanking the beast on both sides. Their outstretched hands do not touch the creature but pin it in place with the invisible power of deepreach while the burrik plunges and snarls.

Now the fifth initiate steps forward. It is hard to tell in the low light, but I think it is Khalon. He faces the beast, standing only a few yards away as it scrabbles to get at him. Then he extends a palm over the sand.

A white-blue light flashes out, momentarily blinding. When it fades, Khalon is holding something in his hand: a long, pointed rod, like a crude javelin. As quick as thought, he has forged a weapon out of the sand. Now he raises it high. A silver flame blooms on the tip of the rod. Khalon throws back his head and bellows a warcry:

"Aurorii chi'ar! Kalimaaa!"

He hurls the javelin; it springs out of his hand with unnatural speed. At the same instant, his companions release the burrik's front feet so that it rears up, straining to leap. The weapon plunges into its chest. Then the beast's luminous fur bursts into flame.

I shut my eyes. But I cannot shut out the bone-jarring shriek.

For a long minute I stand rigid, tremoring. I hear the delirium of the crowd; underneath it, the hum of the deepshield over our heads fades. But I do not open my eyes until I feel Rinavi's gentle touch on my shoulder.

"It's over, Mariikel."

I raise my head. The deepshield dome is gone; the arena lights have come back on, white and glaring. The five new Van'shorii look to the stands, acknowledging the storm of applause.

But all I see is the massive, blackened body that lies stretched on the sand, and when I breathe, I inhale the stink of charred flesh.

CHAPTER SEVEN

I collect my belongings from the artists' room and leave the arena level as quickly as possible. But my progress is slowed by the crowd that now pours from the stands back into the corridors. I am in the transport hub, fighting my way towards an elevator, when I hear my name.

"Mariikel! Over here."

I glance around and spot Kilmaya beckoning to me from an alcove between two pillars. Beside her stands a Serix official: Virik, the guild recordmaster and my uncle's superior at the archives. Virik's half-grown daughter, K'nima, is with them too.

I grind my teeth. They want to congratulate me, no doubt, but I am in no mood for pleasantries. And seeing Virik reminds me that I will not have quiet at home tonight, either—Chervani has invited the recordmaster's family to share our festival meal. With an effort of will, I turn and push through the throng to reach the alcove.

"Here is our victorious artist," Kilmaya declares. "Well, how does it feel to be a part of Van'shorvanii?"

"Exhausting," I reply, more bluntly than I intended. Trying to recover my manners, I incline my head towards Virik and his daughter. "Honor with you, recordmaster, K'nima. I hope you both enjoyed the ceremony."

"Very much, markmaker." K'nima ducks her head, bashful. She is one of the newer apprentices at Kilmaya's studio, and she is still in awe of both me and my teacher.

"It was certainly thought-provoking." Virik's tone is dry. His dour, dark-skinned face holds an ambiguous expression.

"The audacity. You caught that line about *acknowledgment*," says Kilmaya. "He doesn't think much of Mekkalluthak's ban; that's clear enough."

Virik's brow furrows. "What the High Councilor thinks of it is irrelevant. Only the warband commanders can submit an appeal, and I doubt they will try. Dragging out the process will only bring more disgrace."

Oh, Ka. I have just remembered that Askko will be at home tonight, too. I do not know how I am going to face him after our quarrel. Keeping up a façade of good humor for our evening guests is going to be unbearable.

Kilmaya gives me a sidelong look. Then, as if following my train of thought: "Have you seen your cousin yet, Mariikel? How did he take the news?"

"He was...upset. Understandably."

"Hakk. Well, he couldn't have been too angry, since you still seem to be in one piece." Kilmaya's mouth twitches in a wry smile. "I'm sure he will forgive you eventually."

"Of course," I reply without much conviction.

My teacher turns back to Virik. "Did you see how they slipped in the 'Aurorii chi'ar' at the end of the battle-dance? That's a statement, now. The faction motto doesn't belong in the ceremony—"

All at once, the desire to be alone overwhelms me like a physical pain. "Forgive me." The words burst out of me. "I have to go."

Virik blinks in mild surprise. "Forgive us for keeping you. I believe we will see you shortly, anyway—at supper, yes?"

"Of course. I will see you then, recordmaster. Honor with you."

Kilmaya narrows her eyes; she looks as if she means to say something more. I do not give her the opportunity. I step back from the alcove, plunge into the milling crowd, and flee.

I arrive home to an empty house; my family must be lingering at the arena. Grateful for that scrap of good fortune, I head to my room and drop my satchel on my bunk. Then I sink to the floor and rest my head in my hands.

My skull still pounds with the noise of drums, and my tunic reeks of kiili oil and scorched burrik hide. Impulsively, I stand up, undo my belt, and pull off the formal tunic with violence. I step over to the washbasin and turn on the water full blast, scrubbing my face and arms until I can no longer feel the slickness of the decorative oil. Then I dry off and go to my closet to change into one of my simple, blue-and-white studio outfits.

Chervani might scold me for wearing my work clothes while company is over, but I do not care. I want the stench of the arena out of my skin. I feel even more unclean than after I visit the Underbelly.

As I rebuckle my belt, my eyes fall on the rough laborer's tunic hanging in the back of my closet. I pause. It is tempting to slip away, if only to be among people who do not know my face or my name. But I do not have the presence of mind for that journey tonight. Besides, I promised Chervani I would be here for supper.

I sigh. Maybe a quiet walk through the sector will help clear my mind.

Pulling my eyes away from my Underbelly tunic, I take down a light hooded cloak instead and throw it over my shoulders. Then I steal out the front door into the dimming streets. I tug the cloak's hood low over my head. Even when I am not committing crimes, I have grown so accustomed to wearing a disguise that I hardly feel safe without one.

Most families are inside now, preparing their celebratory evening meals, but some groups remain out on their porches or in their gardens, talking or drinking together. The murmur of relaxed conversation and the whiff of spiced kol-dawra drifts in the air. I pull my cloak tightly around my shoulders and walk faster.

Leaving Elantii Street behind, I head down a narrower hall into the less wealthy part of the sector. No Serix house is truly poor, of course—in our clan, there are only the well-to-do and the slightly less well-to-do. Still, the houses here are smaller, the gardens more crowded, and the inhabitants pursue less prestigious professions such as ink-making and pen-crafting.

This was also my parents' neighborhood once. Both my father and mother worked at the clan's trallak farms—as I would have, most likely, had they lived. I remember so little about them that I have never grieved over them much. My real parents may not have been able to afford to apprentice me to such a prestigious artist as Kilmaya. Had I not been adopted by my prosperous, record-keeper uncle, I might not be a markmaker at all.

Perhaps that would have been for the best.

My steps slow as I come out of an alley into a more open area, a small round plaza with a modest fountain bubbling in the middle. A display of stars in a blue-black sky plays across the low dome overhead. The sector is too deep inside the ship to have any windows.

Do you want to die on this miserable ship?

Askko's words come back to me as I wander over to the fountain. Watching the reflection of false stars in the dark water, I feel suddenly melancholy. I have never thought of my home as a miserable or stifling place—but then, I have never known anything else. What would it be like to look up at real stars in a true night sky? What would it be like to have a whole plot of ground dedicated to my parents' bones? I have never thought about that before. There are no individual graves on the ships. My parents' remains, reverently burnt to ashes by a van'shor's deepfire, lie mixed with the dust of their kin underneath the Serix ancestor shrine. But there is no space for more than a pinch of ashes from each deceased clan member's body. Even as we ask for the guidance of our forebears, the Fleet itself has room only for the living.

Probably Askko is right. Life would be better on the planets, no matter what it might cost to conquer them. And yet, I cannot imagine leaving the

Akkano'dath for one of the ocean-washed islands that my cousin described. For me, the ancestral planets have always been stories, not places one could actually go. I am beginning to feel the same way about the ancestors themselves. Their protection—is that only a story, too?

For a while I stand in the quiet plaza, mulling. Warm lights shine from the dwellings nearby, but no one is out in the street. An image stirs in my mind: a hazy childhood memory of sitting by this fountain, crying and afraid. I think I was trying to find my parents' old home, but got lost in the winding corridors and sat down in this plaza because it was the only place I recognized.

Now, over the splashing of the water, I hear a faint, rasping, sing-song voice. At first, I think the voice is a part of my memory—but the sound comes from one of the corridors off to my right. I tilt my head to listen, and the words become clearer:

> *Burrik bite, crab claw,*
> *Kharraktyl climbing.*
> *Tunnelbird whistle,*
> *Steelbeetle shining.*

I recognize the song; it is an old children's rhyme. And now I recognize the gravelly voice, too. I come here so seldom, I had nearly forgotten that this place is close to the house of Haza'ruux—the mad markmaker.

Following the sound of the chanting, I step into one of the dim streets adjoining the plaza. Haza'ruux's doorway is set apart from the others, at the very end of the corridor. He has more room for a garden than his neighbors—in fact, I can barely see the door for all the greenery overflowing his porch. It looks wild and forbidding compared to Hakham and Chervani's carefully groomed plants.

Haza'ruux himself sits on the ground among his untamed bushes, lit by the single lamp above his door. A wiry old man wearing a ragged tunic, he rocks back and forth, his bare feet tapping the dirt as he sings:

> *Wolf fang, bear maw,*
> *Silky ech'taani.*
> *Arrowhawk scream,*
> *Soaring c'aani.*

> *Dance, my wild ones.*
> *Battle, my beasts.*
> *Gather for the games*
> *At the stone of the chiefs.*

The song goes on, but the old man switches into a guttural dialect that I do not understand—or else he is simply making up nonsense words. His audience, however, does not seem to mind the gibberish. Three or four children, so young they have no tattoos besides their clan-marks, tumble and play at his feet. As I approach, one youngster grows bold and scrambles up the hermit's back to perch on his shoulders. Haza'ruux leans over slightly to bear the extra weight, but he continues singing, unfazed.

Haza'ruux Serix always seems to be surrounded by children—although as far as I know, he has none of his own. I suspect he keeps company with little ones because they are less afraid of him than adults are. They are not bothered by the fact that he sings to himself or speaks in strange leaps of logic while tending his plants and making his unusual inks. These children are too young to know that the marks swarming over every inch of Haza'ruux's body are, for the most part, unreadable.

The interlocked symbols are so dense that I cannot even make out the color of the underlying skin. I notice, as I have noticed in the past, that they vaguely resemble the ancient sigils painted on the atrium dome. Rumor has it that Haza'ruux can read the archaic marks that the ancestors used. I am not sure whether to believe that—there are many unlikely stories about the old hermit. People call him *rixar'azahl*, the mad markmaker, even though he has never worked in a studio. On rare occasions, when the whim strikes him, he does give out tattoos: small, decorative marks with no legal meaning, which the guild does not bother to regulate. Some people believe that his marks bring good luck. In any case, no one troubles him about his illegible craft. He seems to be his own master, answering to neither guild nor council.

How pleasant to be a madman, I think. *No one expects anything of you.* And I stroll up to the border of his garden.

"Ha'ruux! Ha'ruux!" The boy on his shoulders tugs at the old man's tunic, pointing at me. The other children pause their games to peer upwards, a little curious, but mostly indifferent. They cannot read marks yet—the sigils on my face stating that I am a master artist mean nothing to them. I find their disinterest refreshing.

Haza'ruux breaks off his chant. He looks up at me, three eyes shut, his grin lopsided. "And who are you, little stranger? Come to ruin my songs? Is the old dog howling too loud?"

"Not at all." For some reason, the tension that has gripped my body all day begins to ease. I sit down on the garden path in front of him. "I was only listening. Don't stop."

"Don't stop, he says!" Haza'ruux cackles. "Do you hear that, little ones? He likes our games. This is a strange one, to be sure." Impatiently, he nods at me. "Let Haza'ruux look at you."

With a reluctant hand, I push back my hood. For a minute, the old man gazes at me with all his eyes. His own face, however, is a mystery—the only tattoo I recognize is the Serix symbol on his neck, barely distinguishable from the tangled swirl of all his other marks.

It is disconcerting to be scrutinized by someone whose skin I cannot read in turn. But I meet his gaze without flinching. I find it difficult to be truly afraid of him. The little boy who clings to him begins bouncing up and down on his shoulders. One of the other youngsters, singing a jumbled version of Haza'ruux's rhyme, scoops up dirt from the path and pours it over the hermit's bare toes.

"Hakk, it's you, Flashing Blade." Apparently losing interest in my presence, Haza'ruux bends over to help the children heap dirt on his own feet.

Flashing Blade! I restrain a laugh. The name Mariikel simply means *silver*. I am not sure where Haza'ruux picked up the idea for the more dramatic epithet.

The boy sitting on the hermit's shoulders narrows his eyes in a mock scowl. "We're playing deepcrafters and Devorak," he declares. "I'm a *kharraktyl* warrior. I have poison teeth." Hissing, he clambers over Haza'ruux's head and leaps at me.

With a laugh, I catch him. He shrieks, delighted, kicking and trying to escape. As I tussle with him gently, I notice that his clan-mark is Trechik. This surprises me, for all the other children are Serix. It is unusual for so young a child to be away from his own clan sector at night. I wonder where his parents are.

During the scuffle, the boy's tunic, which is slightly too big for him, slips down off his shoulder—and I catch a glimpse of a fresh memory-mark on his back. He squirms too much for me to read all the sigils, but I gather enough: his father, a Trechik warrior, died in some recent battle. Most likely, the boy's mother is Serix, a widow who has now returned to the sector to live with her family.

Even as I return his playful snarls, my heart sinks. *A child of war.* Is he even aware that he will never see his father again?

The Trechik child finally escapes me and dashes off into the jungle of the garden, joining his playmates. Haza'ruux watches them with a keen eye. He is particularly kind to orphans—at least, he was kind to me, when I was very young. It was Haza'ruux, I now remember, who found me by the fountain the day I was lost and played with me until my aunt came. But I have not spoken to him for years.

The old hermit fingers a flower hanging down from a vine. "Flashing Blade in his dark hood," he murmurs, as if to the flower. "Always running, never resting. He is so tired. His eyes are sad."

I smile at his odd way of speaking. "What are you talking about? What would I have to be sad about?"

Still Haza'ruux addresses the blossom, twirling it between his fingers. "Poor little Flashing Blade. His eyes are too sharp. Ink is too thin for him. Poor Mariikel."

Unease creeps through me. But I push the feeling away and force a laugh. "What?"

Haza'ruux turns his head, as if noticing me for the first time. But now his eyes glitter, and his gaze is fiercely attentive. Everything about his expression says, *You do not fool me. I know you.*

Fear seizes me. Transfixed, I sit wordless before him.

In the street behind me, a woman's voice calls out. The children pause their games and peek out from behind the shrubs. Again the woman calls, and reluctantly the young ones slink out of the underbrush. The little Trechik boy, however, stops and hugs Haza'ruux's leg.

"Don't want to go home," he complains. "I want to sleep at your house. You're funny."

"Hakka, no, Tyotik." With a gentle hand, Haza'ruux pries him away. "Go home to your nakki. The mad markmaker's house—not a good place for sleeping. You would have strange dreams." He watches as the children leave. "Honor with you, little friends. Come back soon. Haza'ruux gets lonely with no one to sing to."

He says all this in his usual sing-song wheeze—no sign of the bitterly intelligent being who glared out at me only a moment before. I shiver. The two of us are alone now, sitting together in the dim garden. I stare at the ground as if waiting for him to dismiss me.

He shuffles his bare toes through the dirt. Even the soles of his feet are covered in swirling patterns of ink. "You are not a child anymore," he rasps. "What brings you to Haza'ruux?"

"I didn't mean to come," I say quietly. "I don't want anything."

A low, hissing laugh escapes him. "Little Flashing Blade. So humble." With a grunt, he stands and turns towards his overgrown porch. "Come."

Dumbfounded, I glance up. Haza'ruux opens the door, beckoning to me. "Come. You are old enough for strange dreams."

No one goes into the mad markmaker's house. Aside from letting the children play in his garden, he does not host gatherings or entertain visitors. No one I know has ever been beyond that shabby door.

It does not seem wise to refuse the invitation. I rise, gather my cloak about me, and follow him inside.

CHAPTER EIGHT

The front room is small, and so dim that I have to open all my eyes wide before I can make out anything. The walls are hung with animal hides; burrik furs drape the worn couch sitting on one end of the room. Tall, potted shrubs crowd the corners, and vines trail down from shelves, as if the garden outside has invaded the house. Here and there on low tables lie dirty dishes, seemingly forgotten in the midst of a hasty meal. An earthy, musty smell hangs over the whole room.

So this is the mysterious mad markmaker's house. I cannot help blinking my lower eyes in disgust. But Haza'ruux does not seem at all self-conscious.

"Chali, Izali," he calls in his crooning way. "Where are you, my sleek ones? We have a guest!"

At first, I think he is talking to some figment of his imagination. But then an overhanging shrub rustles, and two small, cream-colored muzzles emerge from the foliage. The pair of ech'taanin peer at me, then vanish again with a chirp of alarm.

Haza'ruux laughs. He hums to himself as he ambles across the disorderly room towards a tiny kitchen beyond. Baffled, I follow.

What does he want with me?

The kitchen is better lit but still untidy. Plant clippings and gardening tools litter the narrow counters, while a savory aroma of *tavla* meat rises from a small pot simmering on the stove. The smell reminds me that I ate almost nothing for my midday meal, and I feel suddenly famished. But I do not presume to ask for anything—I will be going home soon for supper. Haza'ruux bends over the pot, muttering; he seems to have forgotten my presence.

Too embarrassed to disturb him, I glance around uncertainly. The counter is strewn with bundles of dried roots and leaves, along with bowls of bright-hued pastes and powders. These must be the old man's ink preparations. I have always heard that Haza'ruux's dyes are special—he is practically the only inkmaker who also grows his own plants, and there are rumors that he does not even use trallak bark. Some artists prefer his inks, saying that they are stronger and more vivid than ordinary dyes. I wouldn't know, for Kilmaya never buys them.

Curious, I reach for a bowl of blue paste. A hiss from overhead startles me. I jerk my hand back and look up into the beady gaze of a large, black kharrak-tyl. The reptile clings to the ceiling with its six lobed feet, eyeing me balefully. Its dark tongue flickers from its mouth.

"Kesh, Tasikko," says Haza'ruux with a chuckle. "Flashing Blade is not after your meat." Then, to me: "Do not mind Tasikko. He is old, like Haza'ruux. Not much poison left in his teeth."

Despite this assurance, I retreat to the kitchen doorway. "Please, why am I here?"

"So little patience. Keep looking, Flashing Blade."

"For what?" I blink in confusion. "I'm not looking for anything."

Haza'ruux does not answer. He continues preparing his meal, starting up his nonsense song again. Exasperated, I turn and step out of the kitchen. Pausing in the front room, I survey the disarray. Pity steals through me. The man is probably lonely. How long has he lived in this odd little house in solitude? Who are his family? Does he have any?

Slowly, I pick my way between pots of herbs and heaps of animal skins. Strange that he should have so many of the latter. Normally only the homes of great athletes are decorated with burrik furs; it is bad taste to adorn your dwelling with the skins of beasts that you have not slain yourself. But I cannot imagine Haza'ruux hunting anything.

I am trying to decide whether to clear a place to sit when I notice another doorway on my left; I did not see it when I came in. A curtain half-conceals the warm glow of the room beyond. I glance over my shoulder. Haza'ruux still prattles to himself at the stove.

He did tell you to keep looking. With that justification for my curiosity, I ease forward and pull back the curtain.

It takes me several moments to comprehend what I see. The room is as bright and orderly as the rest of the house is unkempt. A dark, gleaming table stands in the middle of the floor, and tall shelves line the walls. The ceiling is painted in a brilliant array of interlocking designs. I cannot read the sigils—they are too archaic—but the artistry is dazzling.

The artistry. With growing amazement, I scan the contents of the shelves. Ink bottles. Racks of pens. Sharpening stones and mixing bowls. There is no mistaking it: this place is a studio.

But what in Ka's name is it doing here?

I know Haza'ruux gives out decorative marks on occasion, but I have never heard that he owns a studio—much less a magnificent, fully stocked workshop like this. Awed, I venture a few steps into the room. There are hues of ink here that I have never seen before: iridescent golds, radiant oranges, blues and greens so pale they are almost white. I am not an inkmaker, but I know it is extremely difficult to make these lighter colors using the dark-pigmented extract from trallak bark—the refining process takes months. Haza'ruux is either a very patient man, or else he has his own dye-making methods of which the rest of the clan is unaware.

His pens, too, are of the highest quality, extremely old and made from traditional animal bone rather than metal. I marvel at the exquisite designs carved into the pale bone shafts: flowers and leaves, tiny beasts and miniscule hunters, all enmeshed by a web of old-fashioned sigils I cannot read. I feel an urge to pick up the pens, to feel the balance of them in my hand, to test the ink-flow of the tips—but they are too beautiful for me. I do not dare.

Slowly I turn around, taking in the other shelves in the room. Two entire walls are filled—I gasp aloud—with *books*.

They line the shelves in pristine rows, some slender, others thick and ornate. I have never seen so many in one place before. There are a few books in the guild's record hall—faded, unreadable relics which the archivists preserve only to honor the ancestors—but I have never seen one in someone's home before. And yet, somehow, this mad inkmaker has a whole library.

Irresistibly drawn, I approach the shelf and trace the sigils adorning the spine of one of the books with quivering fingers. I cannot tell if the symbols are words or mere decoration.

How old are these? My mind reels. *Can he actually read them?*

A low laugh surprises me, and I whirl around. Haza'ruux stands in the doorway, holding two steaming bowls. His mouth twitches in a crooked smile.

"Who are you?" I blurt out. "How…?"

With a mischievous air, he extends one of the bowls. "Is Flashing Blade hungry?"

The man is impossible. And the food does smell good. "Yes," I admit weakly.

"Did you forget to eat?" He cackles, pleased. "Haza'ruux forgets, too. So many marks, so many thoughts—what is food to us? But now we will eat."

He turns and crosses the front room. Casting a final bewildered glance about the studio, I follow.

Haza'ruux clears a pile of twigs from a low table and sets down the two bowls. Then he lowers himself onto the couch. "Sit now. You have so much to tell Haza'ruux."

"I do?"

"Hakk, yes." For an instant, he pins me with an uncanny stare, like the one he gave me in the garden. Then his expression shifts back to a lopsided grin. "But eat first." He pushes one of the bowls towards me, his eyes sparking with silent laughter.

I sit down. I feel, inexplicably, like a fumbling apprentice in the presence of a master. I have no idea what he wants, which both irritates and unnerves me. And yet, I sense behind his shifting moods an underlying benevolence. I remember the children playing at his feet, and the Trechik boy clinging to his shoulders.

Glad for an excuse not to speak, I reach for the bowl on the table. It is a thick tavla stew seasoned with savory herbs. I begin to eat, and to my great relief, Haza'ruux does as well. The food is simple but satisfying, and I realize again just how hungry I am. After a minute, the vines on the shelves above us rustle; the two pale-furred ech'taanin spring down to perch on the hermit's shoulders. Almost at the same moment, I hear a hiss from the floor. The black kharraktyl clambers out from under the table and settles itself at Haza'ruux's feet. The old man begins chattering to his creatures, feeding them bits of meat from his bowl.

I try not to stare. I edge away a bit and attempt to focus on my meal. It occurs to me that I ought to save my appetite for supper at home. But it would be rude to leave now; I should at least eat the food Haza'ruux gave me. As soon as I finish, though, I will find some graceful way to excuse myself.

But again my eyes are drawn to the curtain on the other side of the room. *That's the workshop of a master artist—more than a master. But who are his clients? Why would he keep it hidden?* A slow chill grips my spine. *And why would he show it to me?*

I cannot bear this any longer. I set aside the half-finished bowl of stew. "Thank you for the meal—Haza'ruux." I grope for words. "Please. I don't understand. Why—?"

"Haza'ruux has four eyes," he hisses, as if suddenly offended. "He has watched you for a long time."

I gape. Terror clutches at my stomach again. "What are you talking about?"

He puts down his bowl. The tame ech'taanin scamper back up into the vines, and the kharraktyl retreats under the table with a sullen hiss. Before I can pull away, Haza'ruux reaches out and grasps my hand. His grip is surprisingly strong, yet also precise and controlled. He holds my fingers as if he knows the location of every bone and exactly how hard he would have to squeeze to break them.

"Poor Flashing Blade. He works so hard. All day and all night, at his pens. Tongue is silent, but eyes burn." His voice drops to a guttural whisper, and he places a fingertip squarely between my eyes. "He has marks no one can see."

"Stop it." Shaken, I jerk my hand away and stand. "What do you want?"

He grins, blinking slowly—even his eyelids are tattooed. He laughs his broken laugh. "You did not mean to come, yet here you are. What do *you* want, Flashing Blade?"

"Stop calling me that. I don't want anything. I was only passing by."

The old man's searching expression does not change. I sigh. Perhaps if I tell him a part of the truth, he will be satisfied. "I—I was going to give an honor-mark to my cousin. But the guild put a ban on it. I was…upset about it."

"Hakk! No." Haza'ruux squints in irritation. "I do not mean today only. You have had the madness for a long time."

A fit of trembling seizes me. I back away, nearly tripping over a row of potted herbs on the floor. "I'm not mad!"

He regards me in silence for a while. "Why do you fear Haza'ruux? What harm can he do? No one listens to him—only the children." He tilts his head, smiling.

I stare at him, suffocating with dread.

He knows.

He knows about my work in the Underbelly. What else could he be talking about? But how is that possible? Haza'ruux hardly leaves his own house, much less the clan sector. How could he have found out?

And why does he care? Even through my terror, I still sense the strange kindness in his demeanor. An ache begins to throb in my chest. I should say nothing. I should leave. Why should I trust this half-insane old man with the truth I cannot trust to my own family?

But all at once, the pain of a year's silence crushes me. I am bone-weary of this secret, of living and breathing this falsehood. I cannot help it. I am not strong enough.

"Haza'ruux," I choke. "I think I have broken my oath. I have painted a lie."

He holds my gaze steadily, showing no surprise.

"I think—" My voice breaks. "I think I have given an exile-mark to an innocent man."

Haza'ruux closes all his eyes for a moment. "Tell me."

With a deep, shuddering breath, I sit down again. *What have I done?* But the truth has been spoken now, and it hangs in the air between us. I cannot take it back. So I tell the story.

It was nearly a year ago now that I gave Talorak Tarriks a tattoo of exile.

I had finished my apprenticeship mere weeks before. I had passed my mastery-trial, I had received my new mark, and I was still reveling in the thrill of being, at last, a full-fledged artist of Clan Serix. In addition, Kilmaya had officially named me the heir to her studio. I was almost giddy with happiness in those days. I had my pens and inks; I had the promise of a studio of my own; and I had, as everyone did, the bright dream of a future on the planets—for the war against the half-sights was going well, and there was nothing but good news from our battle fleets.

My joy, however, was short-lived. A few weeks after I became a master artist, I received my first summons to the ship's prison to give an exile-mark.

The message on my datascroll did not name the criminal, but there was nothing unusual about that. For the giving of exile-marks, artists are chosen by lot, and we are not provided with the name or the crime of the outcast until we arrive at the holding cells. Were we to know it beforehand, we might be targeted by the criminal's vengeful friends or kin, so these are measures to protect us. Still, I was nervous on that early morning when I packed my satchel and prepared to go to the prison. Kilmaya clasped my hands, told me to be strong, and assured me that the first time was always the most difficult.

When I arrived at the holding cells, an official met me and gave me the traditional markmaker's robes for the ceremony of exile: a long-sleeved white tunic, a full face mask, and long white gloves that reached my elbows. Again, I knew the disguise was for my own protection. Not even the guards who escorted me to the prisoner would know my true identity. But I also knew that white was the color of the Deep Sleep, the chieftain of the realm of Axdraa'dah—ruthless, honorless, devoid of marks. I was putting on the skin of the spirit of death.

It was the first time in my life, I remember, that I had ever covered all of my tattoos—that I had, in a sense, erased my very self. The gloves were mottled and stained; I told myself the spots were simply old blotches of ink. But I could not help feeling, as I flexed my fingers, that my hands were covered with blood.

When I had dressed, the official handed me off to a pair of waiting guards—burly warriors with Ascendance tattoos—who took me to the cell where the condemned man had been sedated. As I followed them, my heart pounding in the back of my throat, I told myself it would be over quickly. All I needed to do was review the court's sentence, ensure that it had the Serix guild's sigil of approval, and give the mark. It would be the work of half an hour, and then I could put it out of my mind.

The cell was bare but brightly lit, containing nothing but a metal work-table bolted to the floor. A man lay unconscious on the table with restraints strapped over his arms, legs, and chest. I took in the lean, powerful body, the Tarriks clan-mark, the tattoos of honor running up and down his arms—and I froze in horror.

I knew this man.

Talorak Tarriks was well-known in the combat arenas as an excellent warrior and instructor of warriors. In his younger days, he had been responsible for the physical training of the ship's children—Askko and I had both received our first combat lessons under his stern eyes. He was a strict teacher, but always just. He had never refused an honorable challenge, had never struck a treacherous blow. The man was irreproachable.

Talorak had trained me to the best of his ability—ill-suited as I was for even basic fighting—and had served as my witness when I received the standard mark for competency in self-defense. Though I rarely saw him after I graduated from the training arena, I knew that he eventually became a member of the Tarriks clan council. I had never heard anything but praise for his character. So when I saw him lying on that cold worktable, bound and sedated, I thought I must be dreaming. What in Ka's name had he done?

If the guards noticed my shock, they did not comment. One thrust a datascroll into my hands. The document declared that Talorak had been found guilty of killing a man while under the influence of undiluted mindwater.

Mindwater!

I could hardly believe the words in front of my eyes. Mindwater was a potent substance that enhanced a warrior's strength and savagery while fighting. A diluted form of the drug was occasionally given to soldiers before battle, but it was not allowed in arena combat. Undiluted mindwater was always illegal—it could drive a man berserk, leaving him with only the killing instinct of a beast.

Talorak would never have considered drinking mindwater. He'd warned us of its dangers, and would have punished his students severely if he'd found them taking it. And yet, here was the official sentence in my hands, telling me that Talorak had used the drug during a practice match, lost control of himself, and fatally injured a young warrior-in-training. And that was not all. Vials of mindwater had been discovered in Talorak's house. Medical tests had determined that the old trainer had been consuming small amounts of the substance for several weeks. There seemed to be no question of his guilt. He had been formally cast out of Clan Tarriks and sentenced to a life of slave labor in the Underbelly.

Talorak, a murderer? I had not even heard that he had been put on trial. But what could I say? The sentence of exile bore the approval of both the Tarriks clan council and the Serix guild. I had a duty to perform as a painter of truth.

If I'd had all my wits, I might have remembered that no markmaker is required to give a tattoo of exile to someone he knows personally. Somehow, when I had been summoned, the prison officials had overlooked the fact that Talorak had once been my teacher. I could have told them about this mistake.

I could have declined to give the mark and walked away without his fate on my conscience.

But I did not remember this, and as I stood there, mute and aghast, one of the Ascendance guards grunted impatiently. "Do I need to read it to you, markmaker?" He shifted his feet into an aggressive stance, and the light caught the curve of his long spurs.

The jeer snapped me out of my stupor. Trembling, I returned the datascroll. I took out my pens and my inks. And then—the shame will be on me forever—I bent over Talorak's unconscious body and began my work.

My hands shook so badly that I had to use stencils. As I traced the four strangling tendrils, line by line, I choked out the devastating words of exile: *"By this ink, I break the bonds…I cut you off…from the care of your ancestors… from your sons and your daughters…from your brothers and sisters, in blood and in arms…"*

Only once did Talorak stir under my touch. His eyelids flickered, and he looked up into my face. His expression was vacant and confused; I do not think he was truly awake. But that instant of half-awareness, before he succumbed again to the sedative, pierced me like a blade. In that moment, I could not believe he was guilty.

Somehow, I finished the mark. The guards escorted me from the cell, and I took off the pale, ink-splotched cloak and gloves. Then I stumbled back to the Serix sector in a daze of horror. At the studio, Kilmaya gave me one look, embraced me briefly, and told me to go home for the rest of the day. It took all my strength not to break down weeping in her arms.

I could not tell her about Talorak. Unless an artist has some grave reason to doubt the justice of a sentence, he is not supposed to reveal the names of those he has exiled. I had no reason, besides my childhood bias, to believe Talorak was innocent. Who was I to contradict the judgment of the Tarriks council and the Serix guild? So I said nothing.

I attempted, after that, to go on with my life. But my serene world of ink and honor had been shattered. I felt defiled. I had nightmares about Talorak, and about marks of shame bursting out on my body like festering sores. I had not merely painted a pattern on the old warrior's skin; I had cut him off from his ancestors. I had handed him over to the Deep Sleep, to the void of Axdraa'dah. The thought began to torment me: what if he had been innocent, after all?

I had to know. So I began my research.

In secret, I scoured the public archives for records of Talorak's trial. I found the statements of the eyewitnesses who had seen him kill the young athlete and the report by the healer who had found his blood contaminated with mindwater. But in the recording of the trial itself, Talorak repeatedly denied any knowledge of the drug. He did not know how vials of it had appeared in his house. He claimed he had been poisoned. Still, the evidence was against him, and his claims went ignored.

But I saw the old warrior's face in those recordings. It was haggard, tortured with grief, rage, and despair—but it was not the face of a liar.

I discovered that Talorak had been the oldest member on the Tarriks clan council, and one of the few who did not have an Ascendance faction-mark. There had been some enmity between him and the younger councilors over a proposed law—something about lowering the requirements for non-blood members to join the clan. The High Council at the time was urging the warrior clans to allow more adoptions so that people from any bloodline could become soldiers to aid in the war. Most of the warrior clans agreed—but Talorak had spoken against the law, throwing the Tarriks council into turmoil. The old warrior was highly respected and had a loyal following. It seemed possible that his faction would win, and Clan Tarriks would not change its strict adoption rules.

While this debate was still going on, Talorak suddenly went berserk from mindwater and killed one of his own students. His trial and banishment were swift. With Talorak gone and his credibility destroyed, his supporters had been forced to disband. Only one—the commander Jal'thor, a military strategist for the Ascendance but also a vocal advocate for clan tradition—still spoke against the adoption law. But one vote was not enough, and the Tarriks council quietly approved the law without further opposition.

By the end of my research, I felt even more guilt-stricken than before. I was right. There had been something rotten about Talorak's downfall—I could practically smell it, and I had never considered myself politically astute. And yet there had been little outcry at his exile. Besides Jal'thor, no one seemed eager to defend a man who opposed the Ascendance war effort. Not even the Serix guild had questioned the outcome of the trial.

I felt certain now of Talorak's innocence, but the prospect of bringing my suspicions before the guild terrified me. I could prove nothing. And if the Ascendance could arrange the ruin of a man as honorable as Talorak, they could dispose of me, too, if I brought the case to light.

So I clung to my cowardice and remained silent.

Even as I established my own reputation as a master artist, even as I garnered praise from all quarters, I hated myself. I was an oathbreaker, and no one else knew it. But I had neither the courage to tell my story to the guild nor the integrity to give up my profession.

It was during this time that I first decided to venture into the Underbelly. Even now, I cannot clearly remember what possessed me to do such a thing. I had some irrational notion that if I could only find Talorak, speak to him, and discover the truth, then I would finally be at peace. But I think I also had a morbid desire to see the place for myself—to see to what kind of life I had condemned this blameless man.

And that was how I, a son of Clan Serix, descended into the Underbelly and came back again. I told no one that I had gone, or what I had seen there. But if giving Talorak an exile-mark had broken me, then witnessing the suffering of the exiles tore me apart. It scattered the remainder of my honor into the void.

Sitting on the burrik skins in Haza'ruux's house, I fall silent. Telling the story, reliving it, has drained me. I feel weak and listless, as if I have bled out from a deadly wound.

Haza'ruux stirs. He has not said a word through my whole narration, but has only watched me closely. I did not know he was capable of such deep attentiveness.

"Did you find your warrior?" he says at last.

"No. I never did."

"But you went back."

Slowly I raise my head to meet his glinting gaze. "Who told you that?"

"Hakka," he laughs softly. "No man needs to tell Haza'ruux what he can see for himself."

I do not reply. I feel too wretched to explain why I decided to break my oath again by giving marks to the exiles. I still do not fully understand that decision myself. All I know is that every time I set my pen to the skin of an outcast, every time my marks bring life back into a hopeless face, I feel I am making reparation for my crime against Talorak.

I do not share this with Haza'ruux. Perhaps he has already guessed. I am about to ask dully what he plans to do with me, now that he knows my misdeeds. But then, to my mute surprise, he reaches out and places a gentle hand on my chest.

"You are strong, to keep silent so long. Haza'ruux can keep secrets, too. Now you will rest."

He rises, stalks across the cluttered room, and disappears into the kitchen. I remain sitting on the couch, numb.

I have done it now—I have told the truth. But I feel no relief. Even if Haza'ruux does not betray me, I will remain a coward and an oathbreaker. The right thing, I know, would be to go to the guild and turn myself in as a skin-changer and an outlaw. But then I would become an exile myself—and besides the pain that would bring to my family and my teacher, it would do no good for the outcasts. If I am one of them, I cannot give them even the comfort of the marks.

There is no right path. No honor… Despondency overwhelms me, and I can no longer think in words.

Haza'ruux reemerges from the kitchen and sits down beside me. "Drink." He pushes a cup into my hands.

I do not want it—I want no comfort—but neither do I have the will to resist him. I drink. The liquid tastes cool and bitter; my throat seems choked with the stench of the Underbelly. I lower the cup.

"Haza'ruux," I gasp, "there are children there. Who are born there. They have not done a thing wrong in their lives, and they live like beasts—"

"Kesh. Drink." He lifts the cup to my lips and makes me finish it. Then he stands again. "Lie down," he orders.

Without thinking, I obey. I curl up on the burrik furs and close my eyes, wishing the world would dissolve.

By the time he returns, I am so sleepy I cannot even lift my head. It occurs to me that I have been drugged—but I am too far gone already to be more than faintly alarmed. Groggily, I open my eyes. Haza'ruux grasps my right wrist, washing my forearm with a warm, damp cloth. On the table beside him sit pens and ink bottles.

"…What?" My tongue feels leaden. A deep distress wells up in me, but I do not have the power to speak or move.

The old man strokes my forehead. His fingers are callused and warm. "Kesh, little Flashing Blade. Haza'ruux has found you now. He will not harm you."

I am asleep before the first pen pricks my skin.

CHAPTER NINE

I awake out of a deep, soft darkness, feeling luxuriously rested. I cannot remember where I am or what day it is, but I am so comfortable that the ignorance causes me no anxiety. What a strange feeling, waking without anxiety. I feel as if my mind has been purged, washed clean of fear.

With one hand, I rub my eyes. I am lying on the couch in Haza'ruux's house with a thick burrik-fur blanket covering me. The lights in the ceiling have changed from an evening orange to a soft white hue, illuminating the cluttered room. Shabby furniture, trailing vines—but no Haza'ruux. The peculiar silence of emptiness fills the house.

It's morning? I blink in disbelief. *I didn't mean to stay the night…*

And then I remember.

I bolt upright, throw back the blanket, and clutch my right wrist. There is a new mark on my forearm: a wide black band, like a warrior's bracer, made out of closely interwoven lines and pricked by points of color like jewels. The craftsmanship is exquisite. Under ordinary circumstances, my first reaction—my artist's reaction—would be awe and admiration. But all I feel is panic.

I can't read it. I don't recognize any of the sigils. Haza'ruux put me to sleep, like an infant, and gave me a mark—and I have no idea what it means.

Wildly, I spring off the couch. "Haza'ruux!"

There is no answer. Still clutching my arm, I rush to the kitchen, but the door is closed and locked. Furious, I turn to the entrance of the studio and thrust the curtain aside, only to find another locked door behind it. With both fists I pound on the smooth metal.

"Haza'ruux! Are you in there? *Haza'ruux!*"

The only reply is a throaty hiss from overhead. The old kharraktyl clings to the ceiling above me, blinking irritably. I glare back at the creature.

"Axdraa'dah take you. Where's your master?"

The kharraktyl flicks its tongue and crawls away towards another corner of the ceiling. Swiftly I go to the front door, and, opening it just a crack, I peer out into the corridor.

It is full daylight. The shrubs and flowers surrounding the porch bloom vibrantly, lacing the air with fragrance. Further off, I can hear the splashing of the fountain and the footsteps of passersby in the plaza. But Haza'ruux is not in his garden.

Curse him! I shrink back inside, panting. I lean against the door and raise my arm to stare at the dazzling mark.

What do I do?

I tell myself to think rationally. It is not unknown for Haza'ruux to give out decorative tattoos. But even though I cannot read the intertwined patterns, I am certain they are not merely ornamental. The tattoo looks too beautiful to be a shame-mark, yet it cannot possibly be a sign of honor, either. The old man gave it to me after hearing my story of cowardice and crime. What in Ka's name moved him to paint this masterpiece on my skin—against my will, no less, and without the authority of any witness or guild? Can he even give legally binding marks? I have no idea. Until last night, I did not believe he was a true artist at all.

It crosses my mind that perhaps Haza'ruux has gone to the guild to betray me. Yet I cannot believe it. If he had wanted to turn me in, he could have done it last night, while I was drugged and unconscious on his couch. Instead he has left me free to walk away—free, that is, except for this strange mark.

Wherever Haza'ruux went, I do not have time to wait for his return. I have slept away half the day. My aunt and uncle—

Deep Sleep! I clutch my head. Our dinner with the recordmaster's family—I completely missed it. Chervani must be worried sick. Not to mention Kilmaya.

Steeling myself for what promises to be an unpleasant day, I cast my eyes around the disarrayed room. I will have to get the truth out of Haza'ruux later—for now, I must cover the mark until I can decide what to do about it. Even if the sigils are unintelligible, it is still far too conspicuous. I need to avoid drawing attention to myself.

After a few minutes of searching the cluttered space, I find a roll of mark-maker's gauze tucked away on a shelf. I tear off a length and wrap it snugly around my right forearm until the tattoo is entirely hidden. I frown at the bandage—I will have to invent some story about injuring myself. Still, that will be easier than explaining the truth.

As I linger in the house for a moment longer, my eyes fall on the curtained doorway of the studio. The memory of the beauty inside haunts me. The embellished walls, the dazzling array of inks, the carved bone pens. And the books…

What is this place? Who does this old man think he is?

I grip my bandaged arm, suppressing a surge of terror. Then I wrest myself away. I wrap my cloak around me and leave Haza'ruux's house behind.

I consider stopping at home, but if either my aunt or uncle is there, I will have to explain where I was last night—and I do not yet have a convincing story to tell them. So instead I go straight to Rixarii Street.

The markmakers' corridor is busy as usual. As I weave between the knots of people, I try to smooth the wrinkles in my disheveled tunic while keeping my bandaged arm hidden under my cloak. My attempt at composure, however, is shattered almost immediately—as I walk up the street, I suddenly spot Askko in the crowd.

He is standing near the entrance of a Clan Trev'ban studio with a few companions—soldiers, fellow hvoss'kan from his warband, by their marks. His friends laugh, striking combat stances and feinting at each other. A scattering of bystanders watches the impromptu sparring match with admiration.

But Askko hangs back from the group, a sullen glare marring his face. When one of his companions sends a mock blow his way, Askko catches the warrior's arm and shoves him back with less-than-playful violence. Then he happens to glance across the street—and sees me.

Reflexively, I look for somewhere to duck out of sight. But it is too late. Askko's eyes widen, and he strides towards me.

"There you are! Kin's blood, where were you last night?" Then, in a lower tone, seething with reproach: "I see you can't even bear to sleep under the same roof with me."

"Not here, Askko." Fighting with my cousin in private is merely upsetting; fighting with him in the street is a disgrace. "I can explain…"

"No need. I understand. A painter like you can't be seen with a man who's wearing something like *this*."

He raises his forearm, almost thrusting it in my face. A bright new mark, still slick with sealing-glaze, shines on his dark skin.

I stare in confusion. At first, I think it is an honor-mark—the vivid red and violet ink, and the prominent position, imply a tattoo for a major achievement. But as I read the individual symbols, I realize they are mostly decorative. The only meaningful character in the pattern is *valkya*, battle-brother, intertwined with several name-sigils: the names of Askko's fellow hvoss'kan.

It is only a comrade-mark, a personal commemoration between friends. But it is much larger and gaudier than any comrade-mark ought to be. Not only that, but one glance at the thick, bold pen-strokes tells me that this tattoo was made by a Trev'ban artist. Askko has never gone to a Trev'ban studio before—their artists serve the laborer clans, not high-ranking warriors.

"I don't understand." I draw back from his outstretched arm. "What is that?"

"What does it look like?" Askko fumes. "You thought that just because your guild wouldn't acknowledge us, the High Council would abandon us, too?"

"What are you talking about?"

"The High Council. They're still honoring us tonight. We had to have *some* kind of mark."

"They're still—" I gape at him, stunned. The High Council plans to publicly recognize warriors who were turned away by the guild? Why? Are they trying to make the whole affair even more shameful? How could Askko have received a mark for such an event?

And then, as I stare at my cousin's arm again, it becomes clear. The guild does not regulate personal, ornamental tattoos—they cannot prevent Askko or any other warrior from receiving a comrade-mark, even if the battle itself was officially disqualified. But this mark—the longer I look at it, the more it strikes me as a piece of calculated defiance. It is clearly made to resemble an honor-mark from a distance, although it contains none of the formal honor-sigils.

Indignation kindles in my chest. The Trev'ban artist who made this tattoo obviously knew the law well enough to exploit its loopholes. A bitter taste rises in my throat.

"So you think this is a suitable replacement?" My voice comes out grating.

"Oh, I know it's not as pretty as you could have made it." Askko's tone is equally caustic. "But it's still a legal mark—even if your clan doesn't like it."

Your guild. Your clan. The jibes, the twist of his mouth, the scorn in his slitted eyes—deep within me, something snaps. "It's your clan, too, Askko! You are Serix first."

He stiffens and steps back in surprise. Around us, the chatter of the crowd ebbs as people pause to look our way. From across the street, Askko's fellow warriors are watching. My pulse begins to throb.

Idiot! What are you doing?

My cousin widens his stance and draws his arms close to his body, as if readying for a brawl. "None of us can choose our parents. But I can choose to fight for the future of our people. Is that so wrong?"

More passersby stop to stare at us. Not all the onlookers know that we are family, and part of me realizes what we must look like in their eyes: a Serix artist and an Ascendance warrior, quarreling openly in the street. That is not a good scene to make after yesterday's ban.

But another part of me is too furious to care. "Faction cannot come before blood-kin!" I feel my own arms rising into a clumsy combat stance, even though I know my cousin could throw me to the floor with one hand.

"If it is necessary to choose—" Askko breaks off. His eyelids flicker, and he frowns. "What did you do to yourself?"

Confused, I follow his gaze. My cloak has dropped away from my right arm, revealing the wide gauze bandage. With a jolt of fear, I clutch my arm to my chest.

"It's nothing." I tug my cloak more tightly around my shoulders.

"It doesn't look like nothing. Where were you last night, anyway?"

My jaw clenches. I need to walk away before I make an utter fool of myself. "I need to get to work. Honor with you, Askko." Before he can react, I sidestep him to continue down the corridor.

"Hakk, Mariikel!" he calls after me. "What's the matter with you?"

I do not answer. Ignoring the stares of the onlookers, I slip back into the crowd. To my relief, my cousin does not follow. I neither stop nor turn my head until I reach the door of Kilmaya's studio.

At the familiar threshold, I pause to compose myself. I fervently hope Kilmaya is busy with a client. If I can sneak in and begin helping with chores, I can redeem myself a little before she has the chance to interrogate me. Quelling my trepidation, I tap the entry pad and allow the door to slide open.

The waiting room is empty except for the apprentice K'nima, who sits at the small desk where clients sign in. At the sight of me, her eyes widen.

"Markmaker—"

"Kesh." I can only imagine how ridiculous I must look, skulking in so late in the day. I hear a murmur of voices from the open door of the workroom. "Kilmaya's in?" I ask.

"Yes," K'nima says with a quaver. "She's with the T'sarek clients." Giving an anxious, sidelong glance, she mouths the word, *"Deepcrafters."*

Axdraa'dah. I bite back a curse. Of course, I would have to walk in late while Kilmaya is attending to some of our most prestigious customers. It is tempting to turn around and walk back out again before my teacher sees me.

But not in front of an apprentice. I have lost enough dignity today already.

"Thank you," I tell K'nima. I slip off my cloak and hang it on the wall next to my artist's apron. There is no point putting off the inevitable. I don the ink-stained apron and tie the worn strings behind my back. Then, making sure my bandage is still secure on my arm, I approach the workroom door.

Inside, two clients—a young man and a middle-aged woman—stand with their backs to me, conversing with my teacher. Like most T'sarek, they are tall, graceful, and powerfully built: in a word, intimidating. From this angle, I can easily see the vivid tattoos covering the back of the woman's neck. The marks radiate outward from the small silvery disc of her deepcraft implant, scarlet and azure against her jet-black skin. The swirling sigils speak of power.

Kilmaya is speaking graciously with the T'sarek woman—a little too graciously. She only uses that tone with extremely high-ranking clients whom she is anxious to please. And my teacher is not easily daunted.

She spots me, hesitating in the doorway.

"Ah, Mariikel." Her voice is genial, as if pleasantly surprised. She makes a courteous gesture towards the T'sarek woman. "You remember Van'shir Tekra, I'm sure?"

My heart plummets. The tattoo Haza'ruux gave me must be a curse. I have had nothing but foul luck today. Tekra T'sarek is not merely a deepcrafter—she is the High Councilor's wife.

Ancestors help me.

I bow deeply, placing a hand on my clan-mark. "Honor with you, van'shir." My voice comes out as a rasp.

The deepcrafter and her companion—her apprentice, probably—both turn to face me. Tekra smiles briefly. "The same to you, markmaker."

Tekra's arms, from her wrists to her shoulders, are encased in brilliant honor-marks. Although her tattoos mostly commemorate achievements in engineering and deepforging, not combat, she still stands with the athletic poise of a warrior. The violet sigils of the Ascendance are just visible under her clothing, curling around the hollow of her throat.

I swallow hard before speaking. "I hope you found the service here satisfactory."

"Of course. Kilmaya's work never disappoints."

Her voice is rich and pleasing, but there is something aloof in her face, as if she is watching me from behind a mask. Her apprentice, standing at her shoulder, does not bother to hide his expression. His lower eyes are hooded in blatant scorn.

"It was only a minor mark that K'hazot needed," Tekra continues, nodding at her student. "Still, I would never trust my apprentices to anyone else. Even if there is a little ill will between your guild and the faction at the moment."

She is still smiling. But a chill seizes my spine.

From behind Tekra's back, Kilmaya shoots me a murderous glare.

"I—I'm certain it will all be settled quickly," I stammer. "We are always honored to have your business here."

"And I am grateful to work with such worthy artists." She tilts her head, giving me a pointed look. "I hope no one has given you trouble. That's quite a bandage you have there."

My palms grow hot with fear. But I force myself to leave my arms at my sides. "No trouble, van'shir—only my own clumsiness. A small burn. Nothing serious."

"I'm glad to hear it." Tekra turns back towards my teacher. "My thanks again, markmaker."

"The honor is mine, van'shir." Kilmaya's face has turned serene once more. "Give my regards to the High Councilor."

I step out of the doorway as the two women exchange a few more pleasantries. The joints in my legs feel as if they have turned to water. I manage to stand beside the worktable with a polite expression on my face until, at last, the deepcrafter and her apprentice leave the studio.

Then Kilmaya stalks over to the entrance of the workroom and shuts the door. She turns on me, her upper eyes narrowed to thin black slits. "A burn?"

"Yes, teacher."

She jerks a finger towards the door. "We have Tekra T'sarek standing witness in our studio, and you decide you need to vanish for an entire morning because of a *small burn*?"

"I'm sorry, teacher. I can explain."

"You had better. I hope your explanation is not as wretched as your timing."

I stare at the floor. "My family…we had guests over last night. I was helping my aunt prepare the food, and I was making klasindi." I wince. "I spilled hot water on my arm."

"I wish you would let your aunt make the klasindi. What if you spilled it on your hand? I can't afford that, Mariikel—"

All at once she falls silent, and her lips press together in a thin line. After a long moment, she says, "You ate at home last night?"

I feel a flutter of foreboding. "Yes, of course."

"Strange." Her voice turns dry. "I wonder why your family told me otherwise."

I choke slightly.

Kilmaya taps the datascroll tucked into her sash. "I sent you a message when you weren't here to open this morning, but of course, you didn't answer. So I called Chervani. She informed me that you vanished last night after the festival and never came back." My teacher gives me a level stare. "She sounded rather distraught about it."

A sickening heat floods my body. *Idiot.* Of course she would call Chervani. Why didn't I think of that? But it is too late now—my scaffold of lies has already crumbled.

"Well," says Kilmaya, "now that we've cleared that up, would you like to tell me what you were really doing last night?"

I feel as if an iron weight is sitting on my ribs. "I'd…rather not."

"Hm." She regards me with a keen expression, as if taking the measure of my stubbornness. "In that case, at least set my mind at rest and tell me what you did to yourself." She points to my arm. "Since you didn't spill klasindi on it."

"It's nothing. It's only a scrape."

Her brow lowers. "I think you owe me this much, at least—"

"It's my own business, Kilmaya!" Abruptly I turn away and walk to the other side of the worktable. I start collecting used pens and mixing-bowls with a furious energy.

Kilmaya approaches with a steely glint in her eye. "If you are hurt badly enough that it begins affecting your work, it will very quickly *become* my business." She reaches across the table and catches my wrist.

"Please, teacher, no—"

"Stop being such a child." And with a deft movement, she loosens one end of the bandage.

In a moment, the wrapping lies on the table, and Kilmaya is staring at my bare arm. Her fingers tighten on my wrist like a vise. "Skin of the Deep Sleep. What is *that*?"

Haza'ruux's mark engulfs half my forearm, the dark, impossibly intricate lines twisting across my pale skin. Under the bright lamps of the studio, the points of color between the sigils shimmer with iridescent hues: deep blue and emerald, violet and gold.

Kilmaya looks up into my face. "Mariikel. Where did you get this?"

I cannot answer. I cannot stop looking at the mark. It teems with unreadable beauty. It seems almost alive.

"Great Ka. You're shaking." My teacher eases her grip on my wrist. "Come here. Sit down."

All the warmth has drained out of my body. Numbly, I allow her to lead me over to one of the client's chairs. I sit on the edge of it, cradling my arm against my chest.

A hesitant rap sounds on the workroom door. Kilmaya turns, standing between me and the doorway. "What is it?" Her voice is taut.

K'nima opens the door a few inches and peers in. "Teacher, the Gabronik clients are here..."

"Tell them to wait."

The girl retreats and shuts the door.

My teacher turns to face me again. "You are going to explain this to me. And quickly. We have work to do."

I glare past her into empty space. I am afraid even to open my mouth. If I tell the truth, I am lost. But I have no lies left, either.

At last, I say, "It was Haza'ruux."

"Haza'ruux?" She blinks, incredulous. "The old inkmaker?"

I do not have the strength to respond.

My teacher extends her hand. "Can I see it again?"

I stare at her out of a dull, animal terror. If by some chance she can read the strange sigils…if Haza'ruux has written something there about my crimes…

But it is no use now. My rigid body slumps. I hold out my arm.

Kilmaya steps forward and takes my wrist in her hands. Like a healer probing a wound, she presses gently on the newly dyed skin. She turns over my arm and examines the whole tattoo.

"Heart's blood," she breathes at last. "This is Haza'ruux's work?"

Miserably, I nod.

She releases my arm. "Someone should give that man a studio."

I gape at her for a long moment. "You're…you're not angry?"

Kilmaya squints three eyes. "Well, I can't even read it, so I don't know what to be angry about."

A wave of relief surges over me, so powerful that I nearly cry out. I hug my arm to my chest to calm myself.

"I don't understand. What is it for?"

"I don't know," I groan.

"What do you mean, you don't know? You let him give it to you."

"I didn't *let* him! I…fell asleep."

I cannot tell her that I was drugged. It is too humiliating, and it would lead to more questions than I want to answer.

"Where? At his house?" She looks at me askance. "I think you had better start from the beginning, Mariikel."

I rub my eyes and then sit up, a little more composed. In truth, I am almost giddy with relief, but I try not to let it show. If she cannot read the mark, I still have a chance at bluffing my way through this story.

"I was exhausted after the festival yesterday. I went out walking before supper, and I was passing Haza'ruux's house. He saw me and invited me in for a meal." That part, at least, is true. "We ate. And talked." I blink nervously. "Then I—I fell asleep on his couch. I suppose I must have been more tired than I realized. When I woke up this morning, it was past the third hour already. And…I had this." Again I curl my fingers around the tattoo.

"What about Haza'ruux? He didn't bother to explain himself, I suppose?"

"He was gone."

My teacher covers her lower eyes with a hand. "Ancestors help me." For a minute she stands wordless, until at last she drops her hand and glowers at me. "Is that all?"

"Yes, teacher."

"You could have told me that when you came in. You had me frightened, the way you were hiding it."

I stare in bewilderment. She breaks into a laugh.

"By Ka, Mariikel, it's only Haza'ruux. The old fool doesn't mean any harm. You're treating this like the work of a skin-changer."

Skin-changer. Even hearing my teacher mention the word aloud makes my pulse quicken. "But the guild…"

"The guild?" Kilmaya makes a scoffing noise. "The guild doesn't care about Haza'ruux's nonsense. His marks don't *mean* anything."

"But…" Her dismissal makes me incredulous. How can she think this exquisitely crafted mark is meaningless?

Then again, I remind myself, she has no reason to think otherwise. Kilmaya does not know what I confessed to Haza'ruux last night. She has no idea what I have done.

"I admit I have never seen him do anything quite so elaborate." She regards the tattoo critically. "And he certainly chose a prominent place for a decoration."

Another twinge of unease seizes me. The forearm is supposed to be reserved for honor-marks. Haza'ruux must know that.

"It is not usually considered proper to wear such a large decorative piece on the arm like that. But if it's the mad markmaker's work…" The corners of Kilmaya's eyes crease slightly, as if she is both amused and exasperated. "You know how it is. People have strange ideas about the old man. It would be ill luck to erase the mark now."

"You don't believe that." But after last night, I am feeling more than a little superstitious about Haza'ruux. Curiosity overtakes my anxiety. "Why is he even allowed to wear those unreadable marks? I have never understood that. How can he get away with it?"

"Tradition. There has always been a hermit living in that little house. Usually half-witted, too. I suppose they really might have been artists or archivists once. It's only a token role now." She laughs aloud. "But ancestors forbid that we actually change any *laws* about it."

I frown. "What laws?"

"Oh—simply that Clan Serix must have a mad markmaker. We are not allowed to get rid of them." She shuts three eyes humorously. "Still, there have been stranger superstitions enshrined in law. This one is harmless enough."

I grip my wrist tighter. After the things I saw last night—the hidden studio, the shelves of ancient books—such a statute hardly seems frivolous. If anything, it makes me even more uneasy. "I've never heard of that law."

"It's in the archives somewhere." Kilmaya waves a dismissive hand. "I had a friend who studied such things once. I don't know much about it myself—it's not as if it affects the studios at all."

Before I can reply, there is a tapping on the door again. K'nima peeks into the workroom. "Forgive me, teacher…"

"Oh, Axdraa'dah." Kilmaya swears under her breath. "I'm sorry, K'nima. Tell them I'm coming."

The apprentice nods in visible relief and shuts the door.

"Enough of this," my teacher scolds. "We have clients." She shoos me out of the chair.

I stand up, but my legs are still shaky. "You're not going to do anything?"

"What do you expect me to do? The mark is not illegal. No one's going to punish you for it."

"If it's only decorative, can't you…" My tongue seizes up. I find I cannot speak the words aloud.

"Remove it?" My teacher regards me with something between shock and reproach. "Are you serious, Mariikel? Does it bother you that much?"

"I…" I find I have no answer. Even ornamental tattoos, which have no legal significance, are almost never erased. But I am convinced, for my own part, that Haza'ruux's masterpiece is not mere decoration. And I am afraid of it. I am afraid of this beautiful, terrible mark, which I cannot read.

"What am I saying?" All at once Kilmaya shakes her head. "No, I'm not going to remove it. That mark is huge. If I burn the skin off half your arm, you won't be able to use your hand for days. Weeks, probably. I can't spare you from the studio for that long. You have clients, too, you know."

"But what will I tell people?"

"What is there to tell? The mad markmaker has decided to favor you. There are worse fates." Kilmaya gestures toward the cluttered worktable. "I have no objections to Haza'ruux or his marks. But missing three hours at the studio with no warning—that I cannot tolerate, Mariikel." She scowls. "Things are bad enough right now, with the guild's ban. You saw Van'shir Tekra. Our Ascendance clients are not happy. The last thing I need is for one of my artists to make a fool of himself."

I wince. Thoroughly ashamed, I bow and touch my forehead. "I'm very sorry, teacher. It won't happen again."

"Good. Now stop flinching like a frightened ech'taani and go make yourself useful." She strides towards the door, then pauses at the threshold and frowns back at me. "And put on some gloves, will you? Your new ornament might startle the clients."

CHAPTER TEN

When we close the studio for the day and I walk home, I do not bother to cover up Haza'ruux's mark. Now that Kilmaya has seen it, there is little point in trying to hide it from other people. She will no doubt tell her artist friends about it over kol-dawra and klasindi tonight, and the story will be all over the clan sector by tomorrow morning.

There is no real danger of anyone deciphering the archaic sigils. If my teacher cannot read the tattoo, I doubt that anyone else will be able to. Even so, as I hurry down Rixarii Street under the dimming corridor lights, I avoid eye contact, and I must resist the impulse to clutch at my own wrist. I feel as if I am walking about with an open wound on my arm.

It occurs to me, as I leave the studios and turn into the residential district, that this is the night I promised to meet with the young exile, Kophas Tarriks, and start arranging his escape from the Underbelly. But I do not have the energy to think about that right now. Besides, I must go home first. If I fail to appear for supper yet again, after my disappearance last night, I will cause even more trouble than I have already.

When I reach the house, I hesitate before opening the door. I am in for another scolding, I know. Silently cursing Haza'ruux for what must be the dozenth time today, I place my hand on the entry pad.

I try to slip in quietly, but I cannot hush the hiss of the door as it slides closed behind me. I have not even taken two steps into the front room when my aunt peers out from the kitchen doorway.

"Mariikel!" She drops the bundle of *chalka* greens she is holding and emerges from the kitchen. Her eyes are wide with relief, but her voice rings with a sharpness I know well.

Reflexively I grasp my arm, hiding the new mark. "I'm sorry, nakki—"

"Come here, dako." Her tone softens into an exasperated fondness. Before I can protest, she steps forward and wraps me in an embrace. I tense. This was not quite the reception I expected, even from Chervani.

89

She pulls back and regards me with a rueful squint. "You know, when you were younger, it was only Askko I had to worry about, running off and getting himself into scrapes. But now you are almost as bad."

"Forgive me." I bow my head humbly. "I didn't mean to. Honestly."

"Oh, I know. I heard about your visit to the mad markmaker."

"Hakk...you did?" I knew there would be rumors, but I did not expect them to fly so fast.

Chervani laughs. "Your teacher sent me a message me to say you were all right. You *did* have me worried last night. Not to mention that you abandoned us to a most embarrassing evening with Virik and Kandri. I kept assuring them you were about to arrive, and you never did."

I wince again. "I'm sorry."

"I know. You were overtired yesterday. I'm simply glad that if you had to disappear, you were at old Haza'ruux's place and not lost or trampled somewhere under the arena. Now." She gives me a mock-stern glare. "Let's see this mark that ruined my Van'shorvanii dinner. It had better be impressive."

With trepidation, I let my hand drop from my right arm. Chervani looks down—and her gentle eyes grow round with unfeigned shock. "Oh, dako." With slow fingers, she takes my wrist, as if irresistibly drawn to touch the twining sigils. "It's beautiful." She is still holding my arm when my uncle emerges from the hall. "Hakham," she cries. "Come see what old Haza'ruux made for him. Have you ever seen anything like it?"

For the next several minutes, I endure both my aunt and uncle examining my arm and exclaiming over it in wonder while I grit my teeth and try not to drown in secret dread. But they, like Kilmaya, glean no meaning from the archaic designs.

"Perhaps he wanted to point out who the best artist in the sector is," Chervani muses. "Even if the rest of the clan hasn't realized it yet."

"Nakki! Don't say that. It's not an honor-mark."

"He's right," says Hakham. "The old hermit has no authority to give real marks." His mouth tightens. "At least it's Serix handiwork."

Displeasure edges his words. At first, I think he is upset with me—but then Chervani draws a breath, fixing my uncle with a steady gaze.

"It's Askko's last evening with us. Please."

Hakham's expression hardens. I sense tension between them, the heavy atmosphere of an argument that has already been resolved, but not happily. My belly twinges. My aunt and uncle rarely quarrel.

At last Hakham exhales. "I'm aware. I hope *he* remembers that, too." Then he turns and disappears down the hall.

Chervani glances at me, anxious. "Askko got a mark today as well. Did you hear?"

"I saw it." The pit in my stomach deepens. "I met Askko on my way to work today."

My uncle's anger is clear now. For his son to go to a Trev'ban studio is humiliating—but especially for a mark that was, for all intents and purposes, made in defiance of the guild's ban. With a pang, I remember how proudly Hakham spoke of Askko only two days ago, when he first arrived home. But now my cousin has become a source of shame to the household—again.

Chervani sighs. "I made Hakham promise to be civil. We are going to have *one* pleasant meal together—I am determined." Touching my arm again, she musters a smile. "Come help with supper."

Guilt assails me. I have been so busy with my own troubles that I have not even thought about how my family must be taking the news of Askko's mark-ban. My aunt puts on a brave face, but it must be extremely painful for both her and Hakham. I haven't helped matters, either, with my unexplained disappearances.

My promise to meet with Kophas pricks at my conscience again—but I cannot go to the Underbelly tonight. I have far more pressing problems here at home. The least I can do, for the moment, is to be an obedient son.

I take her hand. "Of course, nakki."

To my relief, Chervani does not ask me anything more about Haza'ruux as I help her chop chalka greens and season the tavla roast. When the food is ready, Hakham emerges from his study, and we sit down together at the table. Miika, drawn by the savory aroma of the meat, pads into the room and settles herself on the floor beside my chair. There is no sign of Askko yet, and no one mentions his absence—though Chervani keeps glancing towards the front door with increasing anxiety. I feel sorry for her, but for myself, I would not be disappointed if my cousin did not appear. I am not looking forward to facing him again.

We have already started eating when the front door opens and a heavy step sounds in the adjacent room. Then Askko's broad-shouldered frame darkens the kitchen doorway. Miika barks once, scrambling to her feet to greet her master. But Askko does not even bend down to pet the old hound. He stands glaring, legs braced and fists clenched, as if expecting a challenge.

I feel the urge to sink down in my seat and disappear. I know that look. That was how Askko walked into the house four years ago, when he first received his adoption-mark into Clan Trechik to begin his warrior training. Hakham was furious—the Trechik, while not quite as lowly as a laborer clan, were nowhere near as prestigious as the Serix. But there was nothing my uncle could do: Askko was of age, the mark was legal, and there was no erasing it.

But the latent fury that hangs in the air now is even worse. Hakham's face has gone perfectly still. Askko, meanwhile, almost shakes with stifled rage. But his eyelids flicker with some deeper emotion—fear? Shame?

I swallow a bite of suddenly tasteless meat. My cousin usually finds a way to take out such feelings on me.

"Askko!" Chervani breaks the strained silence, her voice bright. "We were just wondering when you'd come. Sit down, dako."

At last Askko tears his gaze away from his father and lowers himself into the empty seat. He is not trying to hide the new tattoo on his arm, but neither is he flaunting it. For one fleeting moment, I begin to hope that no one will mention it at all.

Then Askko's eyes flick towards me—and his nostrils widen with a sharp intake of breath. He stares at my wrist, transfixed.

"What," he growls, "is *that*?"

I groan. Once more, I relate my story about Haza'ruux. But all through the telling, I am keenly aware of Askko's mounting fury: the tightness of his jaw, the dire glitter in his eye. And I can guess what he is thinking.

I've outdone him again. I managed to gain a magnificent tattoo from a man who is possibly the most skilled artist in the clan—while my cousin, after all his service on the planets, was compelled to go to a Trev'ban studio for a mockery of an honor-mark. Once again, I have usurped his parents' favor. And the worst of it is, I did not even try.

For one maddening instant, I want to tell Askko the truth—that I am just as angry and ashamed of my new mark as he is of his own. But I cannot admit that. I do not even have the freedom to defend myself.

When I finish my story, Askko stares at me as if he is trying to decide whether it is worth the trouble to throttle me. Then all at once he gives a derisive laugh. He pulls out the dagger from his belt, stabs a thick slice of meat from the serving platter, and drops it onto his plate. "You must not be expecting to earn many real honors, if you're filling up your skin with ornaments already."

"Askko!" Chervani narrows her eyes.

Heat floods my chest, but I keep my voice level. "There's nothing wrong with ornaments. You have a few yourself."

It is petty of me to bait him, but I have had my fill of humiliation today. Askko's nostrils flare. The gaudy new tattoo on his forearm spasms as he clenches his fist. "I *earned* this, little painter. What did you do for yours?"

"Kesh." Hakham cuts in. "That is enough." He pauses, his gaze downcast.

"I was about to ask you, Mariikel, if you are coming with us to the ceremony tonight."

"What ceremony?"

"For Askko, of course." Chervani, too, seems uncomfortable. "The High Council will be honoring him and the other hvoss'kan."

Of course—Askko mentioned that before. I glance at my uncle and aunt in astonishment. "You're still going?"

My uncle avoids meeting my eyes. "The High Council will be recognizing their general service to the Fleet, not any...particular conflict."

"It's a public ceremony," says Chervani quietly. "All the warriors will have family or clanmates with them. We can't let Askko go alone."

Blood-kin comes before faction. Bitterly, I remember the words I used against my cousin only this morning. The saying cuts both ways.

Across the table, Askko glares at me with thinly veiled fury.

Hakham breaks the painful quiet. "If you do not feel you should go, Mariikel, we understand. No one will hold it against you."

No one except Askko. With an effort of will, I choke back my resentment. "That is kind of you."

"But it *is* his last night home." Chervani gives me another entreating look. She wants peace between us so badly. But for once, I do not feel inclined to give in to her.

"I will see him in the morning, then." I slip out of my seat and stand. "Enjoy the ceremony." Ignoring Askko's livid expression, I turn my back and leave the room.

Later that evening, my family departs for the High Council ceremony, and I go to bed early. But despite the quiet of the empty house, I cannot sleep. Besides my lingering bitterness over my cousin, I keep thinking about Haza'ruux. In my mind I recall every word I confessed at his house last night, relive every stinging surge of shame. How could I have been such a fool? The old man only has half his wits; everyone knows that. Even if he does not intend to betray me, he might do it purely by accident.

That is what I tell myself as I lie on my bunk, gazing at my new mark and tracing the sigils with one finger. Yet I do not believe my own words. Haza'ruux is not insane; I know that now. But this thought only unsettles me more.

I will myself to think about something else, but the only image that rises in its place is the face of the young Tarriks exile. Where is Kophas tonight? Is he at our meeting place in the Underbelly, waiting vainly for me to appear?

Oathbreaker... I groan into my blanket. I have failed to keep my word even to an outcast.

Sheer exhaustion claims me at last, but my dreams are uneasy. Very early in the morning—the ceiling panels still glow dark blue—I wake to the sound of metal clinking against metal.

I turn my head. On the other side of the room, Askko sits on the edge of his bunk, his full travelling pack at his feet. He is putting on his armor, the light ceremonial gear that warriors wear for formal occasions. I watch him silently through half-open eyes. Piece by piece, he buckles on the gauntlets, the long, smooth greaves, the breastplate emblazoned with the sigil of the Ascendance. The metal glints cool and hard in the muted light.

It has been a long time since I have seen my cousin in his armor. It suits him. He looks strong, striking—honorable. I feel a tightness in my chest.

Askko has not noticed that I am awake. He buckles the clasps of the shoulder pieces, fastens his belt, clips on his handgun and dagger in their decorated sheaths. Then he kneels by the bed and prostrates himself on the floor. With one hand, he covers the Serix mark on the side of his neck. He stays in that position, unmoving, for a long time.

He prays in silence, but I do not need to hear his words. I know the invocation well.

Serixan, my ancestors, I call on you. By the bond of this clan-mark, hear me. Fill the blood of my heart with strength. Guide all my striving in honor. Let me carry the truth in my flesh. Guard my mind and my body from lies...

My throat clenches, and my skin grows hot. My flesh is full of lies.

I do not know what Askko did on the planets, nor whether he violated the honor-code. But if he is an oathbreaker, he is no worse a man than I am. He may even be a better one. Askko is willing to lay down his life for the cause he has chosen. That is more than I have done.

At last, my cousin raises his head from the floor and climbs to his feet. With a smooth motion, he shoulders his heavy pack. Then he gazes around the room as if to fix it in his memory. His glance falls on me.

Quickly I shut all my eyes, feigning sleep. Askko's armor creaks as he approaches my bunk. For a moment he stands silent at my bedside—and then he turns and walks away. The bedchamber door hisses open and shut, and his footsteps fade.

I lie with my eyes closed, warring with myself. Then I fling back my blanket and sit up. Askko is a soldier—if I do not make peace with him now, I may never see him again.

I get up and head into the front room. The door to the street stands open; it is still dim outside. In the lamplight of the porch, I can see my family standing in the garden, saying their farewells. With a hesitant step, I approach the door.

Chervani embraces her son, smiling, but her face looks strained. As Askko pulls away, he murmurs something and brushes his fingers against the faded child-mark on her shoulder. Chervani grips his hand and holds it there, too distraught to speak.

When Chervani releases him, Hakham steps forward. In his hands he holds the ceremonial sword that usually hangs in our front room. I feel a twinge of relief—Chervani must have convinced father and son to reconcile, if Hakham is blessing him with the ancestral blade. My uncle presents the weapon to Askko, who bows briefly and touches his forehead to the sigil-etched steel.

"Honor with you, Askko." Hakham's voice catches. "Claim a home for us. I want to live by the ocean when I am old."

"You will, *nakko*." Askko rises and places a hand on his breastplate, over the sigil of the Ascendance. Then my cousin sees me standing in the doorway. "Mariikel." His voice turns gruff. "I thought you were asleep."

"Not with the racket you made putting on that armor," I retort.

He relaxes a little. He approaches the porch step and, in a tentative gesture, offers his hands. I reach out; we grasp each other's forearms. His gauntlets feel cold under my fingers.

"Askko…" *Please pray for me, brother.* These are the first words that come to mind, but it would be too strange to speak them aloud. Instead, I say softly: "I wanted to give you a mark."

"The ban wasn't your fault. You were following orders." Unhappiness flickers in his eyes for an instant, but it does not seem directed at me. "I know what that is like."

The regret in his voice moves me. It crosses my mind that I was also under orders when I gave Talorak his exile-mark. On an impulse, I let go of Askko's arm. I touch his forehead and trace the mastery-mark on his brow—the sign of the warrior. "Honor with you, hvoss'ka."

A startled look crosses his face. I have never addressed him by his warrior's rank before.

"And with you, markmaker." He smiles. It is enough. We release each other, and he steps away.

Askko hefts the pack on his shoulders and steps out into the street. His armor rings faintly as he strides down the corridor; he waves back to us once. Then he turns a corner, and he is gone.

CHAPTER ELEVEN

For the next several days, I play the dutiful markmaker. I go to the studio; I serve my clients; I return home in the evening at a reasonable hour. I stay away from the Underbelly, and I do not seek out Haza'ruux.

However, I cannot avoid the stir that my new tattoo causes at the studio. I can hardly get through a day without a client commenting on it or a few fellow artists dropping by to see it. They admire the craftsmanship and congratulate me—mostly in jest—on gaining the mad markmaker's favor. I attempt to laugh along with them. Internally, I am quaking with terror.

After a few days pass, however, and no guild official appears to arrest me, my trepidation begins to fade. Perhaps the old hermit was being sincere when he said he would keep my secret, though why he would want to protect me, I have no idea. I want to return to the Underbelly—my broken promise to Kophas still weighs on my mind—but I do not feel safe doing it until I know more about Haza'ruux and his marks.

My new tattoo is not decoration; of that I am certain. I need to find out what it means. But I am reluctant to go back to the artist himself. I still do not know what he wants, and I do not like the thought that he has power over me now, knowing my story. Even if I had the courage to ask him about my tattoo, I doubt he would give me a straight answer.

So instead, I go to the archives.

The Serix record hall stands directly across from the guild hall in the great Tralkanii Plaza at the far end of Rixarii Street. I make my way there one afternoon after work—weaving through the usual crowd of artists, record-keepers, and guild officials, and passing between the four age-gnarled trallak trees that stand in the center of the plaza. The record hall itself, a magnificently painted edifice with wide double doors, is the pride of Clan Serix. Of all the ships in the Fleet, we have the oldest and most extensive collection of mark-records: images of every legally binding tattoo given by every Serix artist, going back dozens of generations. Clan Trev'ban keeps their records with us as well, and we even have sizeable archives from other artist clans on other ships. In short, the Serix library is unequalled. I only hope it will have what I am looking for.

I climb the steps of the wide porch, then enter the record hall and approach the front desk to reserve a private study room. While the archivist at the desk checks me in, I let my gaze wander down the long, narrow room, pretending to admire the finely painted pillars, the neat rows of display desks, the glass cases holding the clan's small but precious collection of real books. In reality, I am keeping a wary eye out for my uncle. This is his primary place of work— though he sometimes supervises a mark-scanning station at the ship's docks, verifying the identities of people travelling to and from the *Akkano'dath*. I hope he is at the docks this afternoon.

I am in luck, for once: my uncle is nowhere in sight, and I escape into a study room without having to answer any awkward questions. Then I sit down in the center of the huge, semicircular display desk, scan my mastery-mark to access the archives, and plunge into my studies.

I first consult as many dictionaries as I can find. Some of the records in our library are so old that they do not use the current, standardized sigils. The archivists have compiled glossaries to translate these obscure historical symbols. If Haza'ruux's marks are related to an older form of the Noxxiin language, then I may find a clue to their meaning here.

But over the course of the next hour, as I pore over several hundred years' worth of tattoos, my hope wavers and begins to fade. Even the oldest translatable marks, dating back to the second or third century of the Wandering, bear little resemblance to the exquisite, interlocking lines that now encircle my right arm. Haza'ruux's pen-strokes are so tightly woven that I cannot tell where one sigil ends and another begins. Only the slight variation of the symbols, the irregular dots and flecks that keep the pattern from being perfectly symmetrical, convince me that the marks must be words and not decoration.

Either Haza'ruux is using sigils that are older than the Fleet itself, or the writing system is of his own invention.

Frustrated, I abandon the dictionaries and start a new search. Haza'ruux has lived in that strange little house of his since before I was born; he must have given out many other tattoos over the years. Unfortunately, our clan's archivists are only meticulous about documenting marks with legal meaning. The law does not require them to keep track of ornamental pieces. So when I attempt to research other marks given by Haza'ruux, the results are meager. Of the few tattoos I do find, none are comparable to mine in size or intricacy, and most are decades old; their bearers are deceased. It seems the mad markmaker does not bestow his favors often.

Once more I clear my screen and lean back in my seat. *The mad markmakers...* Kilmaya mentioned something about an old clan law protecting them.

That still puzzles me. I know our laws as well as any Serix artist—why have I never heard of this one before?

I bend over the desk again and pull up the Serix clan code. For several minutes, I sift through an unhelpful assortment of marriage regulations, adoption requirements, the list of crimes punishable by shame-mark, exile, or mark-stripping... I hurriedly skip over that last section. But my search remains in vain. When I reach the end of the document, I have not found a single law that mentions the mad markmakers.

I growl deep in my throat, disgusted. *What am I missing?*

A quiet knock disturbs the study room's silence. I start and turn away from the screen. Before I can rise, the door slides open—and Hakham steps through with a pleased expression on his face.

"Honor with you, Mariikel."

"Na'thalo." I leap out of my seat. "I thought—I was only—"

"Forgive me for disturbing you." The corners of my uncle's eyes wrinkle in amusement. "I just came in from the docks and saw your name in the register. You haven't visited the archives in a while." His gaze drifts to the screens that I am vainly trying to hide behind my back. "Were you looking for something in particular?"

A lie rises to my lips, but something stops me from uttering it. Hakham does not appear suspicious—and why should he? He knows nothing of the confession I made to Haza'ruux. And if anyone can help me track down obscure clan regulations, it would be my uncle.

"There was, actually." Choking back my fear, I gesture towards the open documents cluttering the display—the archaic dictionaries, the Serix clan code. "I was trying to find out more about Haza'ruux's marks."

"Hakka. Curious about your new ornament?"

"Yes." I muster an embarrassed smile. "I wanted to see if there were other pieces like it. And...I heard there were old clan laws about the mad markmakers in the archives."

"Oh? Who told you that?"

I hesitate, surprised at his frown. "Kilmaya."

"Kilmaya knows?" Hakham steps forward, examining my displays, and sighs. "You are determined, aren't you? I suppose telling you can't do any real harm."

"Telling me what?"

"There is a record. But you won't be able to find it, with only your markmaker's access."

He taps the display, activating the desk's scanner, and lets it read both the record-keeper's tattoo on his brow and the Serix clan-mark on his neck. Once the scanner acknowledges him, my uncle opens a new search and sketches the sigil rixar'azahl—"mad markmaker"—into the entry space. "Now try it."

Mystified and a little apprehensive, I run the search. A single result appears on the screen. It is not an ordinary document, but rather an image: a scan of an age-darkened sheet of paper, covered in a script so old-fashioned that it takes me a minute to decipher the title.

"*The Blood-oath of Clan Serix to the Line of the Rixar'azahl*." My lips curl in a grimace. "What in Ka's name is this?"

"A relic of the ancestors. Rescued from the fallen ship *Draalyariik*, during the Tekkal Rebellion. Year 336 of the Wandering." Hakham's tone turns rueful. "One of our few surviving manuscripts from that great library."

I stare at the image in amazement. The archives of the *Draalyariik* are legendary. Our Serix forerunners used to live on that ship, before it was destroyed in one of the clan wars that plagued the Fleet's early centuries. "We still have it? The physical manuscript?"

"Oh, yes. It's in one of our storerooms, with a number of other fragile artifacts."

"In the storerooms?" I turn to face him, incredulous. "Why isn't it displayed in the hall?"

"Because...well, here is the translation." He scrolls down to a second, cleaner page with ordinary sigils. "Read it for yourself."

More baffled than ever, I return my attention to the words on the screen:

> *Aitalo, chief of Clan Serix, together with the councilors of the Markmaker Guild, here states the ancient rights of the Rixar'azahl, to be forever honored and protected on the ship Draalyariik and throughout the Fleet.*
>
> *One house in the Serix sector is to be dedicated, solely and solemnly, to the ancestors of the clan. It is to be inhabited by the Rixar'azahl alone, as preserved and sacred ground. No one may enter the house without the express permission of the Rixar'azahl. The house may not be given to or purchased by any other member of the clan, for any reason.*

I frown. So Kilmaya was right when she said there has always been a mad markmaker in Haza'ruux's dwelling. "Dedicated to the ancestors. Is it a shrine, then?"

"It could be called that. Though there are no ancestral ashes kept there—as far as anyone knows." Hakham squints, as if in distaste. "But that is not the difficulty. Keep reading."

> *The Rixar'azahlii are exempt from the mark-laws of the*

clans; they are to practice their own craft in freedom. Neither the chieftains of Clan Serix nor the councilors of the Guild may command the Rixar'azahl to make or erase any mark. No mark given by the Rixar'azahl is to be altered or removed by any other artist, under any circumstances.

A faint chill tingles down my spine. I glance at the iridescent tattoo on my right arm. Only a few days ago, I tried to ask my teacher to erase it. "No removal under any circumstances? Is that law still valid?"

"Evidently." With a grunt, Hakham takes a seat in my empty chair. "It has never been repealed."

"But why? If they are only ornaments..."

"Indeed. Why protect marks with no legal meaning? We don't know." He spreads his hands in annoyance. "That is not the only privilege they have, either. The Rixar'azahlii are allowed to choose their own apprentices, to inherit the house and continue the line. No one can gainsay that choice or select an apprentice for them—not even the guild. And the punishment for violating any of these rights? Exile, apparently."

"What?" I stiffen. "Why?"

"Who knows? If we had more documents from this era, we might be able to discover the law's origin. But we have lost so much of our history—like all the clans." Hakham leans back in the chair with a wry expression. "All we know is that our ancestors swore on their hearts' blood to preserve these hermit-artists. There is no provision for retracting the oath. We can only obey."

"But if it's that important, why have I never heard of it before?" I gesture to my mastery-mark. "Why didn't I have access?"

My uncle looks discomfited. "It's...something of an embarrassment. If it were widely known that we have an order of artists who are not regulated by the guild...well, you can imagine the scandal. Not that there is anything illegal about it," he adds. "Since they only give ornaments. But not everyone would understand that. There are some clans who would use any excuse to undermine our authority."

Like Clan Trev'ban? The lower-ranking artists might well cause an uproar if they knew Clan Serix had granted one of its own such sweeping freedoms. "So these laws about the mad markmakers are supposed to be a secret?"

"Not exactly. They *are* in the archives—as you can see. But to keep the peace, we do not advertise their existence." He smiles sardonically. "The guild lets the hermits be, the clan treats their marks like good-luck charms, and we all keep the oath our ancestors made."

"I see." But the explanation does not satisfy me. I am still convinced that my tattoo is no mere decoration. And the thought that Haza'ruux has authority comparable to the guild's only deepens my unease. If that is the case, why has he taken no action to punish me for my crimes?

Hakham chuckles at my furrowed brow. "No need to be alarmed. The mad markmakers are a peculiarity of our clan, that's all. They may really bring good luck—who can tell?" He stands and closes the documents on the screen. "Shall we head home, if you're finished here? Chervani will be expecting us."

For the next few days, I have no chance to return to the archives. Even though Askko and his fellow soldiers have gone back to the war, the conflict over the honor-marks, apparently, is not over. On the tenth day of Akk'aal, the guild sends out another announcement: decorative tattoos, like the comrade-marks that Askko and his companions received, are no longer free of regulation. Artists must now submit their designs to a guild official for approval.

"I thought something like this might happen," Kilmaya comments as we open the studio the morning we read the news. "It's ridiculous, of course. The guild doesn't want to look at every little ornament coming out of the Trev'ban shops. But they can't let themselves be made fools of, either."

"It seems a bit drastic to me." I put on my apron and tie the strings behind my back. "Can't they simply punish the artists who made the imitation honor-marks? Their intention was clear enough."

Kilmaya scoffs. "Certainly, but the guild can't discipline an artist for something that wasn't a crime ten days ago. I think Mekkalluthak is more concerned about the future. If the Ascendance is willing to treat ornaments as honor-marks now...well, they wouldn't need the guild's approval for anything, would they?"

"I suppose not." I find it difficult to believe that Ascendance soldiers would truly stoop to such humiliating measures—but then, Askko did, even when he plainly did not want to. It is unsettling to think that the faction holds more sway over its warriors than guild law.

My teacher exhales. "This new ruling will stop them for now, at any rate. Show them that we're serious. Perhaps the guild will repeal it when the faction decides to behave itself. Hakk, but the Trev'ban artists aren't going to be happy." She smirks. "They get a fair amount of income from decorative marks—more than Serix studios do. But not all their clients will want to go through the hassle of these new restrictions, I'd imagine."

I feel a touch of dismay. Kilmaya is right: because Clan Trev'ban's clients are lower-ranking, their markmakers rarely give out honor-marks or other tattoos for prestigious accomplishments. They tend to make up the difference in ornamental work. "They're going to lose business."

"They asked for it." My teacher squints her lower eyes, dismissive. "If they are going to skirt the law, there will be consequences."

I cannot argue with that. And yet, only one Trev'ban studio made the mock honor-marks, and now all the clan's artists are going to suffer for it—though I do not know what else I would have done in the guildmaster's position.

Over the next week, I detect a palpable increase in tension between Serix and Trev'ban artists. When I pass the studios each day, walking to and from work, my clan-mark draws resentful stares from the lower-ranking markmakers and their clients. Once, when I greet a young Trev'ban woman with a pleasant, "Honor with you," I receive a hard, appraising look in reply.

"And with you, guildmaster," she says—cool and deliberately insolent, without so much as a nod of courtesy. Then she turns and disappears into a studio, leaving me standing dumbfounded in the street.

For a minute, I do not even understand her insult. And then it hits me: my mastery-mark indicates that I have voting privileges in the guild, something most Trev'ban artists do not. She must think I had a hand in passing the new regulations. I have not attended a guild assembly for months, but this aggrieved young Trev'ban does not know that.

I try not to let it bother me. Kilmaya assures me the discontent will blow over eventually. "It's hardly the first time the Trev'ban have chafed at a guild ruling. They're only jealous of us, as usual. They will get over it."

I want to share my teacher's confidence—but a few days later, another disturbing piece of news emerges. One early morning, I am preparing breakfast for myself while my uncle sits at the kitchen table, reading on his datascroll. Of a sudden, he exhales loudly and mutters, "Fools."

I turn, surprised at his outburst. Hakham gestures at the report, his lower eyes hooded in disgust. "Clan Trev'ban seems determined to sell itself to the Ascendance."

"What have they done now?"

"Two of their artists—they've given each other the faction-mark."

"What?" No markmaker may swear allegiance to any political faction. Our ancestors learned long ago that when artists join factions, false marks flourish. No matter the party's intention, there is too much risk to our honor. Markmakers must be impartial. "Why would they do that?"

Hakham scoffs. "Why do you think? They say that forbidding artists from joining the Ascendance is creating unnecessary divisions. We must all be 'as one clan' to reclaim the planets, apparently." He pushes the datascroll away. "Idiots. To throw away their mastery-marks simply to gain the favor of a faction. If that is how they regard the craft, good riddance to them."

I pick up the datascroll and glance over the report with dismay. "What will happen to them now?"

"They'll be banned from the studios, of course. If they thought their stunt was going to change any laws, they are sorely mistaken." With a grunt of scorn, Hakham gets up from the table. "They'll be expelled from the guild before the day's out. I hope they enjoy the rest of their lives as inkmakers."

The rebellious artists are from the same Trev'ban studio that gave Askko the imitation honor-mark. I wonder if Hakham read that, too. But I decide not to mention it—it is still a painful subject.

Later that morning, when I arrive in Rixarii Street, I can immediately sense disturbance in the air. The hour is still early, and most studios have not opened their doors yet, but the corridor is packed with clients—Trev'ban clients. The crowd gathers around one of the Trev'ban studios, and the low rumble of talk is not the sound of a festival throng.

The defiant artists. I forgot that the expulsion would be a public event. I have seen shame-marking ceremonies only rarely, and I have never witnessed one in Rixarii Street before. It seems the guild is not wasting any time with their punishment.

I tell myself I should not stop to watch—this crowd is not going to welcome a Serix artist, especially now—but a morbid curiosity slows my steps. I slip past a group of agitated laborers from Clan Tizzan and climb the porch of one of the workshops on the opposite side of the corridor.

In the middle of the crowd, just in front of their studio, the two Trev'ban artists kneel in the street. Next to them stand a guild official and a Serix artist whom I recognize—Narrik, one of the markmakers who was at the bond-kindling. Surrounding the group are four or five other Serix members: guild guards, by their sharpened spurs and the ceremonial swords at their belts. They have not drawn their weapons, but they keep a stern eye on the restless spectators.

My gaze returns to the two Trev'ban artists, on their knees before the door of their own studio. From this distance, I can easily see the bright violet sigils of the new faction-marks on their chests. The markmakers are bound with hobbles but appear to await their humiliation with a brazen calm. Both are young men, only a handful of years older than I am. The younger of the two has only had his mastery-mark for a matter of months.

I stare, transfixed with dread. What would it be like to have my profession taken away from me after so many arduous years of apprenticeship? This punishment is not as severe as it might be—these men will remain members of their clan, though they will have to find another livelihood. Still, Rixarii Street is home to me, as it is to these artists. Being forbidden from the studios would be as painful as being disowned by my family. What would possess a young markmaker to defy the guild so flagrantly, to break his hard-won oath...?

At that thought, I catch myself. I am one to talk.

The guild official is saying something—a formal decree of expulsion, probably. I cannot hear the words over the muttering of the crowd. But now Narrik, the Serix markmaker, steps forward with pen in hand. Leaning over the first of the two kneeling artists, he touches the tip to his brow. The young man stiffens but does not try to pull away. Narrik's voice rings out harshly:

"This was a mark of truth. You have marred and dishonored it..."

The throng stirs. I sense the shifting of feet and the tensing of muscles, the faint hiss of breath through bared teeth. It occurs to me that many of the people in the crowd are clients of these two dissident artists, and some are likely Ascendance members as well. The guild has every justification to expel these markmakers, but that does not mean their patrons are going to look on with complacence. There is a reason the guild guards are here.

Narrik finishes painting the shame-sigils over the artists' mastery-marks; then he steps back with an air of finality. The younger Trev'ban looks shaken, as if he has only just realized the gravity of his actions, now that they are tattooed on his skin. But the older artist's expression hardens into a glare. A wild light glitters in his eyes, and his nostrils widen in a deep breath.

"Aurorii chi'ar!"

His shout pierces the heavy air. Narrik and the guild official startle, and the crowd ripples with a low exclamation. Then, from somewhere in the throng, a lone voice echoes the Ascendance slogan:

"Aurorii! Aurorii chi'ar!"

The guild guards swivel to find the offender. But more voices join in, taking up the faction chant, heckling and calling. The throng presses closer around the artists.

"Hakk, Serixan! Got something against the faction-mark? Want to shame us, too?"

"Don't you care if we ever see the planets?"

"Deep Sleep take you, skin-changers!"

"Kesh!" One of the Serix guards roars a rebuke and lashes out with a spurred foot. His blow clips one of the hecklers in the chest, sending him reeling back into the crowd. "Respect to the markmaker. This is guild business."

The onlookers fall back, sullen but chastened. The other guards move forward, scowling, urging the gathering to break up. In twos and threes the spectators shuffle away until only the disgraced artists are left, still kneeling in the street before the Serix officials. Narrik glares down at them. When he speaks, his voice drips contempt.

"Get out."

Slowly, the Trev'ban markmakers rise, the younger one shaky and staring, but the elder still unabashed. For a long, brazen moment he holds Narrik's gaze—until one of the guards grips him roughly by the shoulder and shoves him away.

The officials disperse; an early morning quiet falls over Rixarii Street once more. But the silence is a frigid one. The only people left in the corridor are Trev'ban markmakers. They watch from the doorways of their studios, narrow-eyed and tight-lipped. Some of them are watching me.

I swallow hard and step off the porch. Justice has been done; the guild has reasserted its authority. But I wonder whether the spectacle has done more harm than good.

CHAPTER TWELVE

When I arrive at Kilmaya's studio, I find my teacher sitting in the front room with her friend Rinavi, chatting over steaming cups of klasindi. Both women glance up as I enter.

"Ah, quiet one." Kilmaya lifts her cup in greeting. "Honor with you this morning."

"And with you, teacher. Rinavi." I touch my brow to them both. The warm scent of klasindi and the atmosphere of ease in the studio are disconcerting after the tension in the street.

Rinavi smiles up at me, the wrinkles creasing at the corners of her eyes. "That's a grim face you're wearing, Mariikel. Something the matter?"

"Oh, he's probably heard the news, is all. You know how he frets." Kilmaya sips her drink and casts me a sidelong glance. "It's only a couple of hotheaded Trev'banin. The guild will take care of them shortly."

"They already have." I drop my satchel and reach for my artist's apron on the wall. "I saw it. On my way here."

My teacher blinks. "Did you? Ancestors, that was quick. I suppose they wanted to have it over with." She leans back in her seat. "I'm rather sorry I missed it. I can't even remember the last time there was a shame-marking in Rixarii Street. Did they make a good show of it?"

Her tone is half jesting, but that only irritates me more. "I don't know. I didn't stop to watch."

I do not know what compels me to lie to her. Maybe I fear she will mock my anxieties again if I describe the defiance of the Trev'ban artists and the agitation of the crowd. Or maybe telling falsehoods has simply become instinctive.

"Hakk, well. They *were* asking for it." Kilmaya sniffs and sets down her cup. "Those two fools were the ones who started the trouble in the first place. Now that they're gone, perhaps we'll have some peace again."

"I hope so," Rinavi chuckles. "My apprentices have been distracted ever since Van'shorvanii. Did I tell you that Brekko and Takiro both came in yesterday with daggers at their belts?"

Kilmaya laughs aloud. "They've seen the Trev'ban artists doing that, haven't they? Well, they are only boys, after all. They are bound to get a little excited when people are looking for a fight. They'll learn."

I pull my datascroll from my bag and begin checking the day's appointments, brooding over my teacher's words. What will Rinavi's apprentices learn, exactly? That Serix markmakers need not carry weapons because we have the force of the law? That is the kind of respect the guild's authority is supposed to inspire—but I am beginning to wonder how effective it is.

"This always happens when there is some controversy in the guild," Kilmaya goes on. "You remember how bad it was with Toh Maas. There were more daggers in Rixarii Street than in the arenas. And people were angry enough to use them, too." She tilts back her head, finishing the last of her klasindi. "Not on markmakers, though. There would have been real trouble then."

"Thank the ancestors it hasn't come to that," Rinavi says.

"Even these Ascendance zealots are not *that* thick-headed." Kilmaya stands and glances at me brightly. "Klasindi, Mariikel, before we open? You look as if you could use some."

The remainder of the workday is uneventful. Clients come and go peacefully, and no one mentions the expelled Trev'ban artists except to laugh at their foolhardiness. I try to push away my disquiet and get on with my work.

Today I am giving out combat-marks to a whole class of children who have passed the first level of their physical training. They are a rowdy, excitable group, and very young. In the past year, most of the warrior clans have lowered the age at which children are required to learn basic hand-to-hand techniques. Already they are being prepared for a life of war.

This saddens me as I ink the small tattoos of accomplishment onto their slender arms. Several of the children are Tarriks, and seeing the Tarriks clan-mark reminds me once again of Talorak. It also reminds me that Kophas is still waiting for me to return to the Underbelly and give him false marks.

I have not visited the exiles recently for fear of Haza'ruux and what he knows about me. But the more I reflect, the less I believe he would betray me. The old hermit has had ample opportunity to turn me in, and yet has made no move to do so. I do not know what he wants, but I cannot help remembering his gentleness when I all but gave my life into his hands. *Now you will rest*, he said. For all his strangeness, there was no malice in him.

Besides, I told Kophas I would help him, and I am already two weeks late for our agreed meeting. The desperate young warrior kneeling before me, gripping my hands in supplication, whispering, *Let me live*—that memory still sears my mind. If I do not keep my promise to him, I will merely be submitting to cowardice again.

At the end of the day, while Kilmaya is busy with our last client, I quietly pack my satchel with tools, chemicals, and bandages. Then, when the studio closes, I make my way down to the atrium garden for my long trek to the Underbelly.

At the corner of the slums that serves as my illicit studio, a small crowd huddles—eight or ten exiles, both men and women, and a few children. They are waiting for me; someone saw me coming and spread the word. When I step out of the shadowed alley, they greet me with relief, with unfeigned joy.

"Markmaker!"

"You came."

"We were afraid something had happened to you."

I allow them to cluster around me, touching my hands, my feet, my tunic. Their clothes are filthy; the stench fills my nostrils. But their faces—oh, kin's heart, the look in their eyes.

"One at a time," I beg. My voice is hoarse, but only because I am trying to keep myself from crying.

The exiles back away obediently, giving me room to hang up my lamp and spread out my tools. Then they come forward in pairs or small groups—the laborer with his friend, the mother with her shy, ragged children. Honor-marks, clan-marks, child-marks. They ask, and I take up my pens and paint.

A strange ease fills my body as I work. I have not felt so light or calm in days. Perhaps this, more than anything else, is the reason I keep coming to the Underbelly. In this place, among these people, I may have to hide my face—but I do not have to lie.

Sinking myself into the rhythm of pen-strokes and the cadence of ceremonial words, I lose track of the time. I almost forget why I came. But finally, when the last of the crowd disperses, a tall, lean figure steps into the lamplight and stands before me.

Kophas Tarriks seems more haggard than when I saw him last. His eyes have dulled, and hunger haunts the sharpened lines of his face. "Markmaker." He bows, unsteady. "I thought you might have decided not to come back."

"I was delayed. But I keep my word." Glancing around at the shadows, I ask, "Do you have a place where we can talk?"

"Yes."

"Take me there." I sling my satchel over my shoulder and extinguish my lamp.

The young warrior leads me into the dark. After a long, maze-like route through the slums, he stops at one of makeshift shelters. The shack is little more than a few pieces of scrap metal propped against each other with a tattered curtain for a door. "Here," he says with a catch in his voice. He ducks inside.

The interior is black, damp, and foul-smelling. I switch on my lamp again and survey the tiny space: a pile of rags in one corner for a bed, a water flask, a few battered metal containers—his food stash, perhaps—and little else. The shelter is barely private, either. Through the thin walls, I can hear the wailing of an infant in the adjacent shack. It reminds me of Lakkia Penthar and her baby. I hope they are both still alive.

The Tarriks exile crouches uneasily in a corner. Neither of us can stand upright in this space. "This is all I have," he mutters.

I smile grimly. If he still has enough pride to feel ashamed, then he has not lived here long at all. "It will serve." I draw the curtain closed and sit down on the cold, dirty floor across from him.

"Forgive me." He stares at the ground, as if uncertain how to begin. "I don't think I've even told you my name."

"Kophas Tarriks. Your parents are Fenrik and Skesha. They raise dalrikhani war-hounds for the clan. You served in the Kento-Chi'ar warband under Valk'taro Tokkorak Tarriks. You were working towards your hvoss'ka rank."

He glances up, startled. Then his expression shifts into a look of grudging respect. "You're good."

"I do my research."

With a grimace, he puts a hand over the exile-mark on his neck. "This mark is a lie. What they put in the records is a lie. I didn't abandon my post."

"But you did disobey your commander. You told me that yourself."

He bares his teeth in a faint snarl. "Killing prisoners is not a warrior's work. It doesn't matter that they were only half-sights. The order was not honorable."

"Erasing all your marks is not honorable, either."

"Says the skin-changer. *You* have false marks. I know that's a mask you're wearing. No laborer could paint marks like the ones you give."

I almost lift a hand to touch the synthetic skin covering my face, but I restrain myself in time. "Are you certain you want this? Do you have any idea what it will involve?"

"I know the dangers, markmaker." He lowers his eyes. "Tell me what to do, and I will do it."

I gaze at him for a minute in silence. It crosses my mind that, except for his filthy skin and clothing, Kophas resembles a younger version of Askko. He is not as strongly built as my cousin, but his tattoos are similar: the warrior-mark on his brow, the violet trident of the Ascendance at his throat. But this man—unlike Askko—chose the honor-code over his faction.

A pang passes through me. I must admire his courage for that, at least.

"The process will take weeks," I say. "Have you ever had a mark removed before?"

"No, of course not."

I put down my lamp and open my satchel to pull out two small, dark bottles. I set one of them on the floor between us. "This is *grekyaa* oil. It breaks down the sealing-glaze over the mark. That is the first step."

Kophas nods, his eyes bright and nervous.

I place the other bottle on the floor. "And this is *thuriiklesh*."

Skin-eater. He flinches at the name.

"It is an acid. It burns away the first layer of skin, and the mark with it. It would probably keep eating through to the bone if you left it on too long."

That last part is an exaggeration, perhaps, but I want to scare him. I want to test his resolve. I frighten myself a little, simply showing him these chemicals. Both substances are strictly regulated by the artists' guild; only markmakers can buy them. It is, in fact, illegal for me to take them out of the studio.

"Burning the mark takes only a minute or two." I pause significantly. "But it hurts."

He looks insulted. "I can put up with pain."

"I am more concerned about infection. With the proper ointments, the skin should heal over in a matter of days, but you have to keep the wound clean." I glance around at the slanting walls of the shack, the grimy condensation dripping from the low ceiling. "That won't be easy to do here."

"I'll manage. I'm strong. I don't get sick."

I frown, skeptical. Perhaps that was true when he was eating full meals and sleeping in a dry, warm bed at night. "There is another problem. You work in a labor crew, yes?"

"Yes." Shame chokes him again. "In the sewage sector."

"The taskmasters are going to notice if you have bandages. And they will certainly notice when your marks have been changed." I take a breath. "Once I begin, you will not be able to work any longer. You'll have to stay in hiding until I am finished."

"I know. I've been thinking about that. I don't think it will be a problem— the taskmasters don't care much if exiles go missing." His mouth twists in a bitter expression. "They'll simply think I've fallen ill, or died. But they won't send anyone looking for me."

I nod without speaking. I believe him.

"Food will be a problem, though," he goes on. "And water. If I can't work for it, someone will have to bring it." He winces, humiliated by the thought. "I could ask someone on my crew, I suppose. There are a few people I think I could trust..."

"I'll bring you food. It's better if no one else is involved."

Kophas pauses, giving me a questioning look. "I'm going to owe you quite the debt at the end of this, aren't I?" He exhales. "Very well. How long do you think I'll have to hide?"

"I don't know. It depends how often I'm able to come, and how quickly you heal." I ponder. "A month, perhaps, to remove the marks. And another month to make the new ones."

His eyes widen slightly in dismay. But he nods, uncomplaining. Then, in a low voice: "What will the new marks be?"

"I haven't decided." I try to sound unconcerned. In reality, that is another problem I have not yet solved: I can forge marks that look real, but if I cannot create a set of official records to go with them, Kophas will stand little chance of getting off the ship.

"When can you start?" Kophas's voice is hoarse.

"Tonight. If you are ready." I touch the caps of the bottles. He stares at them with dread, as if they might burst into flame. "There is one more thing. You cannot tell anyone that I am doing this for you. You understand?"

"I understand. You can't do this for everyone. If I may ask, markmaker... why are you doing it for me?"

I pause. I cannot tell him about Talorak. But I feel he deserves some explanation—some reason to trust that I will keep my word. At last I say simply, "You remind me of someone I used to know." I reach into my satchel and begin pulling out tools and bandages. "Now. Where do you want to start?"

Kophas shivers, as if rousing himself from dark thoughts. "I may still need to work for a few days. I want to save up some rations." He holds himself stiffly, clenching his fists and glaring at the floor. "If you are going to begin, it should be somewhere inconspicuous. Like my back."

I regard him in silence, a pain unfolding in my chest. "You want to start with your memory-marks?"

He blinks, his jaw quivering with tension. Anguish brims in his eyes. "They will have to go sometime."

His shame pierces me, takes away my breath. In my mind, a silent cry rises: *Don't do this.* But I do not know if the words are meant for him or for me.

I collect myself. We are already resolved; we cannot turn back now. "All right. Show me, then."

Kophas unclenches his hands. Slowly he unties the strip of cloth that serves as his belt. Half-standing, he pulls off his ragged tunic. Then he sits down again, naked except for a short kilt.

His body is trim and athletic, although his ribs are beginning to stand out in pronounced lines. But he still looks like a warrior. The mark of the Ascendance dominates his chest like a six-pointed, purple talon, or a jagged wound.

"Turn around," I order.

He obeys. I adjust the angle of my lamp so that it shines on his dark shoulders. Then I lean forward and examine his marks.

I saw them before, of course, when I looked up his records. But at the time I was searching for honor- and shame-marks; I did not pay much attention to his family tattoos. On his upper back are two marks for deceased grandparents and one, slightly less elaborate, for an uncle. All three relatives died either of old age or in honorable combat.

With trepidation I touch the finely wrought sigils. I expected to start by removing a less important mark—a decorative pattern, perhaps, or some minor childhood accomplishment. That would not have been as bad as stripping the names of his ancestors. I feel like an executioner.

"These are large marks. If you still have to work for a few days…it's going to be very painful for you to move if I take these."

"Not those." His voice is taut. "The smaller one. Further down."

I glance downward and readjust my lamp. Then I see it: on his lower back, a delicate, pale blue design, no larger than the tip of my finger. The mark contains only a date and two simple sigils:

Avakali—Sister.

My gut wrenches. *Oh, Ka.* Why did it have to be something like this?

"I'm sorry." I don't even want to touch this mark. My hands would desecrate it.

"It's all right. She was only a year old. I was young, too. I don't remember much."

Briefly I compare the date on the memory-mark to Kophas's clan symbol. He would have been nine when his infant sister died—old enough, certainly, to understand. Old enough to grieve.

Kophas wraps his arms around his knees. When he speaks, his voice is low and harsh. "Get on with it, rethurax."

Skin-changer. The name stabs me like a blade. I do not think I understood until this moment what that word truly means.

With slow movements, I clean the area around the mark with a damp cloth. Then I take my artist's gloves from my bag and pull them on—I can't afford to burn holes in my disguise. I have only worked with erasing chemicals a few times, mostly to repair tattoos that have been damaged by wounds or burns. I have never deliberately and irrevocably destroyed a true mark. It is the one crime I have not yet committed as an artist.

My hands shake as I uncap the grekyaa oil and brush it over the tiny, graceful blue sigils. When the sealing-glaze has dissolved, I wash Kophas' skin again, this time in a strong disinfectant. The sharp smell of it stings my throat as I bend over my work. When his back is clean and dry, I open the bottle of thuriiklesh. I dip my brush in the thick white paste.

The memory-mark is so small that it only needs a daub or two of the acid. Kophas shivers at its touch, and he inhales sharply. His back muscles tense.

There are no ceremonial words to say when erasing a mark. How could there be? But as I watch the white acid eat into Kophas' skin, dissolving his sister's name, I think to myself: *This was a mark of truth. May the breaking of it be for justice.*

Silently, I wash off the acid, scrape away the dead skin, and clean and bandage the wound. Through it all, Kophas does not make a sound. I pretend not to notice when his shoulders begin quivering with unvoiced cries.

CHAPTER THIRTEEN

When I emerge from the Underbelly into the silent atrium gardens, it is well past the thirteenth hour. Hurriedly I change back into my ordinary clothes. I have stayed out later than I intended. If I am exhausted at the studio tomorrow, Kilmaya will notice.

I make my way down the garden paths, trying to put the memory of Kophas out of my mind. He stoically accepted the healing ointment I left with him for his wound, but I could tell that his grief was as heavy as my own. Now, as I leave the atrium, I find myself wringing my hands.

These are the hands of a skin-changer now. These hands have destroyed the truth.

I am so absorbed in myself that I almost fail to notice the figures standing at the transport hub gate.

"Hakka! Stop a moment."

I halt in the entryway, startled. Two Clan Trechik guards, a man and a woman, stand blocking my way—not in a hostile manner, but looking more vigilant than usual. There are always a few security guards in the transport hub, but typically the night shift stays in the gatehouse. I do not think I have ever seen them standing in front of the entrance—not at this late hour, when the hub is deserted.

I almost clutch at my satchel, but I stop myself. I must be calm. "Good evening. Honor with you, Trechikan."

"And with you, Serix." The female guard frowns. "Where are you going at this hour?"

"Home." I try to keep my voice relaxed, but my pulse rises. Both guards have Ascendance marks.

"It's late, markmaker." Her tone is not friendly. "What brings you this far from your sector?"

"I...I was waiting for someone." I drop my eyes, feigning embarrassment. "She never came."

"Hakk." The male guard gives a short, sympathetic laugh. "Better luck another time."

The Trechik woman, however, shifts her feet into the faintest hint of a fighting stance—a subtle threat. "I would hurry home. Walk safely, Serix."

I thank the guards and hurry past them into the transport hub. In the elevator, I lean against the wall and exhale a shaky breath. The way the Trechik woman addressed me… I am a Serix markmaker; strangers treat me with respect and deference. This guard was almost hostile.

It's the Trev'ban artists the guild cast out. People are still upset. But that does not give security guards permission to harass Serix members. I must be more cautious on my trips to the Underbelly—especially since I will be going more frequently now for Kophas. I may need to find another entrance. The atrium gardens are too public.

When the elevator doors open, I hurry back to the Serix sector and pass through the gate. There are no guards here—only the ancestor shrine looming in the middle of the silent plaza, with soft blue lamps glowing between the pillars. My step stutters and halts.

Serixan, my ancestors…

The prayer dies as quickly as it rises to my lips. What can I say? The ashes of my parents, grandparents, and all my other forebears who have lived on the Fleet lie at rest in this shrine, but I have long since lost the right to address them. Giving marks to the exiles was one thing; at least those were true. But to *erase* a mark, a bond between kin, a sacred memory in the flesh…

With a shudder, I hurry past the shrine. Why am I worrying over my ancestors now? They have neither helped nor harmed me—and I am too far along this treacherous path to turn back.

I make my way to Elantii Street. The corridors are dim and empty—but when I reach home, I find the lights in the front room still on. Chervani sits on the couch, writing something with a stylus and datascroll. At the sight of me, she springs up.

"There you are, dako." Relief rings in her voice. "Are you all right?"

"Of course, nakki." Surprised and a little perplexed, I allow her to embrace me. "Were you waiting up for me? There's no need for that."

"I know. I was up anyway—I wanted to finish a letter to Askko." But she holds my arms and looks into my face, the corners of her eyes creased in worry. "I wish you would take your scroll with you when you are out so late."

"Did I leave it off again? I'm sorry." I feel a twinge of guilt. The truth is that I left my datascroll at the studio deliberately. But at the moment I am more concerned about my aunt. She is not scolding me. In fact, she looks almost frightened. "Is something wrong?"

"Wrong? No." But her voice belies her words. "Did anyone try to stop you on your way home?"

The question startles me. *How did she know?* I briefly consider telling her about the guards at the transport gate. But Chervani doesn't know that I left the clan sector tonight; she probably thinks I stayed late at the studio, or was praying at the ancestor shrine. "No. Who would stop me? Is there something going on?"

Her shoulders relax. "Oh. It's nothing." She sounds embarrassed now. But her eyes stray to the front room table. There is a small chip of wood sitting on it, like a piece of bark torn from a shrub or tree. Shame-faced, she picks up the bark and hands it to me. "I found this on the porch when I came home this evening. There's a strange marking on it—I couldn't read it. Hakham couldn't, either. We didn't know what to make of it." She pauses, then says in a lower tone, "I thought it might be a threat from some Trev'ban artist. Meant for you."

I turn the wood fragment over in my palm. Painted on its surface is a complex sigil like the spindly bloom of a flower. I cannot read it. But I instantly recognize the artist's hand. My stomach lurches.

Haza'ruux.

"Does it mean anything to you?" Chervani watches my face.

I rub the bark's rough edges with my thumb. If Haza'ruux wanted to talk to me, he could have sent me a message on my datascroll. He didn't have to leave cryptic symbols on my doorstep to frighten my family. "No." I attempt to sound calm, though unease roils in my belly. "It's some sort of joke."

"I hope so. Hakham told me it was probably nothing. But with all these ill feelings between the studios lately... I wish you would at least carry a dagger when you are out."

I laugh. "I don't think that will be necessary."

"Other artists are doing it. You haven't noticed?"

"People always do that when there is a quarrel in the guild." The words are Kilmaya's, not mine, but I hope they will reassure my aunt. "It's only a show."

She stares at me, unconvinced. With a sigh, I relent. "All right, nakki. If it makes you feel better, I will carry a dagger."

"Thank you." She pulls me into another embrace. Remorse chokes me. Chervani worries about me walking back and forth to work. If she knew where I had been tonight...

If you are ever caught, it will crush her.

I stand back from my aunt and squint in attempted humor. "Only a very small dagger. You know I'm useless with blades. I'm more of a danger to myself than anyone else."

She scowls, but her eyes are smiling. "Go to bed, Mariikel." She waves me away, as if I am merely a precocious child again.

She has not noticed that I am still holding the painted chip of wood. I obey her and go to my room before my guilt betrays me.

The next day, at the studio, I can hardly keep my mind on my work. As soon as we close, I head down to the mad markmaker's house with the bark fragment clutched in my fist. It occurs to me that I am probably doing exactly what Haza'ruux intended me to do. But I do not care. As much as I dread facing him again, I need to know what he wants from me. I need to know if my secret is still safe.

As I turn down the final corridor, I see Haza'ruux sitting in his garden with a child in his lap. My fingers tighten around the piece of bark. A part of me secretly hoped he would not be at home. Now that I see him again, all I can think of is the moment I told him I was a criminal.

He knows.

But now that I am standing in front of his house, I am too ashamed to flee. I inhale deeply and stride forward.

He sits cross-legged on his garden path, holding the same little Trechik boy he was playing with the last time I came. Haza'ruux's gentleness is strangely mesmerizing. He reaches over the child's shoulder, tracing something in the dirt with his finger. The Trechik boy grimaces at the ground, concentrating.

This eccentric old inkmaker who spends his days playing with children—can this possibly be the same man protected by those baffling, ancient laws? Neither the hermit nor the boy seems to have noticed me. Without ceremony, I walk up to the old man and drop the wood chip in the dirt before him.

"I believe this is yours." I try to sound irritated. But my voice quavers.

Haza'ruux does not even look up. He flicks the bark off his drawing and retraces a line in the soil. The child in his lap glances at me. "Hi, Blade."

The boy recognizes me from last time—something more than Haza'ruux deigns to do, apparently.

"Haza'ruux. Did you leave this note at my house?"

The old hermit does not pay me the slightest attention. He finishes his sketch, then leans back and lets the child look at it. The boy squints, then says, "What's that one?"

"Light," Haza'ruux answers.

I stare at the drawing on the path. It is an ordinary sigil—*liir*, the basic symbol for brightness or radiance.

The child points to the glowing orange panels in the ceiling. "Like that light?"

"Yes."

"Let me try." The boy scrambles off Haza'ruux's lap, flops down on the path, and begins making a clumsy copy in the dirt.

"Haza'ruux." Fury wells up in my throat. "I know you put the sigil on that bark. I know you want something from me." Without even meaning to, I find I am clutching my right arm, hiding the elaborate tattoo. "Speak to me!"

The child tugs on Haza'ruux's hand. "Look! I did it."

Haza'ruux glances at the wobbly sigil in the path and smiles. Then, at last, he turns to me. "Tyotik is learning to read. Will you join us, Flashing Blade?"

I laugh, angry and incredulous. "You're not going to tell me anything, are you?"

Little Tyotik blinks at me. "Blade is big. He can read already." Evidently, he is jealous of his teacher's attention.

The old man places a hand on Tyotik's shoulder, grinning. "Flashing Blade is not so big as he looks. He can read a little—but not as well as Haza'ruux." He fixes me with one of his piercing gazes. "Sit down and learn with us."

"I don't have time for your games." What did I expect to accomplish with this conversation? Maybe he is half-witted, after all. I shift my feet and turn away.

Haza'ruux chuckles. The sternness that had appeared in his face melts back into mischief. Smoothing the dirt with one hand, he brushes away the sigils. "Don't you want to know? Flashing Blade cannot rest until he knows."

Before I can reply, Tyotik pulls on the hermit's ragged tunic. "Ha'ruux, show me another one."

Haza'ruux turns his attention to the impatient child. "Draw 'light' again. Flashing Blade must learn with us."

While Tyotik busies himself in the dirt, I exhale in exasperation. "I know how to read."

"Then read this." On another part of the path, Haza'ruux begins sketching a figure—not slowly, as he did for Tyotik, but with the rapid strokes of a long-practiced master. The sigil he draws vaguely resembles the light-mark, but it has more curved lines, with a greater variation of thickness. He pauses, glancing at the boy.

"Done!" Tyotik calls. He stands back proudly from his own sketch.

The child's drawing is barely legible. But Haza'ruux only says, "Very good." He places one finger on Tyotik's sigil. "Liir." Then he places his other hand beside the second, more complex mark. "*Lirii'hir.*"

He looks up. I cannot read his expression—but it is clear to me what I have just seen. Unable to help myself, I crouch down and trace my finger in the air over the graceful sketch. Already, my eyes flick over the lines, memorizing their placement, angles, and thickness.

"Lirii'hir," I murmur. "This is an ancient sigil for light?"

"Sunlight," he murmurs. "From a clear sky." With his fingertip he crosses one of the lines with a short, curving slash. "*Mahak.* Strikes—" He begins another sigil, interwoven with the first. "—*kell-kantajiin,* the warrior's blade. It shines, blinding his foes." He adds a final complex flourish. "Like the sea waves."

Dazzled, I stare at the pattern that has bloomed in the dirt before me. *Mahak, lirii'hir, kell-kantajiin...* The words are all new to me—but then I realize I have seen these symbols before.

"That's it. That's the note you left at my house." I snatch the wood fragment from the ground and compare the sigils. The lines on the wood are much finer, but the mark is the same. My brow furrows. "I don't understand. What does this have to do with...?"

Haza'ruux tilts his head in amusement. He says nothing. Tyotik, bored, stomps on his own drawing, scattering dirt on both of us. Then, all at once, I laugh.

"It's my name." I hold the bark out in my palm. "It's my ancient name, isn't it? *Maha'lirii'kell*—Flashing Blade. The sunlight on the sword and the sea..."

Haza'ruux smiles. He smooths a spot of soil next to the densely intricate symbol and points to it. "You try."

I stay with Haza'ruux for over an hour, long after he has sent Tyotik, protesting, home to bed. The old man shows me dozens of ancient sigils, tracing each one carefully in the packed dirt of the path. I study them, enthralled. Even the simplest of words—*leaf, water, hand*—each has an archaic grace, a nuance of meaning and line that delights me. Only when Haza'ruux declares that I have learned enough for one night do I remember why I came.

Haza'ruux climbs to his feet and brushes his soiled hands on his tunic. I rise with him, a little unsteady—I feel almost drunk. Around us, the vines and bushes whisper in a breeze from the air vents.

"Thank you for showing me the sigils. They are very beautiful." I pause. The street behind us is dim and deserted, but I am still afraid to speak here, in the open. "Haza'ruux—I wanted to ask you..." I extend my arm. "Your mark..."

"No." He pushes my hand away. "Sigil poems are too hard for you."

"What?" I stare at the intricate tattoo on my wrist. "This is a poem?"

Haza'ruux turns away, setting foot on his porch.

"Wait! What does it mean?"

The hermit's eyes narrow in exasperation. "Did you not listen? You are too young to read that mark." He pauses, distracted by a flower on a swaying vine. "You must read some of Haza'ruux's books first."

My breath catches in my throat. "Books? You will show me how to read your books?"

"Come in the morning. Before your work." It is a command, not an invitation. Flicking a dismissive hand in my direction, he turns and opens the door. "Now go away. Haza'ruux must dream tonight."

"But I—"

The door closes. I am alone in the dark, rustling garden.

My shoulders slump. I do not know whether to be relieved or infuriated. I told this man my most shameful secret, and he gave me an unreadable mark—and this is all the explanation he offers?

Slowly I turn and walk down the garden path, touching the unkempt shrubs, scuffing my feet in the dirt where we had our writing lesson. Haza'ruux did seem willing—determined, even—to show me more of the ancient sigils. Is that what he wants from me? Is that what he demands in return for keeping my secret?

I do not know. But it seems that I have a new teacher.

CHAPTER FOURTEEN

For the next few weeks, I almost forget to feel guilty or anxious. I am too busy.

In the mornings, I get up early to go to the mad markmaker's house. At first, I am nervous about entering, considering what happened to me last time. But when he takes me into his beautiful studio, sits me down at the worktable made of real, glossy wood, and sets a book of sigils before me... well, my fear quickly fades.

Mark by mark, he shows me the language of the ancestors, explaining sounds, syllables, and meanings. I diligently copy the symbols with a stylus and datascroll—he will not let me touch his pens or inks yet. Haza'ruux proves to be a demanding teacher. To my surprise, when we are deeply engaged in reading, writing, or translating, his irrational persona drops away. His directions are clear, his critiques precise. He does not let me get away with a single lazy stroke. And often, when I exclaim over the beauty of a line or the eloquence of a sigil, his eyes shine with a delight that is utterly familiar to me—the joy of an artist sharing his work with a kindred mind.

It makes me wonder, again, why he hides his studio, why he puts on his half-witted act. Even as I begin to trust the old hermit, he continues to puzzle me. He does not speak about either my crimes or the mark that he gave me. He asks me nothing of my daily activities. His only concern, apparently, is that I learn to master the ancient marks.

Now and then, during our sessions, I remember the mysterious old laws that my uncle showed me in the archives—the decree that grants the mad markmakers total liberty in choosing their successors. I wonder sometimes if Haza'ruux is training me for that end. The idea disturbs me. If I became the next hermit-artist of Clan Serix, I might have the freedom to continue my work among the exiles—but I would have to give up my position in Rixarii Street and my partnership with Kilmaya. I cannot bear the thought of leaving my teacher.

In any case, I have no desire to live as a mad markmaker, strange and solitary, friendless except for the clan's children. So far, Hazaruux has not declared his intention for me, nor made me take any oaths of apprenticeship. I am presumably free to leave his tutelage whenever I please.

But I do not want to. Not yet. I am learning so much that I am almost happy again.

At the end of each lesson, Haza'ruux shows me passages from one or two of his books. At first, they are impossible for me to translate on my own—but as the days pass, I begin to recognize more symbols in the dense, calligraphic lines. And even when I cannot understand the books, it is a joy simply to run my fingers along the delicate, browning pages, to inhale their musty fragrance.

The passages he shows me are excerpts from legends about the ancestral planets. They are very ancient texts—some predate the construction of the Fleet, he tells me. I am not sure whether to believe this. If it is true, then Haza'ruux's collection is more valuable than all the Serix archives put together. My uncle Hakham, or any other record-keeper, would be overjoyed simply to lay hands on a text written before the Wandering—even if he could not read it.

And yet, Haza'ruux makes me promise not to tell anyone about his books. I do not quite understand why. The stories are mostly legends from the ancestral clans, fantastical tales about warriors with animal tattoos and supernatural powers. Many of them sound like the stories of the mythical Devorak cult. There is even mention of a Clan Sko'larik, a name that is often associated with those savage, beast-worshipping warriors. But these texts do not mention the word *Devorak*. Instead they use another term, which I have never heard before: *Arimaas*.

I ask Haza'ruux if this is an older, alternate name for the Devorak cult. To my surprise, he bares his teeth, and his eyes glitter with sudden anger. "No! Arimaas and Devorak, they are not the same. Clan Sko'larik did not drink Noxxiin blood or worship the beasts. The Keepers of the Arimaas were markmakers and warriors—great guardians. Do not slander them with the name of Devorak." And he spits on the floor in fierce disdain.

"All right. I was only asking." I do not see why he should get so upset over the details of a myth. I have never heard that Clan Sko'larik had an order of markmaker-guardians—how was I supposed to know?

I cannot fathom the hermit's whims and moods, nor why he considers these tales important. Despite my excitement at reading such ancient texts, I am a little disappointed in their content. I had hoped that Haza'ruux's books would have history in them, not fantasy. Still, I do not complain. Every sigil he teaches me brings me one step closer to reading the mark on my own arm—and that I am determined to understand.

In the meantime, I have more than enough to worry about in my work at the studio. Despite Kilmaya's predictions, the tension between Serix and Trev'ban artists shows no signs of abating. A few days after I begin my lessons with Haza'ruux, fighting breaks out in Rixarii Street.

Kilmaya blames it on the High Councilor. Evidently Valo T'sarek made a public comment about the expelled Trev'ban artists, praising their loyalty to the Ascendance cause, and a few overzealous faction members took this as encouragement to defy the guild further. A group of rabble-rousers began frequenting the studios, brazenly demanding the reinstatement of the expelled markmakers. The guild ignored them for a few days, but when the agitators refused to leave on their own, Serix officials sent guild guards to remove them by force. The Ascendance members resisted—out of bravado, according to my teacher—and the fight turned into a general brawl as clients of both artist clans joined in. Eventually the agitators were subdued, but not before several people received serious injuries.

I did not see the fight, but I witness the aftermath. The morning after the conflict, I turn into Rixarii Street to find more guards patrolling the corridor. They are not from the guild; they are regular security forces from Clan Trechik. The warriors greet me civilly as I pass—but I notice, with alarm, that all of them carry handguns at their belts along with their ordinary swords and daggers.

"What's going on?" I ask Kilmaya when I reach the studio. "What are all those Trechik warriors doing here?"

My teacher narrows her eyes. "Keeping the peace, supposedly. The ship council sent them—they seem to think the guild's guards are not sufficient, after yesterday."

"Oh." My distress abates a little. "Well, if it keeps more clients from getting hurt..."

"Hakk. We'll see," Kilmaya snorts. "I say let people have a bit of a sparring match, if they're angry. It's only natural, and they'll come to their senses faster afterwards. I'd rather have that than cowards' weapons in Rixarii Street. I don't care if those firearms are standard equipment now, or whatever excuse those Ascendance councilors make. Do they really think that's going to make our clients feel *safer*?"

I sense she is about to plunge into one of her tirades on the idiocy of the Ascendance leadership, so I hurriedly steer the conversation in a more mundane direction. I have had my fill of my teacher's harangues on that particular topic.

Not that I disagree with her. As the days pass, and the Trechik guards remain in Rixarii Street, my own unease continues to grow. Most of the new guards have Acendance faction-marks; I cannot imagine that they sympathize much with Clan Serix or the guild. I begin to wonder if they were sent to protect the Trev'ban workshops rather than the studios as a whole.

Even outside the clan sector, I no longer feel quite safe. I have always been accustomed, when walking in the public areas of the ship, to receiving respectful nods from strangers. But now, in many places, the looks that my clan-mark earns me are cold, or fearful, or resentful. One late night, when crossing the atrium on my way back from the Underbelly, I run into an intoxicated pair of Ascendance warriors-in-training. They are sober enough to recognize that I am Serix, and drunk enough to call me a traitor and try to grab me. I dodge them without much trouble—but while I do not use my dagger, I am glad, for once, that I have it.

How many ordinary Noxxiin now think, as Askko thought, that the markmaker guild is endangering our future on the planets? *Planet*—it is such a heady word. I begin to wonder how much people will do for the sake of that word.

Despite the unrest, I still go to the Underbelly every few days to keep working on Kophas's marks. I carry two bags with me now: one for my markmaking supplies and one full of food and water for Kophas. The extra weight on my shoulders as I climb down the many ladders only reminds me that I am now wholly responsible for this young man's life. If something were to happen to me, if I were to stop coming, he would starve—or else he would have to return to his labor crew and give up the hope of ever escaping.

I am glad that Kophas is relatively young. If he were older, he would have more tattoos, and the process of removing them would be even more brutal and tedious. During every visit, I clean all his wounds and check them for signs of infection before I start on a new mark. Through all this, Kophas remains uncomplaining. His body is bony now, and his face hollow despite the food I bring. He has to stay in hiding—he cannot safely leave his shelter lest the other exiles see that his marks are being changed. I admire his endurance, but I can tell the isolation is wearing on him, too.

While I work on his marks or wash his wounds, I tell him I have determined that it is too risky to create an entirely original set of tattoos. "There's no plausible way I can forge a false record for the archives—I don't have the proper imaging equipment. Anyway, there are too many safeguards in place."

"Then what do we do?"

I hesitate. "I'll have to copy an existing set of marks."

"An existing set?" He sounds appalled. "You mean I'm going to be walking through the ship with another man's tattoos? What happens if we cross paths?"

"You won't. I can guarantee it."

Horrified comprehension steals over his face. "You're turning me into a dead man."

He has understood my problem: I cannot involve some living, innocent stranger in my crimes. But if I can find the record of a recently deceased, low-ranking laborer—someone resembling Kophas in age and build—then all I must do is copy the marks accurately and bypass certain archive security measures to remove the death date from the records. It will not be easy, but it is more feasible than creating a wholly new set of documents.

It is not a perfect plan: Kophas could still be caught, if some official decides to examine his false tattoos closely. But the ruse might work long enough for him to get off the ship. Once he sets foot on a planet, his records will no longer matter.

"Well, I suppose it's fitting," Kophas growls. He eyes me with a mixture of distaste and respect. "You have no limits, do you, rethurax?"

I swallow hard and do not answer. He is right. I had thought, after erasing a mark for the first time, that there was no worse crime I could commit. Now I am planning to forge the tattoos of a dead man. I am inventing new kinds of sacrilege.

One evening, after giving tattoos to the exiles for about an hour, I make my way to Kophas's shelter as usual and tap quietly on the wall. There is no answer. I knock a little louder; the sheet metal rings under my knuckles.

"Kophas?"

Still, there is no response. I draw back the curtain and switch on my lamp to peer inside.

He is lying on the floor, limbs outstretched, ragged blanket flung to one side. At my entrance, he startles awake, wincing in the lamplight.

"Rethurax." Blearily, he rolls over and pushes himself upright. "Forgive me. I didn't hear…"

The air in the shelter is foul and stifling—more so than usual. I set my lamp and my bags on the floor and kneel at his side. "Are you all right?"

"I'm…thirsty." His eyes are glassy, his breathing irregular. "Do you have water? Mine's gone. I drank it all…yesterday."

I touch the side of his face. Even through the fabric of my disguise, I can feel the radiating heat of his skin. "Axdraa'dah. I knew this would happen.

You're burning." I take one of the water flasks from my heavy bag, give him a long drink, and then ease him back down on his bed of rags. "Do any of your wounds feel inflamed? Never mind. I'll check them all."

He lies listless while I take off his bandages, one by one, to wash the raw skin underneath. I find the infected wound on his chest: it is from my visit two days ago, when I removed his Ascendance tattoo. I grimace. Of course, it would have to be the faction-mark. The acid-burned skin is swollen, oozing a pale gray discharge.

When I clean the wound, Kophas jerks away and groans. It is the first time I have ever heard him cry out.

"I'm sorry." I am shaking, too, but with anger and fear. *This is my fault. I should have come yesterday. I should have covered it better. I should have left you with medicine...*

I rub disinfectant into the wound and smear a healing ointment over his chest before bandaging it again. Finally, I pull the blanket over his lean frame. "Can you eat anything? I brought tavla." I pull the packages of dried meat from my satchel, along with the fruit and other goods I brought for him.

"No." Kophas does not even glance at the food. He lies with all his eyes closed, panting.

"Try to eat if you can." I place the parcels at his side. "I'll be back to-morrow. With medicine." I gather the ointments and soiled bandages. Under the blanket, Kophas stirs and turns his head. His eyes open, round and fever-bright.

"Markmaker," he gasps. "Don't go yet."

I frown. "I'm not going to work on you when you're like this."

"I know." His face contorts, desperation mingled with shame. "Can you stay? For a short while?"

I pause, surprised. He has never requested my company before. But now he is miserably ill—and, I realize, he has hardly ventured outside his own cramped, filthy shelter for weeks. The confinement alone would be enough to drive a man mad. *How has he endured it?* Slowly I set my bag aside. "I can stay."

He relaxes. His eyes flicker shut again. "Talk to me."

For a minute I sit in silence, unsure what to say. I do not want to talk about myself—the less Kophas knows about my true identity, the better. Neither do I want to ask him about his past; that would only stir up painful memories. At last, I say quietly, "Did you ever see one of the planets? With your warband?"

"No. Only stations and asteroid mines."

"My brother is a warrior. He's been on Kol'ihaz." My own words surprise me; I have not thought about Askko for days. "He told me about it."

Kophas turns, his face gaunt with hunger—but not a hunger for food. "What was it like?"

I tell him about the island, the ocean, the sunrises—every detail I can recall from Askko's stories. I wish now that I had listened to his tales more closely. For each marvel I describe—the boundless horizon, the red evening sky, the floating clouds of mist that pour out water on the sea—Kophas drinks in my words with reverent attention. The strength of his yearning puts an ache into my own chest.

"I want to see that." He moves under the blanket. Pain glitters in his eyes. "I don't want to die here, markmaker."

"Kesh. You won't. Not if I can help it."

"What else did your brother tell you?"

"I don't remember much else." Again I fall silent. Clearly, Kophas does not want me to leave yet. But what else can I safely tell him? Then an idea strikes me. "I know a poem from the planets. A very old one. At least—the man who taught it to me said it was that old."

I am not exactly breaking my promise to Haza'ruux. The old hermit only made me swear to tell no one about his books. But this is a poem I learned from Haza'ruux himself—a song, in fact, that I heard him sing under his breath during one of our lessons. I asked for the meaning of the haunting tune, and he translated it for me.

Now, Kophas blinks up at me, waiting. I take a breath and, in a low voice, begin:

> At the foot of Quiriil Mountain,
>   At the crest of the holy hills,
>   The trallak groves are burning,
>   Smoking and staining the sky.
> On the high seat, dark ash settles,
>   And blood seeps into the stones.
>
> The strength of Sko'larik is wasted:
>   Our champions fall at the gate,
> And the Keepers lie slain on the threshold.
>   Blades pierce the hide of the burrik,
>   The kharraktyl's venom has failed,
>   The arrowhawk falls from the wing.
>   Their bodies lie broken, dishonored,
>   And the light in their flesh fades,
>   Never to be rekindled.

For the pens have been crushed, and the ink spilled,
The rites burned, and the dream-halls smashed.
The Arimaas has left us,
For we bear the curse of our kings.
With our blood, we pay for their evil,
While our warriors devour each other,
And feed on our own children's flesh.

May the name of Sko'larik be cursed.
Let this mark be cut out of our bodies,
Cut out and forgotten forever.
Nameless we go down to Axdrad'dah,
And lie down in the dark, without dreams.
Death is our heritage now,
The only gift left for our children.
Our ancestors leave us no blessings:
Only shame and the taste of blood.

With a shiver, I fall quiet. I have never recited the poem aloud before. It has an entirely new meaning here, in the Underbelly, that it did not have in Haza'ruux's beautiful studio. "Forgive me. I forgot how sad it was."

Kophas stares into space as if transfixed. When he speaks, his voice is both hollow and strangely earnest: "It was fitting." After a moment, his brow furrows. "Sko'larik. Isn't that another name for the Devorak? Seems strange to mourn the death of a clan of cannibals."

"They weren't cannibals." The quickness of my own response surprises me. "At least, not all of them. There are different versions of the myths."

"There are? I've never heard them."

"They're very old and...obscure." A sufficiently vague explanation for something I do not understand well myself. "In some stories, the Sko'larik warriors used their animal signs, their marks of power, to fight for worthy causes."

"Honorable Devorak?" Kophas lets out a weak laugh. "Now *that* would be a story." He shifts under the blanket again. "Do you know any tales about them?"

"A few."

"Tell me one." His eyes drift shut again.

I hesitate. I did promise Haza'ruux that I would not tell anyone about his library—but Kophas does not need to know where the tales came from. "Do you know the story of Arkhalo, the first death pilgrim?"

"A death pilgrim?" Kophas blinks up at me wryly. "Are all your stories sad, markmaker?"

"It's about an exile. One who wins back his honor."

The young warrior's face clouds. Then he drops his gaze and pulls his blanket closer around his shoulders. "I could listen to that."

Outside the dim shelter, I can hear the distant clank and hiss of machinery; the fetid smell of the Underbelly fills my nostrils. I shut my eyes and picture Haza'ruux's studio instead. The bright murals, the fragrance of ink, the fragile, browned pages of a book under my fingertips—and through it all, the rasping voice of the mad markmaker, telling me a tale.

"There once was a warrior named Arkhalo, who sought a mark of power from the Keepers of the Arimaas, the markmaker-guardians of Clan Sko'larik. Because of his strength and ferocity, he won the most powerful mark of them all, the sign of the burrik. But there was pride in him, too, and rashness. Once, while staying at the court of a neighboring chieftain, he was demonstrating his skill with the javelin while he drew on the strength of the Arimaas. One of his javelins went astray, struck the chieftain's son, and slew him.

"For this crime, the Keepers drove Arkhalo into exile, defacing his clan-mark and tattooing his misdeed upon his face. Despairing, cut off from his kin, Arkhalo offered himself as a slave to the chieftain whose son he had killed. And the chieftain, wanting him to die a shameful death, sent Arkhalo to hunt down a great and cunning burrik that plagued the mountain roads and lived on Noxxiin flesh.

"So Arkhalo obeyed: armed with nothing but his Arimaas mark, he went out to meet the beast." My voice has warmed to the tale, to the cadence of the words. "For three days beast and Noxxiin struggled, tooth and claw, until the mountain ran violet with their blood. But at last, the warrior dealt the burrik a grievous blow, and the beast fell, never to rise. And Arkhalo—victorious but feeling his heart's blood pouring from his many wounds—sank to the ground in weakness, and breathed his last.

"Hunters discovered the bodies of the burrik and the warrior and brought them back to the chieftain. When they washed Arkhalo's body, cleansing it of the blackened blood, they discovered Arkhalo's clan-mark had been restored, whole and unmarred, and the tattoo of his crime had vanished. For even when all the living turned away from him, the ancestors looked with favor on his courage. And so he became the first Death Pilgrim: for he was willing to journey even to the brink of Axdraa'dah to redeem the honor he had lost."

I fall silent at last. I glance at Kophas—and I find, to my chagrin, that he has fallen asleep.

Moving softly, I gather up the last of my tools and pick up my satchels. Then I gaze at Kophas for a long moment. His nostrils flicker as he breathes steadily, in and out. I resist the urge to pull the tattered blanket closer around him. I do not want to wake him.

For the next few days, I visit Kophas every evening. I bring him food and water and medicine, and I tell him tales of Clan Sko'larik and the Arimaas warriors. Slowly, the infection in his chest subsides, the wound heals, and I resume erasing his marks. We are more at ease with each other after his illness—a little more like friends.

Finally, the day comes when I have erased all his tattoos except his clan-mark. It was not a conscious decision on my part, to leave it for last. Perhaps I avoided it out of some remnant of guilt and reluctance. Or perhaps I unwittingly imitated the ceremony of mark-stripping—a brutal form of execution, reserved for the most heinous criminals. I have never seen a mark-stripping before, and I hope I never will. But I know that the clan-mark is the last tattoo to be cut out of the condemned man's flesh.

Now, as I clean the side of Kophas's neck, I allow my eyes to linger on the symbol—the double-pronged mark of Clan Tarriks, with the tendriled sigil of exile running through it like a scar. It is still painfully similar to the mark I gave Talorak. I brush the grekyaa oil over it, wondering where the old warrior is now. Is he slaving away somewhere in the labyrinth of the Underbelly, beaten and spat upon by taskmasters? Or has he already died, ending his undeserved shame? I will probably never know.

I take a long time to clean off the sealing-glaze—longer than I need to. Finally, I open the bottle of thuriiklesh and dip my brush in the acid.

Kophas stirs. "Do you think they will forgive me?"

I pause, holding the brush inches from his skin. "Who?"

"My ancestors." His voice is quiet. He does not seem agitated, only sad.

I lower the brush. "You are in exile now because you followed the honor-code. Your ancestors must know that." The certainty in my own words surprises me. "I think they will not judge you too harshly."

"I hope not." His eyelids flicker. "I will make it up to them someday. By my heart's blood, I swear it." Bowing his head, he says, "Go on."

Silently I apply the acid. I watch the clan-mark shrivel and dissolve into a small welter of burned flesh. I dreaded this moment—dreaded the act of cutting Kophas off from his ancestors—but now that I have done it, I do not feel much emotion at all. It is only another piece of blistered skin.

In a matter of minutes, I clean and bind up the wound. When I finish, Kophas lifts a tentative hand to his neck. "It's done," he murmurs, as if in disbelief.

"It's done." I turn away and drop my tools into my satchel.

He stretches out his arms, turning them over in wonder. The wounds from his honor-marks have healed, leaving his arms black and bare. With a tremor in his voice, he says, "I must look like a newborn."

"Or the Deep Sleep," I say dryly.

Kophas gives a harsh laugh. "I like that better." For another moment he stares at his bare skin. "The Van'shorii say that if your ancestors reject you, when you die, the Deep Sleep comes and strips your marks." He clasps his hands together tightly. "Do you suppose that's true?"

"I don't know. I'm not a van'shor."

"Well—if I die tonight, the Deep Sleep will not have much work to do on me. I am more ready than most."

He is trying to make a joke, but the bitterness in his voice belies him. A faint shock runs through me at his words. The unease stays with me as I leave his shelter and wend my way back through the slums.

I have prepared a man's body for death. I am the Deep Sleep's apprentice.

CHAPTER FIFTEEN

"A re you ready for the guild assembly this evening?" Kilmaya asks when I come into work one day.

"Assembly?" I set my satchel down on the worktable. My mind is still swimming with ancient marks from my early-morning lesson with Haza'ruux.

Kilmaya regards me with a longsuffering expression. "You haven't read your messages this morning, have you?"

"No."

"I'll spare you the trouble, then. Mekkalluthak has summoned all artists with a guild vote to an emergency meeting."

I blink at the quiet studio around us. "There's an emergency?"

"I know you are absent-minded, but surely you have noticed that our street has been full of guards lately? Guards with guns?"

"Has something happened? Have they hurt someone?"

"Not yet, but they've been throttling our business. Half of our Ascendance clients have been going to the Trev'ban studios, and those who don't wear the faction-mark have been frightened off by the *army* out there." She gestures towards the door in disgust. "Mekkalluthak asked the ship council to remove them over a week ago. They've refused—they claim they are still protecting clients from the unrest." Again she scoffs. "If there's unrest, it's their own fault. For once I'll be glad to sit through one of Mekkalluthak's speeches, if he can get the guild to agree on what to do about it."

"Can we do anything?"

"Hakk, yes." A cunning expression flits across her face. "Did you think banning that one honor-mark was the only move the guild had? We have stronger weapons. But Mekkalluthak wants the consensus of his artists before using them."

With a sinking heart, I turn on my datascroll and glance through my list of clients for the day. But I am thinking of Kophas. I had hoped to make a start on his new tattoos tonight. "This is serious, isn't it? I suppose they expect everyone to come?"

"It certainly is serious. The Ascendance has no business antagonizing us so openly."

I sigh. Has it only been a little over a month since Askko came to claim his honor-mark? How did that one brief event turn into this mess? "You said this was going to blow over."

"It will. But it will do no harm to strike the Ascendance where they will feel it." She says this eagerly, like a warrior mocking an opponent before a sparring match. "The only good thing about this whole business is that I haven't had to paint an Ascendance mark in days."

"I wouldn't mind if that continued."

Kilmaya laughs. "You are not the only one."

The guild hall is already packed when Kilmaya and I reach it that evening. The round, compact auditorium echoes with chatter as the markmakers—about a hundred in all—mingle on the council floor and in the tiered seats. These are the best artists in the guild, all the men and women skilled enough to earn the privilege of a vote.

It still feels strange to be counted as one of them. As I descend one of the aisles, I find my eyes drawn towards the mural on the dome. A huge, stylized painting of a trallak leaf—the guild's symbol—spans the ceiling, surrounded by a series of vivid scenes: farmers tending their crops, pilots navigating, warriors clashing, deepcrafters wielding flame. Every clan, every way of life, every kind of honorable achievement—all are represented here.

I remember the awe I felt when I first saw this place: *This is our world. This is what it means to be Noxxiin. And we, Clan Serix, are its guardians.*

That thought used to fill me with a joy so fierce it was almost painful. But that was before I saw the Underbelly, before I knew the truths even the guild does not bother to record—like how many exiles' lives it costs to keep our ship operational, and how many children are born to those exiles, who will never bear a clan-mark. Gazing up at the ancient mural now, I feel no pride. I only remember that I am an imposter, a skin-changer. Is my clan's heritage a sham, as well? A show of honor, without substance?

I have never questioned the honor of the guild before—not consciously, at least. But it was these councilors, in this room, who must have approved the exile-marks given to Talorak and Kophas. How could such a thing have happened unless they were deceived, or falsehood had corrupted their judgment?

Kilmaya spots Rinavi and some of her other friends on the stairs and goes to greet them. I do not join her. Ill at ease, I weave my way through the press to find an empty seat. I remember another reason why I have not visited this hall in a long time. It is not simply because I dislike guild meetings. If my crimes against the craft are ever discovered, this is the room in which I will be tried and condemned.

I take my place, about halfway up the tiers of seats. Built into the armrest is a small screen displaying the schedule of tonight's assembly. There is a stylus as well for writing in our votes. Absently I pick up the stylus and begin fidgeting with it, tracing invisible patterns on the armrest. Haza'ruux has been critiquing my execution of some of his ancient marks; I might as well take this idle moment to practice.

When the councilors call the assembly to order, Kilmaya finds me and claims the seat beside me. Her eyes sparkle, as they always do when she has been gossiping with her fellow artists. "Hakka, Clan Serix is full of fire tonight. When we're done here, the Ascendance is going to be sorry their soldiers ever set foot in our sector. But what's the matter with you?" She scrutinizes me. "Are you feeling all right?"

I shake my head. "It's nothing." Fortunately I am spared the trial of lying any further. At that moment, an elderly councilwoman rises for the opening invocation:

"Serixan, our ancestors, hear us!"

Her voice rings reedy but clear in the crowded auditorium. The assembly falls into a hush as she continues. "By the bonds of our clan-marks, we call on you. Look upon this council, these markmakers and keepers of truth. Into our hands you have trusted your honorable law. Now grant us wisdom, the unerring blade of your justice..."

In silence, palms to their necks, the assembled artists listen to the prayer. Surreptitiously I scan faces. The vast majority of them, of course, are Serix—though I do spot the Trev'ban clan leader and a few of his artists in the top tier of seats, on the opposite side of the room. Their posture is reverent, but their expressions are hard and aloof.

I wonder how the Trev'ban artists feel about the fact that the invocation is addressed to our ancestors and not theirs. It is rare for a Trev'ban markmaker to pass the skill-trials necessary to gain a vote in the guild, but I have sometimes questioned whether that is truly because of their lesser skill, or because Serix councilors oversee the trials.

The invocation ends, and the crowd settles into quiet expectation. Another councilor—a middle-aged man with deep violet skin—rises from the table in the center of the floor. His build is slender, but he moves with a suppleness and ease that remind me of an athlete in his prime. His sleeveless white robe sets off the multitude of honor-marks swarming his arms.

Stepping onto the speaker's dais, Mekkalluthak Serix raises his face to the assembly.

"Artists of the guild." His gravelly voice is firm and biting. "Several weeks ago, I sat at this honored table, listening to the hearing of an event that the Ascendance presumed to call a military victory. I did not know, then, the extent of the turmoil that hearing would cause. My only thought was for the law that always binds me in this assembly—to discover the truth."

"A safe beginning," Kilmaya mutters. Yet despite her mocking tone, she watches him intently.

"And what was this truth we discovered?" the guildmaster continues. "Simply that the battle was no battle at all—nothing to merit a mark of valor. We judged as the law prescribed, and that should have been the end of the matter."

A murmur of anticipation stirs the crowd. Slowly Mekkalluthak turns on the dais, his stern gaze sweeping his audience. "What has the Ascendance done since that day? They have mocked our law. They have honored the warriors we found dishonorable. Their faction members have taunted us in the streets and threatened our clients with violence. And now their soldiers patrol our studios day and night—soldiers bearing firearms, cowards' weapons, not even fit for true warriors. Soldiers that the ship's authorities refuse to remove despite repeated requests."

He pauses, allowing the crowd to ripple with incensed agreement. I glance at the people near me; all are captive listeners. I have heard Mekkalluthak speak before, but rarely with such passion and power. I find myself wondering what Haza'ruux would think—I have never heard him speak of the Ascendance, for good or for ill.

Mekkalluthak goes on. "I thank all of you for your perseverance in this trial—your devotion to truth in the flesh."

I hold my face very still, so as not to wince involuntarily.

"Perhaps some of you thought this disturbance would pass when anger cooled and reason prevailed. But that has not happened. Instead we continue to witness disturbances in our street, insolence from the faction, and even dissension from within the ranks of our own artists."

I risk a glance at the Trev'ban markmakers on the other side of the room. They are scowling—Mekkalluthak's meaning is clear enough.

"It is our duty, as keepers of truth, to correct the clans when they stray from the path of honor." The guildmaster's voice rises, takes on a grating edge. "There comes a time when, in the face of lies and half-lies, it is no longer enough for us to go about our daily work, plying our pens and inks. If we continue to allow the Ascendance to intimidate us with their mockery, with their show of force, then they will continue to demand that we bend to their will, whether it is honorable or not." The guildmaster bares his teeth, his eyes narrowing to slits. "But the path of falsehood is the path of the Deep Sleep. If we acquiesce—if we do not speak out—our marks will lose their meaning. We will become no better than our half-sight enemies, with their markless skin and deceitful tongues. In fact, we will be worse, if we make marks for deeds that never happened—fashioning a mask of honor for a heart of shame!"

The crowd replies with a rumble of fury. Beside me, Kilmaya slowly clenches her fists. But I only sit mute, listening to the uproar with a strange, cold anger. Wittingly or unwittingly, the guild has already ordered its artists to create false marks—as I, who painted one of them, should know.

What about Talorak, guildmaster? Where were you and your speeches then?

"This is the path the Ascendance would have us take," Mekkalluthak resumes with a hint of a snarl. "They demand our allegiance in word and in ink. But artists cannot not take faction-marks!" With both hands, he pulls opens the front of his robe, exposing the dark violet skin of his chest. "Our chests are bare because our hearts must be pure and impartial. This is the law of our ancestors. To reject it is to reject the very foundation of our craft."

Clan Serix clamors in agreement. But the Trev'ban leader and his companions remain silent.

"We are artists!" Mekkalluthak cries. "We are hunters of truth. We cannot abandon this pursuit, even in the face of danger. By trade, we are not warriors, but now, Serixan, we must fight. We must draw our own kind of weapons in defense of the ancient law."

Kilmaya leans forward. The collective hiss of the assembly sounds like a sharp breeze.

"This is why you are here tonight. I bring you the proposal of the guild council." Mekkalluthak inhales deeply. "A ban on honor-marks for all Ascendance warriors. No matter the battle, no matter the enemy—until the faction agrees to remove their troops from our street and treat us with the respect that is our due."

A babble of noise wells up from the crowd—shock, consternation. At the council table, the rest of the guild members sit silent and stone-faced.

"Proposal of the council?" Kilmaya says under her breath. "That sounds like your handiwork, Kallu."

Mekkalluthak waits until the uproar has spent itself. Then he raises his hands in a conciliatory gesture. "I know your concerns. I know your hearts, Serixan. You are truth-painters. You are saying to yourselves: what precedent is there for such a ban in our laws? What if we cause injustice? What of the honorable individuals within the Ascendance, whom we must refuse along with the rest? It is a hard thing to make them suffer for the folly of their leaders. True, this is an evil—but only a temporary one. The Ascendance will find itself confronted with the fury of its own warriors. They will be forced to consider their own reckless disregard for the honor-code. For a long time now, they have shut out all but the flattering and the submissive from their hearing. But we will *make* them listen to the voice of the law. That is the duty we are sworn to, by our heart's blood, by the ink of our flesh!"

The assembly roars. But I put my face in my hands, trying to quell a dread I cannot explain. The warriors of the Ascendance, the High Councilor, the rebellious Trev'ban artists—all of these swear by their heart's blood, too.

"The guild is prepared to pass this measure—but we cannot do so without your consent." The guildmaster's voice turns quieter, graver. "This ban will touch us all. Yes, it will hurt our business for a time. But as you all know well, wealth means nothing if it is not held with honor. And honor requires sacrifice: of goods, of security, sometimes of blood. And it is not gained in a few short months of raiding alien cities." Again Mekkalluthak pauses, surveying the eager audience. "The goal of the Ascendance, to retake our ancient home, is a noble one. But in pursuit of that end, we must not lose our honor. If we do not speak the truth—in words, in ink, in the flesh—we are not worthy to walk the halls of our own ships, much less breathe free air under the skies of our forefathers!"

The assembly cheers. Around me, people spring from their seats. The auditorium echoes with shouts and the stamping of feet—but I notice, when I glance across the room, that the Trev'ban markmakers have not stirred.

I sink back in my chair. *Honor. Always honor. What is this thing that maddens us all?*

Mekkalluthak raises his arms to the crowd. "Clan-brothers, clan-sisters—the choice is in your hands." He sweeps off the dais, crying, "Let the vote be taken!"

Around me, many artists pick up their styluses and mark the screens on their seats. The room still rings with noise, the heated arguments of neighbor with neighbor. At the central table, the councilors remain intent on their own displays, watching the votes come in.

Beside me, Kilmaya fingers her stylus for a long moment and at last leans over her screen. I cannot help raising my eyes to watch. She sketches the sigil for "yes" and enters her vote.

Even you, teacher? I grip my own stylus, but my hand feels paralyzed. Loathing fills my throat. Mekkalluthak has stirred the clan's anger as easily as an Ascendance zealot riling his followers. Is the guild only another faction to be swayed by wrath and resentment? How do we know we have the sanction of the ancestors? Our opponents claim it, too.

What kind of vote is this, guildmaster? How can we refuse?

My hand hovers over the screen. Then, without touching the surface, I put the stylus down. What right do I have, after all, to act as a member of this assembly? I enter a blank vote and sink back into my seat.

Kilmaya reaches out and grips my arm in a reassuring manner. I do not have the strength to muster a smile in return.

Several minutes pass while the artists finish making their decisions. An anxious buzz of chatter fills the room. At last, Mekkalluthak rises, and a breathless silence falls. The guildmaster leans both hands against the council table. His stance reminds me of a predator's crouch, coiled and taut.

"The measure is passed."

Shouts throb in the air. I close my eyes.

"From this moment—until the Ascendance stops flaunting our law—no faction warrior will receive an honor-mark. Any artist found trespassing this ban will be duly punished." In a ceremonial gesture, Mekkalluthak touches the guildmaster's mark on his brow and then the clan tattoo on his neck. "This is the order of the guild!"

Lacking the will to move, I remain frozen in my seat while people rise, filing out into the aisles and up towards the hall door. Kilmaya puts a hand on my shoulder and says something, but I do not hear it. She disappears into the throng. For what seems like a long time, I watch the mingling crowd, not really seeing it.

I think of Mekkalluthak and Askko, of their equal and opposite convictions. Both of them lay claim to honor. Both of them would fight for it to the death. I am an oathbreaker now; I have given up the ancestors' favor. But I have seen anguish in the eyes of a girl named Lakkia Penthar, and I have given a clan-mark to her bastard child. And neither the guild nor the Ascendance would have lifted a finger to help her.

CHAPTER SIXTEEN

At last, I make my way out of the auditorium. The air in the room seems too thick to breathe, but I have no desire to go home yet, either. The memory of Haza'ruux's cluttered front room, with its hanging vines and burrik pelts, flits through my mind. How strange that the mad markmaker's house should seem like a refuge now.

I cross the pillared foyer of the guild hall and step out into the plaza. The corridor lights glow with the warm gold of evening, deepening the shadows under the branches of the four gnarled trallak trees. Artists and councilors still linger in the plaza, talking in animated tones.

"Why, there he is. Mariikel!"

Kilmaya's voice cuts through the chatter of the crowd. Unwillingly, I raise my eyes. She stands under the violet-black foliage of one of the trallaks, engaged in conversation with none other than Mekkalluthak. This surprises me, but only for a moment. I often forget that Kilmaya and Mekkelluthak are the same age; they were peers once, artists apprenticed to the same master, and Kilmaya still considers him a friend.

Kilmaya beckons to me. It is too late to walk away. "Honor with you, guildmaster," I say, touching my clan-mark as I approach.

"And with you, Mariikel." Mekkalluthak smiles. "I think I have not seen you since you received your mark of mastery."

"It has been a long time." I try to let myself relax. But in the presence of this man, my limbs grow taut and my stomach uneasy. His eyes no longer flash with fury, and his gravelly voice is pleasant, even kind. But I cannot forget the power he wields, nor the way he dominated this assembly only a few minutes ago.

Kilmaya puts a hand on my arm. "Mariikel is the pillar of my studio. I could not get through the day without him. Though if you try to talk to him about anything besides the marks, his mind wanders." Her tone is teasing—she is showing me off.

I manage a wan smile. "I was listening very closely tonight."

"I should hope so! I was just telling Mekkalluthak that he has utterly outdone himself. Only he could manage to get people *excited* about the prospect of losing more business."

Her sarcasm startles me. But the guildmaster only gives her an indulgent glance. "A temporary inconvenience, Kilmaya."

"Hakk!" She squints three eyes shrewdly. "Easy for you to say, Kallu. You are not the one with a half-empty studio."

"Better half-empty than dishonorable." Mekkalluthak's tone is mild, but his eyes grow serious. "Thank you for coming, Mariikel. It is a good thing you have done tonight for Clan Serix."

He thinks I voted for the ban. Inwardly I flinch, but I manage to maintain my composure. "Thank you, guildmaster. I am honored to be here."

"And I am grateful. I know this has not been an easy time for you. I understand you have a brother in an Ascendance warband."

"That is true." What has Kilmaya been telling him?

"I want you to know that it pained me to deny an honor-mark to a member of our own clan. I am sure it pained you as well."

His gracious manner unnerves me—he did not show any compassion for Ascendance warriors a few minutes ago, when he was addressing the assembly. I drop my eyes. I do not want to talk about Askko. "We do what we must for the truth, guildmaster."

"Spoken like an artist. I was asking your teacher about you just now. I heard you have been unusually favored."

"Favored?" I blink in confusion.

He gestures towards my arm. "By the mad markmaker."

Reflexively, I cover Haza'ruux's tattoo with my hand. But Mekkalluthak only laughs. "I'm not going to make you erase it. I could not, anyway. The mad markmaker's tattoos are protected. Not even a guildmaster can interfere."

"Really?" I stare at him, pretending I have never heard of that archaic section of the clan code. I do not want him to know that I have been reading up on it. "I...I did not know that."

"It is an ancient tradition. But he gives out so few marks that it is seldom relevant." His face creases into an expression of chagrin. "So you must forgive my curiosity. May I?"

Cold fear seizes me. The guildmaster of Clan Serix has asked to look at the mark that probably tells the story of my crimes. I doubt that Mekkalluthak will be able to read the ancient sigils, but he was an accomplished artist, too, in his own day. How can I be sure?

"Of course." I laugh as if I am merely embarrassed and hold out my arm. I cannot quite keep it from trembling.

The guildmaster takes my wrist in his hands. His fingers are not calloused, as an artist's ought to be, yet he examines the sigils with the keen gaze of an experienced markmaker. For one long and agonizing moment, I am sure I am lost. But then he sighs and lets go of me. "That Haza'ruux—he's a strange one. It is masterful work. Have you spoken to him since he gave it to you?"

"No." Kilmaya does not know about my early-morning visits to Haza'ruux's house. I do not want to make her angry—and I have no desire to explain my lessons to the guildmaster, either.

Mekkalluthak's eyelids flicker. He seems faintly displeased. "You should. I would not pass up the chance, if I were you. Haza'ruux does not favor many people." There is a sharpness in his words that bewilders me. And then, all at once, I recognize it.

He's jealous!

The master of Clan Serix, envious of *me*? What could I possibly have that he wants—except, apparently, a tattoo from the mad markmaker? I think of Mekkalluthak's ringing voice during the assembly, and the surging of the crowd, and I am very afraid. The last thing I need is the attention of this man. But now it is too late.

Haza'ruux, what have you done to me?

Kilmaya seizes the opportunity to rescue me. "We must bid you good-night, Mekkalluthak. I'm sure we all need our rest. It will be a lively day tomorrow when word of this ban reaches the High Council."

"That it will." The guildmaster still stares at me with an unsettling intensity. "Goodnight to both of you. Honor with you."

"And with you." I incline my head, and together, Kilmaya and I make our way out of the plaza into Rixarii Street.

The corridor is deserted except for the ever-present guards. I wonder if any rumor of the ban has reached them yet. But the warriors take little notice of us, only giving perfunctory nods as we pass. In silence we walk down the dimming street, between the rows of empty studios.

"Well," Kilmaya says at last. "I suppose we should prepare ourselves for a slow day tomorrow."

"Another one?" I grumble.

"Such is the order of the guild."

We turn down a corridor into the residential district. The gardens and pillared halls are quiet, but here and there stand groups of people talking in earnest tones. Among the clan, at least, the news is already spreading.

"Teacher, what do you think of the ban?"

She gives me a keen glance. "I voted for it, if that's what you're wondering."

"Then you think it's a good idea?"

Kilmaya sighs. "The faction seems to want to keep the studios under guard indefinitely. And they have the power to do it, since they control ship security. Something had to be done—something they could not simply ignore." She squints, dismissive. "If they didn't want to anger the guild, they should have stopped provoking us."

I do not find her words very comforting. "Has the guild ever banned honor-marks for an entire faction before?"

"Not that I know of. But there have never been battle-armed troops at the studios before, either—not in our lifetimes, at least. A year ago, not even the most privileged of warriors would have dared carry a firearm in our street. And now look at them. Do they think they are guarding a prison? They should be ashamed of themselves."

We have reached Kilmaya's own house now. But she halts at the edge of her garden and does not go in yet.

"Teacher, what do you think the faction will do?"

"To start with?" She cracks a smile. "Probably call us arrogant, narrow-minded fools."

I gaze at her in the lamplight. "I don't see what is amusing about that."

"That's because you're young. This is the first time you've seen a real clash of clans. It is only frightening if you've never watched the game before." She reaches out and touches my arm. "This will pass, Mariikel. But the marks endure. No matter who rules, we will always need good painters of truth. You do well to concentrate on your work."

Good painters of truth. Oh, teacher, if only you knew… With one hand I grasp my right arm, covering Haza'ruux's tattoo. Suddenly, one of Mekkalluthak's comments comes back to me.

"Teacher, did you know about Haza'ruux's marks?"

She frowns, confused. "What about them?"

"That they are protected. The guildmaster said he cannot order them to be erased."

"Oh, that." She laughs shortly. "I don't know where Kallu dug up that old law. Most likely it is no longer valid." She flicks a hand, exasperated. "Mekkalluthak has been obsessed with Haza'ruux since before you were born."

"Obsessed?" I clutch my arm more tightly. "He's your friend, isn't he? The one who studied the mad markmakers."

"Yes. He nearly became a hermit himself, he spent so much time in the archives. He even tried to become Haza'ruux's apprentice once."

"What?" I try to imagine grave Mekkalluthak, in his white councilor's robe, sitting at the mad markmaker's feet in his wild garden. The image is too incongruous for me to sustain. "What happened?"

"Haza'ruux would not take him." Her smirk fades, turns pensive. "It upset him very much. He gave up studio work and decided to become a councilor after that."

I watch my teacher standing in her serene garden under the soft orange lights of the corridor. Her eyelids flicker at some unspoken memory. It occurs to me, with a slight shock, that although I have been Kilmaya's student for years, there are still things I do not know about her. There is some history between Kilmaya and Mekkalluthak and Haza'ruux—and now I have been drawn into it, too.

I laugh nervously. "So that's why he asked about me."

"Oh, yes. He is quite envious of your new decoration. I doubt he will do anything to you for the time being, however. He has enough troubles on hand." She gives me a shrewd look. "Although, to be safe, you probably shouldn't tell him about your lessons."

"Lessons?" I step back in shock. "What lessons?"

Kilmaya sighs. "I'm not blind, Mariikel. I have seen every tattoo you've given out these past weeks. Your hand is improving, and Ka knows *I* haven't taught you anything recently. Your marks have a new grace to them—an archaic grace, I might call it."

She does not sound upset. But in my shame and confusion, I do not know how to react. I should have known this would happen. I thought I could keep the mad markmaker's influence out of my pen-strokes in the studio. The differences are so subtle that only a master artist would be able to notice them. But Kilmaya, of course, is just such an artist.

I lower my head. "I'm sorry. I should not have—I should not have tried to deceive you."

"No. You shouldn't have." She regards me with a searching expression. "I am not angry, Mariikel, but I am surprised. Why didn't you tell me?"

Because I have to know. I have to know why Haza'ruux honored me when I told him of my crimes. I cannot say this, of course. Yet I am not prepared to spin a convincing lie. So I must give a part of the truth. "I—his marks are so beautiful. He offered to teach me. I didn't know what you would think. I know they are only ornaments, but…"

She tilts her head, bemused. "Did you think I would be jealous? Great Ka, Mariikel. I do not mind if you have another teacher. I am glad you have found something to challenge yourself. Even if they are only ornaments."

"You don't mind?" Incredulous, I straighten. "I—I may go on, then? With my lessons?"

"Yes. I suspect you would anyway, even if I told you not to." She smiles wryly. "You're not my apprentice anymore, quiet one. You are free to pursue the craft as you see fit. I am happy for you." She turns towards her door. "Goodnight, Mariikel."

143

The warmth of gratitude floods my chest. "Goodnight, teacher."

When she has gone in, I walk down the street towards my own house, dazed. What Kilmaya said is true—as a master artist, I am no longer under obligation to obey her except in matters of guild law. But I cannot help desiring her approval. Now it seems I have it.

I am so delighted that, for a few minutes, I almost forget the ban that was passed tonight in the guild hall of Clan Serix.

CHAPTER SEVENTEEN

"Haza'ruux, did you ever know Mekkalluthak? The guildmaster?"

The following morning, I sit in the old hermit's studio, preparing for our lesson. Haza'ruux pulls a heavy, decorated tome from one of his shelves. He scowls at my question. "Why does Flashing Blade want to know about guilds and masters? He has enough to learn."

"I heard he once asked you to teach him."

Haza'ruux pauses and regards me with one of his piercing stares. "What else did Flashing Blade hear?"

"That you sent him away." I hold his gaze, unflinching. "Why?"

His tattooed brow furrows. "He was not worthy."

"Not worthy?" I may not care for Mekkalluthak's new ban, but he is still the clan's leader. I have never heard that he did anything dishonorable. How can it be that I, the criminal, am worthy of the mad markmaker's knowledge when Mekkalluthak was not?

"What do you mean?"

He sniffs. "It is time for Haza'ruux to ask questions now." He sets the thick book on the worktable and opens to a page of dense sigils. "Read."

I sigh. When Haza'ruux closes a discussion, it stays closed. I will have to try him again another time. If I do not know why Mekkalluthak envies me, how will I be able to protect myself?

I turn my attention to the page in front of me. It is the same manuscript we started yesterday: a detailed account of the rise and fall of Clan Sko'larik. I place my finger on the smooth, browning page and begin the painstaking task of translation. Yesterday we left off in the middle of a description of the *arimaa'rix*—the magical marks of power, which the Keepers of the Arimaas granted to warriors. Each tattoo depicted a certain animal, and each granted a different set of abilities. Haltingly, I read out the list:

"*Rix tyal'shivii*: the mark of the arrowhawk. Bestows swiftness and flight. *Rix harraktii*: the mark of the kharraktyl. Bestows climbing and venom. *Rix hazari-ruux*: the mark of the mad dog. Bestows battle-rage and..." I trail off, uncertain. "Battle-rage and luck?"

Haza'ruux chuckles. "That is correct."

Rix hazari-ruux. I blink at the sigils. A revelation steals over me. "That's your name. Isn't it? You're named after a mark of power?"

His eyes glint with mingled mischief and satisfaction. "It is the custom." He has that piercing, knowing look, the one that always unsettles me. *Haza'ruux. Mad Dog*. A strange name—yet fitting. Certainly it suits him better than Flashing Blade suits me.

"Whose custom? The mad mar—I mean...the artists who lived in this house before you?"

He bares his teeth in a grin. "You may call us the mad markmakers. We are not ashamed." He touches the row of sigils on the page. "Yes. We take the names of beasts to honor the bearers of the Arimaas." He speaks the word with a peculiar, throaty rasp; his eyes grow round and solemn. "They were great artists and noble warriors."

I consider reminding him that the Arimaas is only a myth. But then another thought rises to my mind. "Haza'ruux, if they were such noble warriors, why do their stories sound so similar to the legends of the Devorak? They both used these animal signs, these marks of power." I push the book away from me slightly. "You keep saying the Arimaas and the Devorak are not the same. But I don't understand the difference."

"You do not understand?" The old man's nostrils flare. "The difference is simple, Flashing Blade. The Devorak is a corruption of the Arimaas." He taps the page again. "Here. This part will tell you more."

I continue deciphering the convoluted text. The passage describes the grueling tests, both physical and mental, that initiates had to complete before meriting a mark of power. Winning an Arimaas tattoo was the greatest honor a warrior could achieve—and it was by distributing them that Clan Sko'larik eventually rose to supreme power. The Keepers of the Arimaas became not only artists, but also chieftains and rulers.

I glance up from the page, dissatisfied. "This doesn't explain the Devorak."

"There were two ways to obtain a mark of power." Haza'ruux's voice sinks to a snarl. "The true way—and the way of defilement. Some of the warriors who failed to pass the trials made their own corrupted rites. They hunted down Arimaas bearers—warriors or Keepers—and slew them. And they drank their blood like beasts to gain their powers."

"Oh." His ferocious expression takes me aback. The old man's genuine anger when he speaks of the Devorak is always disconcerting.

"But the Devorak did not have pure hearts, or the strength of mind, to

MARY JESSICA WOODS

bear the power well. The Arimaas is meant to be given. To seize the gift for one's own, unworthily—that brings madness."

"I see." I do not quite see, but for the moment, I decide not to inquire further. "It seems strange that no one knows the stories of the Arimaas. These myths—were they lost somehow?"

"Lost. Hakk, yes." Haza'ruux laughs, brief and bitter. "That is its own story. Keep reading, Flashing Blade."

With a sigh, I turn back to the book. The passage describes how the Keepers ruled over the clans for many generations, training Arimaas warriors and defending the Noxxiin people from the savagery of the Devorak. And yet, over the centuries, some of the Keepers began to abandon their strict disciplines and traditions of honor. Instead they tyrannized the clans they had once protected, oppressing the people with their armies of magically enhanced warriors. The clans had no way to fight back or remove them from power until the arrival of the alien Syr and the fearsome weapon they brought, known as....

"*T'vanasyra.*" I stumble over the unfamiliar word. "What is that? I don't know that sigil."

"You do," Haza'ruux replies. "We call it *van'shorakk* now. Deepcraft."

"What?" I stare at the page before me. "The Syr? What do they have to do with deepcraft, of all things?"

"They brought it to our homeworld. They built the first bonds, the machines in the flesh."

I gape at him, incredulous. The sacred art of the Van'shorii, invented by aliens? "That's absurd. *We* invented deepcraft—I mean, the ancestors did. To fight off the Syr and the other invaders."

Haza'ruux chuckles. "How better to fight the Syr than with their own weapon?"

Anger floods my chest. Now he is simply being irreverent. Perhaps he does not care for the deepcrafters and their influence in the Fleet—neither do I, for that matter—but that is no reason to slander their ancestors. "How can you say such a thing?"

"Say what? That the Van'shorii stole their craft from another race? If they did, do you think they would admit it?" Haza'ruux holds my gaze for a minute, grinning—then tosses back his head and laughs aloud. "Come, Flashing Blade, it is a story. Did you forget?"

My skin prickles with embarrassment. How could I let the old man upset me with one of his ridiculous fables? "No. Of course not."

He waves a hand at the book. "Then read."

Grumbling under my breath, I turn to the manuscript once more. The story—the *myth*, I remind myself forcefully—goes on. During the first battles with the Syr, the clans discovered the mysterious implants that allowed the invaders to control matter and energy with their minds. Over time, the Noxxiin learned how to build their own deepcraft bonds. The Keepers were divided: some called the machines a dangerous sacrilege, but others encouraged the new technology. For even the Keepers were afraid of the Syr and their weapons, and some no longer trusted that the strength of the Arimaas would save them.

Thus the Van'shorii—armed with deepfire, deepreach, and all the other powers of the bond—fought alongside the Arimaas warriors to drive the alien Syr from their home planet. For a while they were victorious, and they brought peace to the Noxxiin people.

But this peace was false and festering. Fear and envy grew up between the Keepers and the Van'shorii; before long, another war erupted. The deepcrafters took up the cause of the oppressed clans—and after many bloody years of conflict, the Van'shorii defeated Clan Sko'larik, overthrew the Keepers, and outlawed the marks of power, the mysteries of the Arimaas.

The story rings familiar in my mind. Replace the Keepers with the Devorak chieftains, and it would be the legend we remember every year at Van'shorvanii, celebrating the victory of the deepcrafters over a cult of supernatural warriors...

I shake myself out of the thought. No one knows how the Van'shorii began; even the story told during the festival is only a legend. Their true origins are lost, along with the rest of our ancient history. I restrain a growl of frustration. Once again, I wish Haza'ruux's books would not mix myth and history as if they were equal.

Haza'ruux tilts his head. "What is it, Flashing Blade?"

"I've...never heard that version of the story before." All at once a memory returns to me: sitting in the dark of the Underbelly, in Kophas's shelter, softly chanting a lament about blood and ash and the destruction of a clan. "Is that what the song is about? *The pens have been crushed, and the ink spilled, the rites burned, and the dream-halls smashed.* Is that talking about the Arimaas being... outlawed?"

"Hakka. Yes." The old man's eyes brighten; he seems pleased I remembered the song. But then his smile fades. He fingers one of the exquisitely crafted pens that lies on the table, running his thumb over the tiny bone carvings. "The Van'shorii declared the ancient rites unclean. They hunted down and slaughtered all the bearers of the Arimaas—even those who had worn their marks with honor." His voice drops. "The name of Sko'larik was forbidden. The remnant of the clan was scattered, forced to renounce their own ancestors."

Haza'ruux falls silent, staring at the pen in his hand with a kind of desolation. I regard him for a minute, unsettled again. Is he fooling me, putting on another act? Or does he truly think the deepcrafters wiped out the ancient clan of Sko'larik? Has he been studying these myths for so long he believes they are real?

Cautiously I clear my throat. "That is a sad story."

"Few remember it." Haza'ruux reaches over and closes the heavy book. "But that is enough stories for one morning."

He picks up the tome to return it to the shelf. Still mulling, I rise from my seat. What would the Van'shorii do if they knew Haza'ruux was teaching this less-than-flattering account of their order's origins? Probably it is a good thing that everyone thinks him a madman.

Thinking of the deepcrafters reminds me of the Ascendance—and that reminds me of the guild assembly last night. I grimace. I would rather keep reading myths, even sacrilegious ones, than go to the studios today. "Haza'ruux, did you hear about the new ban that was declared last night?"

He grunts. "What ban is this?"

"We are no longer allowed to give honor-marks to Ascendance warriors."

The hermit shoots me a keen glance. "Why is Flashing Blade concerned?"

"Why? I'm an artist. I have to be concerned."

Haza'ruux runs his fingers down the spine of his book. He does not reply.

"Mekkalluthak said it was the only way to protect the clan's honor. But won't it simply make the faction angrier with us?"

"Factions and bans—people are always getting angry." He glowers at me. "Do not become distracted, Flashing Blade. We have more important work."

I sigh. Arguing with the mad markmaker is futile.

When I reach Rixarii Street, I can immediately sense the effect of the ban. There are more guards than yesterday; every Trev'ban studio seems to have its own contingent. The warriors are more heavily armed than they were before, too: many wear helmets and breastplates now, emblazoned with the sigil of the Ascendance. Their hands rest close to the blades and firearms at their belts, as if they expect a brawl to break out at any moment.

My muscles tense as I walk between the rows of shops. The guards have dropped the pretense of courtesy. When I pass, they do not bow or touch their clan-marks. They only give me frigid glares. One young Trechik warrior eyes me as I approach—and then leans forward, clears his throat, and spits in my path.

I halt, inhaling sharply. If I respond to the insult, I will only draw attention to myself—and I have a feeling that the other warriors will not be inclined to help me. So I ignore the insolent guard and continue walking. Suddenly, I am worried about Kilmaya.

She sits behind the display desk in the studio, unscathed—looking bored, in fact. She is sharpening pens, a menial chore that she usually leaves to the apprentices. I look at her askance.

"I told the apprentices to stay home," she explains. "No sense in their getting stabbed or trampled. *They* didn't vote on the ban." She narrows three eyes at me. "Enjoy yourself at the mad markmaker's?"

"Yes." I gesture towards the display desk. "Do we even have any appointments today?"

"We do. But it will be interesting to see whether they show up." She examines a pen-tip critically. "Look at this edge. I knew K'nima was leaving them a little dull." She beckons me to sit and join her, then says, "Since it seems it will be a quiet day, we may as well catch up on chores."

I stifle a groan. "Is this what it's going to be like for the whole ban? Why come in at all?"

"Oh, it is part of the statement, of course. We are here to serve our clients. If they do not come out of fear of the guards—well, it is their shame, not ours." She taps the desk. "Are you going to stand there complaining, or are you going to help me?"

I drop my satchel on the floor, and pick up a pen and a sharpening stone. It is going to be a long day.

By the time the fifth hour strikes, Kilmaya and I have cleaned the studio and reorganized our entire inventory of inks and tools. Only two of our six scheduled clients have appeared for their appointments. Now, I lean in the open doorway, anxious and bored to distraction. The street is eerily quiet. Further up the corridor, where the Trev'ban artists have their studios, I can see a slow but steady trickle of clients coming and going. The guards treat them respectfully. But the Serix studios are empty. Our markmakers linger in their doorways, talking in small groups or watching the Ascendance guards. I stamp my feet nervously and go back inside.

"I don't like this."

"At least it's quiet." Kilmaya, having finally run out of things to clean, reads at the display desk. "There's a protest outside the High Council chamber right now. Ascendance warriors, clamoring for them to do something about the ban. I wouldn't want to set foot outside the sector today, I think." She leans back in her seat. "Hakk, well. We are safe enough here."

I sigh and gaze out the door again, wondering how much more suspense

I can bear. How long will the ban last? Weeks? Months? It does not seem the wills on either side will break any time soon.

"Patience, Mariikel," says Kilmaya. "It's no use fretting. People will come to their senses eventually. Everyone needs marks."

Far up the street, I sense a stir, a faint commotion as the sparse crowd parts suddenly. They make way for a group of four T'sarek deepcrafters, who march down the corridor with purposeful strides. Even at this distance, the Van'shorii are unmistakable with their athletic builds and glimmering, silver tunics. Long, white tongues of flame hover in their hands.

I feel a thrill of fear. Deepcrafters rarely show their powers except in public ceremonies. *What's going on?*

Seeing my transfixed expression, Kilmaya gets up and joins me at the door. At the sight of the deepcrafters, she draws in a breath. Swiftly and steadily the Van'shorii walk past the Trev'ban studios, not even glancing at the guards who bow and touch their clan-marks as they pass. As they approach, I finally notice the two figures walking in the deepcrafters' midst. Kilmaya recognizes them a moment before I do.

"It's Tekra T'sarek." Her voice is taut. "And Shekali."

The wife and daughter of High Councilor Valo. They are Kilmaya's clients—but they have never come to the studio with a bodyguard of deepcraft warriors.

"Did they have an appointment today?" I whisper.

"No." Her eyes are wide.

At the door of our studio, the bodyguards come to a halt. They are still holding their slender white flames; I can feel the heat of them from my place in the doorway. The deepcrafters' faces are impassive except for the pale, luminescent tattoos on their brows and cheekbones.

T'vanasyra...the craft of the Syr... There is something cold and unnatural in the light of their silver fire, and in the eerie similarity of the deepcrafters' features. Standing this close to them, I could almost believe that deepcraft is of alien origin.

I risk a look at Tekra T'sarek. She is not using her powers; her facial tattoos are not illuminated. But the muted wrath in her eyes is almost more intimidating.

A tense muscle twitches in my teacher's face, but she keeps her usual composure. She steps forward, inclines her head, and says in her most gracious tone, "This is unexpected, Van'shir Tekra."

"I imagine it is," says Tekra. An icy edge rings in her voice. "I am sorry I did not warn you ahead of time. But I thought, today, you would not be too busy."

I glance at her daughter, Shekali. She is a young woman, hardly more than a girl, with an unusually slight frame for a T'sarek. She wears the marks of a bondmaker's apprentice. I remember that Shekali is the only one of Tekra's children who cannot wield deepcraft: she is not genetically fit for an implant. There is no shame in that, of course—most ordinary people cannot use deepcraft, either—but Shekali is the daughter of two high-ranking T'sarek deepcrafters. In her own family, she was born a disappointment. Now, she stands beside her mother with a dull expression on her young face. I feel a twinge of trepidation.

Everyone in the corridor, artist and guard alike, is watching Kilmaya now. And the four T'sarek warriors still hold their flames.

"Please, come in." With one hand, my teacher makes a gesture of welcome. "I'm afraid the studio is too small for your escort, however."

There is a steely undertone in these last words, a silent warning. Tekra narrows her eyes. For a moment, I am afraid she will refuse. But then she blinks, and the four deepcrafters simultaneously extinguish their flames. The glowing tattoos on their faces fade. As one, the bodyguards step back from the door.

Kilmaya and I also stand aside while Tekra and her daughter enter the studio. My teacher closes the door behind us. She turns to her clients. "How may I serve you today?"

"Hakka." Tekra laughs. The sound is pleasant yet does nothing to diffuse the tension. "I am glad you are not refusing us outright. This ban! There have been all kinds of rumors this morning."

"The guild's decree applies only to warriors," says Kilmaya. "As neither you nor Shekali is in the military, there should be no trouble." The words themselves are cordial—but the two women exchange them like the first feints of a sparring match. They stare at each other with barely concealed hostility. Between them, Shekali gazes at the floor, her eyes half-lidded. She has not said a word yet.

"I am relieved to hear it," says Tekra. "I could not bear going to any lesser studio." Flattery—yet barbed. She places her hand on her daughter's shoulder. "Shekali wishes to receive the faction-mark."

A brief and heavy silence falls. No one needs to ask which faction. I watch Kilmaya's eyelids flutter as she tries to conceal her surprise. "Is she of age?"

"Of course. You ought to know."

I glance at the date-sigil in Shekali's clan-mark. She is, by a slim margin, legally old enough to declare her allegiance to a political group. Still, it is not customary for one so young to receive a faction-mark. Shekali remains staring at the ground, wordless. A sudden fear twists my stomach.

Several emotions flit across my teacher's face, too quickly for me to identify. She seems wary, like an animal circling a trap. But at last she turns to the daughter. "Is this your wish, Shekali T'sarek? To receive the mark of the Ascendance?"

For the first time, Shekali raises her eyes. "Yes, markmaker." Her expression is stoic—nothing more. But all at once my heart races, and my palms grow hot.

She doesn't want it. She has not truly consented. Don't do this!

If Kilmaya sees the dismay on my face, she does not acknowledge it. Instead she sighs. "Very well, then. I will be with you in a moment." She turns back to Tekra. "Please sit, van'shir. I'm afraid my apprentices are out today—can I bring you anything to drink while you wait?"

"Please do. I know you keep a good kol-dawra on hand, Kilmaya."

"Certainly." My teacher inclines her head, then glances up at me. "Mariikel, will you take Shekali inside? And prepare the inks."

For a moment I cannot move. Is it possible Kilmaya does not see what is happening here?

"Mariikel!" she snaps.

"Yes," I murmur, and my limbs unfreeze. Without looking at either Tekra or my teacher, I invite Shekali to enter the workroom. "This way."

Slowly, she precedes me into the room and sits down in one of the client's chairs. She stares into space with a blank expression. As I take inks and tools down from the shelves, fear gnaws at my heart. *Don't do this. Not a false mark. Not again.* It does not matter that Kilmaya will be holding the pen this time. If I say nothing, I am equally guilty.

Finally, I cannot bear it. I glance towards the front room; Kilmaya and Tekra are still talking. I put down the bottle of violet ink, step over to the chair, and look down into the young woman's vacant eyes. "Are you nervous?"

She flinches. "No." The word is almost inaudible.

"You know that no one can give you a faction-mark without your consent."

Confusion flickers in her face. "I did consent."

I glance over my shoulder again. Then I place my hand on the armrest of the chair and say, very softly: "You are doing this of your own free will?"

She tilts her head upwards, looking at me. Pain brims in her dark eyes, and shame, and helpless rage. Her throat quivers as she swallows, regains control of herself. "Of course I am."

I know a lie when I hear one. I want to take her hand, beg her not to let us do this violence to her will. But what can I say? She is the daughter of the Ascendance High Councilor. If I try to defend her from her own parents, I will only cause her more grief. I understand, too, why Kilmaya did not refuse to paint this mark. As long as Shekali gives consent, the request is legal—and my teacher cannot deny a lawful mark of allegiance without denying the legitimacy of the faction itself. Yet the fact that the tattoo is lawful does not make it truthful.

I feel as if someone has driven a dagger into my chest. *Not again. No, not again.* But the same powerlessness that gripped me when I gave Talorak his exile-mark steals over me once more. I turn away from Shekali and walk back into the front room, feeling numb.

"Teacher," I say. "She is ready for you."

CHAPTER EIGHTEEN

After the T'sarek women depart—Shekali with the sigil of the Ascendance on her chest, and Tekra with a triumphant smirk on her lips—the rest of the day passes without incident. But Kilmaya and I avoid each other in resentful silence. We both know Tekra's visit was a show of force, but there was nothing we could do except submit. I pack up early, making sure to fill my satchel with the inks and pens I need for tonight. With a curt farewell, I take my leave and step out into the unnaturally quiet corridor.

I am determined to start painting Kophas's new marks tonight. But it is probably unwise for me to venture into the public areas of the ship. I might be accosted by a band of angry Ascendance zealots before I even reach the Underbelly. Fortunately, on my datascroll, I have a map of all the ship's maintenance tunnels, which I acquired when I first began my illegal profession. There are several maintenance doors in the Serix sector, and in the past few weeks I have scouted them out, searching for the most inconspicuous entrance.

My destination is at the far end of the sector, close to Haza'ruux's house. With swift steps, I leave Rixarii Street and make my way through the residential district, only stopping at home to pick up my stash of food and water for Kophas. Then, loaded down with supplies, I continue my route through the sector. The corridors are still quiet; most people have not yet returned home from their daily work. I am grateful for this—but then, as I approach the small plaza adjacent to Haza'ruux's house, I hear a burst of noise: a child's piercing yell and a scuffle of feet.

I enter the plaza to find three young children fighting beside the fountain. Two of them grapple on the floor while a third looks on, shouting. At first, I think they are only roughhousing—but then one of the boys kicks the other in the stomach with a ferocity that is not mere play. The hurt child shrieks. And then I recognize him: it is Tyotik, the little boy Haza'ruux has been teaching.

155

"Hakk! What's going on here?"

Startled, the other two children look up. At the sight of an unfamiliar, disapproving adult, they scramble backwards. With guilt branded on their young faces, they turn and flee down a corridor.

Tyotik stumbles to his feet, his arms wrapped around his skinny chest. "Blade!" he wails. To my utter surprise, he run towards me and collides with my legs. He clings to my knees, sobbing. "Tell them I'm Serix. Tell them!"

I crouch down, and after a moment of hesitation, I wrap him in a gentle hug. He seems more upset than hurt. "Kesh, now. What happened?"

"They said I'm not Serix." His small body quivers with rage. "They said I have a bad mark. Like the soldiers."

"Soldiers? What soldiers?"

"The ones in the painting street." He starts crying outright.

Suddenly I understand. Tyotik has a Trechik mark on his neck, and most of the Ascendance guards in Rixarii Street are from Clan Trechik, too. Tyotik's companions must have heard someone complaining about them and decided to take matters into their own hands. Anger pierces my chest. Has this conflict turned even the clan's children against each other?

"Tyotik." I pull him away from me so that I can look him in the face. His upper eyes are still squeezed shut in fury. "You don't have a bad mark. Your clan-mark is Trechik because your father was Trechik. There is nothing wrong with that."

Tyotik scowls. "Nakki said my nakko isn't coming back. I don't want to be Trechik."

I sigh and glance around the plaza. Where is Tyotik's mother? Has she not explained this matter to her son? No doubt she is still grieving her fallen husband. "There's nothing I can do, Tyotik. It's…it's the law. It's the way things are."

"But I want to be *Serix*!" He stamps his feet. "All my friends are Serix. And nakki. And Ha'ruux. And you." He flings himself into my arms again.

I embrace him in what I hope is a comforting manner. When his tantrum subsides, I pull him away from me once more. "Tyotik. Look at me. You are still Serix by blood. That will always be true no matter what marks you have." A thought strikes me, and I smile at him. "Have you seen Haza'ruux today?"

"No," he says mournfully.

"What do you think he would tell you?"

"I don't know." The boy hangs his head, kicking at the pavement. "He says my writing is messy."

"It's all right. He tells me that, too." I squeeze his shoulder. "I will tell you a secret. If Haza'ruux is teaching you how to write, it means he thinks you are very smart. Is he teaching any of your other friends?"

The boy frowns, then brightens a little. "I don't think so."

"There you are, then." I release him and stand up. "Go on home. Everything will be all right."

He blinks, nods, and hugs me again. Then, as if suddenly shy, he darts away into one of the nearby houses. I look after him with a puzzled smile, until the memory of why I am here descends on me once more, and my heart grows heavy.

That is the truth, no matter what marks you have. Have I stooped to corrupting children now? What kind of artist am I? *One hunting for justice,* I remind myself. Breathing deeply, I leave the fountain and the plaza behind and continue on my way to the Underbelly.

The entrance to the maintenance shaft is nearby, in a dead-end corridor full of storage crates. I change into my disguise behind a stack of boxes and, using my false marks, bypass the scanner on the maintenance shaft door. I step into the tunnel and shut the door firmly behind me.

These tunnels are luxurious compared to the route I normally take to the Underbelly: they are dry, well-lit, and comfortably warm. I take out my datascroll and pull up my map of the maintenance shafts. These tunnels extend for miles, connecting every level of the ship, and I do not have time to get lost.

I make my way deeper into the winding metal labyrinth, using elevators to descend through each level. For most of my journey, the hum of the machinery in the walls is my only companion. But now and then, when I reach an intersection or an elevator hub, labor crews pass me in twos and threes. Some greet me, but most ignore me altogether. I am glad, as usual, that my disguise is so effective: I appear so low-ranking that even these common laborers hardly deign to speak to me.

As I descend, Shekali T'sarek returns to my mind. The memory of her desolate face fuels my anger and determination. Barely a woman, she is already a pawn in this wretched game between the Ascendance and Clan Serix. I wonder if her parents persuaded her that joining the faction was the honorable thing to do, or if they threatened her, or if they bothered to consult her at all. And Kilmaya allowed it. I allowed it. For what purpose? To keep the High Council from accusing us of rebellion? A lie to defend against a lie—how can that be right?

And yet, I am doing much the same thing, changing Kophas Tarriks's skin. Forging a falsehood to free a falsely condemned man—it is all so wrong. Something stronger than the markmakers' oath drives me to this madness.

But the oath I have broken belongs to the honor-code, the law of the ancestors. If I cannot follow that...then what am I following?

My darkening thoughts haunt me until I arrive at a narrow, dingy tunnel with a rusted hatch in the floor. On the adjacent wall, built into the panel, is another mark-scanner. It appears old and corroded; I can only hope it still works. I place my palm on the entry pad. For a moment nothing happens—and then the scanner blinks, acknowledging my mastery-mark, and I hear the clank of the hatch bolts sliding.

I exhale softly. It would have been a long trek to the next entrance if this door had not opened. I bend down and wrench the rusted handle to force open the hatch. A cold wind and a foul smell of chemicals wafts up into my face. Holding my breath, I peer into the darkness below. A short ladder extends down to a barely visible platform. I have reached the Underbelly.

I step onto the ladder and close the hatch behind me, then climb down. My heavy bags swing against my sides, tugging me off balance as I clamber down the rungs. But my steps are swift and sure—I have grown used to the extra weight. I do not need my map now, either; I know my way from here. Several ladders and half an hour later, I reach the ground floor of the slums. Then I find Kophas's shelter and rap softly on the wall.

"Come in," he calls at once.

Relieved, I duck inside. I pull my lamp out of my satchel and switch it on. The young exile sits against the wall, his blanket wrapped around his shoulders. He winces at the light.

"Where have you been?" His voice sounds gravelly, as if he has not spoken for days—which is most likely the case. "I ran out of food two days ago."

"I'm sorry. I was delayed. I couldn't help it." I rummage in my other bag and toss him a package. "Yekri fruit."

Hunger glints in his eyes. Without complaint, he tears into the package. As he bolts down the fresh berries, I watch him with anxiety. Even with the food I have brought, he is still bone-gaunt, and his black skin is dull and grimy. No matter what marks I give him, he will still look like an exile.

I push away my worries as I unpack the rest of his rations and set them on the floor. "How is your neck?" I nod at the bandage wrapped around his throat.

"Better." He swallows the last handful of fruit and wipes his mouth with the back of a hand. "I think it's nearly healed."

"Let me look at it."

I unwrap the gauze and examine the side of his neck, where I removed his clan-mark. The healing ointment has done its work well this time. The new skin is smooth and dark; only when I shine my lamp directly on it can I discern a faint scar.

"It looks good." I wipe away a stray fleck of ointment. "I think it's ready."

He stiffens a little. "Did you...find records to use?"

"Yes." That has been my primary work the past few days. "I'll show them to you."

I reach for my datascroll and pull up the mark-records that I downloaded from my uncle's display desk. Copying records from the archives without the proper permission is illegal, of course. But I do not feel very guilty about it— only about deceiving my uncle. If he knew he were harboring a skin-changer...

I hand the datascroll to Kophas. "Dirak Tizzan," I say. "Construction worker, about your age. He died two months ago in a dock accident."

Kophas stares at the records with revulsion. For a minute, he struggles to speak. "A Tizzan?" he says at last.

I sigh. "We've discussed this. You will escape notice much more easily if you are from a laborer clan."

"I know. It's not that. It's..." He pauses for a long time, gazing at the mark-records in dread. "His family..."

I press my lips together in a tight frown. "Let's hope you never meet them." I begin taking inks and tools from my bag. "Study those marks well. You'll need to know them—at least until you reach the planets."

He grimaces. But the mention of the planets brings a spark of bitter determination back into his face. "I'm ready."

I wipe his neck free from grime, open my inks, and pick up my pen. Despite my resolve, my fingers tremble slightly. It is so strange to give this mark to a grown man. Only infants should receive this kind of clan tattoo. By my hand, this exile is about to be reborn.

In silence I trace the outline of the Tizzan symbol, the single downward slash flanked by several small, spur-like crescents. With excruciating caution, I fill in the sweeps of color and the miniscule verity lines, glancing at the mark-records occasionally for reference. The style is awkward for me to imitate: the dead man's marks were made by a Trev'ban studio, and their artists use thicker strokes than I am accustomed to. So I work slowly, sinking myself into the challenge. If I concentrate deeply enough, I can almost forget the magnitude of the crime.

When the tattoo is finished and I apply the sealing-glaze, I do not say the usual words. I will not invoke the ancestors to bless this false ink—I have worked enough sacrilege tonight. Instead, for this lawless mark, I invent my own ceremony. "You are a son of Clan Tizzan," I say. "Your name is Dirak." Gripping his shoulder, I meet his wide-eyed gaze. "Welcome back to the living."

CHAPTER NINETEEN

The days at Kilmaya's studio become maddeningly dull. I spend my time cleaning and organizing and, on rare occasions, attending to a client. A few patrons still brave the hostile glares of the security guards for the sake of a Serix mark. But the work is so slow that Kilmaya begins leaving me to watch the studio alone while she gossips with her fellow artists. I do not mind. We have not been on good terms since she gave Shekali the faction-mark.

The ongoing tension of the guild's ban wears on everyone's tempers. Even at home, I do not get much of a reprieve. My uncle frequently comments on the reports from the rest of the ship, which tell of continuing protests and discontent from Ascendance warriors. Chervani, meanwhile, keeps fretting about my safety despite the fact that I dutifully carry my dagger. In my opinion, she should be more concerned about Hakham—he refuses to carry any kind of weapon, whether at the record hall or the security stations at the docks. He still puts his trust in his Serix clan-mark. Like my aunt, I wonder how long that symbol will provide us protection.

One evening I return home from work—tired and irritable from another tedious day with few clients—to find an unexpected guest. Hakham sits on the half-circle of couches in the front room, a glass of kol-dawra in hand. Across from him, leaning forward in earnest conversation, is Virik, the recordmaster of the guild.

Both men glance up as the front door slides shut behind me. I halt, embarrassed. I have not seen the recordmaster since he congratulated me after the Van'shorvanii ceremony, when my response was flustered and discourteous—not to mention that I completely missed the festival meal my family hosted for him.

Hakham lifts a hand in greeting. He looks tired in his reserved, tight-lipped way. "Honor with you, Mariikel. Join us for a drink?"

"Of course, na'thalo. Thank you." I accept more out of politeness than a real desire for the liquor. Although it is hardly the first time Virik has been a guest in our house, his status in the clan still demands a certain courtesy—and I should probably try to make up for my earlier blunders.

I slip my satchel to the floor. Under the table, Miika whuffs and thumps her tail sleepily in greeting. I nod to Virik, brushing my fingertips against my clan-mark. "Good evening, recordmaster. It's an honor to have you. What brings you tonight?"

"Nothing but the promise of a good bottle of kol-dawra." Virik blinks, his dark-skinned face even more dour than my uncle's. "Ancestors know we could all use some right now."

Hakham grasps the flask on the table and pours the liquor into an empty cup for me. I take a seat beside him, summoning the energy to assume my mask of good manners. Miika turns her head to lick my sandals; I push her away gently with one foot. She has been seeking more attention than usual ever since Askko left. I wonder if she misses her master.

The thought of my cousin, far away on his ocean-washed island, causes a pang in my chest. What is he doing now? Does he know about the guild's declaration and the turmoil on his home ship? What would he think of it all?

"So," Virik asks, "how goes the sparring match?"

I take the offered glass from my uncle. The harsh aroma of undiluted kol-dawra stings my nostrils. "I'm sorry?"

"I mean the ban," says Virik. "You artists are taking the brunt of everyone's grudges. How are things at the studios? Kilmaya still has my K'nima staying home."

"Oh." I take a tiny sip of kol-dawra, wince, and swallow. It is true that Kilmaya has not yet told our apprentices, including the recordmaster's daughter, to come back to work—but that is mostly because we have so little for them to do. "It's been quiet, really. There haven't been any more fights in the street. Not since the Trechik guards arrived."

"No, I don't suppose there would be. Even those Ascendance zealots know they are not immune to bullets." Virik reaches for his own drink, then leans back, frowning. "I've heard you're losing clients, though."

"Some. A number of our Ascendance clients have been going to Trev'ban studios instead."

The statement is deliberately vague. In truth, Kilmaya and I have only served two Ascendance members since the latest ban, and one of them was Shekali T'sarek. The rest of our patrons who belong to the faction—even people from high-ranking clans, who would ordinarily spurn the idea of going to a lesser workshop—seem to have abandoned us without a second thought. But I am reluctant to admit just how empty our studio has been the past several days.

Hakham scoffs. "It's not as if Clan Trev'ban can give them the honor-marks they want. Their artists are bound by the ban as much as ours. What point do they think they are making?"

"It's no secret that the Trev'ban leadership would like to support the Ascendance more openly—if they could get away with it." Virik hoods his lower eyes. "Half of them are faction members in all but ink. And the other half are happy to use the turmoil to pressure the guild in other ways. Have you heard about this latest petition they submitted?"

My uncle grunts in affirmation, but I only frown. "No, I haven't."

"They are demanding that the guild allow Trev'ban artists to help judge the mastery-trials. It's about voting privileges, of course. They only want to give the vote to more of their own."

I regard the recordmaster, wondering at his scathing tone. To me it seems only natural that the Trev'ban markmakers would want more of a say in what happens in their studios, especially with the guild's recent restrictions. But I do not think my opinion would be welcome in this conversation.

"They complain that *we* give the vote based on clan, not merit," Virik grumbles. "How much Trev'ban artists know about true merit is debatable. Also, they might stand a better chance of gaining the guild's favor if they weren't aspiring faction members. But that does not seem to have occurred to them."

He downs the last of his kol-dawra and sets the cup on the table with a clack. Then the front door shushes open, and my aunt steps into the room. She is wearing one of her plain, dark-brown working tunics, still stained with soil and sap from the trallak farms. Her eyes widen when she spots Virik.

"Recordmaster!" She hurries over, bobbing her head in deference. "I didn't know you were coming by."

Virik's irritated expression relaxes. "Honor with you, Chervani. Please, don't trouble yourself. I'll be taking my leave soon."

"You're certainly welcome to stay for supper if you would like." Chervani gestures towards me in a teasing manner. "Mariikel has decided to appear this time. He has been even more elusive since he began studying with old Haza'ruux, but we do still see him occasionally."

I choke in the midst of another burning sip of kol-dawra. I told my family about my lessons with Haza'ruux, but there was no need to announce them to the recordmaster.

Virik sends me a curious glance. "Is that so? I did hear something about the mark the old man gave you. Quite impressive. So he is teaching you now, too?"

"Sometimes. A few new techniques." I place my cup back on the table, trying to keep my hand from shaking. I would rather talk about anything, even guild politics, besides my connection to Haza'ruux.

Virik only laughs. "What? Not interested in becoming a mad markmaker, then?"

"No, recordmaster." I offer a strained smile. "That is not my plan."

I am glad that Virik does not seem to take the matter too seriously—and yet his words leave me with a faint chill. Haza'ruux has been teaching me far more than a few new techniques. I am a full apprentice to him in all but name. He has never said that he is preparing me to be his successor, but I cannot imagine what other purpose he might have. I need to reread the old manuscript that my uncle once showed me in the archives. If the mad markmaker offers me a formal apprenticeship, does the law of the ancestors require that I accept?

"Mariikel?" Chervani's voice breaks through my brooding. From her arch tone, it is not the first time she has tried to get my attention. "I asked you a question, dako. The studios, how were they today?"

I shiver, returning to myself. "What? They were fine. There wasn't any trouble today."

"That's good." Her shoulders drop a fraction, releasing tension. Chervani has been even more concerned for me than usual after hearing how Tekra T'sarek nearly threatened our workshop with a contingent of deepcrafters. But my answer seems to reassure her for now. She steps around behind the couch, placing a hand on my uncle's shoulder. "And the docks, Hakham?"

"Also uneventful." Hakham cracks a dry smile, reaching up to clasp her hand. "Really, Chervani. The faction may be upset, but there is only so much they can do. The ship council is not allowed to drive me from my post simply because of my clan-mark. Besides, they cannot run dock security with mark-scanners alone." He nods to Virik. "Serix archivists are the best trained to recognize forgeries, and the Ascendance knows it. They are not about to replace us."

"I would like to see them try." Virik gets to his feet with a dismissive grunt. "Well, I should be going—my family will be expecting me. Honor with you all."

"And with you, recordmaster," Chervani returns. "Give our greetings to Kandri and K'nima."

"I will." Virik nods briefly towards me. "Best of luck at the studios. K'nima has missed the work. She hopes to return soon." He touches the side of his neck in farewell. "May the ancestors grant us some peace, for all our sakes."

"Ancestors grant it," I murmur. But I do not raise a hand to my clan-mark. I am not confident the prayer will be answered.

Chervani's accusation that I have become even more elusive is truer than I like to admit. Sometimes I do not see my aunt and uncle for days on end. Every morning, I leave the house before they are awake to study with Haza'ruux. In the evenings, after work, I often go straight to the Underbelly to continue painting Kophas's new marks. I return home late, drop into an exhausted sleep for a few hours, and then rise to do it all over again.

But I am glad of the work. The challenge of forging a complete set of tattoos, which must fool both the idle glance and the security officials at the docks, fills me with a new fire and focus. While I paint, I rehearse with Kophas his new history: he is now Dirak Tizzan, a young dock worker looking to join a labor crew on the planets. Clan Tizzan are asteroid miners, scrap collectors, and construction workers, so they always swarm the docks. It is also a large clan, so the chances of Kophas meeting anyone who knew the real Dirak Tizzan are low. As long as he maintains his cover and does not attract attention, he should be able to get on a shuttle unquestioned.

Meanwhile, in Haza'ruux's hidden studio, I continue to struggle my way through old manuscripts and myths. Despite my growing unease that the hermit views me as his successor, I still admire his craftsmanship and cannot help wanting to master it. But I am frustrated with the endless fables of the Arimaas. When I ask him whether he has any real histories on his shelf of books, he merely flashes one of his manic grins and chides me for my impatience.

One morning, after our usual writing practice, he reads to me from a manuscript in verse. The text is part of an epic poetic cycle about the glory days of Clan Sko'larik, before the corruption of the Keepers. The old man's voice rings gravelly but resonant as he recites the rhythmic lines:

> *On Valtha, the holy hill,*
> *They built the great dreaming-hall,*
> *With pillars of fragrant kriar wood*
> *And lintels of shining trallak.*
> *On the walls, and swarming the pillars,*
> *They carved the signs of the beasts:*
> *Burrik and hawk and shadewolf,*
> *All the creatures of power.*
> *And here, on the fragrant floors,*
> *The Keepers lay down, and they dreamed.*
> *Deep in the dream they wandered,*
> *Watching the distant lands*

And touching their warriors' spirits,
Guiding them from afar.

I am supposed to read the text along with him and stop him when he reaches a sigil I do not understand. Instead, I fidget with my stylus, staring at the intricate lines of the tattoo on my right arm. I have been studying with Haza'ruux every day for over a month now, yet the mark he gave me is still a mystery. With effort, I can identify a handful of sigils, but they are so tightly intertwined with other, unknown symbols that I can make no sense of them. Perhaps the whole mark is gibberish after all. Haza'ruux has not mentioned my crimes since I first confessed my story to him. It is almost as if he has forgotten it.

I have long overcome my fear that he might betray me to the guild. But other fears grow in its stead. The thought that Haza'ruux might be training me to take his place, to become the next mad markmaker, still haunts me. Is the mark he gave me a tattoo of apprenticeship? Am I bound to his service even though I never agreed?

Even if that is the case, I do not understand why he would choose me, an admitted oathbreaker, to learn the language and legends he protects. And how did he find out about my work in the Underbelly? He *knew*—before I confessed to him that night, he already knew. Every time I remember that fact, I feel a chill deep in my belly.

Does he know what I am doing now, with Kophas? Why hasn't he tried to stop me?

I realize the room is silent. With a start, I glance up. Haza'ruux is looking at me with hooded eyes. "Flashing Blade is not listening," he growls.

I open my mouth to apologize. But all my fear and frustration well up in my throat. Why should I wear a mask for Haza'ruux? He knows what I am. "I want to read something else."

"Something else?" He tilts his head, eyes glittering.

I curl my fingers into a fist and hold up my right arm between us. "I want to read this." I try to control the tremor in my tone. "You said it was a poem."

"You are not ready to read that."

"That's what you said last time. I could do it if you would help me."

He frowns more deeply. "No."

"Why?" I push back my stool abruptly and stand. "Why in Ka's name did you give it to me if I'm not meant to read it?"

Haza'ruux rests his hand on the open book. He regards me without anger. "Can a day-old child read the sigils of his clan-mark?"

"I'm not a child. You owe me an explanation."

He squints his upper eyes. "Haza'ruux owes you nothing. You are the one in debt."

Unease clutches at my belly. *Idiot.* "You are welcome to turn me in any-time," I say bitterly. "I won't stop you."

"Brave little Flashing Blade," he mocks. But then he chuckles, and his eyes relax. "Do not fear. Your secret is safe with Haza'ruux. But if you want to read poems, you must learn your sigils first."

"When?" I hold out my arm again. "When will you teach me how to read this?"

"When you are ready." He flicks a hand at my stool. "Sit, now."

I glare at him furiously, but at last I sit down, defeated. "Is this the payment for my debt? Listening to your stories?"

His mouth twitches in a grin. "Perhaps."

"I could leave." The threat is only half-serious, but if he is truly determined to make me his apprentice, how hard will he try to keep me? "What if I don't come back tomorrow?"

Haza'ruux blinks, undisturbed. "Flashing Blade may leave whenever he likes." He turns back to his book. "But then he will never learn."

As he begins reading again, I restrain a groan. He knows me too well. I cannot stop coming until I find out what my mark means. Until then, I must endure whatever he deigns to teach me.

Two weeks have passed since the ban, and it is another predictably slow day at the studio. Kilmaya is out, as usual. I sit at the table in the workroom, pretending to mix inks. In reality, I am studying the sigil poem on my arm. Haza'ruux's refusal to tell me what it means has only increased my resolve to translate it. However, the most I can do is pick out the few sigils I recognize and copy them out separately on my datascroll. The task is slow and proba-bly futile—but it is less mind-numbing than checking inventory again, and less disheartening than reading yet another report about guild quarrels and Ascendance protests.

When I hear the front door open, I am glad for the excuse to get up. It might only be Kilmaya, but it might also be a client. I slide off my seat and step into the front room. At once, I halt in my tracks.

Standing in the middle of the room, with his long white tunic and regal bearing, is Mekkalluthak Serix.

"Guildmaster!" I bow my head. "Honor with you. How may I serve you?"

"Honor with you, Mariikel. It is good to see you." His voice is warm and genuine. He stands poised, relaxed—yet there is a charged air about him, an unwavering intensity in his gaze, that overawes me. The elegance of his many honor-marks, vivid against his violet skin, only adds to the effect. Up close, he reminds me of a deepcrafter—unusually small and slender for a van'shor, perhaps, but with the same perceptiveness, the same natural assumption of authority.

It is no wonder that this man persuaded Clan Serix to vote for his ban.

The guildmaster glances around the empty studio. "Where is Kilmaya?"

"She is—out. I'm sure she is nearby. I can find her. It will only take a moment."

"Don't trouble yourself." He holds up a hand, smiling. "I will see her soon enough, I'm sure. Besides, I came to ask after you."

A jolt runs down my spine. "Me?" I try to sound merely puzzled, not alarmed. I do not entirely succeed.

The guildmaster chuckles. "Well, not only you. I want to visit all the clan's artists. I know the ban has taken its toll on the studios—I want to encourage everyone, in person."

I relax a little, though I am still bewildered. I have rarely seen Mekkalluthak making rounds at the studios, and never by himself—he always has an escort. But then, Clan Serix has never openly defied the ruling faction before, either. "Thank you. That is very good of you."

"Certainly." He tilts his head at me. "So? How are you faring?"

I gesture at the pristine but empty room. "As well as can be expected. It is…" I cough. "It is rather dull, actually."

"I can imagine. I know the news from the rest of the ship seems unsettling. But it is good news for us, in truth."

I squint. "I hope you are right."

"Every day that passes puts more pressure on the faction. Their warriors are growing impatient. They live for honor-marks—they will only put up with this ban for so long."

"I suppose." His words remind me of Askko and his explosive anger when he learned that the guild had turned him away. If that is happening all across the ship, I can only imagine the turmoil. But the thought also makes me uneasy. Is Mekkalluthak deliberately inciting rebellion among the warrior clans?

"We have allies emerging, as well," the guildmaster continues. "The longer the authorities occupy our sector, the clearer their true motive becomes. They want to bend us to their will. People are beginning to see that. There is a contingent in Clan Tarriks that has been particularly vocal—a respected valk'taro named Jal'thor and some of his followers."

Jal'thor? I blink—he was of one of Talorak's supporters in the Tarriks clan council. I came across his name more than once when researching Talorak's trial; he was one of the few people who attempted to defend the old warrior. And now, apparently, he is coming to the defense of Clan Serix.

A rare warmth of hope stirs in my chest. "That seems like good news."

"It is. Clan Tarriks has been under Ascendance control since before the war. The fact that one of their own commanders is willing to speak against them now...well, let us say things are shifting in our favor."

"That is encouraging." I muster a smile. "Thank you for telling me."

"Of course. Thank you for your patience." Mekkalluthak inclines his head, touching his clan-mark. "The guild could not fight this battle without you."

His gesture of deference embarrasses me. I do not know how to respond, so I bow more deeply and hope that will satisfy him. When I rise, he is smiling again, with a keen glint in his eyes. "But as for you," he goes on. "Things cannot be so dull for you as you say."

"What do you mean?"

"Well, you are taking lessons from Haza'ruux. At least, so I've heard." He watches me closely. "Are the rumors untrue?"

Silently I curse my teacher and her gossiping tongue. But then, it may not be her fault—anyone who was paying attention might have noticed my daily trips to the mad markmaker's house. "It is...not untrue. He...offered to show me a few techniques. For ornamental marks." I have an overwhelming urge to hide my right arm behind my back. But I clench my fist and resist.

"Hakka." Mekkalluthak sounds impressed. "He must think a great deal of you." His smile is still pleasant, but my palms prickle with unease. According to Kilmaya, this man once tried to become Haza'ruux's apprentice and failed. Does he view me as some sort of rival?

"It's nothing. They are only decorations."

"Legally, perhaps. But there is no shame in that. His sigils do share similarities with some ancient scripts. It is good to remember the craft of our ancestors." His tone is earnest. He shifts his weight from foot to foot as if restraining a nervous energy. "Tell me what you are learning."

"Hakk, well—" I nearly choke. What can I say? I cannot tell him about Haza'ruux's books; the old hermit made me promise that much. But I must give some answer. "He...it's an older form of writing. As you said."

"Like your mark?" He points at my wrist. "Can you read it yet?"

Involuntarily, I clutch at my arm. "No—I mean—no. It's too complex for me still." As soon as the words leave my mouth, I curse inwardly. I have just admitted that the mark is not meaningless.

"Ah." Mekkalluthak lowers his hand. His eyelids twitch, a flicker of disappointment. "Well, if you ever learn what it says, I would be curious to hear about it. The work of the mad markmakers has always been an interest of mine."

I grip my arm so tightly that my fingers begin to tingle. "I will be sure to let you know."

"Very good." But the words ring false. He stares at me as if dissatisfied.

Then he exhales and smiles again, but this time I can tell it is a mask. "I have other studios to visit. But I look forward to speaking with you again sometime. Give my greeting to your teacher, will you?"

"Of course."

"Until then, Mariikel. Honor with you."

"And with you, guildmaster." I force myself to let go of my own arm so that I can touch my clan-mark. I see Mekkalluthak to the door. Then I lean my back against it, feeling shaky.

The guildmaster knows something—about Haza'ruux, at least, if not my criminal activities. Despite the political uproar over the ban, this is the second time that he has singled me out, asking about the mad markmaker. And his interest is more than mere curiosity. Behind his gracious manners, I sense a determination that will not be thwarted.

But why? What in Ka's name does Haza'ruux have that he wants?

I glare down at the sigil poem on my arm. For all its beauty, it has caused me nothing but trouble. I cannot afford the scrutiny of the guildmaster—not when I am actively trying to smuggle an exile out of the Underbelly. But neither can I stop going to Haza'ruux for my daily lessons. Without his help, I will never learn the meaning of my mark.

I groan aloud and let my arm drop. How, by the empty skin of the Deep Sleep, did I get myself into this mess?

The door opens behind me. I curse in surprise, only to find myself face to face with Kilmaya. "What's the matter with you?"

"Nothing." I rub my arm. "You startled me."

She harrumphs and then glances down the street. "Was that Mekkalluthak I saw coming out of here?"

"Yes. He said he was visiting the studios. To encourage us."

"I see." Her eyelids flicker in irritation. "How generous of him. I wonder how he finds the time." And she sweeps past me into the workroom.

I look after her with a sinking feeling. I want to ask her again about Haza'ruux and Mekkalluthak, but she is clearly in no mood to talk. I pull a cloth out of my apron pocket and begin dusting a shelf. The shelf doesn't need it—I must have cleaned it a dozen times this week. But I have nothing else to do.

CHAPTER TWENTY

The next morning, when I knock on Haza'ruux's door, there is no answer. I wait for a minute, standing among the fragrant vine-blossoms that surround his porch. The street is quiet at this early hour. The air vents whisper in the ceiling, and in the plaza behind me, the fountain bubbles softly. I knock again. Still no response.

Should I leave? It is not like Haza'ruux to keep me waiting; he probably isn't home. It would not surprise me if he chose to disappear without a word. He is the mad markmaker, after all.

Still, I am reluctant to go. I have nothing to look forward to at the studios except another long day of boredom and worry. As exasperating as Haza'ruux can be, his lessons at least give me something to occupy my mind. In frustration, I tap the entry pad on the wall.

The door slides open with a soft rush of air. Taken aback, I stand frozen on the porch. Does Haza'ruux usually leave his door unlocked? I wouldn't know—I have never tried to enter on my own before. But it would seem strange; he is so careful to keep his precious library a secret.

I peer into the front room. The lights are dimmed, but otherwise the cluttered space looks the same as usual. Tasikko, the old kharraktyl, clings to the middle of the ceiling, upside-down. The reptile flicks its tongue, looses a throaty hiss, and retreats into a vine-shrouded corner.

I feel a sudden twinge of worry. *Is he ill?* I have never known Haza'ruux to be sick before, but he is an elderly man. And he does not have any family to care for him. I step inside, hoping my previous visits satisfy the ancient law that no one may enter uninvited.

"Haza'ruux?" Vines rustle and a soft chittering sounds in the shadows— the hermit's pet ech'taanin, no doubt. No one else responds to my greeting. But a light glows from behind the curtain leading to the studio. I shut the front door behind me and draw the curtain aside.

The pristine room is brightly lit but empty. The worktable—a huge, solid piece of furniture—has been pushed against one wall, leaving the middle of the floor clear. In the center of the room, in the space the table usually occupies, there is a hatch in the floor. It is a plain, metal trap door, like an entrance leading down to a storage room—surprisingly mundane, compared to the rest of the embellished studio.

Is Haza'ruux down in the storage room? Perhaps that is why he did not hear my knock. Or perhaps—unease grips me again—perhaps he fell and injured himself, and could not climb back out. I drop my satchel and crouch down to lift the trap door. The thick metal hatch appears heavy, but I have little trouble pulling it open. My arms are fit and hardened from my near-daily climbs to the Underbelly.

"Haza'ruux?"

No answer. I widen my upper eyes, trying to make out the room below. A steep stepladder descends into a dimly lit space—a dark floor tinged with a reddish glow. I do not see Haza'ruux. I open the hatch all the way and let it rest on the floor. Then I step onto the ladder and climb down. The air in the storage room feels warmer than the studio—heavy and still, with an acrid, smoky aroma. I drop to the floor and turn around.

I blink, waiting for my eyes to adjust to the dim light. I am in a low, circular room, supported by concentric rings of slender pillars. Tiny red lamps set into the ceiling glow with a steady radiance. In the center of the room is an open space—like a clearing in a grove of slender trees—with more red lamps hung round it. A wide, shallow bowl full of powdery ashes sits on the floor.

What is this place?

Amazed but wary, I glance around. Haza'ruux is not here, and I can see no other doors or passageways. My nostrils flare as I inhale the room's bitter fragrance: spicy but subtle, with an underlying sweetness.

I should go. Something about this room makes me nervous; it looks like a place that Haza'ruux would not want me to see. He must have forgotten I was coming this morning—as unlikely as that seems. Yet I cannot bring myself to leave. Instead, I reach out and touch one of the slender pillars. To my surprise, the surface feels grooved and slightly rough under my fingers. It is not metal. The pillar is made of wood—dark, polished wood, carved with a web of intricate patterns. I turn and scan the room again. The floor, the walls, the ceiling: every inch of this room is paneled with real wood.

Staggered, I take a step back. I have never seen so much decorative wood in one place before. It is a luxury item; only a wealthy artist or councilor could afford to install paneling like this. Again I turn my eyes to the walls. Hundreds of small, square panels, each about the size of my hand, line the curve of the room. They have carvings on them, too. In the dim light, I have to open all my eyes wide to examine them.

Each square bears an exquisite carving of an animal: a burrik, a wolf, a kharraktyl, a serpent. Here is an arrowhawk, and here a sleek ech'taani. Other carvings depict delicate flying insects, or strange water-creatures with fins and needle-like teeth. Even in the flat, red lamplight, the carvings are so sharply detailed that I can distinguish the individual strands of feather and fur.

The artistry astounds me. For several minutes I stand in mute admiration, my eyes roving over the wall. *Who carved all these?* Then I notice that each panel has a sigil inscribed in the corner. The script is archaic, but I recognize it from Haza'ruux's lessons: a date-sigil. With my fingertip, I trace the engraved lines: *Year 522 of the Wandering.*

A chill trails down my spine. *Is that the date this was carved?* Slowly I draw my hand away from the panel. If that is true, this engraving was made over four hundred years ago.

I glance at the surrounding panels. They have similar dates, separated by gaps of thirty or forty years. Intrigued, I begin pacing along the curve of the room, following the dates forward. *Year 634. Year 741. Year 809.* And then, just as the panels reach the present century, the images end abruptly, leaving a blank stretch of wall. I pause to study the final carving. The fierce figure of a snarling war-hound glares back at me, teeth bared and hackles raised. The date-sigil in the corner reads, *Year 918 of the Wandering.*

That was more than fifty years ago—before my time, but not before Haza'ruux's. Perhaps he fashioned this last carving?

Haza'ruux. Rix hazari-ruux. The mark of the mad dog.

I stare at the carving again. With a jolt of clarity, I realize: these panels are not mere decoration. They are a record. Haza'ruux once said that every artist who lives in this house chooses the name of a beast in honor of the Arimaas warriors. These images—these must be the symbols of the mad markmakers.

Is it possible? I gaze at the rows of panels, covering my mouth with one hand. *How far back does this record go? Is the line of mad markmakers as old as the Fleet itself?*

Both Kilmaya and my uncle said that Clan Serix has always had a mad markmaker, but seeing the proof of it carved into these ancient panels leaves me shaken. The myths of Clan Sko'larik, of the Arimaas—they are not merely the obsession of one old hermit. This house truly belongs to an unbroken line of artists, going back hundreds of years, who have dedicated their lives to the preservation of these stories.

But...why?

I feel a little dizzy. I have the urge to kneel down and say a prayer to my Serix ancestors, if only to apologize for intruding on this archaic sanctuary. But I am too bewildered to think clearly. *I should go.*

I back away from the wall and head for the ladder. As I cross the opening in the middle of the room, I raise my eyes to the ceiling. In the crimson glow of the lamps, I can see every chiseled line on the panels above me: more carven animals, leaping and dancing, wreathed by a ring of dense, unreadable marks. But sitting in the middle of the ring, dominating the pattern, is a sigil that I recognize instantly. I stumble and nearly cry out.

What in Ka's name...?

It is the mark of exile.

I stare at the ceiling, too shocked even to breathe. The sign of the un-clanned—what is it doing here, in this ancient clan shrine, of all places? Then my mind begins to register the details of the carving. It is not exactly the same as the modern exile-sigil; it is more elaborate, less stark and spare. But the main lines—the swirling, tendril-like arms, the small double crossbar—it is, without doubt, an embellished version of the same mark. But it is not a sign of shame here. The symbol is clearly in a place of honor—painstaking-ly carved and decorated, ringed by lamps and pillars and the wild, exulting beasts of the Arimaas.

An inarticulate fear surges in my throat like a wave of nausea. I lurch to-wards the ladder. I don't know what this place is—but I cannot stay here any longer.

I scramble up the ladder and emerge, gasping, into the studio. The cooler, fresher air clears my head at once. With all the force I can muster, I slam the hatch door closed. For a while I crouch on hands and knees, breathing deeply, until the sickening tug of vertigo fades.

What did I just see?

I'm not sure I want to know.

CHAPTER TWENTY-ONE

For the next few days, Haza'ruux continues to be away from home—or at least, when I knock on his door, no one answers. I am too afraid to venture inside again.

The memory of that strange, hidden shrine underneath his studio haunts me. The exile-mark carved into the ceiling like a desecration...what can it possibly mean? Who are the mad markmakers, really, and what kind of cult has the hermit drawn me into? Am I wearing a sacrilege in my own flesh as well, in the exquisite, unreadable mark?

My fears make me increasingly reluctant to continue my morning lessons. But as long as Haza'ruux is gone, it seems my studies are suspended, anyway. Part of me is relieved—but another part worries about him. The mad markmaker is free to go where he pleases, but with the current unrest, he may not be safe outside the clan sector. What if he has been accosted by Ascendance zealots in some obscure corridor of the ship? Are things so bad that faction members would attack an old man simply because he wears a Serix clan-mark?

I tell myself to stop fretting. Haza'ruux is eccentric, but he is not foolish—he can take care of himself. His prolonged absence is probably another test of my patience. Still, I cannot help wondering about it. Has he ever disappeared like this before? His neighbors might know. Yet I am embarrassed to knock on strangers' doors and ask if they know the whereabouts of the clan half-wit.

Early one morning, I am turning away from Haza'ruux's porch yet again when a familiar young shout breaks the stillness of the corridor.

"It's Blade!"

I raise my head just in time to see little Tyotik sprinting towards me. With a shriek of delight, he tackles my knees. I stagger back on the garden path. The boy grins up at me, unabashed. "Hi, Blade."

"Well, hello," I gasp. "What are you doing up so early?"

A quiet laugh pulls my attention away from the child. I glance up to see a young Serix woman standing on a nearby porch; she has just stepped out of the house. Her dark-skinned face looks tired, but she regards me with a mixture of amusement and interest.

"So you're Blade. I've been wondering." She walks over to join me in the mad markmaker's garden.

I take in her tattoos: the inkmaker's mark on her brow, the Trechik adoption-mark on her neck, and the marriage-mark on her hand—with the death-sigil that indicates she has been recently widowed. With a pang, I realize who she is. "You're Tyotik's mother?"

"Yes." Her weary features crease in another smile. "He's been telling me a lot about you, markmaker."

"Has he now?" I strive, without much success, to disentangle myself from the boy's grip. He has wrapped all his limbs around my legs and only giggles as I try to shake him off.

"Blade is brave. He stopped Tiro and Nallak from hitting me. *And* he says I'm Serix like you, nakki."

Mortified, I raise my palms in apology to his mother. "I didn't mean—I only told him—"

"It's all right. You don't need to explain." To my surprise, her eyes soften with unspoken gratitude. "I'm Kana. What is your name?"

"Honor with you, Kana. I'm glad to meet you." I attempt to regain my composure, but it is difficult with Tyotik climbing up my back by way of my satchel. "My name is Mariikel."

"No, it's not!" Tyotik hollers. "His name is Blade. Ha'ruux said so."

Kana chuckles. "Haza'ruux says a lot of strange things. Come here, you little kharraktyl, and leave the poor markmaker alone."

The young woman pries her son away from me and lifts him into her arms. He struggles, kicking in protest, until Kana starts tickling his bare feet. After a minute of mingled screams and laughter, Tyotik quiets and snuggles against his mother's shoulder. Kana turns to me again, her expression bright and curious. "So you're the one who's been coming to learn from Haza'ruux?"

"That's right." Does the whole clan know of my lessons now?

"Nakki!" Tyotik tugs on his mother's tunic. "I want to see Ha'ruux. Can I go play with him?"

"Not today. We're going to the Trechik sector to visit your *ji-nakko* and *ji-nakki*, remember? They want to see you, too."

I hear the catch in her voice as she mentions her deceased husband's parents. Sympathy throbs in my chest. To have family in two different clans—especially now, with all the tension between Clan Serix and the rest of the ship—cannot be easy for her. I admire her courage in venturing outside the sector at all.

"Why?" Tyotik pouts. "Blade gets to see Ha'ruux. I haven't seen him in a long time."

The boy's comment causes me a prick of anxiety—it seems to confirm the old hermit's disappearance.

"I haven't seen him, either, to tell the truth." Hesitantly, I address Kana: "Do you know where Haza'ruux has been lately? He hasn't been at home the past few days."

"Oh. He does that." Kana sends a wistful glance around the lush garden. "I grew up on this street. I've known him to be gone for weeks at a time, until you could hardly see his door for the vines growing over it. He never tells anyone where he goes. But he always comes back. Are you worried about him?"

"I was—a little."

"He will be all right. He's the mad markmaker." She pauses, then resumes with a smile, "I can see why he has taken you on. You are kind, like he is."

My fingers clench around my satchel strap. "I'm not his apprentice."

"Forgive me. I meant no offense." But she sounds more amused than apologetic. She hefts Tyotik in her arms again—the boy vainly attempts to fling himself backwards, out of her grip. "We have to go. But I'm glad to finally meet you, Blade."

I suppress my discomfort at the nickname and touch my clan-mark politely. "You as well, Kana. Honor with you. And...be careful outside the sector today."

Her arms tighten around her squirming child; she blinks in quiet thanks. "I will."

Kana turns away. Tyotik waves to me enthusiastically over her shoulder. Then the pair of them round the street corner and disappear, leaving me alone in the gray lamp-glow of the morning.

With Haza'ruux's lessons suspended, I resign myself to the slow days at the studio. But—to my surprise and relief—business picks up again. After nearly a month of the guild's ban, some of Kilmaya's usual customers muster their courage and come back again. There are even a number of Ascendance members who, dissatisfied with the service of the Trev'ban artists, start returning to Serix studios. Although we still cannot offer military honor-marks, we can give them clan- and marriage- and mastery-marks, and all the other day-to-day symbols.

The increase in work, and the evidence that the ban is having the desired effect, put both me and Kilmaya in better spirits. My teacher seems optimistic, too, about the end of the conflict. "What did I tell you?" she says. "The

Ascendance cannot keep people away from us forever. We are past the worst of it now. Another week or two, and we will see the end of this farce."

I am not so sure. At home, my uncle tells me that Clan Trev'ban's petition—to have more say in determining their artists' voting privileges—was struck down by Mekkalluthak and the other Serix councilors. The Trev'ban leadership is not happy, and Hakham does not think the Ascendance is ready to back down; he predicts there will be more trouble.

I hope that my teacher is right, and my uncle is wrong. I am weary of the tension and hostility haunting Rixarii Street. And the sooner this unrest runs its course, the sooner and more safely I can help Kophas get off the ship. Lately, I have gone to the Underbelly only for him—I have not given marks to other exiles. My energy only extends so far.

I have reached the subconscious decision that once I finish forging Kophas's tattoos, I will not go back to the Underbelly again—not for a while, at least. I must find out what Haza'ruux really wants. Mekkalluthak worries me, too. Once this business with the ban is over, I have a bad feeling the guildmaster will continue pestering me about the mad markmaker. I do not yet know how I will dissuade him.

I ache for a simple moment of peace—like the morning I woke up in Haza'ruux's house, after my confession. But now there is no rest, and no one to turn to.

One morning I decide, for the first time in many weeks, to sleep in instead of going to the mad markmaker's. He has not been home for days—what is the point? So I spend an extra hour in bed, and for once, I awake feeling refreshed. *You've been overworking*, I tell myself as I slip out of my bunk. If I would allow myself more rest, perhaps I could approach my troubles with a clearer head. I stretch my limbs, feeling unusually buoyant.

I go into the kitchen, where my aunt is eating her morning meal of spice-preserved tavla and freshly brewed klasindi. Miika crouches underneath the table, her dark ears pricked, hopeful for scraps. At my entrance, Chervani glances up and cries out in surprise. "Mariikel! I thought you had gone already."

I smile as I sit down beside her. "Not today. I decided to sleep for once."

"Good for you." The corners of her upper eyes crease in a fond but chiding expression. "I wouldn't mind if you did that more often, dako. I know those lessons are important to you, but honestly—if it weren't for the food that disappears every day, I could almost forget you still live here."

I wince. My uncle and aunt have encouraged my extra studies, but I still feel guilty about my constant absence from home. I will have to make up for that, too, once I finish Kophas's marks. "Forgive me. It's not only my lessons. Everything has been so strange at the studio this past month. I've been distracted. And worried."

"Hakk, well. You have reason enough for that."

Something damp nudges my hand; I glance down to see Miika nosing at me. Automatically I reach out to stroke the dog's sleek head. I find my gaze lingering on her lanky frame and whiplike tail. Her fangs gleam half-exposed as she pants, eager for attention.

The image of a bristling, snarling war-hound, chiseled into a dark wood panel, surfaces in my memory. *Haza'ruux. Mad Dog...*

"Dako?" Chervani peers keenly into my face. "You're not ill, are you?"

I shiver and pull myself back to the present. "No, nakki. Only tired." Giving Miika a last pat on her gaunt shoulder, I offer my aunt a reassuring smile. "But I think the trouble is nearly over. Our clients are coming back."

"I heard that. I'm so glad."

"Me, too." Miika wanders away, claws clicking against the floor. I reach for the bowl of yekri fruit on the table. "People are tired of this ban. Kilmaya thinks it will probably be lifted soon. She said—"

"Mariikel."

At my uncle's taut voice, I pause and look up. Hakham has appeared in the kitchen doorway, holding his datascroll in one hand. His face is rigid with anger, his nostrils flared. "Have you seen this?" he asks.

"What is it?"

He lifts the datascroll; the screen displays some kind of report. "They have destroyed a studio now."

"What?" My body stiffens. "Who? What happened?"

"It was last night." My uncle approaches the table and hands his device to me. "Some group of young Ascendance members—warriors-in-training, it says—came into Rixarii Street after hours and broke into a studio." His voice tremors with muted rage. "They smashed everything. They weren't even trying to steal."

"Kin's heart," Chervani murmurs.

I try to read the report, but I am so agitated that I can hardly comprehend the sigils on the screen. "What about the security guards? Didn't anyone stop them?"

"The guards did arrest them. But not in time to save the studio—apparently." His eyes narrow to slits.

"Was anyone hurt?" Chervani asks.

"No. But the damages are going to be expensive; it will take weeks to repair. Hakk!" he growls. "They had better make these criminals pay for it.

There will be shame-marks for this. And if those idiot Trev'ban artists are somehow involved—"

I put down the datascroll; my pulse races with fear and fury. "I have to go."

"Now?" Chervani catches my hand as I stand abruptly. "You haven't even eaten, dako." The glimmer of anxiety in her eyes belies her words. She does not want me going anywhere near Rixarii Street today. But I have no choice.

"Kilmaya will be there. I can't leave her alone." Then, only stopping to retrieve my satchel, I rush out the door.

The hour is early, but Rixarii Street is already crowded. Breathless, I slow my jog and halt at the edge of the commotion. The throng consists mostly of artists and security guards, but there are people here from all over the clan sector as well, drawn by the news of the vandalism.

With growing anxiety, I weave my way through the crowd. People talk loudly, angrily, shoving for a view. Near Kilmaya's workshop, the crowd turns into a crush. Surely Hakham would have told me if it were our own studio that had been destroyed? But I am too small to see over the heads of the throng, and neither can I force myself to the front for a better vantage point.

I backtrack and fight my way to the corridor wall. Between two shop-fronts, I find a series of narrow rungs built into the side of the hallway: a maintenance ladder leading up to the support beams. My months of clambering up and down the ladders of the Underbelly have served me well. Without a second thought, I grip the rungs and scale the side of the wall. Then, climbing up into the support beams that span the corridor ceiling, I look down from my perch into the street.

Below me, the crowd presses against a barrier that has been set up in front of one of the studios. It is not Kilmaya's—it is the shop across from hers, belonging to her elderly friend Rinavi. A pang of horror racks my chest. The door of the studio has been smashed in; broken bottles and spilled ink litter the front step. Across the whole front of the shop, painted in crude, sweeping strokes, sprawls the violet double-trident of the Ascendance.

My palms grow hot, and my throat closes with rage. Rinavi is one of the oldest artists on Rixarii Street, praised and respected by peers and clients alike. She is an honorable, gentle woman, and not politically outspoken. She has done nothing to provoke this. Besides, this wanton destruction is not merely an insult to my clan—it is a sacrilege against the craft of markmaking itself. No artist, Serix or Trev'ban, should ever be treated like this.

Scanning the sea of tattooed heads below me, I spot Kilmaya standing near the doorway of our studio. Rinavi is with her. My teacher rests a hand on the older artist's shoulder, as if trying to pull her friend away from the crowd.

Quickly I crawl across the connecting beams and drop down on our own front step. As I straighten my tunic, Kilmaya turns and startles at the sight of me. "Great Ka, where did you come from?"

I nod towards the ceiling.

"What are you now, a kharraktyl?" The words are facetious, but her voice rings brittle.

"I couldn't get through. It was the quickest way here." Ignoring her surprise, I step towards Rinavi, who stands in a trance, staring at the wreckage of her own studio. A new contingent of guards pushes through the throng: guild security, by the trallak-leaf tattoos on their brows. They seem to be arguing with the Trechik guards by the barricade.

Gingerly I place a hand on the elderly artist's shoulder. "Rinavi?"

Her eyelids flicker spasmodically, and she seems to look through instead of at me. In one hand she clutches half of a shattered pen. "How?" I can barely hear her over the din of the crowd. "Who could have done this?"

The mob surges around us. Kilmaya gives her friend's shoulder another tug. "Come. Do you want to be trampled? The guild guards will take care of the studio. Come inside."

Together we pull Rinavi into the safety of our own front room. Kilmaya slaps the entry pad; the door shuts, muting the noise outside to a low roar. Then she sits Rinavi down on one of the benches. "You rest now. I'll brew some klasindi, and then we will see about speaking to those guild officials. If there's anything left to salvage, they will find it for you."

Rinavi still grips the broken pen in her hand. Violet ink seeps from the shattered shaft onto her fingers, but she seems not to notice. "My clients. I will have to tell them...not to come..."

"Nonsense." Kilmaya gently pulls the pen-shaft from her grasp. "We'll tell them to come here. Mariikel and I can make the room. No need for you to lose more work than you have already." She wraps the pen in a piece of gauze from her apron pocket, then sets it on the front desk. A dark splotch seeps through the white fabric, like a bloom of blood.

"Mariikel," Kilmaya snaps. "Get her something for her hands."

"Yes, teacher." Her command stirs me into motion. While Kilmaya disappears into the workroom, I pull a clean rag from a neatly folded stack and offer it to Rinavi. The elderly markmaker does not appear to see me. She stares at the opposite wall, her breathing harsh, her teeth bared in an unconscious grimace.

"Rinavi?" I say. "You need to clean your hands. Before that ink sets."

She does not reply. Hesitant, I kneel at her feet. Unfolding her clenched hands, I wipe the violet stain from her palms and her slender, callused fingers.

Anger swells beneath my ribs. These hands have never painted falsehood. They have only fashioned truth, honor, beauty in the flesh. I can still remember her gentle touch, her quiet cheer when she stood beside me in the arena at Van'shorvanii. But now her skin is cold under my fingers and damp with the smeared violet dye.

For the pens have been crushed, and the ink spilled...

I wipe away the last of the ink and wrap the older artist's hands in my own. "Rinavi. They caught the men who did it. The guild will see justice done. I know they will."

The words are poor comfort to an artist who has just seen the place of her life's work defaced and dishonored. But Rinavi finally meets my gaze. Her eyelids still quiver uncontrollably. "How did it come to this?"

"I'm sorry. I wish I knew."

I release her hands and rise, crumpling the stained rag in my fist. Then I turn and head back into the workroom. Kilmaya stands at the washbasin, filling a small jug with heated water for klasindi. I join her, dropping my rag in the basin to let it soak.

"Ascendance *axnakkan*." My teacher spits the words, low but vehement. "And Rinavi. Of all the people to..."

I shut off the steaming water. "What happens now?"

"The vandals have been taken into Trechik custody; they'll be brought before the ship council later." Kilmaya pulls out a handful of dried klasindi pods from a cabinet and drops them into the jug. Her hands shake even as her voice remains deadly calm. "Mekkalluthak wants them handed over to Clan Serix to receive shame-marks. He's demanded as much in a public statement."

"They can't deny us that." Kilmaya does not respond; her expression darkens. I grip the edge of the washbasin. "Can they?"

"They might try," she growls. "I am not sure the faction believes the law still applies to them." She glares down at the jug in her hands. The warm, subtle fragrance of the drink fills the room, but the scent does not appear to calm her. "Something will have to be done. You heard what Mekkalluthak said at the last assembly. We must make good on our threats. If the Ascendance refuses to punish these vandals, we may have to take even more drastic measures."

"More drastic?" The guild's ban on honor-marks was unprecedented. "Like what?"

"Ka only knows." My teacher turns away towards the door; her face is grim. "I hope we do not have to find out."

Eventually the crowd outside disperses, and a maintenance crew begins cleaning up the debris from the damaged workshop. But the disturbance once again leaves us with a dearth of clients. Instead, our studio becomes a gathering-place as Serix artists stop by to offer consolation to Rinavi, then stay to speculate about politics with Kilmaya.

Everyone waits for news of the vandals and their punishment. The latest reports announce that the perpetrators have been brought before the ship council, who will decide whether to hand them over to Clan Serix as requested. In the meantime, Valo T'sarek releases a statement expressing his disappointment in the destruction and his hope for resolution between the Ascendance and the guild. Mekkalluthak immediately responds with another public message, which Kilmaya reads aloud from her datascroll as our fellow artists cluster around the worktable:

"There can be no resolution without justice. These faction members have transgressed the law of our ancestors, dishonoring with violence the sanctuary of truth in the flesh. If Valo T'sarek truly wishes for peace, he will appear before the clans at the ship's council and advise them to hand over these criminals for the shamemarks they have already earned. If he does not—we will know his words to be sigils without substance, an ink that does not bind. For his own sake, and the sake of all those who bear the mark of his faction, I pray he proves otherwise."

The markmakers who fill the room murmur with agitation.

"What is he going to do? Another ban?" exclaims Narrik. The ill-tempered artist looks even more agitated than usual. "As if we haven't lost enough business. Does he expect us to run studios without clients?"

"What would you have him do?" Kilmaya sets the datascroll aside. "He hasn't said anything about another ban. But even if he did...perhaps, in the circumstances, it would be warranted."

Noise engulfs the room as the gathering erupts into heated debate. Sick at heart, I slip away and retreat into our storeroom. I have heard enough.

By the end of the workday, I feel exhausted, though I have done nothing except pretend to take inventory and listen to Kilmaya argue with her peers. It is a relief to pack my bag, leave Rixarii Street, and head down to the maintenance shaft at the far end of the clan sector. No matter the outcome of this latest standoff, I am determined that Kophas should not suffer any more delay on my account. Hurrying through the narrow tunnels, I reach the Underbelly without incident and arrive at Kophas's shelter.

I have made all his major tattoos now—the clan-mark, the mastery-mark, two memory-marks, and a handful of minor honor-sigils for childhood accomplishments. My final task is to copy a few ornamental marks. Kophas sits before me in the cramped shack, one leg outstretched for me to work on, the other leg curled to his chest. We are both quiet this evening: I am concentrating on my pens, and the young exile seems even more morose than usual. But as I trace a band of interlocking, blue-and-white lines around his ankle, he breathes deeply and stirs.

"I keep thinking," he says in a bitter tone. "I could have avoided this."

I finish a stroke and look up. "Avoided what?"

"The Underbelly. The skin-changing. Everything. I could be on a planet now with my warband. I could have my hvoss'ka rank. I could have honor-marks." His jaw tightens, and his eyelids tremor. "I could have had everything if I had simply let those half-sights die."

I sit up, disquieted. Kophas has not mentioned the cause of his exile since the day we first met. I have never brought it up, either—I always assumed the subject would be too painful. But Kophas goes on, his voice taut. "They were unarmed, so we took them prisoner—as the code prescribes." His lips pull back from his teeth in a soundless snarl. "We put them in a storeroom, to keep them out of the way while we secured the station. Thirty, forty of them, all packed in. We kept them like that for...I don't know. Four or five days. The room stank like—like animals."

He clamps a fist to his mouth. I remain silent, my pen poised but motionless. In the long pause, the distant machinery of the Underbelly creaks and clangs.

"I was guarding them. I had to request food and water for them when no one else brought it. And then, when the order came to bring them down to the docks... I thought we must be moving them to another ship. So I told them... I tried to make them understand they had nothing to fear." His eyes grow wide and glaring, fixed on an invisible memory. "We put them in the airlock, as ordered. But there was no ship waiting. There never had been."

He trembles, his arms locked tight around his bent knee. I feel a prickle of horror as his meaning sinks in. Death by the void—we do not even execute our own criminals that way. And this is how the Ascendance disposes of unarmed half-sight civilians?

"I tried to stop it, when I realized what was happening. I fought the other guards. But it was too late already." He sinks his face into his hands. "Deep Sleep, I was so stupid."

"Why? Why were they killed?"

"I don't know. We weren't told. It might have been something about the rations—between us and the prisoners, supplies were running a little low. But that's not enough reason to—" He breaks off, steadies himself. "I know they were only half-sights. I know how badly we need to win this war. But Ka, their faces." Another cry chokes him. "I'd given my word they would be safe."

I regard him, unable to speak. I have never seen a person, either Noxxiin or half-sight, die. I have never watched anyone be cast out of an airlock to suffocate instantly in the frozen void. How do I even begin to console him?

"At least you tried to save them. In that, you acted with honor."

Kophas barks a laugh. "And we can see how much good that has done me." He spreads out his arms until his fingertips nearly touch the walls of the shelter. "Here I am, sitting in rags. Wearing a dead man's marks." He bares his teeth in a manic grin. "So honorable."

"It's nearly over. Think of the planets."

"They are very far away, markmaker." He hides his face again, resting his forehead on his knee.

I can think of no response. Wordlessly, I refill my pen with ink. I am about to resume my work when he lifts his head and speaks again.

"My family—I was never allowed to see them before I was exiled." His voice is quiet, but grief glitters in his eyes. "They still think I am a traitor and a coward. That is all they will remember." He slams a fist against the flimsy wall. The sheet metal clangs and echoes. "They'll never *know*. They will never know the truth."

He bows his head. I sit motionless, my pen frozen in my hand. His agony stirs the familiar ache in my own chest—the pain of bearing falsehood in my body. "You are still honorable," I say after a long silence. "No matter who knows it." As I look at him, a thought comes back to me—something that Haza'ruux said on the night that I first confided in him. It seems a long time ago now. "You have honor-marks no one can see."

"What's the point of that?" Then he shakes his head. "I'm sorry. I'm being ungrateful."

"Don't think of it. I am glad to serve you."

He blinks, gazing at me with a baffled expression. "You're a strange one, skin-changer." Finally, gesturing at his outstretched leg, he mutters, "Well, go on and finish it."

I lean over and set my pen to his skin again. I add the last few embellishments to the decorative mark, then apply the sealing-glaze and tie a clean piece of gauze around his ankle. "It's done." I pull off my markmaking gloves. "You're a new man, Dirak Tizzan."

He shuts his eyes in a grimace. "I suppose I will have to get used to that name."

"Yes. And quickly." I wipe down my pens and cap my inks. "But don't head off to the docks just yet. You may have new marks, but you still look like an exile. And smell like one." I gesture at his grimy tunic. "I'm going to bring you new clothes."

He groans. "When?"

"Tomorrow." I rise and settle my satchel over my shoulder. "One more day, and you will be a free man. I swear it."

CHAPTER TWENTY-TWO

The next morning, I awake with a sharp sense of anticipation that borders on dread. It takes me a moment to remember why. Staring at the muted blue glow of my ceiling, I inhale, and then release my breath slowly.

Today you repay the debt.

I roll out of my bunk and rest my feet on the chilly floor. It has been over a year since I gave Talorak his exile-mark, a year since my first descent into the Underbelly. At last, I am helping someone escape from that wretched place. My work—my crimes—will finally bring about some real good.

I stand up, switch on the light, and step over to my closet. I take down my laborer's disguise and an extra tunic. It is an old one, rather worn, which Askko outgrew years ago. It will be a little short on Kophas, too, but it will serve. I fold the clothes into my satchel.

I rummage in a drawer, pull out a small, bulging pouch, and empty its contents. The hard, red-brown coins clack against the floor. Simply to reassure myself, I count them: five hundred *os'tekta* in pure, polished karu wood. I traded in my own credits for the coins weeks ago. It is not an extraordinary amount of money—I could buy a few high-quality pens for this sum. But for Kophas, it will buy weeks of food, lodging, and most importantly, a seat on a transport shuttle bound for the planets.

I sweep the coins back into the pouch. It feels strange to touch so much wood—I rarely use hard currency in my daily business. A memory of the hidden room in Haza'ruux's house, with its wooden pillars and animal carvings, looms in my mind.

I bury the money deep in my satchel, then stand up and begin dressing myself for the day. There is nothing left to prepare. Last night, when I came home late, I slipped into the study and logged into Hakham's display desk with a forged version of his mastery-mark. Markmakers cannot change information in the archives, but record-keepers of sufficient rank can—so I used my uncle's access to find Dirak Tizzan's official record and erase the date of his death. I can only hope that no one will notice the discrepancy until Kophas is safely off the ship.

When I emerge from my room, I hear the murmur of my aunt and uncle's voices in the kitchen. As I enter, they both look up at me from their places at table. Hakham frowns darkly, one hand poised over his datascroll. Chervani sits across from him, her shoulders tense. Their plates of meat and fruit appear untouched.

"What's happened?" I ask.

My uncle's brow furrows. "You don't know?"

"It's something about the vandals, isn't it?" I did my best to put that trouble out of my mind last night.

"That's old news already," Hakham scoffs. "You didn't hear? The ship council let them go yesterday with only a fine to pay for the damaged studio." He sends me a baleful glance. "No shame-marks."

"Hakka, no." Kilmaya's prediction was right; once again, the guild's demands have been ignored. With a sinking heart, I take a seat at the table. "Why? How can they get away with that?"

"Because the guild is to blame for provoking them, obviously." Hakham's tone grates with sarcasm. "*We* are the ones unjustly withholding honor-marks."

"Of course." Bitterness seeps into my voice. With a pang, I remember the promise I made to Rinavi yesterday, that the guild would see justice done. Now the elderly artist will not even have that small comfort.

"Naturally, the guildmaster warned that he was prepared to pass even harsher measures against the faction if the ship council did not...reconsider their decision." My uncle clasps his hands together, eyes fixed on the tabletop. He seems to be weighing his words. "There have been...rumors...that he intends to place a total mark-ban on all Ascendance members."

Chervani shifts, her expression taut. My breath hisses as I suck in air through my teeth. Banning faction members from the studios entirely, cutting off their access to all marks—that would almost be equivalent to mass exile. "The guild wouldn't do that. They *can't* do that. I don't think they even have the authority."

"That hasn't stopped the rumors," Hakham growls. "And as if that weren't enough—" He gestures, disgusted, at the datascroll on the table. "Now Clan Trev'ban has released this absurd declaration."

"Declaration? About what?"

Chervani rubs a hand over her eyes, and I realize she has not yet said a word. When she finally speaks, her voice is subdued: "They say they are leaving the guild."

"Leaving?" I blink several times, mute with astonishment. "How? To do what?"

"To start their own, evidently." Hakham bares his teeth in disdain. "You would not believe—hakk, read it for yourself." He slides his datascroll across to me. Below the embellished spearhead design of the Trev'ban clan symbol, a long document fills the screen.

> *The council of Clan Trev'ban to the honorable people of the Akkano'dath:*
>
> *During these past months, Clan Trev'ban has looked on in distress as the guild of markmakers has issued restriction after restriction upon the courageous warriors of the Ascendance. For months, Clan Serix has heaped humiliation on the very people who are shedding their heart's blood to win back our ancestral home. Now they threaten all who bear the faction-mark, the sign of hope in the flesh for the future of the Noxxiin people.*
>
> *We of Clan Trev'ban have protested these unreasonable bans, but we have been unable to act—for the guild has long been governed not by merit, but merely by an old and failing bloodline. Clan Serix claims to act in the name of the law. But does not the law itself state that markmakers must remain impartial in their judgements, unbiased towards any clan or faction? Yet the guild has made clear its bias by its willingness to withhold merited marks from thousands of honorable Noxxiin. They would even cut off the youngest and most innocent children from the bond of the ancestors by refusing them clan-marks. The Serix claim to be the guardians of truth in the flesh, but they have revealed themselves to be only the guardians of their own ill-held power.*
>
> *For this reason, on this day, the eighth of Kaichilaal in the year 965 of the Wandering, the council of Clan Trev'ban declares independence from this sham of a guild. We will no longer play a part in their bans and threats of bans. We will return to the ancient artists' code of truth, merit, and honor. We will give justice once more to the Noxxiin people, and to our warriors who even now are fighting for our home soil...*

The document continues, but I have read enough. I raise my eyes from the screen to stare at Hakham. My limbs have gone cold. "This is insanity. There can't be more than one markmakers' guild."

"Of course not. It's rebellion. They are inviting war. And that is exactly what we will get if Mekkalluthak does not discipline them quickly."

I slump in my seat, feeling dazed. Yesterday a single studio was vandalized, and now we are talking of war? "What can he do at this point? If Clan Trev'ban does not acknowledge the guild's authority..."

Hakham snorts. "The guild still owns Rixarii Street. They have every right to go into the studios and confiscate supplies. The Trev'ban can't give marks without pens or ink."

I spread my hands in exasperation. "Will they even be able to get close to them? With all those Ascendance guards still patrolling the street?"

My uncle glances away. "I am sure the guild officials will have an armed escort as well."

His voice holds a note of trepidation. I do not have to ask why. The guild may have its own small security force, but its role is more ceremonial than practical. They are trained to fight, but they are not nearly as skilled as soldiers from warrior clans like Trechik or Tarriks. If serious violence breaks out, the guild escort will stand little chance against the Ascendance guards.

Hakham shakes his head and sighs. "The guards do not have the authority to interfere. The studios are guild property—if Clan Trev'ban refuses to follow the law, they have the right to evict them."

"And what if they do?" Chervani breaks in with unexpected vehemence. "Has no one thought of their clients?"

Hakham and I both turn to look at her. My aunt's face, ordinarily gentle, has hardened with anger. Deep lines crease the dark gray skin of her brow. "My laborers at the trallak farms. Most of them go to Clan Trev'ban for their marks. I know one girl who was to be married this month. And another man whose wife is about to have a child. They are not even Ascendance members. What will they do if their artists are thrown out on the street? Go markless, like exiles, until the guild and the council have finished their quarrel? How long will that take?"

Hakham scowls. "We are not preventing anyone from getting ordinary marks. Our own studios are still open—"

"You *know* the laborer clans cannot afford Serix prices," Chervani snaps. "And even if the guild agreed to lower them, we still would not have enough artists to serve all those people. Clan Trev'ban has twice as many markmakers as we do. If they leave, there will be thousands of clients who have nowhere to go."

Hakham only glowers. "Perhaps the Trev'ban council should have thought of that before writing this idiotic declaration." His chair grates against the floor as he pushes back from the table, stands, and stalks from the kitchen. I remain seated with Chervani, slightly taken aback. It has been a long time since I last saw my aunt and uncle argue in earnest.

After a brief silence, Chervani turns to me with a pained expression. "Are you going in today? People have already taken to the streets. Everyone is so angry..."

"I have to go." I hate to see her distraught, but I have no choice in this matter. "Unless the guild tells us otherwise."

She shuts her eyes for a moment and then lays a hand on my arm. Her fingers feel cold against my skin. "Be careful, Mariikel."

After a hurried breakfast, I collect my satchel, fasten my dagger to my belt, and head to Rixarii Street. The corridor is even more crowded than it was yesterday. Lines of clients—men, women, and even children—cluster at the entrance of every Trev'ban studio, trying to push their way inside. Other groups gather in the middle of the street, stamping and shouting rhythmically:

"Justice to our warriors! Down with the bans!"

"Stand with Trev'ban!"

"Aurorii—chi'ar! Aurorii—chi'ar!"

The rabble-rousers are mostly young people from laborer clans—farmers, mechanics, maintenance workers—and many of them are showing off the Ascendance marks on their chests. Tattoos gleam with the sheen of kiili oil, and an oppressive sweetness hangs in the air. The familiar perfume is jarring.

My limbs tense, and my hand drifts to the hilt of my dagger. Avoiding eye contact, I lower my head and begin threading my way through the throng. But I have hardly gone a dozen steps when someone appears in front of me, blocking my path.

"Hakka, Serix!" A heavyset laborer with a Tizzan clan-mark stands over me, fists clenched and nostrils wide. He wears only a sparring kilt, leaving his chest and his vivid faction-mark exposed. "Decided to show your face, skin-changer?"

My heart pounds, and my fingers curl around my satchel strap. Hearing a stranger call me skin-changer is unsettling, even though I know he only said it to provoke me. He has no idea that it is, in fact, the truth. "Please let me pass. I have no quarrel with you, Tizzan."

"I have one with *you*, painter. You'd keep our children unclanned, would you? Treat us all like filth?"

The man lunges forward. My hand darts out to block the blow. My fingers clamp around his wrist, and I jerk his arm upward, throwing off his balance.

The laborer stumbles, eyes wide—he did not anticipate the strength of my grip. Frankly, I am a little shocked as well. But the advantage only lasts for an instant. Snarling, the Tizzan tears his arm out of my grasp. Then he leans back, coiling one leg for a kick.

I am about to dodge and draw my dagger when another figure barges through the crowd towards my attacker. "Hands off!" It is one of the

Ascendance guards, a stern-faced Trechik woman. She grabs the laborer by the shoulder and pulls him away. "Respect to the markmaker."

The laborer bares his teeth in a snarl. "Are you lot defending them now, too?"

"I'm saving *your* skin, you fool." The woman shifts her feet into an aggressive stance, and her hand slips down to the holster of the small gun at her belt. "Do you know what the fine is for injuring a markmaker? I doubt you can afford it."

The Tizzan hisses. But his eyes are fixed on the guard's firearm. He backs off—though not before turning in my direction one last time. "Axdraa'dah take you." He spits on the floor between us. Hot moisture settles on my feet. Before I can react, the man leaps away and disappears into the milling, noisy mass of the crowd. The Trechik woman looks after him, her lower eyes squinted in distaste.

Slowly I rise from my defensive crouch. "Thank you," I stammer.

The woman turns her weary glare on me. The sigil of the Ascendance gleams dully on her breastplate. "Don't thank me, Serix. I am only trying to keep this rabble from turning into something worse. And your guild isn't helping."

The strain in her voice betrays some other emotion besides resentment—can it be fear? I blink, startled. It crosses my mind that the Ascendance guards might in fact be anxious to prevent more violence—if they cannot control the angry crowd, they will be blamed.

I release the hilt of my dagger and incline my head in a wary nod. "My thanks, anyway. Honor with you."

She does not return the expression. Instead she jerks her head, gesturing down the corridor. "You'd better go, painter. Don't make me rescue you again."

Several people nearby turn in our direction—my Serix clan-mark draws hostile stares. I duck past the guard and hurry down the packed hallway. The Ascendance war-cry still echoes from the crowd behind me.

"Aurorii—chi'ar! Aurorii—chi'ar!"

I reach Kilmaya's studio without further incident. There are fewer people here—the protesters have not ventured this far, and Serix workshops, once again, seem to be empty of clients. A barricade still stands around the ruin of Rinavi's studio. The debris has been cleared out of the street, but the crude painting of the faction-mark remains sprawled over the broken door, staining the wall with splotches of dark purple.

I tear my gaze away and approach our own studio. Kilmaya stands in the open doorway, looking out towards the shouting crowd. She greets me with a hooded glance. "I see you made it in one piece." Her glib words cannot hide the tension in her voice.

"Barely." My pulse still pounds, and my limbs begin to shake. I squeeze the strap of my satchel to steady myself. "Is the guild really going to confiscate the Trev'ban studios?"

"I don't know that they have another choice. They will have to do something—we cannot afford to show weakness now, with Clan Trev'ban in open rebellion. But sending guild guards into that mob..." She shakes her head. "I am not sure I would want to watch."

I gesture to the deserted portion of the corridor. "Another quiet day for us, I suppose?"

Kilmaya's eyes narrow in a humorless glare. "Let us hope it stays quiet."

The day drags on. By mid-afternoon, the number of protesters in the street has only increased, and they have started to spill over into the Serix section of the corridor as well. Ascendance members and Trev'ban clients mill about, still raising occasional chants and war-cries. For once, I am grateful for the Ascendance troops and their guns. But even if the guards are deterring violence, they do not disperse the people.

I sit on our porch, arms resting on my knees, watching the crowd. I prefer being out in the street to being cooped up in the studio; at least here I can see what is happening. Behind me, the door stands open, and I can hear Kilmaya, Narrik, and Rinavi discussing the latest reports from the guild.

"High Councilor Valo is stepping in. He's called for a negotiation."

"Between the guild and Clan Trev'ban? The High Council wants us to meet those oathbreakers on equal terms?"

"Has the guildmaster responded?"

"Not yet. He is stalling for time, most likely."

"Trev'ban axnakkan. Deep Sleep take them all."

Listening to the conversation, I feel my spirits sink even lower. I want to be home, or at Haza'ruux's house, or even in the Underbelly—anywhere I could escape from the guild, the faction, and this whole wretched conflict. As I watch the restive crowd in the corridor, I wonder if this is how Askko feels in the calm before battle. All at once I wish that my spirited, planet-strong cousin were beside me now. *But he would not be on your side,* I remind myself with a wrench of sadness. *He would be on theirs.*

I am about to go inside when a stir from the throng catches my attention. People move and murmur, looking towards something coming up the street from the sector gate. I climb to my feet for a better view. In the distance, the crowd makes way for a contingent of warriors—twenty or thirty of them, heavily armored, marching three abreast as they plow through the packed street.

My heart leaps into my throat. "Who is that?" I exclaim.

The conversation in the studio breaks off, and Kilmaya steps up beside me. "What's the matter, Mariikel?"

I nod towards the approaching warriors. The soldiers march at a rapid, measured pace, their heavy boots ringing against the floor. Unlike the other guards in the street, these warriors sport full battle gear: gleaming black breastplates, gauntlets and greaves, helmets that fit closely around their faces, revealing only their stern, unblinking eyes. They carry javelins and tall oval shields that swarm with sigils of strength, protection, and honor—and the angular, double-pronged clan symbol of Clan Tarriks.

"Tarriks elite," Kilmaya breathes. "A valk'taro's escort. Ancestors, what are they doing here?"

"More Ascendance?" Narrik joins us on the porch, his face rigid with alarm. Rinavi shuffles forward to peer outside as well.

Kilmaya narrows her eyes. "That's clan gear they're wearing, not the faction armor. Still..."

She does not have to finish her thought. Like all the warrior clans now, most Tarriks members are also Ascendance. But if these soldiers have faction-marks, they do not show them—and the swift, aggressive way they move through the crowd hints they are not friendly to the protesters, either.

About thirty paces away, the Tarriks troops halt. The man in the lead—a tall, maroon-skinned warrior with a slender sword belted at his waist—steps forward into the space the crowd has cleared. When he removes his helmet, I can see, even from this distance, the mastery-mark of a warband commander on his brow.

"I am Valk'taro Jal'thor of Clan Tarriks." The commander's harsh voice booms through the corridor; a hush falls over the crowd. "On behalf of the markmaker guild, my warriors are to take over the security of Rixarii Street."

A murmur of consternation rises from the throng. One or two nearby Ascendance guards shift their stances, staring at the Tarriks warriors. Clearly, they were not warned of this change in security.

"Jal'thor," I murmur in wonder. "I recognize his name—I have seen this man's face before, in the recordings I watched of Talorak's trial many months ago. Although an Ascendance commander, he was also one of the old trainer's close friends and supporters.

"You know him?" Kilmaya asks, her voice sharp with surprise.

"What? No." I falter for an instant. "I—the guildmaster mentioned him to me. He said he objected to the way the faction has been treating the guild."

"Mekkalluthak told you?" Kilmaya squints in skepticism, then glances out into the street again. Jal'thor pulls his sleek, embellished helmet back over his head. His black armor glints under the corridor lights. "Well, then. Someone is taking a stand for us, at last."

"Isn't he Ascendance?" Narrik hisses. "What in Ka's name is he doing?"

We watch, transfixed, as Jal'thor strides forward several paces, stopping in front of the barricade that surrounds Rinavi's ruined studio. For a moment, the commander glares at the Ascendance symbol splashed across the wall. His shoulders rise and fall, as if in a deep breath.

Of a sudden he whirls to face the apprehensive crowd. One armored foot slams on the floor with a clang. "Out!" he barks. "Hvoss'kan, clear this rabble. Secure the studios."

A rumble sweeps through the assembly—confusion, alarm. People back away from the Tarriks warriors, but here and there I spot someone sinking into a combat crouch, or placing a hand on a sheathed dagger. The Ascendance guards glance from Jal'thor to the angry crowd, as if unsure which side they ought to confront. All through the corridor, Serix artists peer out of their doorways, regarding the newly arrived warriors with amazement.

Slender fingers grasp my arm. I jump, but it is only Rinavi, steadying herself against me. "Did the guildmaster send for them?"

"If he did, I hope he knew what he was doing." Kilmaya does not take her eyes off the warriors. "They might have come of their own accord. Either way, they are risking much to be here."

"Do they have the authority for this?" Narrik mutters. "To send away the other guards?"

"Well, Jal'thor certainly outranks them all," Kilmaya replies. "But I doubt he is here with the permission of the faction."

Another surge of noise disturbs the crowd. One of the Ascendance guards pushes through the throng and approaches Jal'thor. It is the Trechik woman I met earlier today, the one who intervened between me and the angry laborer; apparently she holds some authority here. Now she scowls as she halts in front of Jal'thor, her stance tense and wary. "Valk'taro." She touches her clan-mark in deference, even as her glare betrays suspicion. "What is the meaning of this?"

Jal'thor's reply is too low for me to catch the words, but the way he stands over the Trechik woman makes it clear he has no intention of leaving. The conversation continues, inaudible. Around us, the crowd begins to murmur again, pressing closer to the contingent of Tarriks soldiers.

Kilmaya steps off the porch, maneuvering for a better view. Narrik follows her, and after a moment, Rinavi leaves my side to join them as well. Other Serix artists emerge from their doorways into the street. The stoic troop of

Tarriks warriors with their black armor and sigil-embellished shields carry no firearms—only javelins and short swords, daggers and throwing hatchets. Jal'thor's followers bear only honorable weapons. But more Ascendance guards push through the spectators, their hands resting on the guns at their belts.

A heaviness constricts my chest. I want to grasp Kilmaya's arm and pull her back into the shelter of the studio, but she would think me a coward.

Half a dozen Ascendance guards have gathered in the middle of the corridor, facing off with the Tarriks warband. Jal'thor and the Trechik leader are still talking, but the woman makes angry gestures towards the studios while Jal'thor's replies sound curt and harsh. Armor creaks as soldiers on both sides shift, almost imperceptibly, into defensive stances.

"Teacher?" I call.

If she hears me, she does not acknowledge it. Instead she remains standing beside Rinavi and Narrik, transfixed on the scene before us. The Trechik leader raises her voice, but Jal'thor does not back down. Meanwhile, the crowd's murmur increases to a dull roar:

"*What is he doing?*"

"*He has deserted the faction...*"

"*They are seizing the studios!*"

"Traitor! Traitor!"

The shout springs up, clear and passionate, from somewhere in the throng. The Tarriks warriors stir, teeth bared, heads swiveling as if to find the culprit. The Ascendance guards brace themselves, feet wide apart, hands hovering over the hilts of their short swords.

"Teacher?" I step forward and reach for her now. "Should we go inside?"

A cry rings out, and a clang like struck metal. At the same instant, one of the Tarriks warriors lifts his shield. Two Ascendance guards lunge forward. I hear the screech of armored boots against the floor, the slither of drawn blades. A woman's yell cuts through the noise—the Trechik leader, shrill with panic:

"*Stand down!*"

The soldiers collide.

The corridor erupts; the two opposing lines dissolve into a grappling mass of warriors. Behind them, the crowd surges forward, charging into the fray with fists or drawn daggers.

"Hold the studios! Aurorii chi'ar!"

A wall of people bears down on us. I do not think. I spring past Rinavi and Narrik to grab Kilmaya's arm.

And then I hear gunfire.

The blast rings out, so close and shattering that the sound vibrates in my ribs. Shrieks pierce the clamor. I shove my teacher through the doorway of the studio. Too surprised to resist, she stumbles and falls. I leap in after her, then turn to shut the door.

The street seethes with motion—a crush of bodies, a swell of screams, punctuated by the deafening bark of gunfire. Some protesters brandish weapons while others flee in terror. One brawny laborer, armed with a hatchet, scrambles out of the stampede and makes a dash for our studio porch. I cannot tell if he is attacking or seeking shelter—and I am not about to wait to find out. I slam my hand down on the entry pad.

The door hisses shut. I slump to my knees, panting. But Kilmaya scrambles up, her eyes wild. "Rinavi!" She lunges for the door.

"No!" Fiercely I grapple against her and block the way. "It's not safe."

She bares her teeth; spittle flecks my face as she tries to tear away. "Let go of me, Mariikel!"

I throw my weight forward, bearing her down to the floor. Then, gripping both her arms, I pin her against the side of the front desk. "Are you insane? They will tear you apart!"

She cries out; her face contorts with pain. All at once I am conscious of how hard my fingers are digging into her arms. With a start, I let go. Kilmaya crouches, cradling her wrist to her chest, staring at me in shock.

"I'm sorry," I gasp. "Did I hurt you?"

She does not answer. Outside, the sounds of the riot are already subsiding. I can still hear shouting, but not the crash of blades or the rattle of gunfire. Slowly, still blocking the doorway, I get up and palm the entry pad, then peer around the edge of the door.

The skirmish has broken up; it seems the Tarriks warband has won. I see an Ascendance guard on his knees, surrendering his firearm to Jal'thor—who promptly drops the weapon and spits on it. Other warriors subdue angry laborers, or help frightened people to their feet. Nearby, I spot Rinavi, leaning on the arm of a younger markmaker. The elderly artist appears stunned, but otherwise unharmed.

Thank the ancestors. I release a shaky breath. "Teacher, she's here. She's all right."

Kilmaya joins me in the doorway. To my surprise, she does not rush out into the corridor to greet her friend. Instead she stares in the opposite direction, her gaze fixed on a cluster of Tarriks warriors who bend over a body sprawled on the floor. When one soldier stands to bark an order, I glimpse the blue-and-white tunic of a Serix markmaker, stained with violet blood. And I recognize the honor-marks adorning one limp, outflung arm.

Narrik.

My teacher sobs. "Oh, Ka." She buries her face in her hands.

CHAPTER TWENTY-THREE

An hour later, Mekkalluthak summons the artists of Clan Serix to an emergency assembly.

The guild hall is crowded and hot. I am alone; Kilmaya left to take Rinavi home. I sit with my head in my hands, my eyes closed. Around me, people speculate and argue. Some say that a civilian, one of the protesters, threw something at the Tarriks warriors—a dagger or a piece of debris. Others insist it was the Ascendance guards who moved first. I find I do not care to know how the riot started. It ended with more studios damaged, several civilians injured—and Narrik Serix dead, with a stray Ascendance bullet in his back.

I cannot unsee the older artist's body, bloodied and broken as Jal'thor's warriors lifted it from the corridor floor. I did not know Narrik well, nor even particularly like him. But he was still my teacher's friend, a fellow artist, and a clanmate. My blood-kin. In my mind I keep replaying the first few moments of the riot—the clash of weapons, the surge of the crowd, my fingers closing around Kilmaya's arm as I snatched her out of harm's way. Could I have pulled Narrik to safety, too? The memory is already a blur.

When the auditorium falls suddenly quiet, I know that Mekkalluthak has entered. I raise my head. On the floor below, the guildmaster steps onto the speaker's dais, his eyes narrowed in restrained fury. His chest swells with a breath.

"Markmakers of Serix!"

His voice splinters the silence. The whole crowd seems to shudder.

"If any of you, before today, had doubts about the intentions of the Ascendance, let your eyes be opened now. You have seen the truth. You have seen Serix blood spilled on Serix ground!"

The assembly roars. The suffocating air rings with shouts of rage.

"They have kept soldiers in our street, carrying dangerous and dishonorable weapons. They have terrorized our clients and choked our business. They have allowed our studios to be destroyed and refused to punish those responsible. And today—today, in the street that should be most inviolate, they have slain an artist. They have laid hands on our blood-kin!"

Another cry of fury from the crowd. In the seats near me, I can hear someone weeping.

Mekkalluthak clenches his hands at his sides. "The faction must be held responsible. If they had withdrawn their troops weeks ago, as we requested—if they had controlled the crowds and kept the peace, as they claimed they would—if they had not been carrying cowards' weapons, unfit for true warriors—our clan-brother Narrik would still be among us. But as it is—" the guildmaster pauses, surveying his audience with a glare. "As it is, the Ascendance have proven themselves faithless at every turn. We demand justice: justice for our dead, for the trampling of our ancient rights. The people responsible for this violence, warriors and laborers alike, must be arrested and brought to trial."

"*Mark-stripped!*" a maddened voice shouts. "*Strip them!*"

Like a warcry, other artists take up the words. In moments, the whole hall is shouting. I shrink in my seat, my skin tingling. I have never been in a roomful of people clamoring for blood.

Mekkalluthak raises both hands for silence. "We will have justice. I swear, we will have justice."

Slowly, the noise ebbs. The guildmaster lowers his arms. He breathes deeply for several moments before speaking again.

"We have tried every legal recourse to discourage the faction from this path. But they are no longer interested in law, or the honor-code, or truth in the flesh. Even the High Councilor himself, instead of defending the rights of the guild as is his duty, demands that we negotiate with the dissidents of Clan Trev'ban, who have broken their oaths and turned their backs on the craft of our ancestors."

Another rumble of anger rises at the mention of Clan Trev'ban. Was it only this morning that they declared their secession from the guild? It seems an age ago. I wonder, suddenly, if there were any Trev'ban artists who were as horrified by the announcement as I was—markmakers who only wished to ply their craft and serve their clients, who had no desire to be caught up in this sickening squabble. What would I do if I were Trev'ban, and I found myself forced to choose between allegiance to the guild and loyalty to my own clan?

Faction cannot come before blood-kin...

"The truth has now become brutally clear." Mekkalluthak raises his voice over the muttering assembly. "The Ascendance wants marks for their own ends, regardless of honor or shame." With one fist, he strikes his own chest. "They will not rest until every artist on this ship submits to a faction-mark!"

Another long cry bursts from the crowd. I cover my face again.

"We are in a grave position. It requires grave action. For the time being, Rixarii Street is secure—Valk'taro Jal'thor and his warriors, who courageously came to our aid today, have agreed to remain and guard our sector until the conflict with the faction is resolved. But it is clear, after today, that even this may not be enough to deter violence." He bows his head for a moment. "So it is with great regret that I announce a temporary suspension of studio work. Until our grievances have been addressed, we will not give marks to Ascendance members—or anyone else. The studios will be closed."

A hubbub of disbelief, dismay. Mekkalluthak waits for it to subside. "I cannot risk you artists," he says firmly. "Your knowledge, your honor, the skill of your hands: *you* are the heart-treasure of this clan. I am grateful for your valor, your willingness to stand for the truth—but we need you alive."

I pay no attention to the guildmaster's praise. *He is banning every mark, for everyone, until the faction listens.* I should be horrified, but instead I feel only a cowardly sense of relief. I can stay home until this whole wretched conflict is over.

Mekkalluthak goes on, his tone driving and relentless. "The length of this suspension depends entirely upon the High Council. Valo T'sarek has neglected his oath to guard the law, standing by idly while we have suffered violence and indignity. Now we give him a final chance to make amends. The guild councilors and I have submitted a formal demand: if the High Council does not give us justice, we will call on all the clans of the Fleet to consider whether Valo T'sarek is fit to rule at all."

Exclamations of shock. Murmurs surge up around me.

"*An assembly of the clans?*"

"*Deposing the High Councilor?*"

"*But the war...the planets...*"

"This is no treason or rebellion." The guildmaster raises his hands. "There are measures in our law against the tyranny of factions. And yes, I will dare to say it: we are living under a tyrannical faction now. If their desires were honorable, why would they need to persecute the clan that keeps the truth?

"The Ascendance claims that we are sowing division at a time when we most need unity. But it is *they* who have broken the peace between clans by rejecting the way of the ancestors. If we allow our people to continue down this path, we will destroy ourselves long before the half-sights can. How can our warriors fight with falsehood in their flesh? How can we live under sunlight if we are living lies? If we take the planets but lose our honor, we have gained *nothing.*"

His voice drops to a hiss of fury. In the face of his wrath, the assembly trembles. But I only hear his powerful, grating tone, and see the grandeur of his figure: slender but violet-skinned, the color of glory and blood. A terrifying thought drifts into my mind.

This man could make us do anything. We would follow him into Axdraa'dah.

On the floor, Mekkalluthak says a few closing words before stepping off the dais. But I do not hear him. My body is rigid. I feel I am staring out over the edge of some abyss—an abyss I have been approaching for a long time, but which I have denied until now. The words that come back to haunt me are my own, flung at my soldier cousin in a moment of anger:

War! Do you think of nothing else?

In a daze, I look around at the assembled artists. We are not fighters. We have no real weapons—but a terrible conviction seizes me.

We are all at war now.

I rise from my seat and stumble through the crowd to make my escape.

I return to the studios only to retrieve my satchel. Then, in the dimming lamplight of evening, I go to the Underbelly.

I am glad, now, that I discovered my alternate route through the maintenance shafts. There is no way I could show my face outside the Serix sector today. All the same, I hope this will be my last journey to the Underbelly for a long time—perhaps forever. I want to put my crimes behind me. I want to rest.

I descend the maze of maintenance tunnels, climb down the ladders in the foul-smelling dark, and set foot among the slums of the exiles. Condensation drips from the beams. The rank chill seeps through the rough fabric of my laborer's tunic. Shrieks echo from an alleyway where two half-grown boys fight over a scrap of food, kicking and clawing at each other like beasts. At the foot of a pillar, an old woman in a threadbare cloak lies shivering, her stare vacant and corpselike.

I wend my way between the shelters, feeling detached and appalled. Is it possible I have grown *used* to this? Fear, bloodshed, disease, death: these things are ordinary in the Underbelly. The quarrels of guild and faction would seem petty to these people, incomprehensible. Mekkalluthak complained of the persecutions Clan Serix has suffered—but even the violence today in Rixarii Street hardly compares to the everyday brutality of an exile's life. These people live in the shadow of the Deep Sleep. They know the gnawing, wordless sound of his voice; they bear his sign in their flesh, pale and sinuous, clinging to their bodies like a parasite...

Like the mark chiseled into the ceiling in Haza'ruux's hidden room. The memory shoots a chill down my spine. I nearly stumble over a heap of scrap in the cramped alleyway. I catch myself against the wall of a shack, breathing hard.

Why would the mad markmaker have the symbol of exile carved into his secret shrine? I still have no idea—I have not let myself think about it. But I feel that mark is haunting me, twining invisibly around my own throat, dragging me towards a fate I do not want or understand.

Pull yourself together. I stand upright, wiping grime off my gloved hand. I need to focus. Kophas needs me to focus. I cannot fail him.

I thrust Haza'ruux out of my thoughts and resume my trek through the slums. An exile shuffles past, brushing against me in the narrow street, but I keep my eyes lowered. I do not want to see his mark.

When I reach Kophas's shelter, I find him awake and alert. He leans forward eagerly, blinking in the glare of my lamp as I enter. "Markmaker. Thank the ancestors. You have the clothing?"

"Yes." I find myself smiling. I do not think I have ever been so glad to see him. I sit down on the floor and pull the extra tunic out of my bag. "It's a little worn, but it should help you pass unnoticed. I'm sorry I didn't have any sandals that would fit you. You'll have to use your own for a while longer."

He nods and accepts the folded tunic. "I'll manage. Thank you."

"I also brought this." I reach into my satchel again and retrieve the pouch of money. The coins inside clack softly as I drop it into his hands.

His four eyes widen. "How much is this?"

"Five hundred os'tekta."

"I can't take this from you." He looks mortified. "You've done so much already."

"You'll need it," I insist.

"But I can't repay this—"

"You never could."

He blinks, his pride still smarting. But at last he sighs. "Very well." Then, putting the money aside, he regards me with a searching expression. "Who *are* you, markmaker?"

"My name is not important." I fasten the straps of my satchel, avoiding his gaze. "It is safer if you don't know."

"I didn't mean that. I didn't want to question you before. But now…" He looks down at his arms, at the tattoos that are not his own. "You're not what

I imagined a skin-changer would be. You don't want money. You don't want anything." His eyes burn with bewilderment. "Why do you do this?"

I hold my breath. He has trusted me with his life—he deserves the truth.

"I knew someone who was unjustly exiled. A Tarriks warrior, like you. I came here looking for him. I never found him, but..." My voice fades.

Kophas gazes at me with wonder. "That's why you serve the exiles? For his sake?"

Unable to speak, I lower my head.

"Heart's blood." In the glow of the lamplight, his face his grave. "You are a brave man."

I say nothing. Instead I exhale and shake off my discomfiture. "In any case—it's done. You're free to go."

Kophas grips my arm. I flinch, but he holds on. "You don't have to worry. If I am caught—"

"You won't be caught. Your marks are as good as real. I've altered the records, too. Even if they check you at the docks, they shouldn't stop you." I pause, realizing that my outburst was more for my own reassurance than his. "You won't be caught."

His grip eases. "I was going to say—if I am caught, I won't betray you." He lets go of my arm and places two fingers on the side of his neck. "By my ancestors' blood, I swear it."

I wince, wondering about the validity of an oath sworn on a false clan-mark. But I decide not to remind him. He is sincere, and for that I am grateful. "Thank you."

For a moment we sit in silence. Kophas stirs. "This is farewell, then."

"Yes." But I am reluctant to leave. "Be careful when you go up. There's unrest on the ship right now. The markmaker guild..." I break off. "What are you doing?"

Kophas bows down, stretching himself on the filthy floor. Reverently, he grasps my ankles and touches his forehead to my feet.

"No. Hakk, no. Please don't." I pull away. I endure gestures of homage from the other exiles because they do not truly know me. But Kophas is like a friend now.

The young warrior lets go and raises his face. "When I kneel on the soil of our ancestors, I will remember you, markmaker."

I clench my teeth, restraining the cry that throbs in my throat. "You will be there before I am."

He gets up, blinks, and collects himself. "Honor with you, then."

"And with you. I wish you many more honor-marks—real ones. Farewell, Kophas Tarriks." I rise, tear myself away, and duck out of the shelter.

For a few minutes I wander down the alleys, hardly noticing where I am going. The air vibrates with the rumble of machinery; my sandals squelch in puddles of filth. I am dizzy with relief—Kophas is free. I have kept my promise. And yet I feel unspeakably sad.

When at last I reach the route leading up to the maintenance shafts, I grasp the rusty ladder and halt. I rest my forehead against a cold rung. My legs buckle. I squeeze the bars until my fingers ache.

Oh, Talorak. Forgive me. It should have been you.

I lean against the ladder, weeping softly. My muffled cries echo in the darkness. Then, somewhere behind me, a footstep scrapes against metal. I raise my head. Several feet away, a ragged figure stands huddled against a pillar. In the poor light, I cannot see the exile's face. This outcast must have followed me, hoping to ask for a mark. Guilt pricks at my conscience—I have not served anyone here besides Kophas for weeks.

I smooth a hand over the thin fabric of my mask, trying to salvage my composure. "Can I help you?"

"Markmaker." A woman's voice—young, but hard and bitter. Slowly she leaves the shelter of the pillar. She wears a frayed shawl that covers most of her face and carries a bundle bound to her chest. I glimpse the smooth curve of a tiny head: a baby.

My tension eases. This, at least, I can do. "Do you need a clan-mark?"

"No. You gave him one already."

"I did?" I glance at the woman more closely. I can only see the glitter of her eyes under her shawl. "Have I served you before?"

"You don't remember?"

She does sound familiar. But I have seen many desperate young mothers in the Underbelly. "I'm sorry..."

With one hand, she draws back her head covering. Her skin is black, her features hunger-sharp. "Lakkia," she says. "I am Lakkia Penthar."

Of course, I remember her now: I gave a mark to her infant son on the same night that I first met Kophas. I have thought about her, too, since then—more than once. But I did not ever expect to see her again. "Yes. Yes, I remember you. What can I do for you?"

"I—" She breaks off. She seems to struggle with a bout of shame or anger. Then: "I need your help."

I brace myself for her request—food and water, or medicine for her child. It is not the first time an exile has asked me for supplies. I usually refuse; if I were to start giving away rations to everyone, I would soon be overwhelmed. But for this woman, in this moment, I pause. "What do you need?"

Again she hesitates. In the sling, her infant snuffles; she hugs him closer. "I want to change my marks."

"What?" I step back. "No! I don't do that."

"You're doing it for that warrior."

How did you find out? I nearly say the words aloud, but think better of it. I should have known that rumors would spread no matter how I tried to be discreet. Irritation rises in my gut; my palms grow hot. "It's too dangerous. He was willing to take the risks—but he only had himself to care for. I can't do it for you. Not with your child."

She gazes at me with muted fury. Silence stretches between us, disturbed by the distant clang and rumble of machines. Softly, she says, "You want him to die here?"

"No." I restrain a groan. "But there are some things I cannot do."

For a long moment, she falls quiet. "If you won't change my marks, will you at least take him with you?"

I frown. "What?"

"Out of the Underbelly." Her voice tremors. "He only has a clan-mark. You wouldn't need to erase anything."

"What do you mean? I can't raise him."

"But someone could. If you could find someone…"

My mind reels; I grip the ladder again to steady myself. Find a Penthar family who would be willing to adopt the child of an exile? Would it even be possible? Clan Penthar are farmers—Chervani might know someone. But even then, it would have to be done in secret. If anyone discovered the truth…

What am I thinking?

"No!" I turn vehemently on Lakkia. "I can't."

"Why not?" Her eyes remain slitted and stubborn, but her jaw trembles.

"I simply can't. I'm sorry."

Her face grows slack. She stands cradling her child. "Why do you come here? Do you think your inks are enough for us, markmaker?"

Anguish unfolds in my chest. *No, Lakkia. They have never been enough.* "I do what I can."

She stares at me. Her eyes are four dark pools of reproach. "Axariix."

Coward. I inhale sharply; air hisses through my teeth. "Please go."

Lakkia does not move.

I step forward. "Go! Get out of here. I can't help you."

Without a word, she turns and walks away into the shadows. I stand, breathing heavily, listening to the shuffle of her bare feet against the hard and filthy floor. Then she is gone.

What is wrong with me? I have never raised my voice at an exile before. All at once, I cry out savagely and slam my fist against a nearby pillar. Pain spasms through my hand, but I do not care. I lean against the ladder again. I breathe the cold, damp air and listen to the vague roar of the forges far above. I stand that way for a long time.

CHAPTER TWENTY-FOUR

The trek back up to the Serix sector leaves me little strength for sadness. By the time I reach the exit of the maintenance shaft, I have managed to put Lakkia and her baby out of my mind. My great task of forgery is over. Kophas's fate is out of my hands now. I do not have to return to the Underbelly ever again, if I so choose.

I stop at the shaft door to listen and make sure no one is standing in the hallway beyond. All is quiet. I ease the door open and slip out into the storage space. Behind the crates, I change out of my disguise. Then I walk out into the dark plaza. A few warm lights shine from the houses; the painted doors glow with color. In the fountain, water laps softly.

I gaze up at the stars projected across the dome overhead. Soon enough, Kophas will be looking up at the real stars, with his feet on the surface of a planet. And all my toil will have meant something.

A hiss breaks the quiet. "Flashing Blade."

I cry out. In the hallway across from me, a figure emerges from the shadows. Even as I fumble for my dagger, I realize who it is. "Haza'ruux. Oh, Ka. It's you."

He stalks across the plaza and stands before me. I stare at him, still shaking. *Was he waiting for me here?* That is a terrifying thought. I did not even know he had returned home.

He regards me through narrowed eyes. "Where have you been?"

I stutter like an idiot. Of course, Haza'ruux knows about my work in the Underbelly. But I have never told him about Kophas or my scheme to help him escape.

"Two days you have not come," he says. "What is keeping you? We have work."

Then I realize he is not talking about the Underbelly at all. He's talking about our lessons. Some of my courage returns—and with it, a flood of indignation. "Where have I been? Where have *I* been? What about you? I cannot help it if *you* disappear."

He scowls. "Haza'ruux has been home for two days."

"Do you even know what has happened in the past two days?" I whisper—I do not want to disturb the people in the houses nearby—but my voice quivers with anger. "There are riots at the studios. One of our artists has been killed. Our clan is on the brink of defying the High Council." I jab a finger at my own chest. "I've had other worries besides your old books!"

He receives my outburst in silence. After a moment, he says, "You will come in the morning."

"No. I won't." I plant my feet wide apart in a fighting stance. "I'm sick of your games, old man. What is all this about? What do you want from me?"

He says nothing, only gazes solemnly into my face. His calm is infuriating.

"I have been coming for weeks, asking no questions, reading your old stories." I clench my fist and raise my right arm. "Why haven't you told me the meaning of my mark? And why does the guildmaster keep asking me about it?"

Haza'ruux's brow lowers. "What have you told him?"

"Nothing! But only because I know nothing. Who *are* you? You and your books—and your wooden room—" I falter. I did not mean to mention the hidden chamber under his studio. But the old hermit does not react with anger or surprise.

"Hakka. You have been in the dreaming-room, then?"

Is that what he calls it? An inexplicable chill grips me. "I'm sorry. I didn't mean to intrude. You weren't home—"

"Do not fear." He waves a hand. "Haza'ruux meant for you to see it." He fixes me with one of his fierce, burning looks. "You want to know the meaning of your mark?"

"I—" The directness of his question astounds me. "Yes. Of course."

"Come, then." Swiftly he turns and strides towards his own house.

Astonished, I follow. Could it be that he is going to give me a straight answer, for once? Yet I feel disquieted. What could my mark have to do with that strange wooden room and its unsettling carvings?

I'm not sure I want to know. But it seems I am about to find out.

We pass through the unkempt garden; leaves and vines rustle under our feet. The old hermit opens the door and steps into the front room. He does not sing to himself or call to his pets, but instead goes straight into his studio and turns up the lights. The huge worktable still stands against one wall. In the middle of the floor, the trap door lies open. Involuntarily, I halt on the threshold, gazing at the hatch with dread.

Haza'ruux does not seem to notice my hesitation. From one of the shelves, he pulls down a slim book with a polished, dark cover. Then he points to a rack of his antique pens. "Bring one of those. And ink."

I draw a quick breath. Haza'ruux has never allowed me to touch his mark-making supplies before. Then the rest of his words register in my mind. "Bring them? Where are we going?"

He walks over to the open hatch and steps down onto the ladder.

Fear dispels my momentary eagerness. I grip the doorframe. "Can't we do it here?"

Haza'ruux only frowns. "You will understand better in the dreaming-room." Then he climbs down and disappears.

I remain standing in the doorway. I do not want to go back into that oppressive, ancient little room with its uncanny carvings. But I tell myself this is merely another of the old man's whims. I can endure it, if it means learning the truth about my mark.

I set down my satchel by the door. Then I step over to the shelves and take down a bottle of black ink. Finally, I choose a pen from the rack. The pale bone shaft is elaborately carved, the tip chiseled out of a real burrik's tooth. The tool feels light, but also sturdy and well balanced. I wonder how old it is.

I turn away from the shelf and approach the trap door. Even standing on the edge of it, I catch a whiff of the room's smoky aroma. Then, holding both pen and ink in one hand, I turn around and descend the ladder.

When I reach the floor, I find Haza'ruux standing in the central area of the chamber; the book he brought lies at his feet. He takes the pen and ink bottle from my hands, then nods up at the hatch. "Shut the door."

My body grows rigid. "I would rather leave it open."

"Do you want to learn from Haza'ruux or not?"

I swallow my groan. *What am I doing?* With slow movements, I ascend the ladder and reach up to grip the handle on the underside of the hatch. Then I pull it closed. The light from the studio above vanishes, leaving only the dim reddish glow of the dreaming-room's lamps. I feel as if I have cut myself off from the realm of the living.

Haza'ruux now sits cross-legged in the middle of the room, underneath the carving that eerily resembles an exile-mark. The book lies open on the floor before him. "Come," he says. "Sit."

I obey. I do not want to look at the engravings around me, so instead I fix my eyes on the book. The pages, to my surprise, are empty.

Haza'ruux regards me with a grave expression. "Have you tried to read your mark, Flashing Blade?"

"Yes. I've seen my name-sigil and a few other signs. But I can't—I can't make any sense out of them."

"I will help you. Give me your arm."

I realize I am holding my right arm cradled against my chest, as if guarding a wound. I glance up at Haza'ruux. His gaze is steady, calm and piercingly clear. I realize he knows how afraid I am. He has always known. Even before I wandered into his garden on that first night, heartsick as a lost child, he recognized my pain.

Kesh, little Flashing Blade. Haza'ruux has found you now. He will not harm you.

Gradually I extend my hand. "Teacher," I whisper. It is the first time I have called him by that title. "Show me where it starts."

He reaches out and touches a spot on my wrist where a complex, swooping sigil nests in a ring of twisting lines. "Here," he says.

And we begin.

For the next hour, I forget the world outside of the ancient dreaming-room. I forget the violence I witnessed in Rixarii Street this morning; I forget Mekkalluthak's threat to rebel against the Ascendance. I even forget, for a while, that I am a skin-changer. In this moment, only the ancient sigils matter—their grace and nuance, the visible music of pen-strokes.

One by one, Haza'ruux shows me how to distinguish the tangled symbols. I copy them individually into the blank book with pen and ink. His tools are a delight to use—sturdy in the hand yet perfectly balanced, so that the flow of ink on the page feels as effortless as thought. I have never written on true paper before, but it seems so natural that I soon cease to notice the novelty.

I refocus on the symbols. Even with my rudimentary knowledge of the ancestors' script, I can tell that taking the sigils apart like this destroys much of the poetry's subtlety. This mark was made by a master, and it is meant to be read by one. But I do not have the eye for such complexity. I wonder if I ever will.

When I finish copying out the sigils in neat rows, Haza'ruux turns to the next blank page in the book. "Now write the meaning."

I blink slowly. My writing hand aches, and I feel exhausted. So much has happened today—and now I must translate the most complicated piece of archaic poetry that I have ever seen? But I do not complain. From some deep well of strength, I summon the energy. I put the pen to paper once more.

Line by line, the poem unfolds before me. Haza'ruux helps when I need it, but for the most part he remains quiet. He seems to be watching me more closely than the text. The parchment fills up with writing: ordinary marks, clumsier and less eloquent than the ancient ones. But the narrative they tell is stranger and more haunting than any fable or myth I have ever read:

In the garden of the Place of Dreams
The Keeper roamed, howling.
Long and lonely he sang, but no creature called back to him,

Neither beast, nor bird, nor creeping thing:
The garden lay empty.
In the twilight, before the star-rising,
The Keeper, weary of wandering and singing in vain,
Crossed over a mountain, and looked on the valley below.
Bare stone it was, and metal, and nothing grew there,
Neither fragrant kriar, nor fruitful yekri.
The valley was full of Noxxiin Aurorii—
The Children of the Stars—
But they saw no stars now.
They stood, men, women, and children, without speaking,
All clans, all ranks, all ages,
And in their flesh, their marks bled like open wounds.
Rich violet staining the skin, soaking the ground,
Racing in rivulets down to the bowl of the valley.
And the blood filled the valley, and made a great sea,
Ever-growing, washing against the rock.
The blood-sea swallowed the people, one by one,
Elders and infants, warriors and craftsmen alike.

On the mountain, the Keeper raged and screamed his sorrow.
But even as he howled, and ground his teeth,
He gazed again out across the valley.
On a far ridge stood a man with silver skin.
And he, too, bore marks that poured blood.
But his eyes shone,
And he wept aloud as he watched his people drown.
Then he stepped down from his mountain, into the sea.
The blood covered his feet, and his knees, and then his chest,
And still he waded deeper, until it swallowed him.
Down into the reeking sea, the Silver One walked.
The blood did not choke his throat, nor blind his eyes:
He could see through it.

In the deepest part of the sea, he paused,
And a great abyss opened at his feet:
The gate of Axdraa'dah, the Place of No Dreams.
Darker than all color the chasm stood,
Pouring out the mist of pain and forgetting.
Yet the Silver One did not halt.
He stepped forward and plunged into the chasm,

And fell for a thousand days,
His bright body cleaving the darkness, a blade of light.

At last he came to rest in a silent place,
A black plain, unending, heaped with bodies:
Men and women and children, lifeless, markless.
The Silver One stood among them.
He still wore his marks like wounds, and still they bled,
Rich, burning violet running down the skin.
He bent down and touched the bare corpses,
And on the throat of each man, woman, and child,
He painted a sign in his own blood.
Each body that he marked began to breathe,
And though they did not wake, they dreamed.

The Place of No Dreams shuddered at this music.
Out of the plain, a towering figure rose.
His skin shone white and empty, like polished bone,
And his eyes glowed with the color of oblivion.
The Deep Sleep looked down at the Silver One,
And said in his un-voice, in soundless words:
"Who are you, then, you skin-changer?
You dare give signs to the children of Axdraa'dah?"
And the Silver One replied:
"These are your people no longer. You have no claim.
They bear my mark now, the blood of Flashing Blade."

The Deep Sleep roared, laughing his noteless laugh,
And he reached out
To strip Flashing Blade's marks, to end his life.
But when he touched the bright body,
The violet blood flowed over his bone-white hand,
And stained his empty skin.
The Unmarked One, the Chief of the Undreaming Realm,
Opened his mouth and screamed.
The sound shook the great chasm of Axdraa'dah,
And stirred the dreaming people—men, women, and children—
And they awoke.

After I trace the final sigil, I set down my pen on the wooden floor. For a long moment, I stare at the page, and then at the swirling tattoo on my arm.

My hand trembles. "What is this?" My voice is so dry, the words come out as a croak.

"It is my dream."

"Your dream?"

"I saw you," he rasps. "Long before you came to me, I saw you in this dream."

I shake my head. The images of the poem, lurid as a nightmare, linger in my mind. "What in Ka's name are you talking about?"

"Do you remember nothing? You have read of this. The Keeper of the Arimaas can walk in dreams and see the truth of hearts."

Ice settles in my veins. "Haza'ruux." I struggle to keep my voice level. "The Arimaas is only a story."

He shuts three eyes. A crooked smile breaks across his face. "Then Haza'ruux is only a story." He gets up from the floor and pulls at his shabby tunic.

"What are you doing?"

He pays me no attention. Slowly he tugs off the tunic and stands before me, wearing only a light kilt. His torso is thin and wiry—surprisingly athletic, for as old as he must be. Tattoos encase his chest and stomach, so dense that I cannot even tell the color of the skin underneath. But the lines are not merely sigils. In the center of his chest, the patterns coalesce into an image: a lean, four-legged beast, crouching with bared teeth and wild eyes—a raving war-hound.

Mad Dog.

It is the same dog-figure that I saw carved on the wall in this room, only more elaborate, more lifelike, more terrifyingly beautiful. Then I look closer. On the war-hound's forehead, blazing in pale ink like a deformed star, is the uncanny sigil. It is identical to the symbol etched into the ceiling, the one that looks like the exile-mark, with its sweeping, entangling limbs.

I yell and scramble to my feet, backing away. I stumble against the pillars behind me. "What—what is this?"

Haza'ruux places his hands on his chest. "The marks do not lie. You have four eyes, Flashing Blade. Do not close them to the truth."

"You're mad."

He laughs. "You wanted to understand, yes? The Arimaas is true. Clan Sko'larik was real. So were their marks of power."

"That's not possible."

His brow lowers. "Haza'ruux will show you what is possible."

Spreading his feet in a warrior's stance, he closes his eyes and draws a deep breath. Then, on his chest, the mark of the war-hound begins to glow. It is not the faint, silvery phosphorescence of a deepcrafter's tattoo. An intense, violet-white radiance pours from his skin, flooding the dim chamber with light. Every carving in the wooden walls stands out in stark relief. Then Haza'ruux bares his teeth. A guttural, bone-chilling snarl rips the air—a sound no Noxxiin should be able to make.

The radiance pulses through Haza'ruux's web of tattoos, spreading from his chest to the rest of his body. Then the brightness seems to lift from his skin, encasing him in a blinding shroud of light. The shroud resolves into a shape: a glowing, shaggy body, a blunt and beastly head, gaping jaws, and two eyes burning like the deep fire of the stars.

My limbs feel like water. I sink to my knees. Through the translucent, beastly shroud, I can still see the old markmaker's face. He looks ecstatic, as if possessed by some fierce and unspeakable joy.

I cover my eyes and bow my head to the floor. Even when the brilliance fades, I remain prostrate, trembling. After a minute, I hear his feet—his natural feet—shuffling towards me. I flinch away. "Don't touch me."

He halts. I stagger up and back away from him. His marks are dull again, the beastly tattoo still visible, but shadowy now in the reddish lamplight. Sadness lingers in his eyes. He looks old and weary.

"You're a deepcrafter," I whisper.

Vehemently he shakes his head. "I am a Keeper. The Arimaas needs no machines in the flesh like the Van'shorii have. The rite of the Keepers is pure."

"I don't understand. How is that possible?"

"You do not need to understand how. Only know that the Arimaas is true. It was not lost when Clan Sko'larik was destroyed. The honorable Keepers went into hiding and preserved the rites—even as their own mark became a sign of shame among the clans."

He touches the pale, twining sigil on his chest. I feel a settling sensation in my own body—as if some missing shard of a thought has drifted, at last, into place.

"You have wondered about this sign, yes?" A bitter smile stirs his lips. "You know it as the mark of exile. But in truth, it is the sign of the Keepers."

"That can't be. I never saw that mark in your books. You never taught it to me."

"Not true." He picks up the pen and open book from the floor where I abandoned them. Then he places the book between us and crouches down, turns to another blank page. "You know the parts, Flashing Blade, but you have not seen the whole."

Haza'ruux begins tracing an archaic sigil on the parchment: a single, sinuous line that doubles back on itself. "The order." He starts a new line, curving downwards from the first. "Of the bearers." With smooth strokes he adds yet another upswept branch. "Of the gift." He adds two tiny crossbars to the central line. "Of the Arimaas."

I watch through a haze of incredulity. The four sigils have fused into that awful whole, unfolding like a flower both alien and familiar. I can see the meaning now. But I still do not want to believe it.

Haza'ruux sets down the pen. "When the deepcrafters came to power, they hunted down all who bore this mark. In time, it became the sign of banishment for any who were cast out of the clans. People forgot the truth of the Arimaas, forgot what this mark had meant before." His brow creases in a brief, pained expression. "Even our clan, the blood-kin of Sko'larik, have forgotten."

"Blood-kin?" My voice rings hollow.

"Of course." The old man sends me a penetrating glance, as if to say, *Have you learned nothing?* "The Sko'larik did not die out, though they were forced to renounce their name. Their descendants established a new clan of markmakers." In a reverent gesture, he brushes two fingers against the side of his neck. "They called themselves Serix—'true blood,' in the ancient tongue."

Truth in the flesh. Cold dread washes over me. *We are the children of Sko'larik?* I want to deny his insane tale. But I find I can say nothing.

Haza'ruux goes on: "When our people built the Fleet and left the home planets, the Keepers came with them." With a wave of his arm, he indicates the animal carvings on the walls. "Every artist who has lived in this house has borne a mark of power."

"The mad markmakers…"

"That is what others call us—as it must be, to keep the marks safe. The true heritage of Clan Serix—it does not lie with guilds or councils. It lies with *us*, the Keepers. With the Arimaas."

My vision swims. I want to run. I want to leave this horrible room, this nightmare, and never return. But I cannot move because of the question burning on my heart. "Why are you telling me this?"

"In times past, there were three people who were allowed to know the truth of the Arimaas. The Keeper, the Keeper's apprentice, and the chieftain of the clan."

Horror prickles my skin. All at once, I have a vision of myself as an old and withered hermit, covered in cryptic tattoos, singing nonsense songs while tending an unruly garden. It is not the first time that fear has crossed my mind—but the full truth of the mad markmakers' craft is more terrible than I ever dreamed. *No. Oh Ka, no.* I bow my head and brace both hands against the floor. "Please," I sob. "Please, Haza'ruux. I don't want this. I can't be your apprentice."

"Little Flashing Blade." Affection warms his rough voice. Leaving his book on the floor, he kneels before me and grasps my shoulders. I try to pull away, but he holds on tighter. "You are not my apprentice. If you were, I would have seen your creature—your Arimaas sign—in my dream. No, Mariikel. You are our chieftain."

"What?" In utter bewilderment, I stare into his face.

"A true chieftain sees like a Keeper does—through ink and skin, to the deep heart. This is the sight that you have. You have gone down into the dark to make a clan out of those who are like the dead. This is a chieftain's work."

"Stop calling me that!" I wrench myself out of his grip and press my back against the wall. "I am a criminal. A liar. A *skin-changer*!"

Haza'ruux gives me a look of fathomless grief. "You suffer because your heart's blood burns. The truth—you do not wear it on your skin alone. It is a fire in your flesh."

The words seem to strike me in my vitals. A great, unvoiced cry swells in my chest. But then I glance down and see the sigil poem—the nightmare-mark—that still twines around my arm. "What have you done to me?" I shriek. "Have you put your sorcery into my skin, too?"

"No, Flashing Blade." A smile flits across his face. "It is only an honor-mark."

Another scream rises in my throat, but I choke it down. "I didn't ask for this."

"It is not your place to ask. Only to receive."

"I am not who you think I am!"

"Kesh." His voice cuts like a lash. "Enough. There is more I must tell you. Be still and listen."

I flinch. My eyes are drawn back to the tattoo of the war-hound on his chest, shifting subtly as he breathes. I remember the awful radiance it poured out a moment ago, that deluge of light—and I shut my mouth.

"The Arimaas is a great strength but also a great burden. It can be corrupted—as you have read." The hermit's lips curl in a grimace. "It has been many generations since Clan Serix had a leader strong enough to bear this knowledge. But if the chieftain is worthy, and the clan is in danger—then the Keeper may choose to share the truth."

I am not a chieftain! I want to protest again, but I do not dare. "What danger?"

"I have walked in other dreams these past days." His voice drops to a rasp. "I saw the ancient stronghold of Clan Sko'larik. I stood in the dreaming-hall of the Keepers. It was burning." His eyes glitter, as if reflecting the unseen flames. "Many nights, I have seen this. There is something coming—a great grief for the clan. I do not know when, or how. But there will be suffering and terrible shame." He turns to me again. "Clan Serix will need a true chieftain."

I shake my head and press my back against the wall. The ridges of the panels dig into my spine. "You have the wrong man."

Haza'ruux glowers. "There is no falsehood in the Place of Dreams."

"You're insane. Your dream is wrong. And I want nothing to do with it."

Wearily the hermit rises. He rests one hand on a slender pillar. "Go now. Sleep. You have seen enough for one night."

I climb to my feet. I grip my wrist until it aches—as if I could wring Haza'ruux's ink out of my skin. In a hoarse voice I say, "I'm not coming back."

He regards me with hooded eyes. "You may run, Flashing Blade, but you will not escape the bonds of your own blood. I do not tell you what you will be—I tell you what you already are."

"Axdraa'dah take you, old man."

I make a dart for the ladder. Haza'ruux does not stop me. I scramble up the rungs, thrust the hatch open, and burst out into the studio above. Then I stumble into the adjacent room and out the front door. I trip over the vines that snake across the path, falling hard to my hands and knees. In a paroxysm of terror, I scrabble upright. Even the mad markmaker's garden is trying to drag me down into insanity.

In the street, I start to run. I do not stop until I find myself in my own quiet corridor, in front of my own home. I fall down panting at the foot of our solid, sane, neatly painted door.

Betray me, Haza'ruux. Betray me now, if you will. I am not going back.

CHAPTER TWENTY-FIVE

For a long time I sit on the step, watching the blue glow of the night-lamps and breathing in the damp, loamy aroma of the garden. But the familiar scent does not soothe me.

The mark of the mad dog...

The great, phantom beast emerging from Haza'ruux's brilliant marks—it was not deepcraft. I have never seen a van'shor do anything like that. The abilities of the Van'shorii are refined and disciplined, but the mad markmaker's display was a raw outpouring of power—like the all-consuming furnace of a star's heart.

The Arimaas.

In my mind, I want to deny it. But I cannot deny the evidence of my senses. My body is still shaking.

I am so angry: at Haza'ruux for luring me into his insane cult, and at myself for trusting him. And as for his talk about my being a chieftain—the thought is so absurd that I could almost laugh. Even if the myths of Clan Sko'larik are true, why should I be entrusted with these secrets? What in the Deep Sleep's name does Haza'ruux expect me to do? It would make far more sense to give this knowledge to someone with authority, someone who would know how to use such a tremendous power. *Like Mekkalluthak.*

A frightening thought strikes me. *Does he know?*

Briefly I think back to my encounters with the guildmaster. I remember his eagerness, barely concealed beneath his gracious manners, to learn about my unusual tattoo. I know that Mekkalluthak has studied the history of the mad markmakers—is it remotely possible that he thinks the Arimaas is real?

It doesn't matter. I cannot tell Mekkalluthak, or anyone else, what I have seen tonight. I wish now that I had never confided in Haza'ruux, nor agreed to let him teach me. I want nothing to do with this insanity; the secrets I carry are heavy enough.

In the lamplight of the porch, I look down at the sigil poem on my arm.

I press my thumb into the exquisitely dyed skin, rubbing in slow circles. I finally know what the tattoo means—but it is an old man's demented dream, little better than a false mark.

A knot hardens in my belly. Let Haza'ruux do what he wills; I am sick of living in fear. I know how to break this bondage, how to put the mad mark-maker and his visions behind me. And it will only take a few daubs of acid.

I rise from the porch and turn my steps towards the studios.

Rixarii Street is still bathed in a dim blue glow; the daylights will not come on for another hour yet. So there is no one in the corridor except the ever-present guards—only they are not the same guards as before. The Ascendance troops are gone; these are Valk'taro Jal'thor's warriors. They stand in twos and threes, leaning on their javelins or long oval shields, watching the street and talking in low tones.

A thread of anxiety pulses in my gut. I know these warriors are here to protect us—at least, that is what Mekkalluthak claimed—but the sight of a standing army at the studios still sickens me. Ascendance or Tarriks, firearms or blades, the differences matter little. Will we never be able to work in peace again?

I duck my head, trying to avoid the warriors' notice. Unfortunately, I have to walk through the middle of the corridor—and I am the only person in the street who is not a soldier. Guards turn their heads as I pass. One man steps away from the wall and into my path.

"Hakk, you." He taps the butt of his javelin against the floor. "Stop there."

I halt. In the dim light, the warrior's dark face seems to melt into the black metal of his helmet, so I can only see the four gleaming points of his eyes. "I am Serix. A markmaker." My voice comes out shrill. "I need something from my studio."

The warrior's gaze flicks over me, checking my clan- and mastery-marks. No doubt he wonders what I could possibly need at this hour. But if he suspects some misdeed, he does not mention it. Instead he only nods and touches his neck in a salute. "Forgive my intrusion, markmaker. You may pass. Honor with you."

I do not even return the farewell. If he knew what I am about to do, would he let me go so readily?

I reach Kilmaya's studio, unlock the door, and burst inside. I turn up the lights and go to the shelf where we keep the supplies for mark-erasing. Then I take down the chemicals, disinfectants, and bandages and set them on the worktable. Already my hands are shaking. The ancient clan laws say that not even the guild can order one of the mad markmaker's tattoos removed. But I am a skin-changer now. Why should that matter to me?

I sit down at the worktable and open the bottle of grekyaa oil. Then I take up a brush to paint the solution on my arm. I hesitate, staring at the gorgeously intertwined symbols on my skin. My name-sigil lies interlocked with a nightmarish spiral of marks: blood, mist, Axdraa'dah...

He saw you marking the skin of the Deep Sleep. Waking the dead.

For an instant, I am back in the Underbelly, sealing Kophas's new, false clan-mark—clapping a hand on his shoulder and saying, *Welcome back to the living.*

"No." I don't care what Haza'ruux saw; he is wrong about me. With trembling fingers, I brush the grekyaa oil on my arm. It feels slick and cool against my skin. Counting under my breath, I force myself to wait the allotted time—it always takes a few minutes for the solution to break down the transparent sealing-glaze.

At last I pick up a cloth and wipe off the oil. The mark still looks as vivid as ever, but that does not surprise me—Haza'ruux's inks are brighter than ordinary dyes, even without a glaze. I wash and disinfect my arm, and pat it dry. Then I uncap the bottle of thuriiklesh.

This is going to hurt.

Breathing deeply, I lay my arm on the table, palm upwards. Once I touch the acid to my skin, I cannot turn back. There will not be any legal consequences for erasing this so-called decorative mark, but people will ask questions—Kilmaya, my family, even Mekkalluthak, if he hears of it. But I can simply tell them that Haza'ruux removed it himself, that he found me unworthy of his lessons after all. And if Haza'ruux should try to punish me—well, I know his secret too. If need be, I can threaten to reveal his precious Arimaas powers to the Van'shorii. He will have no choice but to leave me alone.

I plunge the brush into the bottle and pull it out again, thick with white paste. Then I grit my teeth and smear it on my arm.

I do not belong to you, Haza'ruux!

I lift the brush and wait for the agonizing sting of dissolving skin. For a full minute I stare at my forearm, unbreathing.

I feel nothing. Under the acid, my skin is still whole and smooth.

What is this?

The thuriiklesh is supposed to work instantly. What did I do wrong? Did I not wait long enough for the grekyaa to break down the seal? With feverish movements, I wipe off the acid and apply another layer of oil. My pulse throbs in my temples, and I make myself wait for twice the usual time. Then I clean my arm again and place a daub of thuriiklesh in the middle of Haza'ruux's mark.

Still, nothing happens.

Oh, Ka, no.

I grip the brush harder. I paint acid over the tattoo in broad strokes, pressing hard as if to scour it into my skin. In my haste, my fingers slip, and I smear the paste onto my wrist, beyond the borders of the mark.

At once, the bare skin tingles. I watch as the patch of pale gray flesh darkens with irritation. The burning begins.

I gasp with pain; the brush drops from my hand. The blistering sensation deepens, but I sit paralyzed, watching the acid eat into my wrist. It only burns my unmarked skin—the sigil poem remains completely unharmed. Are Haza'ruux's marks immune to erasing chemicals? Or is this more of his Arimaas magic?

Curse him! The Deep Sleep take him! Curse him!

Through my pain, I fumble for a rag and wipe the acid away. I stagger over to the workroom sink and turn on the faucet. As the water sluices over my raw wrist, I lean over, half snarling and half sobbing. Is this why it is forbidden to remove a mad markmaker's tattoo—because it is, in fact, impossible?

How can he do this to me?

I pull my dripping arm out of the water. The burning has faded a little, but the sigil poem still clings to my skin like some strange and glittering parasite. Horror overwhelms me. *Get it off me. Get it off!*

With my free hand, I grasp the dagger at my belt and tug it out of its sheath. I touch the blade to my skin and hold my arm over the sink. I shudder so hard that I cannot hold my hand steady. Haza'ruux's mark swims before my eyes. Yet even as I stare at it, an image from the poem returns to me, horribly vivid:

And he, too, bore marks that poured blood.

With a clatter, the dagger slips from my fingers and drops into the basin. I sink to the floor, hugging my arm. I do not have the strength to strip my own mark. Most likely I would cut too deep and end up bleeding to death on the studio floor. But I still feel like a coward. I cradle my hand against my chest.

What do I do now? What do I do?

I crouch on the floor for a long time, rigid, until the workroom lights change gradually to a pale daylight hue. It is morning. I have been awake for eighteen hours—a full day. Despair seeps through my body; I want to curl up on the cold tile and sleep. I do not even care if that is how Kilmaya finds me when she comes in for work.

Then a memory filters through my exhausted mind: Kilmaya won't be coming in today. There is no work. Mekkalluthak closed the studios, told the artists to stay home.

I groan and drag myself to my feet. The burned patch on my wrist still stings. I stumble back to the worktable and find a tube of healing ointment to daub onto my arm. The wound is not large, but remains an ugly violet-black, with a rough and blistered surface. I will have to keep it hidden for a while—there is no sense in showing everyone that I tried to erase my own mark. I cut a length of gauze and wrap it around my wrist. It reminds me, eerily, of the time that I tried to hide the mark before, the morning I woke up in Haza'ruux's house. Now I know I will never be rid of it. I will have to wear the mad markmaker's dream for the rest of my life.

Let the Deep Sleep take Haza'ruux, and Mekkalluthak, and the Ascendance, and everyone else. I am going home.

When I finally emerge from the studio and lock the door, it is full daylight. The corridor remains deserted except for the Tarriks warriors, who watch me impassively from behind their shields. The stillness of the street disconcerts me; even the Trev'ban studios remain shut and silent. Perhaps the Trev'ban artists are obeying the guild's order after all—if only because the guild now has warriors worth fearing.

When I reach the residential district, however, I find the streets crowded, mostly with Serix artists. With no work to attend to, they stand in plazas and on porches, talking and debating. Some of the arguments are heated—not everyone agrees, it seems, that Mekkalluthak's threat against the High Council was a wise decision.

Wise or not, in a matter of days, we will find out who has more mettle: Mekkalluthak Serix or Valo T'sarek. I fear the outcome either way.

I have almost reached Elantii Street when I hear my name. "Mariikel?"

In the midst of the busy corridor, I spot Kilmaya, staring at me with a startled expression. My heart sinks further; the last person I want to talk to right now is my teacher. But I do not even have the energy to walk away.

She hurries across the street to stand before me. "There you are. Kin's heart, I'm glad to see you."

I gaze at her dully. I have not seen her since before the assembly last night—she left with Rinavi almost immediately after the riot. That seems like years ago now. "How is Rinavi?"

"She's all right. I stayed with her last night. She wasn't hurt, but Narrik... she has taken it hard. As we all have." Kilmaya rubs her forehead; she looks exhausted and aggrieved. "I was just going over to see his family. You heard the funeral is tonight?"

With a dazed sense of guilt, I remember that Narrik is dead; of course, there must be a funeral. "No. I hadn't heard." I cannot think what else to say.

"I'm glad I found you, then." She looks me over. "Chervani called me last night asking for you. It was late—she was quite worried. Did you get home all right, quiet one?"

"Yes." The lie rises to my lips without thought. But a strange ache pulses under my ribs. I want to kneel down in the street, clasp her hands, and say, *Teacher, I'm in trouble. Please help me.*

"That's good," Kilmaya replies. Yet her frown remains skeptical. "You look terrible. Are you ill?"

I rub my eyes. "I'm only tired."

She inhales sharply. "What did you do to your arm?"

I glance at the bandage on my wrist. It only covers the acid wound; Haza'ruux's tattoo is still visible. I wish I had covered all of it—the sight of that mark is hateful to me now. "I strained my wrist."

"Doing what?" she exclaims. "There's blood on your leg, too. What happened to you?"

I stare down at my feet. A long, dark purple smear runs down my knee. I must have cut it when I tripped and fell in my flight from the mad markmaker's house. I did not even notice until now. "It must have happened yesterday," I say vaguely.

Kilmaya narrows her upper eyes. "Mariikel…"

I am too tired to invent a more elaborate story. "Please, teacher, I need to go home."

"Home?" She sounds baffled. "Where have you been?"

I do not reply. Instead I brush past her, my eyes lowered. She calls after me, but I do not look back.

CHAPTER TWENTY-SIX

When I reach the house, I find it quiet and empty; both my aunt and uncle are away. They must have gone to work despite the turmoil. The studios may be closed, but the security stations and the trallak farms need to keep running, regardless. I am relieved at my family's absence—it means I have a little time before I must face them again.

I sit down heavily on my bunk and unstrap my sandals. A vague unease nags at me; I feel I have forgotten something important. Then it occurs to me: I am missing my artist's satchel. I must have left it behind when I fled Haza'ruux's house last night. Silently I curse. My personal pens and tools are in that bag, but it also contains my Underbelly disguise, the synthetic mask and gloves with their forged marks—the evidence of my crimes. And now Haza'ruux has them.

I have been a fool, but there is nothing I can do about it now. I will have to find a way to retrieve my satchel later. Right now, I simply need to sleep.

I kick off my sandals and then stretch out on my bed. I do not even bother to close my door or dim the lights.

I awake in the late afternoon, groggy and bewildered. My body feels stiff and drained of strength. Something damp bumps my hand, and a whiff of warm air tickles my skin.

I crack open two eyes. A dark, blunt-muzzled creature fills my vision, with pointed ears and a half-open mouth full of fangs. The war-hound looms over me, panting.

I loose a yell and slam my head against the top of the bunk. The lanky dog jumps back, too, with a startled yip. And then I realize the creature is not some vision or nightmare—it is only our own hound, Miika, who stands stiff-legged in the middle of my room, watching me warily.

"Oh, Ka." I wince, rubbing the back of my head. "You scared me."

I slip to the floor and sit with my back against the wall, then hold out a hand, inviting her closer. Miika eyes me, unsure whether I am offering reward or punishment. At last she pads forward, tail swinging cautiously. Her ears flatten against her dark head as I caress her. "There, Miika. Kesh now. I'm sorry."

She settles by my side, pressing her flank against my leg. I ground myself in the sensation of wiry fur against my palm. This is real. This is normal. I am home, and no one is trying to harm me.

Then my gaze falls on my tattooed arm and the bandage tied hastily around my wrist. The skin underneath still stings. A single thought emerges in my mind, startlingly clear:

I need to get off the ship.

I do not know why the idea did not occur to me earlier. Perhaps I was simply too frightened to consider it. I have never left the *Akkano'dath* before; it is the only world I know. To uproot myself, to leave it all behind for some other ship in the Fleet, seems unthinkable. But if Haza'ruux tries to force me into his Arimaas cult... I shudder, remembering the brilliance of his unnatural tattoos. What other choice will I have except to flee?

I give Miika's lean shoulder a final pat, then rise to take off my disheveled tunic—it still smells faintly of the incense from the dreaming-room—and change into fresh clothing. I splash water on my face and wash the dried blood from my knee. A little more alert, I step over to my closet and look through my belongings. I do not own much. It would not be difficult to pack it all in one or two bags if I had to escape the ship.

But what would I tell my family?

A pang constricts my heart. My aunt and uncle would be shocked and grieved if I announced, one day, that I was leaving. They would demand a reason. Kilmaya would be angry, too—I am the heir to her studio. How can I abandon my obligation to her?

It wouldn't be forever, I tell myself. *Haza'ruux is an old man, and even the Arimaas does not make him immortal. A few years away, working for one of the lesser artist clans on the other ships...then I could return.*

This thought only comforts me for a moment. Even after Haza'ruux dies, there will surely be another mad markmaker. Will his successor also track me down, force me to take part in the rites of the Arimaas? Will I have to remain a voluntary exile simply to escape the Keepers and their dreams?

I groan aloud and grip my temples. Under the bandage, my wrist throbs. Then, through my open bedroom door, I hear the sudden click and hiss of the front entrance. The light tap of footsteps sounds in the hall. *Chervani.*

Miika clambers to her feet and pads out into the hall. For a moment I do not follow. But I cannot bear to wait, to pretend that I am not here. I step quietly across the room and pause in the doorway.

My aunt stands with her back to me in the entrance to the kitchen. Her slender shoulders droop, and she leans one hand against the lintel. Miika noses at her other hand, but Chervani ignores the old hound. She looks frail and lost.

"Nakki?"

With a little cry, she turns. Her face contorts; pain glitters in her eyes. "Mariikel."

With a stab of remorse, I realize this is the first time she has seen me since the riot in Rixarii Street. Wordless, I step forward and wrap my arms around her. "I'm all right," I murmur. "I'm all right."

"Where were you?" She leans into my shoulder, sobs shaking her body. "I tried to reach you for hours. People have died now, Mariikel. I only want to know where you are."

"I'm sorry." My throat aches. I embrace her more tightly.

"What happened?" Chervani steps back, still gripping my arms. "What kept you?"

"There was an assembly." I pause, casting about for a plausible lie. "It went late."

"Late! Did it take all night?"

"The guild council...questioned the people who saw the riot. I had to stay."

"One message." The corners of her eyes crease in anguish. "You could have sent us one message, saying you were safe. Is that so much to ask?"

"I'm so sorry, nakki." I have no excuse, no justification for my utter thoughtlessness. I pull her close again. "I'm such a fool."

"Yes, you are." Her voice breaks. But she does not push me away.

At last I release Chervani and step back. She blinks at me, exhausted. I wonder if she slept at all last night.

I cannot keep doing this. I cannot keep lying to her. But what choice do I have now?

"We heard about Narrik." Her voice drops to a grieved murmur. "Kin's heart, Mariikel. How has it come to this?" She takes my hand again. "We'll come with you to the shrine tonight, for the funeral. Ancestors know the whole clan could use the prayers right now."

"Of course." Deep in my belly I feel sick. If the things I saw last night in the dreaming-room were real, and Haza'ruux was telling the truth—then our ancestors were Clan Sko'larik, who were wiped out by the deepcrafters. They could not even save themselves. How can they possibly protect us now?

Chervani still grips my hand, as if afraid to let go. I swallow my unease, muster a smile, and fold my palms around hers. "It's all right. I won't disappear tonight. I promise."

I help Chervani prepare the evening meal. While the tavla broth simmers, my aunt asks about Kilmaya and Rinavi. Otherwise we talk little. When Hakham comes home, all three of us sit down to the first supper that we have shared together in over a week. But the conversation remains subdued, and I feel distant and sick at heart. I focus on my family's voices instead of their words—as if I am trying to fix their tones and inflections in my memory. Hakham sounds irritated. He is telling a story from work—something about the reaction of the clans to Mekkalluthak's latest threat, and how people were openly hostile towards him at the docks.

Chervani's voice rises in distress. "If the guildmaster had been willing to *talk* to Clan Trev'ban instead of bringing in more soldiers, Narrik's children might still have a father. But now he's gone, and his family may not even have the comfort—the right—of placing his ashes with his ancestors. Is there even a deepcrafter on the ship right now who would be willing to perform a Serix funeral?"

"The Van'shorii have a duty to the dead, regardless of clan." Hakham glowers into his bowl; he has barely tasted his meal. "If they neglect it, that is their fault, not ours."

Chervani remains silent, her jaw set in a rare display of obstinacy. After a moment, Hakham groans and rubs his upper eyes. He reaches for Chervani's hand and caresses the marriage-mark on her deep gray skin. "The guild will arrange something for Narrik. They'll find a way."

It occurs to me that whatever happens between the Ascendance and Clan Serix, my family, Kilmaya, Rinavi—everyone I know—will have to go on, day after day, living with the consequences. If I leave the ship, I will be running away. I put down the fragrant cup of klasindi I just raised to my lips. It seems that no matter what I do, I am still playing the coward.

A faint chime sounds from my uncle's bag, which hangs on the back of his chair. He sighs and turns to pull out his datascroll. "It's Virik." He walks into the front room to take the call, leaving me and Chervani in the kitchen. She sends me a pained glance, and I know that she has noticed my silence.

It is no use waiting. I must broach the subject eventually; better to do it now than the night before I leave. "Nakki, I've been thinking of travelling."

Her face slackens. "What?"

"I want to go to another ship for a while. I'm...frustrated. We've had so few clients these past months. And now the guild has told us to stay home altogether. Who knows how long it will last this time? I can't do this anymore. I need to get out of the sector."

"I suppose...I suppose I understand." Her eyelids tremble as she tries to process my outburst. "Do you think that's safe right now? With everything that's happening?"

"I don't see any good in waiting—"

From the front room, Hakham suddenly curses aloud.

Something in his tone makes my skin prickle—a note of raw fear. Chervani and I stare at each other. In silence we listen to the remainder of his conversation, but his terse responses provide little context. When he reenters the kitchen, his movements are swift and his eyes round with dread. He grabs his bag from the chair. "I have to go. Virik's called me in."

"You only just got home," Chervani cries. "What's going on?"

"There's a lockdown. Everyone in the docks has to be fully scanned. Deep Sleep, it's going to be a long night."

Alarm floods my veins. "A lockdown? What for?"

"Some fool has just tried to kill the High Councilor. That's what for." In a voice infused with anger and fear, he says, "Don't leave the house. Either of you." Then he rushes from the kitchen and out the front door.

Almost as soon as Hakham is gone, Chervani leaves, too, making some excuse about warning the neighbors. I do not try to stop her. Instead, I clear the dishes from the abandoned table and put away the half-eaten food. Then I wander into the empty front room and collapse on the couch. Miika follows me and lies down at my feet. I pet her absently, mechanically.

I will not be leaving the ship any time soon. The lockdown at the docks may last for days while security tries to find this would-be assassin. Until it lifts, I have nothing to do except worry—and hope that Haza'ruux will leave me alone.

And then I remember Kophas.

Oh, Ka. It has been less than a day since I gave Kophas money and clothing for his escape. Knowing him, he would not waste any time getting out of the Underbelly. He may already be at the docks, searching for a shuttle to board. If he gets caught in the lockdown, all his marks will be scanned and checked against the records. *In which case...* I groan aloud.

He may still escape. My forgeries are excellent; I know for a fact they would fool most ordinary people. But I did not think Kophas would ever have to undergo a full scan—only routine checks of his clan- and mastery-marks. If a sharp-eyed record-keeper examines all his tattoos in detail, he might detect the tiny discrepancies between Kophas's skin and Dirak Tizzan's records.

Is it worth risking another trip to the Underbelly to try to warn Kophas? But no—he has certainly left by now. I have no way to find him. I can only pray he had not yet reached the docks when the lockdown began, and that he has the sense to lay low for a while longer.

I sink my head into my hands. *It wasn't supposed to happen this way.*

With a soft whine, Miika nuzzles my face. I push the dog away and rise. I cannot sit here doing nothing; I may as well try to find out what in Ka's name is going on. I return to my room and search for my datascroll—and then remember that the device is still in my satchel at the mad markmaker's house. Cursing under my breath, I head to my uncle's study instead and turn on his display desk. Then I pull up the latest reports.

The assassination attempt occurred when Valo T'sarek and his personal escort were on their way to the Serix sector—apparently with the intention of meeting Mekkalluthak to negotiate an end to the standoff. A team of laborers had been doing renovations in one of the transport hubs, and somehow the assassin planted a bomb on the empty construction scaffold. It exploded just as the High Councilor and his bodyguards passed underneath. A few of the guards were injured, and one died in the blast. Valo himself, thanks to his deepcraft shields, escaped with mere scratches.

No one knows who set the bomb—it must have been triggered remotely. There are conjectures, of course, that the assassin might have been a member of the construction crew. All the workers assigned to that site have been taken in for questioning, but as I sift through the reports, one name appears repeatedly: Clan Serix.

Statement after statement recalls the irrefutable fact that only yesterday, in public, Mekkalluthak Serix called on the clans to oppose Valo T'sarek. Never mind that his threat involved a lawful process, not murder—that detail has been quickly forgotten. In the eyes of the Ascendance, Mekkalluthak clearly instigated the attack. Whether he arranged it himself or merely inspired someone else is of little consequence.

It does not take long for Mekkalluthak to issue a terse denial: *The guild of markmakers deplores this act of treachery. We neither had knowledge of this plot nor, at any time, intended violence against the High Councilor. At this moment, Serix record-keepers are working with Ascendance security to track down this assassin. We will find this despicable criminal, brand him with shame-marks, and cast him into exile as he deserves.*

There is no mention at all, now, of the High Council's crimes and abuses against Clan Serix. It makes me wonder if Mekkalluthak, too, is frightened.

If the guildmaster is afraid, the clan is in deeper trouble than I even thought possible.

No matter who tried to kill the High Councilor, Mekkalluthak is no longer in a position to make demands. He will have to retract his threat to depose Valo T'sarek. He might even be forced to lift the mark-bans and reopen the studios. It might be the only chance left to appease them.

My mind drifts briefly to Haza'ruux. *Is this what you saw in your dreams, old man? Is this the shame that will come upon us?* Fury and fear well up in my throat. *What am I supposed to do? You are the one with a mark of power—and yet you do nothing. What kind of guardian are you?*

I clench my fists and choke back a cry. Under the bandage on my wrist, my wound stings anew. But being angry at Haza'ruux will solve nothing. If punishment comes, he will suffer with the rest of us. Our only hope is that the real assassin be found and his connection to Clan Serix disproved—if it can be disproved.

For once in my life, I pray that the Ascendance may find their quarry.

CHAPTER TWENTY-SEVEN

It is past the ninth hour when I hear the front door open. I spring to my feet and hurry out of the study. Chervani stands in the hall, looking haggard. "They're blaming Clan Serix," she says.

"I know. I saw."

My aunt stares at me, her lips trembling. "People say the High Council will try to exile us. All of us."

I read those reports, too—Ascendance zealots, calling for radical retaliation. "That's absurd. They can't do that. They are only saying that to frighten people."

Chervani does not respond. Her face is a mask of fear.

"Listen." I reach out and grasp her limp hands. "They can't pin it on us that easily. They will have to show proof. And there isn't any." But my voice sticks in my throat. I remember Talorak and Kophas—I know perfectly well that Ascendance courts do not have trouble finding evidence to suit their needs. "In any case, they can only lawfully punish the assassin. None of *us* have done anything wrong." Again, my gut twinges. If only that last statement were true.

Chervani's eyes remain glazed. "I don't know what to think anymore."

"It will be all right." Gently I squeeze her hands. "Come. We should go to the shrine. The funeral will be starting soon—we should be there."

My aunt takes a deep, shuddering breath. "You're right, dako." She blinks, a little more composed. "The ancestors will shield us. They will guide us even through this."

"Of course they will." I say it to reassure her. But I taste a bitterness in my mouth, as if I have spoken yet another lie.

In the amber light of evening, we leave the house and head towards the entrance of the sector. When we reach the ancestor shrine, we find the plaza packed with other Serix members—young and old, artists and archivists, ink-makers and trallak tenders. Families huddle together, kneeling or prostrate on the floor, all facing the round, pillared structure of the shrine in the middle of the chamber. Despite the crowd, a hush grips the whole room, broken only by the murmur of prayers and the occasional cry of a fussing child.

"Serixan, ancestors, we call on you. By the bonds of our clan-marks, hear us. Shield the children of your heart's blood..."

Dread weighs heavily on my chest as I guide Chervani through the throng. It dawns on me that these people are not only here for Narrik's funeral. They have heard the news about the High Councilor—they are afraid for the clan.

There is something coming.... There will be suffering, and terrible shame...

With a shudder, I drive Haza'ruux's warning from my mind. We have reached the shrine entrance now. Two Tarriks guards, more of Jal'thor's men, flank the doorway, tall and impassive in their black, sigil-etched armor. At the sight of the warriors, my limbs tense—but these soldiers merely salute in respectful silence, touching their clan-marks. It is strange having warriors in the clan sector who are actually here to protect us. Nodding in return, Chervani and I pass through the door into the shrine.

A muted orange glow illuminates the dark heads of the assembled clan members within. The interior of the shrine is even more crowded than the plaza outside, and the air hangs warm and stagnant from the close-packed bodies. I cannot see the front of the room, but I can hear the slow, muffled beat of a drum and the plaintive drone of a solitary raith'aal. A woman sings, her tone steady and piercing, chanting a series of names:

"Telaan, markmaker, son of Alonak and K'thora. Alonak, inkmaker, son of Brethalo and Hiravi. K'thora, record-keeper, daughter of Zirrok and Jaltha..."

The chant is Narrik's lineage—the names of his ancestors. Beside me, my aunt lifts a hand to her neck. I do the same, almost unconsciously. I wonder how long the singer has been here. Chanting the ancestry of the deceased can take hours.

Trying to move quietly, I slip along the wall, looking for a place to stand. Towards the front of the room, near the musicians, I spot Kilmaya. She kneels on the floor beside Rinavi, who sits with her head bowed. My teacher rests one hand on the elderly artist's shoulder.

I approach them, Chervani following close behind. At the shuffle of my footsteps, Kilmaya turns. Her eyelids droop with exhaustion, but she rises to greet us. "Mariikel. Chervani." Briefly she embraces us. "Kin's heart, I'm glad you're here."

I stand mute as my teacher wraps her arms around me. I have rarely seen her look so tired and grieved. But then, Narrik was among her close circle of friends; she has known him since they were both apprentices. All the words of comfort on my tongue dry up, useless as dust. So I say nothing and merely embrace her in return. The weight of Kilmaya's head against my shoulder feels strange. Was her body always so light, so slender-boned? I remember how easily I threw her to the ground during the riot, and a heat of remorse floods my veins.

My teacher lets go of me and returns to her place next to Rinavi. Meanwhile, my aunt kneels on the other side of the elderly markmaker, then takes her hand and murmurs consolation. The drone of the pipe and the chant of names continues, low and relentless; the actual ceremony will not begin for several minutes yet. I remain standing, taking in the dim, stifling chamber while unease seeps into my bones.

I have not been inside the shrine for a long time—not since I began going to the Underbelly. The space has not changed since I visited last, yet it feels foreign. The polished floor of real maroonstone tile, the curving walls adorned with murals of famed artists and clan leaders—everything still looks as I remember it. Overhead, the deep amber glow of the dome shines through an exquisite wooden latticework, which is carved in the shape of the Serix clan symbol surrounded by a spray of trallak leaves. The latticework casts a dappled pattern of gold light and shadow on the crowd below, creating the illusion of a shaded grove.

It is a beautiful room—and I recall, with a pang, that I used to love it here. Growing up, I would stop by often, even when there was no special occasion. The shrine was a refuge, both from the bustle of the studios and from home, where Askko's quarrels and misadventures made for continual disturbance. I used to bring my stylus and datascroll here to practice my sigils, comforted by the nearness of my Serix ancestors—including my own birth parents, whose ashes lay interred under the gleaming stone floor, mingled with the remains of all their forebears.

But now—it is not the room but rather I who have changed. I am a stranger now; I foreswore the right to take refuge here when I first broke my oath as a markmaker. In the truth of my flesh, I am already an exile.

I squeeze my eyes shut. I accepted long ago that, even if I dared to pray, my forebears would no longer acknowledge me. But my family, my teacher, Rinavi, Narrik...what did they do wrong? How have they dishonored the clan, that the ancestors should remain silent in the face of their suffering?

Or is it possible...is it possible that the ashes underneath this room are only ashes, with no power to help or hurt anyone? What if our ancestors have never watched over us at all? *Is there only the Deep Sleep after death?*

After seeing how the outcasts live in the Underbelly, I could almost believe it. And yet that would not explain what I saw last night in the mad markmaker's house—the Arimaas, the awful beauty of light in the flesh, the tattoos rippling with radiance and power.

I cover my face and sink to my knees on the cold stone tile. I do not know what to believe anymore—about the ancestors, the Arimaas, or even myself.

It takes me a minute to notice the room has fallen silent. The music and chanting have stopped, and I hear the rustle of robes as the crowd around me stirs. I open my eyes. People rise and turn to face the door, where a small group of newcomers enters the shrine at a slow processional pace—Narrik's family.

I struggle to my feet. Chervani and Kilmaya rise, too, supporting Rinavi between them. We watch as the family crosses the short distance from the door to the open area at the front of the shrine. Leading the procession is Narrik's wife, a delicate-framed woman with an expression of shock stamped on her fine-featured face. In her hands she clutches a tiny vial made of dark purple glass.

Rinavi moans aloud. Kilmaya wraps an arm around her shoulders, steadying the older artist. My aunt, too, hangs her head in grief. "Poor Dalnari." Even through her whisper, Chervani's voice breaks. "At least the deepcrafters did not refuse them the ashes."

My gaze lingers on the glass bottle in Dalnari's hands. Only yesterday, Narrik Serix was in our studio, drinking klasindi, debating politics with my teacher, grumbling about the bans—an ordinary artist with an artist's concerns. Now the handful of ash inside that jewel-like vial is all that remains of him. Desolation creeps over me again.

Close behind Narrik's widow, two children follow—a boy, little more than a dozen years old, and a girl even younger. The son wears the sigil of a markmaker's apprentice on his brow, and carries a short sword in his hands, the flat of the blade resting against one open palm. He stares at it fixedly as he walks, as if it might fall and shatter on the tile. Beside him, his young sister bares her teeth, trembling; she is trying not to cry.

Behind the children come Narrik's siblings, parents, and several other, more distant relations. Together, the family processes to the front of the shrine, where a pedestal—a simple, fountain-like structure with a fluted column supporting a shallow basin—juts out of the floor. But there is no water in this basin. Instead, the bowl sits dry and empty: it is a funnel to the ash-chamber below the floor, where the remains of our Serix forebears have rested for centuries.

With dreamlike slowness, Dalnari places the ash-vial on the broad rim of the basin. Then she steps back, almost stumbling, to stand between her two children. She waits with head bowed.

An uneasy hush falls over the assembly. People glance from the waiting family to the far wall of the shrine, where a curtain emblazoned with the Serix symbol hangs over the entrance to the small preparation room beyond. Normally, a deepcrafter would preside over the dedication of the sword and the pouring of the ashes. But it seems unlikely that any van'shor will attend this funeral. The family will have to perform the ceremony themselves. So what are they waiting for?

Just as the crowd begins to murmur and grow restless, the curtain to the preparation room stirs. A figure emerges into the dim, gold-dappled light of the shrine—lithe and poised, with deep violet skin.

Mekkalluthak.

A faint ripple of wonder sways the room. It is the guildmaster himself, but not as I have ever seen him before. Instead of the white robe and gold belt of his councilor's garb, he wears only a simple sparring kilt, like a warrior entering the arena. Barefoot and bare-chested, he approaches the pedestal and kneels before it briefly, touching his forehead to the edge of the basin. Amber light glints off the scarlet honor-marks that cover his forearms and shoulders.

I did not expect to see Mekkalluthak tonight. I assumed he would be too busy dealing with the Acendance's latest threats against the clan. But instead he is here—presiding over the funeral in place of the absent deepcrafter. He is not acting as guildmaster now, but as chieftain of Clan Serix.

No, Mariikel. You are our chieftain.

Haza'ruux's bewildering words echo in my mind. I dismiss them with a surge of revulsion. Even if I had such ambitions, I do not possess Mekkalluthak's natural authority, his power with words, his instinctive composure and confidence. Even now, as he rises from the pedestal, he exudes a fierce and silent grace that draws the eyes of the whole assembly. Despite his narrow chest and slender artist's build, there is something primal and warlike about his presence. The way he looks now, I could imagine him as one of the ancient Sko'larik chieftains from Haza'ruux's books—a Keeper, austere and powerful, wielding the fearsome light of the Arimaas.

But then, if Haza'ruux spoke true, the guildmaster *is* Sko'larik. We all are.

Mekkalluthak steps around the pedestal to approach Narrik's family. The guildmaster reaches out to Dalnari, murmuring a greeting and clasping both her forearms. The woman stares at him, stricken. Then, like a taut cord snapping, her whole body seems to collapse. She drops to her knees, still clutching the guildmaster's hands. A cry breaks from her throat—raw, keening, brimming with animal anguish.

In front of me, Rinavi sobs again, and Chervani flinches as if struck by a blow. "Kesh," says Kilmaya. But her tone shakes with repressed emotion.

Mekkalluthak does not pull away from the weeping, shuddering woman. Instead, he crouches down before her, placing one palm over her clan-mark.

For a long minute he kneels there, head bowed and eyes closed, his lips moving in some unheard prayer. The rest of the family look on with awed expressions.

I can guess why. A deepcrafter would never make such a gesture. Laying hands on another person's clan-mark to share in their suffering—that is only fitting between blood-kin. This is a blessing only a chieftain can give. And I have never seen Mekkalluthak give it before.

The effect on the room is palpable. Around me, I hear my fellow Serixan shifting, hissing in wonder, breaking into muffled cries. The fury and grief in the suffocating air sets my teeth on edge; I can almost taste it. Mekkalluthak's gesture draws fear out of the whole clan like poison from a wound. Now their eyes fix on him, hungry, yearning for some word of consolation.

At last Dalnari's keening subsides into silent sobs, and the guildmaster lifts his hand from her neck. Two family members move forward and help her to her feet. Then they retreat a few steps, leaving Mekkalluthak alone in front of the pedestal.

The guildmaster raises his head, gazing at the assembly in silence. The corners of his eyes crease, hinting at pain or unspeakable weariness. Then his expression smooths over, and his composure returns. "Serixan, my people." His voice, though low, cuts the quiet like a blade. "Our clan-brother, Narrik, has shed his heart's blood for truth in the flesh. Mourn him, but do not fear for him. He has given his life for the craft, as a warrior of truth. Even now the ancestors wait to welcome their battle-brother."

I find myself frowning at the words. *Shed his blood for the truth?* Mekkalluthak makes it sound as if the man gave his life willingly—but Narrik did not choose to stand in front of an Ascendance bullet, nor to be trampled by that panicked throng. It was not a battle or a noble sacrifice; it was a horrific accident, hardly a fitting end for an honorable artist.

But you can't say that, can you, guildmaster? And though I do not quite understand why, my heart hardens against him.

Mekkalluthak goes on. "In this dark hour, our enemies stand against us, accusing us of the vilest falsehoods. Do not yield, Serixan. Honor your clan-brother's memory and remain firm in truth. May Narrik grant us all his own courage." He draws a deep breath, nostrils flaring. "Let us call to our forerunners on his behalf. Bring forward the blade of the bloodline."

The assembly, recognizing the formal opening, settles into silence. After a moment, one of the family members touches Narrik's son on the shoulder. The boy starts as if out of a trance. Then, remembering his role, he grips the short sword in his hands more firmly and takes a hesitant step towards Mekkalluthak. He kneels and presents the weapon to the guildmaster. "This is the blade of our bloodline." The boy's voice wavers, high-pitched and uncertain. "I offer it for my father as dethra, a worthy weapon for...for the final combat."

An ache throbs in my throat. The child does not deserve this burden. He is too young to say those words here, in this place. I did not have to say them at my own parents' funeral—but then, I was so young I could barely speak at all. I do not even have a memory of the ceremony.

Mekkalluthak reaches down to take the sword from the boy's outstretched hands. Holding the blade flat, the guildmaster lifts his eyes to the ornate ceiling. "Serixan, ancestors, hear us. Accept this steel from our hands as the sign of our clan-brother's honor. Let him take up this blade in battle against the Deep Sleep. Do not abandon him, the son of your heart's blood, but stand by his side in the combat. Shield him from every deathly blow. Guard his spirit from the void of Axdraa'dah..."

Mekkalluthak's voice rolls on, powerful and sonorous. But I find myself unable to focus on the prayer. Instead, I feel I am back in the dreaming-room, tracing out sigil after sigil of that fearful poem:

And he fell for a thousand days,
His bright body cleaving the darkness, a blade of light.

I gasp, shattering the vision with a shake of my head. Kilmaya glances round at me, her expression concerned. I grimace and turn away.

The dedication of the blade is complete. Mekkalluthak bends down in front of the pedestal and places the sword on two ornate brackets that curve out of the column. Then he rises and stands behind it, facing the assembly. With reverent movements, he grasps the glass vial that sits on the rim of the empty basin.

"Narrik, son of Clan Serix." He removes the stopper from the bottle. "You have preserved your marks of truth. You have kept the bonds. Let heart's blood return to heart's blood. Rest now in the Long Dream's glory, among your own kin."

Mekkalluthak tips the vial. A thin stream of fine, dark gray powder drops noiselessly into the basin. At the sight of it, a collective groan rises from the crowd. Dalnari cries aloud again. Many people sink to their knees, touching their heads to the floor.

I remain standing. It occurs to me in a distant, incongruous way, that the vial in the guildmaster's hands resembles a bottle of markmaker's ink, and the ash is the color of raw trallak dye, fresh from the tree.

And in their flesh, their marks bled like open wounds...

Mekkalluthak, with a deep bow, returns the empty vial to its place on the edge of the basin. A desolate boom echoes through the chamber—the drummer has taken up his mallets once more. The singer raises her voice again, too, in a haunting tune:

> *Blood has returned to blood,*
> *Ash settles to ash.*
> *The light in the flesh has faded, and who will rekindle it?*
> *Come, keepers of the clan:*
> *Do not let us go nameless to Axdraa'dah,*
> *Or lie down in the dreamless dark.*
> *Seal your children with your own sign,*
> *Your indelible mark.*

The chant is familiar; I have heard it at every Serix funeral I have ever been to. But now, a chill settles over my skin. I recognize the words from another poem.

The light in their flesh fades...nameless we go down to Axdraa'dah, and lie down in the dark without dreams...

It is the lament of Clan Sko'larik. Is that where the funeral hymn first came from? *Come, keepers of the clan...* I have never thought anything of those words before, but... Is it possible? Have we been praying to the ancient Keepers, our Sko'larik ancestors, without knowing it? Have we been grieving the loss of the Arimaas all this time?

Through a daze, I stand listening to the mournful, undulating melody. Around me, people stir and begin to leave the shrine. Chervani moves forward to greet Narrik's family, to embrace his devastated wife. Kilmaya and Rinavi approach the pedestal and bow reverently to touch the rim of the polished basin. But I cannot move. I can barely even breathe.

When I finally look up, I find my gaze drawn to Mekkalluthak once more. The guildmaster draws aside the back curtain to return to the preparation chamber. For an instant he pauses to glance over his shoulder—and looks directly at me.

Mekkalluthak's face goes still and cold. Then the moment passes. The guildmaster turns away, slips behind the curtain, and disappears.

CHAPTER TWENTY-EIGHT

When Chervani and I return from the funeral, Hakham still has not come home. Chervani, fretful as ever, wants to wait up for him. I urge her to rest instead, promising to wake her when he arrives. My aunt obeys with little protest—which tells me how fatigued and overwrought she really is.

While Chervani retreats to her own bedchamber, I collapse on the couch in the dimly lit front room. I feel battered, hollowed-out. The Ascendance, my clan, Kophas, Haza'ruux—my anxieties close in around me, obliterating thought. Miika, sensing the disturbance of the house, paces the perimeter of the room for several minutes before settling at my feet to keep vigil. The old hound watches the door, ears pricked in mute patience.

Despite my best efforts, I cannot keep my eyes open. I fall asleep on the couch in the front room, waiting for my uncle.

In my fragmented dreams, Ascendance soldiers search for me in Rixarii Street. I hide in the storeroom in Kilmaya's studio, pouring ink on my skin by the bottle to blot out my tattoos. I feel a tug on my clothes, and I look down. Tyotik, the little Trechik boy, gazes up at me plaintively. "Change *my* mark," he pouts. "I want to be Serix."

With a sickening start, I wake. On the floor, Miika stirs and voices a half-bark deep in her throat. Blearily, I realize that my uncle is home. I shudder and rub my hands over my face as I sit up. "What time is it?" I croak.

"Almost morning." He sounds utterly exhausted. He shuts the door and shuffles over to the couch. Miika rises to greet him, tail lashing, but Hakham ignores her. He crumples into the seat across from me and rests his head in his hands.

For a minute, only the old hound's sigh disturbs the silence as she settles to sleep again. Then at last, I ask the inevitable question: "Is there any news?"

"Plenty. And none of it good." Hakham sits up, letting his head fall back on the cushions. "Hakka, Mariikel. I don't know what we're going to do."

I stare at him, lost for words. Generally my uncle is level-headed and does not bother others with his troubles—at least, he does not share them with me. We have never been close in that way. I can at least attempt to reassure Chervani, but I have no idea how to comfort Hakham.

"You haven't found him, then. The assassin."

He exhales harshly. "We do not even know what we are looking for. Ascendance security is interrogating those construction workers—but so far, they all deny knowing anything about the bomb. Meanwhile we must keep slogging through mark-scans for everyone who was trying to get on or off the ship. It's a nightmare."

"You'll find him," I say, though without much conviction. "Whoever it is, he can't hide forever."

"Maybe he can. If he finds a good enough skin-changer."

I wince. "But you know what forgery looks like."

"I thought I did. Until tonight."

"What do you mean?"

He stares at me. His face twitches, as if he is debating whether to speak. "Oh, Ka," he groans at last. "I don't think we found the assassin. But we found something else." He grips his temples in both hands. "If I tell you this, you must promise not to speak of it to anyone. Not even Chervani. You understand?"

"Yes," I say faintly.

"It might have nothing to do with the bombing at all. But it is the worst possible timing."

His eyes are dark with dread. And looking at him, my calm, confident, intelligent uncle, reduced to this shattered state, I suddenly know what he is about to say. Gazing at this man—who gave me a home, a family, and a craft, who was a father to me when I had none—I am not afraid; I feel only an excruciating remorse.

"We stopped this one laborer," Hakham says hoarsely. "He was only a dock worker. But he was Tizzan, and there were some Tizzan in charge of that scaffold where the bomb went off. So of course, we had to check him thoroughly—simply to say that we did it. So we scanned him and pulled up his records." He rubs his palms over his eyes again. "The marks matched. There weren't any missing verity lines or anything like that. They were legitimate. But there was something strange about them."

I realize, dimly, that he expects some response from me. But I cannot speak. Instead I sit rigid, feeling as though I am watching myself from far away.

"The marks on the man's skin—they seemed better than the ones in the records. An exact copy, but finer craftsmanship. And the laborer himself acted oddly, too. He denied knowing anything about the assassination attempt. But he could not give a clear account of what he had been doing when it occurred. And he seemed reluctant to tell us where he lived, or who his family were—he would only say he worked at the docks.

"So we searched for his name in the dock's records to check his statement. Someone found an accident report. It said that this laborer—Dirak Tizzan—had died in a malfunctioning airlock." His voice grows rough. "Three months ago."

Dirak Tizzan. The name rings in my mind. It never occurred to me to change the dock records. There should never have been any reason to investigate that far.

"Someone must have tampered with the Tizzan's mark-records—made it look like he was alive again. The imposter wouldn't tell us who he really was, even after it was clear that his marks were forged. So we had him taken back to a holding cell at the guild hall." He winces. "We are trying to keep it quiet. We don't want people to hear about this until we find out where he got those marks."

I feel light-headed yet bizarrely detached. "Why not?"

He bares his teeth in a grimace and leans closer. "I will tell you the truth, Mariikel. If the lockdown had not happened, we never would have caught this man. We would have sent him through without a second look. His tattoos were that good." He clasps his knees in a convulsive gesture. "I have seen false marks in my work before, but nothing like this. No half-trained skin-changer made these. It was a master artist—I would swear it." For a moment he struggles to breathe. "They looked like Serix work."

I do not reply.

"I don't want to believe it," my uncle goes on, "but I've seen it with my own eyes. Somewhere on this ship is a Serix artist, or someone trained by a Serix artist, who is giving full sets of false marks. How many other forgeries have slipped past us?" Again he buries his face in his hands. "I don't think a Serix planted that bomb. But I'm almost certain that one made these marks. And if that gets out…"

He does not need to finish. If the High Council finds out that a Serix made illegal tattoos, they will need no other evidence to punish the clan. Forging marks is not merely a crime against the Ascendance. It threatens everyone—because it threatens the truth.

What is the truth? I do not know anymore. I am not sure I ever did.

Hakham stares at the floor, his story finished; he does not seem to notice my silence. I know I should say nothing. If I am to save myself, I need to stand up and leave this room—now, before I do something foolish. But I cannot. My tongue moves, as if by its own power.

"What will happen to him? To the imposter?"

My uncle narrows his eyes in a scowl. "It will depend how he cooperates. If he tells us who made the marks, well—the harsher sentence may fall on the skin-changer, not on him. If he does not tell—" He presses his lips together and falls silent.

My heart throbs, fast and hot, but my hands feel cold, as if they belong to a corpse. "Will he be mark-stripped?"

Hakham avoids my gaze. "That's not for the guild to decide. We must find out his true clan—they have the right to try him first. If he refuses to claim a clan, only then will his sentence fall to the guild. But if he has any connection to the bombing...or if there is a Serix artist involved in this, too... The High Council may overrule everyone and take the case into their own hands."

I feel I am suffocating. As vivid as a nightmare, I see Kophas bowing before me, grasping my filthy ankles. Even now I can feel the grip of his fingers, strong and desperate.

Let me live, markmaker. Let me live.

Hakham stares at me. "Mariikel?"

On weak legs, I stand and look down at my uncle. There is so much to say—so much that is impossible to explain—that we might as well be standing on opposite rims of the pit of Axdraa'dah.

I walk to the front door and tap the entry pad.

"Where are you going?" he demands.

"I don't know." It is the truth. Without another word, I step out and shut the door of my home behind me.

The daylights are just coming on in the corridor, shedding a pale gray radiance on the gardens and painted pillars. There are a few people in the street, but they walk swiftly and silently. I doubt that anyone in the sector slept much last night. Clan Serix is awake—keeping vigil, breathless and afraid. I wander between the houses like a ghost.

There is nowhere to go.

Yet I keep walking—not quickly, but not slowly either. I have a vague, ill-formed thought that I could slip away to the Underbelly, hide until the lockdown is over, and then, perhaps, escape the ship. No one knows yet that I am the skin-changer. But even as I turn the idea over in my mind, I know it is impossible. I remember Kophas's voice, his fervent whisper: *By my ancestors' blood, I swear, I will not betray you.*

I promised him. I promised. He knew the risks; we both did. But it was not supposed to end this way. This task was supposed to be my payment, my reparation for failing Talorak. But now Kophas will die, as Talorak no doubt died. I have led him out of the Underbelly into the clutches of the Deep Sleep.

What am I?

I halt. My steps have led me to the little plaza near Haza'ruux's house. The fountain trickles. The dome glows with the soft, yellow radiance of morning.

My first impulse is to turn away. Why did I come here? I do not want to see Haza'ruux again. Even if he could, in this last hour, offer me sanctuary, I do not want it.

Yet I stand at the edge of the fountain and stare down into the bright and trembling pool. My own face is silhouetted darkly against the reflection of the dome. Slowly I immerse my hands in the water, my wrists limp, my palms turned upward.

I want to live. The words are my own now. But I do not know to whom I am appealing.

"*Hiii-yak!*"

A fierce shout nearby startles me. I step back from the fountain, my hands dripping, before I realize that the voice is a child's. In the corridor, Tyotik Trechik stalks between the houses, a snarl fixed on his lively, dark face. In his hands he wields two slender branches, no doubt broken off from some shrub in Haza'ruux's garden. He does not appear to notice me at first—instead, he springs and tumbles in a battle-dance of his own imagining, dueling an enemy that no one else can see. With a final rush and a yell, he stabs the air with both his weapons—and then falls to the floor in a heap.

He lies still for so long that I wonder if he has fainted. But then he rolls over onto his back, breathing hard. At the sight of me, he sits up and blinks. "Hi, Blade."

A pang of envy makes my throat tighten. What I would give now to be like Tyotik again: playing make-believe in the corridors, ignorant of clan rivalries, of the Ascendance, of the Underbelly. Slowly I crouch down to the boy's level. I cannot manage a smile, but I look him in the eye. "Hello."

"I'm dead." He says this simply. "The burrik killed me."

"Oh." I frown. "I'm sorry to hear that."

"It's all right." He collects his makeshift swords and climbs to his feet. "I'm a death pilgrim." He swings his twigs in the air, enjoying the sound of their whistling.

I tilt my head. "A death pilgrim?"

"You know. I'm a warrior who did something bad, so his clan doesn't like him. Now I have to find a monster to fight. So I can die and be hon—honor-able." He stumbles over the word.

"I see." Emotion washes over me. I ease back on my hocks, down to the floor. "Who told you about death pilgrims?"

"Ha'ruux." He drags his sticks along the floor, looking shy. "He has lots of stories."

"That he does." My voice catches. "So. You're dead now." I wrap my arms around my knees. "Did you get your honor back?"

Tyotik looks down at himself, as if expecting to see tattoos appear on his skinny, markless arms. "I think so."

"That's good." My body quakes, and I clench my teeth.

Tyotik stares at me, wide-eyed and solemn. "You're sad." Slowly he puts down his sticks and hugs my arm. "My nakki is sad sometimes, too."

I cry harder, though still silently. Tyotik climbs into my lap and wraps his arms around my neck. His touch is light and warm. He does not say anything, but simply rests his head on my shoulder and lets me hold him.

After a while my sobs quiet, and I sit for a minute, still pressing him to my chest. He pulls away, blinking. "Are you better?"

"A little." I gaze at the mark on his neck, the sign of Clan Trechik. It is the same tattoo the Ascendance guards wore, the ones who killed Narrik. But this child does not yet see the world in marks alone. "I have to go," I whisper.

"All right." He climbs off my lap and bends down to reclaim his sticks, but I reach out and take hold of his slender hand.

"Can you do something for me?"

He nods.

"Tell Haza'ruux—tell Haza'ruux that I had to go fight the monster."

Tyotik regards me with dark, wondering eyes. "Are you a death pilgrim, too?"

A shiver racks me. "I like to pretend."

"Oh." He considers this. Then he leans over, picks up one of the makeshift swords, and presses it into my hand. "You can have one of mine."

The hour is still early, but the record hall of Clan Serix in Tralkanii Plaza already stands open. Archivists and guild officials hurry in and out of the broad, decorated doors. A small band of Serix guards, tense and alert, flanks the porch. In the middle of the plaza, in the shadow of the aged trallak grove, I halt.

I did not stop at home, nor at Kilmaya's place. I knew that if I spoke to anyone, I would lose my courage. Rixarii Street felt eerily empty when I passed through—no artists, no clients, only the stern, imposing figures of Jal'thor's Tarriks warriors.

Now, as I stand in the trallak grove before the record hall, I look down at the stick Tyotik gave me. The twig looks wispy and foolish, but I do not regret taking it.

Then my eyes fall on my bandaged wrist and the exquisite sigil poem. Underneath the gauze, the acid wound throbs dully. That is my one consolation, in this moment: once I give myself up, I will have nothing more to do with the Arimaas. Haza'ruux will no longer have power over me. The old hermit may possess ancient and terrible magic—but even he cannot rescue me from the law.

It is time to end this.

I set foot on the wide porch and step through the door.

The main archive room opens before me: long and narrow, with brilliantly painted pillars dividing the hall into several airy chambers. But no one seems to be enjoying the building's beauty. Record-keepers sit at rows of display desks, leaning over their screens. Guild officials pace back and forth, pointing at displays, asking questions, conversing in terse exchanges. An air of urgency oppresses the room.

I half-expect to see Kophas somewhere, standing between a pair of guild guards with his hands bound and his feet hobbled. But of course, the holding cells are underneath the guild hall, on the other side of the plaza.

I approach the central display desk, where a harried-looking woman sits, holding a datascroll. She is speaking sharply to someone on the other end of the call. I have to stand before her for several minutes before she finally puts down her device and subjects me to a glare. "The archives are not open to the public today. We are closed for lockdown work. You will have to come back later."

"I don't need to see the archives. My name is Mariikel. I am a markmaker."

"I can see that," the woman snaps. Then her head tilts, and her narrowed eyes relax a little. "You're Hakham's son, aren't you?"

I wince. "Nephew."

"That's right; I always forget. You don't look much like him, do you?" She frowns again. "Well, he's not here. He went home a little while ago."

"I'm not looking for him." The pounding of my heart makes the blood roar faintly in my head. "I—I need to see the recordmaster."

"Virik?" the woman exclaims. "Not a chance. He has enough on his hands."

"I think he will see me. I have information. About the imposter—Dirak Tizzan."

She stiffens and draws a quick breath. "You?"

I blink in affirmation. I do not trust my voice anymore.

She still looks dubious. "The recordmaster is very busy. But if you would like to speak to one of his assistants, we will record your information and pass it on to him. I am sure he will appreciate it."

"No. I can only speak to the recordmaster."

For a minute she regards me, her brow furrowed. "Very well," she says at last and stands. "Follow me." She hurries down the long room, weaving between desks and agitated officials. I follow, trying not to stumble over my own feet. My limbs feel weak and boneless.

At the far end of the hall, we approach a door painted with the sigil of the recordmaster. My eyes linger on the intertwined symbols: the barbed half-circle of *Truth*, the sword-like sweep of *Guardian*. My guts twists again. My clan, my craft—I did not want to betray them. How did I become the enemy, the very threat our recordmaster guards against?

Four armed men stand before the entrance: two Serix guards and two grim, heavyset Tarriks soldiers. As we reach the door, one of the Serix guards shifts his stance. "I am sorry, but the masters cannot be disturbed right now."

"I know," the woman says in a short tone. "This artist has important information on the forgery. He must speak to Virik directly."

The guard frowns but at last nods in assent. He opens the door. Together the woman and I step inside.

In the middle of the chamber, two men study a huge display desk covered with images of tattoos. Virik, his dour face fixed in a grimace of exhaustion, traces one of the images with his finger, speaking earnestly to his companion.

The other man is Mekkalluthak, dressed once more in his white councilor's tunic. Both officials look up and fall silent.

"Guildmaster. Recordmaster." The woman bows. "My apologies for the interruption. This artist insisted on speaking with you. He says he knows something about the imposter."

For a moment, the men simply stare at me. Virik appears surprised and irritated, but Mekkalluthak's expression remains ambiguous. His eyelids twitch. I incline my head and do not look up. Terror numbs me. I did not expect the guildmaster to be here, too.

"Thank you," says Virik stiffly. "You may leave him with us."

The woman salutes, touching her neck. But she turns slowly, with obvious reluctance, and gives me a sidelong glance as she exits and shuts the door.

I stand in silence.

"Hakham told you what happened?" Virik seems displeased. "Well, I suppose I cannot blame him much. Guildmaster, you know Mariikel, I'm sure? He is the nephew of one of my record-keepers."

"Thank you. We know each other well." Mekkalluthak speaks quietly but with a peculiar intensity. I raise my eyes.

"So." Virik subjects me to another glare. "You say know something about this forgery?"

I cannot move. I grip Tyotik's little sword, but my blood has frozen in my veins. My throat refuses to make a sound.

"Well?" Virik grunts.

"You needn't be afraid," says Mekkalluthak. "Whatever you can tell us, we will be grateful. You are doing a great service to the clan."

He assumes his gracious manner with ease, though he, too, looks exhausted. Between the clan funeral and all the turmoil following the assassination attempt, I doubt he slept at all last night.

At last I wet my lips. "Before I speak—if I tell you who made those false marks, will you spare the imposter?" My voice cracks. "Will you promise not to have him executed?"

Virik frowns. "What is that to you?"

"I have to know."

"I can't promise that. That's not up to us. We don't even know who the man is."

Mekkalluthak lifts a hand, and Virik quiets. The guildmaster watches me, his eyes bright and cold. "Who are you to make such a demand?"

A violent trembling grips my body. In my chest, my heart seems to contract. *Oh, my ancestors. Help me.* I sink to my knees. With reverent care, I place Tyotik's twig on the floor before me. Then I raise my head and meet the guildmaster's gaze.

"I am the skin-changer."

CHAPTER TWENTY-NINE

At first, they do not believe me. Virik demands to know who threatened me into making this absurd confession. Then he asks if there is some other artist I am trying to protect. In answer, I begin reciting—in a dull voice but in exhaustive detail—the list of Kophas's false marks. After a minute, Virik cuts me off.

"Did Hakham show you all of that? Is he part of this?"

"My uncle knows nothing. I know those marks because I made them."

The recordmaster is about to burst out again, but Mekkalluthak restrains him with a touch on the arm. "Virik. I think we had better listen. Set up a recording, please."

Virik scowls but inclines his head. "Yes, guildmaster."

"And tell Ikhalo to come in and bind him. Mariikel, you are under arrest—since you are so insistent." He leans across the desk with a dire light in his eyes. For the first time since I entered the room, he looks angry. "And then, you will sit down and tell us what, in the name of Ka and all the ancestors, you have been doing."

As ordered, one of the Serix guards comes into the room, sits me down in a chair, and slips a leather hobbling-strap around my ankles. Not that I could hurt anyone even if I tried—my spurs are short and dull, and my sparring skills almost nonexistent. But I submit to the restraint without protest. While the guard retreats to stand behind my chair, Virik enters a command into the display desk to record the conversation. Then both the recordmaster and the guildmaster sit down across from me.

I find I am oddly calm now, as if the worst is over. I tell them about Talorak—his trial, his exile, my certainty that he had been falsely condemned. My interrogators hear me out with stony faces. Mekkalluthak asks why I did not alert the guild of this incident at the time. For a moment I sit in silence, staring at my limp hands in my lap. "I was afraid. At the time, no one was accusing the Ascendance of false judgments. And I had no evidence—only my own suspicions."

Mekkalluthak's brow lowers. I wonder, suddenly, if he is thinking of Jal'thor, the Tarriks commander who has been defending Clan Serix. Does the guildmaster know of Jal'thor's connection with Talorak—that he, too, believed the old warrior to be innocent? But if Mekkalluthak does know, he remains quiet. He motions for me to go on.

I tell them of my first journey to the Underbelly in search of Talorak. How I could not find him, even after many trips to the realm of the exiles. How instead I found Kophas, and hearing his tale of injustice—so similar to Talorak's—I decided to help him. I say nothing of the other exiles to whom I gave marks. They do not come into this story, and I will not betray them if I can help it. They do not need to suffer any more because of my folly.

Virik listens to my account with muted fury. "It did not occur to you that this Tarriks exile might be lying to you?"

"No. I looked up his records. He seemed to be an honorable man."

"He *seemed* to be?" Virik explodes. "You had no proof. No witnesses. What kind of markmaker are you?"

"A very good one." Mekkalluthak sounds bitterly amused. "He nearly slipped this exile past us all."

Virik glares at the guildmaster in astonishment. But before he can retort, Mekkalluthak leans forward again. "Did anyone help you with this forgery?"

"No. I...I did use my uncle's access to the archives to alter the records. But he didn't know." I hang my head. "No one knew what I was doing."

This is not quite the truth. Haza'ruux knew I was going to the Underbelly, though I never told him about Kophas. But I see no reason to bring him into this, either. The old hermit neither helped nor hindered me in my crime; he does not deserve punishment. And besides, I must avoid talking about the Arimaas. There are still some secrets I do not dare reveal.

Mekkalluthak sits back. He has resumed his impassive expression, but now and then a tiny muscle spasms under the fine, interlocking tattoos around his eyes. On the desk, he clasps his fingers together tightly. "And what did you get out of it? This Kophas Tarriks—what did he do for you?"

"Nothing. What could he do?"

"He's not even a mercenary," Virik growls. "He's simply an idiot." Fuming, he stands up and strides across the room, then turns on me again. "Were there others? Who else have you smuggled out of the Underbelly?"

"No one." This, at least, I can say in truth. "Kophas was the only one."

"And that satisfied you, did it? Do you realize what you've done?"

I lower my gaze, subdued. "I am willing to bear the consequences."

"Consequences! You talk of *consequences*? Do you have any idea what the High Council is going to do when they hear of this?"

I have no answer. The recordmaster opens his mouth and curses me.

"Kesh, Virik." Mekkalluthak rises. "Mariikel, you appear to have admirable but misguided intentions. Even if this Tarriks warrior were exiled unjustly—of which we have no certain proof—you have still broken guild law and your markmaker's oath. That is inexcusable." He draws a deep breath, and his jaw tightens. "Besides that, your admission of guilt will complicate the clan's situation considerably. This bombing that occurred yesterday—"

"I had nothing to do with that."

The guildmaster's brow pinches with weariness. "I would like to believe you. But it probably will not matter."

"What do you mean?"

"You and your Tarriks exile may not have tried to kill the High Councilor. We may or may not be able to prove it. Regardless, you have still defied the authority of the Ascendance in the most flagrant way possible—helping a traitorous warrior escape his sentence. This offence will not be seen as yours alone." His cold glare turns wrathful. "The whole clan will have to bear the weight of it."

Oh, Ka. I feel as if a chasm opens in my belly. It did not even occur to me that the High Council might draw a connection between my crime and the assassination attempt on Valo T'sarek. But of course, they will leap at any chance to accuse Clan Serix of dishonor, and I have given them exactly the opportunity they need. How could I have been such a fool?

But there was no other way to save Kophas.

"I—I didn't think—"

"Of course you didn't." The guildmaster cuts me off. "But it's too late now. We will have to fight those battles when they come. In any case, your crime is extremely serious in itself. Whatever happens, I can tell you now that you will never return to your studio."

"I know." All at once I see myself kneeling in Rixarii Street, under guard, with my family and my teacher looking on, while another artist paints a sigil of shame on my brow. *This was a mark of truth. You have marred and dishonored it.* I grip the sides of my chair. "What will happen to Kophas?"

Mekkalluthak does not answer right away. He looks down at me with a mingling of contempt and desolation. Then he shudders and seems to hear my words. "I do not know."

I close my eyes. I have given everything now. Still it may not be enough.

Mekkalluthak gestures to the Serix guard behind my chair. "Ikhalo, take him to a holding cell for now. Discreetly, please. I must bring this information to the rest of the council." The guildmaster paces around the desk and stands in front of it. The guard grasps my arm.

"Wait. Can I—can I send a message to my family?"

"No," Virik barks. "Your honor is forfeit. You speak to no one."

The guard pulls me to my feet. I do not resist as he leads me, shuffling in my hobbles, to the door. When I glance back, Virik still glowers at me, teeth bared. But Mekkalluthak bends down, reaching for something on the floor. He picks up Tyotik's twig and twirls it between his fingers.

The Serix guard leads me away from the busy main room of the archives and down a deserted hallway. I keep tripping over the awkward constraint of the hobbles, but to my faint surprise, Ikhalo does not chide me or treat me roughly—instead he catches my arm whenever I stumble and lets me lean against him. We enter an elevator, and after descending a single floor, come out into a long, narrow corridor. I do not recognize this place, but it must be a private passage between the record hall and the guild hall. Mekkalluthak must not want my arrest to be known yet.

At the end of the corridor, we pass through another door and enter the lower floor of the guild hall. I have never been here before, either; I only recognize it because of the stylized trallak leaves painted on the walls at regular intervals. The guard takes me down a short hallway to a row of holding cells. He sketches a symbol into an entry pad and opens one of the rooms.

The cell is small and minimally furnished: a cot sits against one wall, a chair and table against the other. In the corner is a cramped washroom. The walls are bare metal, devoid of paintings or sigils. Ikhalo unfastens my hobbles as I stand in the middle of the chamber.

"How long will it take?" I ask.

"Until what?"

"Until they decide what to do with me."

"I couldn't say." He blinks and regards me with an odd expression. He is an older man, and his marks tell me that he has escorted Serix guild members for many years. "I know it's poor comfort now," he says, "but by the skin of the Deep Sleep, that was a brave thing you did."

I stare at him, bewildered. Ikhalo smiles grimly.

"But you did not hear me say that." Touching his clan tattoo, he nods in a quiet gesture of respect. "Honor with you, markmaker." Then he steps out and shuts the cell door. For a moment I stand listless, taking in the bleak room. Then I walk slowly to the cot and sit down.

I went to the record hall thinking only of the moment of confession; I considered nothing after that. I did not think of the imprisonment, the waiting. I did not think of my family, who will now have to endure witnessing my trial and perhaps my banishment or execution. The thought of Hakham, Chervani, and Kilmaya torments me. Even if they hear my whole story, I do not know if they will ever understand.

For myself, though, I am not afraid—not like I was before. Everything is out of my hands now. I still fear pain, certainly. If I receive the death sentence and my marks are stripped from my body, I know I will scream through every moment until the executioner slits my throat and ends my misery. But death—death I cannot bring myself to fear. Even Haza'ruux dreamed that I would face the Deep Sleep willingly. In that much, perhaps, he was right.

I wait. I lie on the cot for a while, exhausted but too anxious to sleep. I get up and pace the room. I lean against the door, listening for any talk or movement outside. I wonder if they have put Kophas in a cell near me. But I can hear nothing except the faint whisper of the air vents in the ceiling.

After a few hours, another guild guard brings me a meal. She refuses to answer my desperate request for news and leaves again without speaking. The food is bland and unappetizing—two strips of boiled tavla and a cluster of underripe yekri fruit—but I eat it anyway. I am hungry, and I have nothing else to do.

As I eat, I notice that the bandage on my wrist is loose and wrinkled. I take a moment to peel it off, wincing as the gauze sticks slightly to the raw skin underneath. My wrist appears swollen and irritated—though the sigil poem remains unharmed and vivid as ever. So much for my one attempt to change my own skin.

I gently rinse my arm at the tiny sink in the washroom and. The healing ointment has rubbed off, and the wound stings worse than ever, as if there is a slow fire burning just under the surface of my skin. I marvel now that Kophas allowed me to put him through this pain for weeks on end. That man has suffered so much for his freedom—all for nothing now. If his clan court is merciful, he will merely be sent back into exile. But if the Ascendance gets its hands on him…I do not want to think about that.

Carefully, I wrap my wrist in the gauze again. The bandage is dirty, but I have nothing else to use. If the swelling does not go down soon, I might have to ask the guards for more healing salve. But for now, I am willing to bear the pain.

Cradling my hurt wrist against my chest, I allow my eyes to dwell on the interlocking lines of the sigil poem. The tattoo is so beautiful. Even though I have translated it—roughly—I could still study it for years and not be able to glean every nuance. But I will never live up to Haza'ruux's strange honor-mark now. Dreams or no dreams, I am going to die as a criminal.

I lean my back against the wall and sink to the floor. I sit and grieve in silence.

Eventually the lights in the cell dim to a deep nighttime blue. I lie down on the cot, staring at the darkened ceiling. For the first time in I cannot remember how long, I raise a sincere prayer to my Serix ancestors—or to anyone dwelling in the Long Dream who might deign to listen. I do not ask for mercy but only the strength to bear whatever comes.

I do not expect to sleep well. But my mind and body are so overwrought that I drift off almost as soon as I have finished my invocation. My rest is deep and dreamless, and I do not wake until the daylights switch back on.

After a while, a guard brings me another meal, but nothing else—no news, no indication of when the guild will summon me to trial. My wrist still hurts, but I cannot bring myself to ask for medicine or a clean bandage.

I finish the meal. Hours pass. It seems strange that no one has come for me yet. Don't the other councilors want to question me as well? But I do not know much about these kinds of proceedings. I might be here for days before anyone summons me—weeks, perhaps. Groaning softly, I lean my forehead against the bare metal of the door. I wonder how my family and my teacher are doing, whether they have heard yet. The thought of my loved ones makes me sick with anguish.

Eventually I grow tired of pacing the cell, but I am too restless to lie down and sleep. I need to occupy my mind. I kneel in the middle of the room, bow my head to the floor, and put my hand over my clan-mark. I do not know if my ancestors are listening, or if they can help me. But I do not know how else to pray.

Honorable ones, I call on you. By the bond of this clan-mark, hear me. I beg you, let Kophas live. Do not let my life be for nothing—

Of a sudden, I hear muffled footsteps in the hallway. Then the lock buzzes, and the door hisses open. I scramble to my feet. A Serix guard—Ikhalo, the older man who first escorted me here—stands in the entrance. "Markmaker." The corners of his eyes crease in sympathy. "Your family is here to see you."

He steps aside. Before I can speak or move, Chervani rushes forward with a piercing cry. Then she is in my arms, clinging to me, weeping bitter, racking sobs.

"Mariikel. My little one. My gentle one."

I hold her tightly, too heart-stricken to respond.

Hakham enters the cell with more reluctance. His upper eyes are narrowed, his face stony. Ikhalo steps to the door again. "Half an hour," he says, and taps the entry pad. The cell door slides closed.

Chervani leans against me heavily, still crying. I lower myself onto the cot so that we can both sit on the edge of it. "Kesh. Please, nakki. Kesh, now."

"Why?" Her fingers dig into my shoulders. "Why, Mariikel? How could you do this to us?"

I do not answer. For a minute I simply hold her in my arms until her violent shuddering subsides. Hakham still stands by the door, cold and aggrieved. He has not said a word yet. I am afraid to meet his gaze, but the silence is unbearable. Finally, I ask: "What did they tell you?"

"Everything." Hakham's expression does not change. "They let us listen to your statement." Then his eyes flash, and his lips curl back in a snarl. "After they had questioned us like *criminals*!"

I flinch. Chervani sobs again. But my uncle's face only contorts with rage. "All this time. All this time, you have been lying to us. My archive access. You used *my* mastery-mark for this. This crime…"

"I'm sorry." There is nothing to say, nothing I can do to repair this breach of trust.

"I remember." Chervani pulls away from me. "I remember when Talorak Tarriks was exiled. I didn't know you gave him the mark, but I knew you were upset. But this…" She clasps my hands, bending over, rocking in her grief. "You didn't have to do this, dako! There must have been another way."

I try to hush her again, murmuring useless words. My throat aches. I want to tell her about Kophas: his suffering, his longing for the planets, the way he wept when I erased his sister's memory-mark. I want to tell her about the other exiles I served: the young mothers, the children, the old men wasting from hunger and disease. *If you could have seen them, nakki, you would have helped them, too.*

"I'm sorry. I didn't mean for things to happen this way."

"And what did you mean to happen?" Hakham's face remains livid. "You have dishonored us. It was bad enough when a son of mine chose to leave us for a lesser clan. But to have a skin-changer living in my own house…" He chokes off the words. Never in my life have I seen Hakham so enraged. But then, this is the man who first taught me the law, who instilled the honor-code in my mind when I was still a child.

"Na'thalo." My voice tremors. "If it were Askko who had been exiled—and you knew the sentence was unjust—what would you have done?"

His nostrils flare as he inhales harshly. He steps forward and raises a hand as if to strike me. But Chervani leaps up and catches his arm.

"Leave him alone!" she screams. "The Ascendance has already taken one of our sons from us. Do you want them to take him, too?"

Hakham grows rigid. He stares at my aunt with unspeakable pain. Then he wrenches his arm away and turns towards the wall. His shoulders are shaking.

"They want to kill you." Chervani sinks to the floor, kneeling before me. "They want to strip your marks."

Despite my earlier resolve, fear tingles down my spine. "Who does?"

"The High Council." Hakham's rage has dissolved; he looks like a broken man. "They ordered the guild to hand you over. But Mekkalluthak will not do it. He says you have the right to be tried by your own clan. He is still holding out."

Mekkalluthak is protecting me? "For how long?"

"I don't know. He closed the clan gate and stationed a band of those Tarriks warriors there. No one can get in or out of the sector."

Ancestors help us. I do not think I have ever heard of a guildmaster closing the sector gate before. Mekkalluthak would not take such a drastic action unless he thought Ascendance troops might come in and seize me by force. "He can't keep it closed forever. What is he going to do?"

"I don't know," Hakham answers.

"The clan is turning against him," Chervani says. "People are frightened. There was a protest today in Rixarii Street. Even the other councilors are abandoning him." She stares up at me, her teeth bared in agony. "They want to give you up."

"Well." My throat tightens. "If it will bring peace…"

"Don't say that! Kin's heart, Mariikel, don't say that." She breaks down weeping again, resting her head on my knees.

Hakham looks on, stricken. "They want to accuse you of conspiring against the High Councilor. You and that Tarriks exile."

"Kophas is not the assassin. He has nothing to do with this."

My uncle shakes his head. "I am not sure it matters anymore."

Silence settles between us, disturbed only by Chervani's stifled moans. I clasp her hands gently. I want to lift her up, to tell her everything will be all right, as I have done in the past. But that would be a lie, and I cannot lie to her anymore.

All at once, I remember the other person I have lied to countless times—my teacher. Fearfully, I raise my eyes to Hakham. "Does Kilmaya know?"

"Yes." He glances away. "She was summoned for questioning, too."

I imagine the guild officials knocking at my teacher's door, telling her that I have been arrested, that I am a skin-changer. The thought becomes too painful. I shut it out. "Have you spoken with her?"

"Only briefly. She…did not want to see us."

I swallow. "Do you think she will see me?"

"I don't know."

Oh, my teacher. Don't leave me. Not like this. "If you see her, can you tell her I am sorry?"

My uncle blinks mutely in assent.

"Tell her…tell her I acted as well as I knew how…when there was no honorable path before me. If I must die for that…" A wave of sorrow strangles me; I cannot finish. "I know I have no excuse. I have shamed you all…"

"No." All at once Chervani lifts her head, gripping my fingers convulsively. Her expression has hardened, and in the depths of her tender eyes glitters something fierce and steely. "No, Mariikel. I am not ashamed of you. I don't care what they do to me; I will not renounce you. Not now, and not…" She lowers her head again, trembling, caressing my hands.

I find myself staring at her shoulder, at the two child-marks on her upper arm: one for Askko, and one, with the sigil of adoption, for me. All at once I feel I cannot breathe. "Nakki," I cry. And to Hakham: "Nakko."

Hakham glances at me, startled. I have never called him *father* before.

"Forgive me. Forgive me." And then I cannot speak anymore.

Hakham stirs. He places his hand on my neck, over my clan-mark. His whisper is rough and unsteady. "Ancestors protect you—" He does not get any farther. He kneels down and embraces me. Chervani murmurs my name over and over. They do not let go of me until the guard returns to the cell.

CHAPTER THIRTY

That night, I dream of home.

I am sitting with my family in our front room, sharing klasindi and spicy alkani wafers. I feel it must be a festival day—Van'shorvanii, or perhaps Dawravanii, the new year's celebration. The room seems to be full of people chattering loudly. Nearby, Hakham and Chervani laugh with Kilmaya. Across the room stands Askko, tall and splendid in his full hvoss'ka armor. He is engaged in conversation with a young couple whose faces I do not recognize—but somehow I know they are my mother and father, my birth parents.

I do not find this strange at all, and neither do I feel the need to speak to them. Instead I feel an intense, almost painful happiness. The guild must have pardoned me. My crimes must have been forgiven. How else could I be here, enjoying a festival meal with my family?

"Hakka, quiet one."

Kilmaya is suddenly sitting beside me, three eyes squinted in amusement. I babble something, begging her forgiveness. Yet she does not seem angry. Her face creases in fond exasperation. "Look at the mess you've made. Now I have to clean it up."

She grasps my right arm. I look down. Haza'ruux's tattoo appears strangely colorless—the intricate patterns have decayed into a chaotic scrawl. Before I can cry out in surprise, Kilmaya rubs my arm with a cloth. The dull ink lifts away from my skin as easily as mud.

A mingled emotion washes over me: horror at the mark's destruction, but relief that I am finally free of it. How could it be so simple to remove?

"Flashing Blade."

A voice ripples the air, so deep and visceral that I feel the vibration of it in my bones. I spring to my feet. Standing on the far side of the room, as if he had walked in through the wall, is Haza'ruux.

He looks like a creature of light—every tattoo in his flesh smolders and flickers with radiance. His four eyes burn violet-white. On his chest, the image of the raving hound snaps and writhes. *"Flashing Blade."* When he speaks, the whole room seems to quake. "What are you doing?"

He approaches me. The people standing between us do not appear to notice him. Compared to the sharp brilliance of the Keeper's body, the other figures seem misty and insubstantial. Haza'ruux passes through them as if they are made of smoke.

I drop to my knees. Kilmaya has disappeared, and so has my family. I know I am having a nightmare, but that knowledge does not lessen my terror. I have never had a dream like this one. The mad markmaker stands before me now, surreally vivid. I can feel his presence, his immediacy, like a white heat in my spirit.

"What have you done? Why are you harming your mark?" With one brilliant hand, he reaches down towards me.

I jerk away. "Get out." I stagger upright and clench my fists. My voice rises to a scream, wild and hoarse. "Leave me alone! Get out of my house!"

The room reels; my vision foams with darkness. For a moment I can only see the mad markmaker, with his bright and terrible face, reaching for me as if from a great distance. But I still shriek in rage. "Get out. Get out. *Get out—*"

I awake with a yell on my cot in the prison. The bare chamber rings with my own voice. Then the echoes die. I am alone.

My heart throbs fiercely in my chest. I lie on the cot for many minutes, shuddering under the thin blanket. After a long time, I raise my right arm and look at it under the muted blue lights. Haza'ruux's mark is still there, dark and twisting on my silver skin.

I hide it again under the blanket. I roll over and stare at the empty wall. But I do not sleep. I am too afraid.

For two days, I see no one except the guards who bring me food. I eat; I try to pray; I sleep only fitfully. Sometimes I dream—but Haza'ruux does not appear to me again.

On the third day, no one comes to my cell at all, not even to give me a meal. When my stomach begins to twist with hunger, I get up and bang on the door. I shout for the guards. When I pause, I think I can hear a metallic pounding from the corridor beyond—as if someone is hitting another door in answer to my cries. But no guard comes.

I lean against the wall, achy and light-headed. The acid wound on my wrist feels even worse now; the skin around it is warm and painful to the touch. The next time someone comes to my cell, I will have to ask for medicine—if there is a next time. Does the guild mean to let me starve here?

Day becomes evening; the cell lights dim to amber. I lie on the cot, dozing uneasily, when I hear the tramp of feet in the hallway. Before I can push myself upright, the door unlocks and hisses open.

Two Tarriks warriors, heavily armored, stand in the corridor. Both wear visored helmets; I cannot see their faces.

"Get up," one soldier says. "The guildmaster will see you now."

Dizzy, I sit up. The warriors do not bother to bind me but simply pull me to my feet with brusque efficiency. I gasp with pain as one strong hand closes around my injured wrist. Gripping my arms, the men push me along in front of them, out of the cell. I stumble once, but they haul me up again before I can fall.

Swiftly the warriors take me down a maze of short corridors. We are still underneath the guild hall, but I do not see any officials, only more guards. A few are Serix, but most are Clan Tarriks—more of Jal'thor's men. They move through the passageways in grim haste. These soldiers, too, are battle-armed. Some carry supply packs on their shoulders, and many—to my surprise—now wear handguns at their belts and larger firearms slung across their backs.

At last, we arrive at an elaborate door painted with Mekkalluthak's name-sigil. One of the warriors raises a hand and is about to knock when the door opens of its own accord. A broad-shouldered, maroon-skinned figure steps out into the corridor—Jal'thor, the leader of the Tarriks warband.

"Valk'taro!" My escort stiffens. Both warriors bow, forcing me to lower my head as well.

When they rise again, I find myself staring up into Jal'thor's stern face. The Tarriks commander stands well over a head taller than me, and combat-marks festoon his muscled arms and shoulders. He squints, mouth tightening in a mirthless expression. His voice, when he speaks, is a curt growl. "So this is our skin-changer."

My legs buckle. *He knows.* This commander is Talorak's friend, the one man who tried to save the old warrior from unjust exile. And now he knows I am the artist who branded his clanmate with a mark of banishment, who condemned him to the Underbelly.

Then—to my utter bewilderment—the commander breaks into a low, rumbling laugh.

I glance up. Jal'thor's frown has melted. "So you are the one whose blood the whole ship is calling for. I admit, I expected someone more impressive." Critically he eyes my cowering posture. "Can you even stand upright? Who taught you your sparring stances, painter?"

His jesting manner takes me aback. After a moment of shock, I swallow hard and still my quaking limbs. "Talorak Tarriks."

Jal'thor's face darkens. "So I heard." A silence. "You didn't learn much from him, did you?"

"No, valk'taro. I was a very poor student in the sparring arena."

"But a gifted one in the studios." Jal'thor tilts his head to one side. I have a fleeting sense that he is testing me. I try to back away, but the warriors tighten their grip on my arms and hold me still.

"Come, markmaker. I am not your enemy." A curious laugh escapes him. "I commend your boldness. As one oathbreaker to another."

I stare at him, baffled. He bares his teeth in a roguish grin.

"The Ascendance has a price on both our heads. But perhaps, if we die, we shall die well." The commander's expression sobers, and some muted emotion flickers in his eyes. "Thank you for searching for Talorak. He was my teacher, too."

For a moment, I cannot speak. "I am sorry I could not find him."

The ghost of a smile lingers on Jal'thor's severe countenance. "You learned more from him than you know, I think."

I do not respond. My guards shift their feet.

"Hakk. Well, skin-changer, I'm glad to have met you. Perhaps, when we have more leisure, I might call upon your services." The facetious glint returns to his eye, and he taps a hand on his armored chest. "I've an old faction-mark that needs removing."

With that parting remark he turns, striding down the hall with a brisk step. Warriors salute him as he passes. Dumbfounded, I watch his broad, retreating back—until my guards tear me away and tug me forward, through the open door of the guildmaster's chamber.

Mekkalluthak's private office is softly lit and tastefully furnished—decorated desks and chairs, inlaid with real wood, stand throughout the room. Paintings line the walls: portraits of past guild leaders. Yet despite the luxury, the chamber looks disarrayed. A miscellaneous pile of crates occupies one corner—clothing, soldiers' ration packs, ammunition. Against the back wall sits a cot, like the one from my prison cell, heaped with rumpled blankets. In an ornate chair in the middle of the room, Mekkalluthak sits alone. His face looks sunken.

One of the warriors touches his neck in a curt salute. "Here is the skin-changer."

"Thank you." Mekkalluthak does not raise his eyes. "Leave us."

With another bow, the soldiers turn and exit the chamber. The door clicks closed behind them. All at once I wish Jal'thor were still here.

"Sit down, Mariikel."

The guildmaster's voice is quiet and expressionless. Slowly I lower myself into a seat across from him. For a long time, he gazes at me in silence. Then his eyelids twitch, and he stirs. "Do you remember receiving your memory-marks when your parents died?"

I blink, taken aback. "No, guildmaster. I was very young."

"I remember." His mouth tightens. "I was the one who gave them to you—when I was still an artist."

What? The skin of my back tingles. *Mekkalluthak painted my memory-marks?* How did I not know that? Hakham and Chervani must know; they would have brought me to the studio, all those years ago. But perhaps they did not like to remind me that I was an orphan. Mekkalluthak would have been quite a young markmaker at the time. He would not have been well known yet.

Now, the guildmaster watches me with half-lidded eyes. "A two-year-old child, bearing the marks of death on his body. I thought it was merely a tragedy then." His face hardens. "I did not think it was an omen."

"What do you mean?"

With one finger, he traces the sigils carved into the armrest of his chair. "I assume no one has told you what happened."

"I heard that the clan sector had been barricaded. And that..." I hesitate. "And that the High Council want me handed over."

"Yes. You and your Tarriks friend have been declared traitors to the Ascendance. But you are in good company." He smirks and spreads out his hands. "So have I."

"What?"

"Oh, it was only a matter of time. If you had not given them an excuse, they would have found another. But it is true: the High Council has ordered my arrest." His eyes glitter. "I am guilty, apparently, of harboring the would-be murderer of Valo T'sarek and the artist who changed his skin."

A coldness settles in my limbs. "Guildmaster. Kophas is not the assassin. You must believe me."

He waves an impatient hand. "*I* believe you. But the Ascendance is determined to find themselves an assassin. And I doubt they will ever find the real one."

"Why not?"

Mekkalluthak's brow lowers. "It would not surprise me if Valo T'sarek arranged this bombing himself—precisely to lay the blame on Clan Serix. I do not know for certain. But for now, there are more important matters. The clan is in danger."

Haza'ruux's gravelly voice rises in my memory: *If the chieftain is worthy, and the clan is in danger...* I shiver. "How?"

"The High Council threatened to bring charges of treachery against anyone who continues to support me. Meanwhile, they are offering safety—asylum, as it were—to any Serix who wants it. At a price." Mekkalluthak bares his teeth. "They are demanding that the whole clan pledge loyalty to the faction."

Horror seizes me. "Everyone? Even the artists?"

"Of course the artists. Us most of all. That is what they have wanted from the beginning." His voice takes on a bitter, ironic note. "Clan Serix has dishonored itself. We no longer stand for the truth—meaning, of course, the will of the Ascendance." Then he grows more serious. "They are afraid of us, Mariikel. Our mark-bans have caused immense disorder on the ship. The clans, the warriors especially, are discontented. Some are on the brink of rebellion—indeed, some have already crossed it. If the High Council allows this conflict to continue, they will have a civil war on their hands, as well as the war with the half-sights. And they cannot afford that. So they must find a way to control the guild instead."

"Guildmaster." I can hardly speak. "This is insanity. If all they want is my blood… My life is not worth this!"

His eyes flicker with a strange expression. "Hakka, Mariikel. You do not even know what you are." Then he shakes his head. "No. Under other circumstances—if you were an ordinary skin-changer—I would not hesitate to hand you over. But you are not ordinary. You choose your crimes carefully, rethurax."

I start to cry out again, but he silences me with a glare. "I have many reasons to want you alive. The first is your testimony about Talorak Tarriks. Combined with Jal'thor's support, we will be able to make a strong case that Talorak was, in fact, exiled for political convenience and not a true crime. If we can bring that evidence before the clans, it will be a great blow to the faction. And this young warrior, Kophas—his story of the half-sight prisoners may be useful, too. There are many things happening in the war that the Ascendance would prefer to keep hidden from the people here on the Fleet."

"You knew." Grievance wells up in me, a fierce heat under my ribs. "How long have you known about Talorak?"

"Not as long as you, evidently." Mekkalluthak shoots me a withering glance. "Jal'thor only came to me with his own testimony a few weeks ago. I cannot be blamed for injustices of which I was not aware. So don't count yourself so righteous, Mariikel. If you had brought your suspicions to the guild months ago—as your duty as an artist demanded—I may have been able to intervene. But you did not."

My duty… I sink back into silence, my indignation dissolving into nauseating shame. I have no one but myself to blame for my cowardice.

"But that is all useless speculation now," Mekkalluthak resumes. "We no longer have the luxury or protection of the law—only the sword." He leans back in his ornate seat. "Jal'thor has fifty of his best warriors guarding the sector gate. The High Council will have to send troops to fight them if they want to get in. By the time they make up their minds to do it, we will be gone."

"We?"

"Jal'thor has access to a personal spacecraft at a maintenance dock. As soon as he makes the proper arrangements, we will board it: you, Kophas, and I. I have contacts in other parts of the Fleet—people who will help us. If necessary, we may even seek refuge on the planets."

I stare at him, aghast. Is this the same man who denounced the Ascendance in fiery words in front of all the artists of Clan Serix? How can he talk of fleeing?

"What about the clan?"

He does not look up at me. But I can see the desolation in his face. "It is better for them to submit for a time and survive. We will return for them. I swear it."

A sour taste rises in my throat. "You are abandoning them."

His eyes flash. "I am *not* abandoning them. I can find us allies. I can raise us an army. But I cannot do either of those things if I am dead or imprisoned." He speaks so forcefully that spittle flecks his dark lips. "You of all people should know that. The clan can endure temporary oppression for a greater good." He gives me a piercing look. "It has before."

A chill grips me. "What are you talking about?"

He laughs, brittle and mirthless. "I think you know what I am talking about. Our ancestors—they did not always bear the name of Serix."

"I don't know what you mean."

"You do not have to play the fool with me. I know perfectly well who Haza'ruux is. And so do you."

I do not reply. But my heart beats with a terrible fear.

"Our true history is not quite as much of a secret as the mad markmakers would like it to be. It is difficult, but not impossible, for a dedicated scholar to piece together the truth—if he is willing to read strange tales." He stares at me, his eyes wide and baleful. "I know what he has been teaching you."

"He is not teaching me anymore. He sent me away."

The guildmaster scowls. "I doubt that very much. That old man has been waiting for decades to choose an apprentice. And I can see better, now," he adds in a softer voice, "why he chose you."

"He's wrong," I say hoarsely. "He made a mistake."

Mekkalluthak ignores me. "You are a bold man, Mariikel. You desire justice. You have no love for the Ascendance. And you know how to keep a secret. That alone makes you dangerous." His voice sinks to a rasp. "And once you have mastered the true craft…the Arimaas…"

This is madness. "Guildmaster, I am not—"

"I know what you are." He points at my arm, at the exquisite tattoo. "You are the next Keeper. But what do you think you are keeping the Arimaas *for*?" Abruptly he stands up; his hands quiver with agitation. "I am not a fool. I understand why it has been kept a secret. But there is a time to preserve knowledge and a time to use it. The mad markmakers have always been guardians of our clan, of our most precious heritage. Everything that we possess is now under threat—our freedom, our marks, our very honor." His nostrils flare; a wild light shines in his face. "What better time to bring back the ancient strength of Clan Sko'larik?"

I do not speak. I have glimpsed what he means, and it terrifies me.

"Now you know why I cannot let you die," says Mekkalluthak. "The day is coming when the clans—all of them—will have to throw off the tyranny of the Ascendance. And they will need our help. Think, Mariikel. Think what would happen if we could raise up warriors to rival the Van'shorii."

I am thinking. I am thinking of all the books Haza'ruux made me read, of the devastating war between the Keepers of the Arimaas and the order of deepcrafters. I do not doubt anymore that the stories are true. Slowly I shake my head. "You are insane."

He barks with laughter. "No. Only practical. A warrior does not leave his best blade to rust in the sheath."

Flashing Blade. I shudder. Does he only see me as a weapon to wield?

I must put an end to this. My wrist throbs with pain, but I clench my fingers into fists. "Guildmaster, I am not Haza'ruux's apprentice. He told me so himself."

Fury contorts his face. "Don't lie to me. What else could you possibly be?"

I open my mouth but find that I have no answer. Haza'ruux said I would be chieftain of the clan—but even if I believed that, I do not dare admit it now, to the guildmaster's face.

Mekkalluthak scoffs at my silence and collapses back into his chair. "No matter. Haza'ruux needs you; that much is clear. If he ever wants you back, he will have to come to me."

The venom in his words takes my breath away. *He is still angry,* I realize, with a faint sense of shock. *He has hated Haza'ruux for all these years.*

"I can't give you what you're looking for," I repeat. "If it's Haza'ruux you really want, why not bring him?"

The guildmaster does not reply—but he shifts in his seat, and I can tell the question nettles him. *But of course.* Trust the mad markmaker to disappear when he is most wanted. "You can't find him, can you?"

Mekkalluthak's glower tells me I have guessed right. "He knows where *you* are, I have no doubt—and what he must do if he wants to continue your training. If nothing else, he cares about preserving his own craft. He will come."

"He won't do it." I could almost laugh. If the guildmaster is trying to use me to lure Haza'ruux out of hiding, he does not understand the old hermit at all. "He would rather kill me."

"Rather than what? Admit that the Arimaas falls under my authority?" Mekkalluthak smiles. "We will see about that. Either he comes with us, or he stays and submits to a faction-mark like the rest of the clan. Which do you think he will choose?"

I do not answer. I am thinking of my family and Kilmaya with the sign of the Ascendance branded on their chests like a violet scar.

"Enough of this." The guildmaster stands and turns away. "I have more preparations to make tonight, before we leave. You will remain in your cell until then. Jal'thor's men will come for you when we are ready."

"No." Through clenched teeth, I whisper, "I am not going."

Mekkalluthak glances back at me. His hooded eyes glint. "You do not have a choice, markmaker."

CHAPTER THIRTY-ONE

The Tarriks warriors return me, cursing and struggling, to my cell. When they leave, I shout and pound the door until my voice fails and my fists are bruised. But no one responds. Shivering, exhausted at last, I fall into a doze on the bare metal floor.

But sleep brings me no peace. Half-dreams of dread weave through my shattered thoughts. In my nightmares, I run through the clan sector, trying to bring my family to Haza'ruux's house—for some reason I think we will be safe there. But every time I look back, Hakham and Chervani have fallen further behind. The walls shift, and the streets change under my feet. I do not know where I am.

Pain pulls me back to consciousness—a deep throbbing in my wounded arm. Groaning, I flex my hand and crack open my eyes. I can see nothing. The cell is completely black.

A power failure?

Staggering to my feet, I put out my hands and feel for the vent above the door. After half a minute of blind terror, I find it. A stream of cool air whispers against my fingers. *Thank the ancestors.* I lean against the wall, dizzy with relief. The ventilation system is still running. So are the gravity generators, for that matter, or else I could not stand upright. Only the lights have gone out. I have no idea what time it is or how long I have been asleep.

With my uninjured arm, I bang on the door. "Hakka! Is anyone there?"

I only hear, as before, a pounding in the corridor like a vehement echo. *Kophas?* I shout his name, but if he responds, I cannot make out any words.

It occurs to me that this power outage might not be an accident. Did Mekkalluthak arrange it to cover his escape? But if that is the case, why haven't his warriors come to fetch us?

My arm grows tired; I kick at the door instead. Then, as I pause for breath, I hear noise outside: a distant crash, a harsh yell. I stiffen. *Jal'thor's men.* They must be in a hurry—are we leaving?

Then, from the corridor, I hear the stark eruption of gunfire.

I jerk away from the door and back into a corner, pressing myself against the walls. Footsteps ring in the hallway and halt in front of my cell. I hear muffled, clipped voices. A bang shakes the wall, then another, and another. With a screech of tortured metal, the door gives way.

A glaring white beam pierces the blackness. I flinch and shade my eyes. A warrior stands in the entrance, hefting a heavy rifle. His helmet lamp shines so brightly that I can only see his silhouette. "Skin-changer filth," he snarls.

Before I can even cry out, he snatches the front of my tunic and hauls me to my feet. He drags me out of the cell and throws me to the floor in the hallway. The cold muzzle of a gun presses into the back of my neck.

"Don't move!"

I crouch on all fours, unbreathing, my pulse hammering in my throat. The corridor is pitch dark except for the warriors' lamps; the beams sweep back and forth across the floor. I cannot tell what is happening, but I do not dare look up.

They can't kill me. Mekkalluthak needs me—

The soldier who holds a gun to my neck shouts to his companion. I hear a metallic clanging and the crash of another door being wrenched open. Then a yell echoes—a high and piercing warcry.

"Kalimaa!"

A thud vibrates the narrow corridor, like someone being thrown bodily against the wall. I hear a burst of scuffling—a shriek—a thick, hideous snapping noise. The soldier guarding me cries out; he lifts his gun from my neck.

I raise my head. In the beam of the helmet lamp, Kophas crouches over the other warrior, who lies crumpled and unmoving. *Dead?* I can't tell. Kophas scrabbles for something at the fallen soldier's belt—jerks out a dagger—then looks up, his face contorted with feral rage.

Behind me, the first soldier roars a curse. "Axdraa'dah—!" And he lifts his rifle to his shoulder to fire on Kophas.

My body moves before I can think. I fling myself backwards and collide with the soldier's knees. He stumbles, nearly falling on top of me, and his shot goes wild. In that instant, Kophas springs. With a shout, he tackles the warrior; the stolen dagger flashes in his hand. The soldier's rifle spins out of his grip and clatters against the wall. The two of them hit the floor, kicking and clawing.

"No!" I shriek. They are going to kill each other. My legs tense to spring forward, to throw myself into the fray of fists of thrashing feet—

Before I can move, Kophas rolls on top of his opponent, pinning him to the floor. He wrests his dagger hand free and thrusts his weapon through the gap between the man's helmet and breastplate. He twists his hand. The warrior screeches, chokes—goes limp.

The hoarse scream petrifies me, touches some primal fear deep in my vitals. I huddle on the floor, stunned. For a moment, Kophas pants, still straddling his fallen opponent. The helmet lamp glares up into his snarling face. Then his features slacken, and he turns to me, wide-eyed.

"Markmaker?"

"Kophas," I gasp.

He drops his dagger, crouches down beside me, and clasps my shoulders. "Are you all right?"

Too shaken to speak, I merely blink. His fingers, hot and wet with blood, squeeze my bare arms. "They told me you had turned yourself in." In the slanted beams of light, he studies me with an expression I cannot read. Then he says, strangely, "I thought you were older."

I stare at him, bewildered. And then I realize this is the first time he has seen me without my disguise. I feel as if I have never seen his face before, either. I have only known him as the powerless exile, sick and starving in his Underbelly hovel. I almost forgot he is Clan Tarriks—an elite warrior, trained from childhood to kill.

"What have you done?" I whisper.

He looks puzzled. "What do you mean?"

"Jal'thor's warriors." My mind reels in horror. Have I just watched a man slay his own clanmates? "The guildmaster sent them for us."

"Hakk." Kophas looses a shaky, mirthless laugh. "These aren't Jal'thor's men." He leans over, picks up the fallen rifle, and hefts it in one hand. Then he flicks a switch, turning on a light on the end of the barrel. He points the beam at the dead warrior's breastplate. The blood-spattered armor bears the familiar double-trident of the Ascendance.

"Faction warriors? How—how did they get in?"

"They must have broken into the sector." Kophas sounds blunt but calm. "I knew something was wrong when the lights went out. If they managed to reach us down here, they've probably taken out most of the guild guards—and Jal'thor's troops, too. We need to get out of here."

"How?"

He puts down the gun and kneels by the corpse again. "If they see our marks, we're dead. We'll need to cover them." He tugs off the warrior's visored helmet and pulls it over his own head. Then he points at the other body lying further down the corridor. "Strip that armor and gear up."

"What?"

"Move! Unless you want to wait for the rest of the warband to show up."

Cowed, I crawl over to the other corpse. The soldier's breastplate is deeply dented, and his head lies twisted at an unnatural angle. I hesitate, loath to touch the body.

"Hurry!" Kophas cries.

Moaning through my teeth, I put my hands on either side of the helmet and pull. The soldier's head falls back limply; four dark, sightless eyes stare up at me. *Oh, Ka.* Nausea rises in my throat as my gaze flicks over the warrior's tattoos: the Penthar clan sigil on one side of his neck, the Trechik adoption-mark on the other. This young man left his birth clan only a year ago to fight for the faction. *Like Askko,* I think, with a sickening in my gut. *Kin's heart, he's no older than I am. What have we done?*

Gagging, I drop the helmet and turn away.

"Markmaker!" Kophas calls again. He pulls on the boots from his own stolen set of armor. "There's no time."

With shaking hands, I try to unbuckle the Ascendance soldier's breastplate. But I do not know what I am doing—I have never worn armor in my life—and the dead warrior's gaze paralyzes me. I find myself mouthing a prayer, begging mercy for both his spirit and my own:

Pentharan, Trechikan, hear me...guard the son of your heart's blood...stand by his side in the combat...

For a few minutes I fumble with the foreign straps and clips. Then Kophas kneels beside me, taking over. With swift ease, he helps me into the breastplate, the shoulder pieces and gauntlets, the heavy, reinforced boots. They are all too large for me; I feel clumsy and dazed. Kophas, however, moves with urgency. "Take this." He thrusts a small gun into my hands.

I look down at the firearm askance. The weapon has the sleek lines and compact barrel of an Arroqi handgun—the same kind that Askko showed me, months ago. "I've never used one."

"You don't need to use it. You only need to look the part." He picks up the helmet from the floor and lowers it over my head. "Don't touch the comm settings. I've adjusted them—we can hear the rest of the warband, but they can't hear us. Understand?"

The visor descends over my eyes. I expect darkness, but instead I wince at the glowing array of sigils projected in front of me. I do not understand the data, but at least I can see the dark hallway more clearly. Through the visor, the corridor—and the bodies of the soldiers, now stripped of their armor—appear to be bathed in a flat, orange glow.

I turn away from the corpses and grip the handgun more tightly. "How do you know there are more warriors?"

Before he can answer, a static noise bursts through the side of my helmet, followed by a clipped voice: "Hvoss'ka Ratokk reporting...Verity Street... clear..."

Kophas grabs my arm. "Let's go."

He pulls me into a run, heading up the corridor. The young warrior jogs light-footed, head swiveling, his rifle raised. I stumble over my armored feet, laboring to keep up. "Where are we going?"

"I don't know yet. We need to find a way outside first."

We arrive at a door that opens into a tight, curving stairwell. Another corpse sprawls across the threshold: a warrior in Tarriks gear, one of Jal'thor's men. Kophas lets out a soft hiss. Briefly he bends down to touch his dead clanmate's shoulder, whispering something I cannot hear—a prayer, perhaps. Then Kophas lifts his hand and signals me to wait. He steps around the fallen warrior and climbs the stairs in a lithe, silent stride. I did not know it was possible to move so quietly in full armor.

While Kophas disappears around the curve of the stairwell, I remain in the hall, panting and staring at the dead Tarriks soldier. Through my helmet, I hear the crackle of comm noise and brief exchanges in military jargon that I cannot comprehend. All at once I wonder where Mekkalluthak is, and Jal'thor, too. Did they escape before the Ascendance troops invaded? Or have they been captured already? Is that why they never came for us?

"Markmaker." Kophas's voice echoes down the stairwell. "All clear."

Swallowing hard, I step over the warrior's body and mount the stairs. Kophas waits on the landing, gazing through another doorway to the room beyond. "Ancestors help us," he mutters. "The Deep Sleep has been walking here tonight."

We look out into the foyer of the guild hall—but I barely recognize it. Makeshift barricades of furniture and crates crisscross the room. The elegant pillars are blackened with scorch marks, and bullet holes riddle the vibrant murals on the walls. On the gleaming tile, now stained with blood and debris, bodies lie strewn: Ascendance soldiers, Tarriks warriors, and guild guards. Directly in front of us, a Serix corpse slumps at the foot of a pillar. I recognize the vacant, upturned face: it is Ikhalo, the guard who spoke kindly to me.

I lean against the doorframe. "Oh, Ka."

"Markmaker." Kophas grips my shoulder, forcing me to turn and face him. "Listen to me. We are on our own now—we can't expect anyone's help. The Ascendance is out for our blood, and I don't plan on letting them have it. Do you know a place we can hide?"

"I don't know. I don't know." In the close confines of the helmet, I gasp for air. Then: "I know a way back to the Underbelly. But it's on the other side of the sector. We'll have to go through the residential district."

He nods. "Take us there. If anyone tries to stop us, I'll handle it." Briefly he claps his hand against the side of my helmet. "Courage, markmaker."

He steps out into the foyer. I follow close behind, trying not to look at the bullet-mangled bodies. Together we clamber through the gaps in the barricades until we reach the main entrance of the guild hall.

The grand, decorated doors have been smashed open, as if by an explosion. Shards of metal and blackened wood crunch under my feet. I can hear noise in the plaza outside—an echoing din of shouting and wailing, punctuated now and then by gunfire. The air smells acrid, like smoke laced with a harsh chemical tang. Kophas pulls me towards the wall, so that we approach the door from the side. Holding his rifle close to his chest, he peers around the damaged lintel.

His armor creaks as he stiffens, and I hear the sharp intake of his breath. "Axdraa'dah."

"What is it?" I step forward, but he puts a hand on my chest.

"I don't think you want to see this."

I push past him to look around the edge of the door.

A shroud of smoke blurs the air, lanced by the swinging beams of headlamps. For a moment, I cannot tell what I am looking at. The plaza mills with people: more Ascendance soldiers, from the look of their armor. Some run in and out of the buildings; across the street, the door to the record hall has also been smashed open. In the middle of the plaza, the ancient branches of the trallak grove, now charred and stripped of leaves, smolder and pour thick, dark smoke towards the ceiling. The pungent fumes of fire retardant sting the back of my throat.

The trallak groves are burning,
Smoking and staining the sky...

"What—" I bend over, hacking on the foul air. "What's going on?"

That is when I notice the bodies that litter the ground—under the trallak trees, near the entrance of the guild hall, broken and bullet-torn. But these corpses wear no armor.

These are not warriors. These are Serix civilians.

A shriek pierces the uproar; my eyes dart to the middle of the plaza. A group of Ascendance warriors trains their firearms on a huddle of civilians—fifteen or twenty of them, both men and women. As I watch, two of the warriors haul a terrified Serix man forward and force him to the ground. Then they hold his arms while a third soldier bends over him. I catch a glimpse of a short, curved dagger in the soldier's hand. I hear the man scream.

My knees lock. I can get no breath in my lungs. Kophas grabs my arm and drags me away from the door. "Their marks," I cry hoarsely. "Deep Sleep, they're stripping their clan-marks!"

"Kesh," Kophas orders. His voice sounds unsteady.

I struggle against his grip. How can this be happening? Mekkalluthak said the High Council merely ordered the clan to pledge allegiance to the faction. Is this the kind of loyalty the Ascendance demands? Must we renounce our bloodline, our very names?

May the name of Sko'larik be cursed.
Let this mark be cut out of our bodies,
Cut out and forgotten forever...

"Ancestors above. It's happening again." Wildly I thrash, trying to break away from Kophas, to fling myself towards the ruined door. "We have to do something!"

With a grunt, Kophas tugs me back and slams me against the wall, pinning me with his whole weight. "Don't be a fool. We can't take on a whole warband—"

The comms in our helmets crackle to life again. "Hvoss'ka...clear. Elantii Street, clear. Moving into Qor'al Plaza..."

My heart seizes. "Did you hear that?"

"What?"

A deep cold floods my whole body; my gun nearly drops from my hand. "Kophas. My family lives on Elantii Street."

He curses softly and releases me. Then he raises his rifle, clasping it against his shoulder. "Let's go."

I spring past him. I burst out of the guild hall and into the turmoil of the plaza, my heart throbbing, my armor clanging around me. I run as I have never run before.

Rixarii Street is choked with troops. Warriors swarm the corridor, breaking into studios or escorting terrified civilians towards the sector gate at gunpoint. The hot air reeks of smoke and blood.

We weave through the chaos, hugging the wall, barely dodging armored figures and trampling boots. Once, we nearly collide with an Ascendance soldier who is dragging a stunned old man from the porch of a studio. "You there! We need more men in the plaza. Go help—"

"Can't," says Kophas. "Hvoss'ka's orders." And we charge past.

When we enter the residential district, the crush disperses abruptly. Between the ransacked homes, the streets lie empty—empty except for the bodies sprawled on the porches, or in the trampled gardens. I see them, but only as in a nightmare, as if they cannot be real. The pounding of my pulse becomes a hammering prayer, an unceasing cry of anguish.

Serixan, ancestors, where are you? How can you let this happen to us?

I stumble around a final corner into Elantii Street. My eyes lock on my home. The front door stands open, smashed.

A yell rips from my throat. I outstrip Kophas and burst into the front room. The lights are out, but with my helmet lamp and visor, I can see the disarray. The low table by the couch has been overturned; broken dishes litter the kitchen floor. Our ancestral sword lies abandoned in a corner, the blade snapped in two pieces. In the middle of the room, Miika sprawls full-length on the dirt-stained tile. Bullet holes riddle her lean, dark flank. The old warhound's eyes shine glassy and glaring, and her tongue lolls from open jaws, still bared in a death-snarl.

"Na'thalo! Nakki!"

No one answers. I dash down the hallway towards their bedroom. The door stands partway open, and the entry pad on the wall has been smashed. Even before I look, I can smell the tang of blood.

Hakham lies crumpled in the middle of the floor. His eyes are open, huge and staring; his limbs are slack. Violet-black stains soak the front of his tunic. Beside him, Chervani lies facedown, her arms outstretched, still reaching for him. Even as I dart forward to turn over her cold body and see the neat, round wound in her forehead, I am shrieking "No!" over and over and over.

I clutch Chervani to my chest. My words dissolve into animal screams. Pain engulfs me, pure and unspeakable—and then boils up into rage. I want to smash bones, to throttle flesh. Every nerve in my body strains towards one desire: *Kill.*

Armored footsteps pound behind me, and a heavy hand falls on my shoulder. Snarling, I leap up and turn on the soldier, my hands reaching for his throat. I don't know where my gun went. But this man is going to die, even if I have to kill him with my teeth.

The warrior grabs me and throws me down. "Markmaker! It's me."

I raise myself from the floor. "Don't touch me!" The words are a raw shriek.

Kophas kneels in front of me. "We have to go. I am sorry."

"Then go. *Go*! Get out of here!"

"I owe you my life. I am not leaving without you."

I bend over Chervani again, sobs racking my body. "I'm not leaving them."

"Markmaker!" He grabs both my shoulders. "They are with the ancestors now. We can do nothing more for them."

I scream and thrash against him. "Leave me alone!"

"Listen to me," Kophas shouts. "Your people are dying as we speak. If you can get us out of the sector, maybe we can save some of them. If you stay here, you're going to be killed. You can't avenge them if you're dead!"

My hot breath fogs my visor. But the word *avenge* pierces the haze of my grief. I stop struggling. "I can't. I can't leave them like this."

"We don't have a choice. Here. We can cover them, at least." He releases me, then strides over to the bunk in the wall, picks up a rumpled blanket, and returns. "Say farewell."

I touch Chervani's face, trailing my fingers down her cool, lifeless cheek. How can it be only days ago that she embraced me, called me her little one? *Nakki. Forgive me, nakki…*

A keening cry rises in my throat. I feel as if a white-hot barb is ripping my chest from the inside out.

Kophas crouches beside me, head bowed. "Heart's blood to heart's blood," he mutters. "Rest now in the Long Dream's glory…"

Still strangled with sobs, I touch my hand to the side of my neck, then brush my fingers against Chervani's clan-mark, then Hakham's. Kophas gives me the blanket, and I pull it over them both. *I will come back for you.* But even as I make the promise, I know I will not be able to keep it.

Kophas lifts me to my feet. Together we heave on the door, dragging it closed despite the damaged runners. I lay my palm on the dented metal and scuffed paint.

My mother. My father. Honor with you.

This is all the funeral I can give to the two people who raised and loved me as their own. I am an orphan twice over now. Even if I survive this night, I will probably never receive memory-marks for my adopted parents—half the artists in the sector must be dead or captured already.

And that is when I remember Kilmaya. I cry aloud.

"What is it?" Kophas retrieves my lost handgun and holds it out to me. My fingers wrap around the grip fiercely—the weapon feels natural in my hand now.

"My teacher. She lives on Dawra Street. Have you heard them say anything about Dawra Street? On the comms?"

"I don't know. I don't know this sector."

"We have to find her. If she is still—" I choke, unable to finish.

Kophas hefts his rifle. "Is she close?"

"It's on our way."

He nods. "Then let's move."

CHAPTER THIRTY-TWO

We plunge back into the nightmare of the streets, running side by side between the shattered houses without speaking. A stinging scent burns the back of my throat; some of the gardens burn, or smolder under the chemical flame retardant spraying from the ceiling. Through the billowing smoke, we glimpse more bodies among the debris: twisted, limp corpses with blood-soaked tunics. Kophas whispers curses as we pass. The only reason I do not collapse to the floor is that I am focused on Kilmaya.

I'm coming, teacher. Ancestors, let her live. Don't take her from me, too.

We hear gunfire up ahead—and screams. Weapons in hand, we dash down the hallway and round the corner into Dawra Street.

The corridor teems with Ascendance soldiers. Some break into the houses while others stand guard over civilians huddled in the middle of the street. A woman's shriek sends a jolt through my body; I glance around wildly.

Kophas grips my arm, restraining me. "I think we're too late."

"No!" I shake him off and strain to see past the troops. Kilmaya's house stands further up the street, but the crush is too thick for me to force my way through, and I have no time to waste. I thrust my handgun into its holster, sit down against the wall, and start pulling off my heavy armored boots.

Kophas gives a start. "What are you doing?"

"I can't climb with these." With a final tug, I toss the boots aside.

"What?"

Without answering, I spring up and scan the wall. There are no maintenance ladders nearby, but the ornamental ledges surrounding the door of one house look sturdy enough to serve as handholds. I grab the ledges and clamber up the wall onto the slender support beams. The girders here are narrower than the ones in Rixarii Street—more decorative than functional—but they still hold my weight.

From the web of beams, I can see Kilmaya's house. The door is still standing. But even as I watch, two soldiers break off from the milling mass of troops and jog towards my teacher's home, guns raised.

I do not even have to think. My body, agile in fury, weaves between the girders, crossing the length of the hallway in a matter of seconds. When I am crouching directly above the two warriors who batter at Kilmaya's door, I draw my gun. What I told Kophas was true—I have never used one before. But I lean down from the beam, jerk on the trigger, and fire.

My shot goes wild, pinging off the floor. But the soldiers yell and leap back. Twice more I fire, and twice I miss. One of the warriors looks up at the ceiling now, pointing. The other aims his rifle at my head.

I try to pull away behind the beam, but it is too narrow to provide any useful cover. Surprise was my lone advantage, and now I have lost it. Bullets whine past me; I twist to one side, nearly losing my balance. Panting, I fumble with my gun. If I am going to die today, I want to die fighting.

A sharp crack sounds nearby—once, twice. I flatten myself against the beam. When I open my eyes again, I find I am looking down at the bodies of the two soldiers, sprawled on Kilmaya's porch. I gasp and glance around. Below me, Kophas dashes into view, his rifle still pressed to his shoulder. He shakes a fist at me. I can just hear his shout over the din of the crowd.

"Deep Sleep, get down, you idiot!"

I do not need any further encouragement. Scrambling over the girders, I reach the wall and slide until my feet touch the top of Kilmaya's doorway. Then I jump the rest of the way. I land on the porch, between the bodies of the dead warriors, and crash to my knees. Kophas drags me upright.

"What are you doing? They're going to see us!"

Behind him, the corridor still seethes with turmoil. If anyone saw Kophas shoot the two soldiers, they have not yet raised the alarm. Gasping, I reach for the door. "My teacher's in there."

Kophas growls another curse but releases me. "Hurry!"

I slam my fist on the entry pad, but the door does not budge. Of course, it is locked. With both hands, I pound on it. "Kilmaya," I scream. "It's me. It's Mariikel."

Kophas shoves me aside. He coils one leg, then whirls and delivers a blow to the door with his boot. Already dented, the door shudders; a dark gap appears at the edge of the frame. Kophas wedges the butt of his rifle into the opening, then heaves on the weapon. With a screech, the door slides open. We tumble inwards, into the dark house.

I leap to my feet in the front room. There is no need to search any further. Kilmaya stands at the threshold of her bedroom—eyes slitted in rage, teeth bared, trembling but erect. In one hand she grips a slim, antique sword: her family's funeral-blade. Now my teacher raises the weapon, pointing it at us defiantly. The tip wavers; I can see her arm trembling. "I'm no warrior. Only an old painter. But by the blood of my ancestors, I will not disgrace my marks." Her chest heaves, and her voice sounds brittle. "Do what you came for."

"Teacher." I drop my gun, and with two hands thrust my visor back. "It's me."

Her face slackens. "Mariikel?"

I lunge forward to catch her as she collapses. We sink to the floor. I hold her against my chest, as I held Chervani. But Kilmaya is warm, and breathing, and shuddering with cries.

"You're alive," I whisper.

Weeping into my shoulder, she cannot say anything. "Mariikel," she gasps finally. "How did you get here? What's going on?"

"We're going to get you out of here. My friend Kophas will help us. He's a warrior; he helped me escape."

Behind us, gunfire rips into the front of the house. Instinctively I push Kilmaya down, throwing my body across hers. I glance back over my shoulder towards the door. Without the visor's aid, I can no longer see well, but in the beam of my headlamp I can just make out Kophas, flattened against the wall.

"They've seen us," he snaps. He ducks around the edge of the door for an instant, then fires off a rifle shot. A second volley of bullets rattles the house in reply. Kophas leaps backwards into safety. "Markmaker, throw me your gun."

I grope around on the floor until I find the handgun, then slide it across to him. Still crouched against the wall, he catches the weapon. "I can hold them off for a minute as long as they don't charge us. But when my ammo runs out—"

Gunfire spatters through the door again. Outside, soldiers shout and jeer. My heart grows cold.

Staying low to the floor, I turn back to Kilmaya. She is trying hard not to whimper. I wrap her in my arms—because there is nothing else to do. I have failed again. The soldiers will have to shoot me first to get to her. But she is still going to die. "Teacher. Forgive me."

She huddles against my chest. "I am glad you are here."

We all meet the Deep Sleep alone. But I do not say it aloud. I merely embrace her more tightly. Over our heads, Ascendance bullets slam into the walls. Kophas roars a battle-cry. I bow my head and shut all my eyes.

Then, from the corridor outside, a scream rises. Long and full-throated, it drowns out the sharp crack of gunfire. It does not sound like a Noxxiin voice at all. It sounds like a beast, shrieking in rage.

A jolt streaks through me—a shock of hope. I release Kilmaya and raise my head. "Haza'ruux," I whisper. Then I shout it: "Haza'ruux!"

Outside, the soldiers stop firing. The eerie howl still resounds in the corridor. Leaving Kilmaya, I reach as if by instinct for her fallen sword. Then I scramble to the open door and join Kophas. He crouches flat against the floor, staring out into the street.

"Who...what *is* that?"

I look out. Except for the pinpoints of the warriors' headlamps, the street is pitch-black—but I have no trouble spotting Haza'ruux. He stands in the beams overhead, his torso bare, and every tattoo on his body radiates light. As he tilts back his head, howling, tongues of brightness like violet flames ripple along his skin. In his hands, he grips twin knives with broad, curved blades. Everyone in the street, Serix and Ascendance alike, gazes at him, petrified.

At last, his long wail fades. Snarling, he springs from the beams. On all fours he lands among the Ascendance soldiers. He wears no armor, carries no weapons besides his knives. The warriors shout and turn their guns on him. With a deep-throated growl, Haza'ruux charges the nearest soldier. Point-blank, the man pulls the trigger—and nothing happens. Haza'ruux collides with him and hurls him to the ground.

A flurry of gunfire erupts. But like a radiant, vengeful phantom, Haza'ruux whirls and dodges between the soldiers, unharmed. Bullets do not seem to touch him. Several times, warriors try to approach him, only to find their weapons misfiring or exploding in their own faces.

"Their guns keep jamming," Kophas cries, incredulous.

A memory returns to me, unbidden, a line of sigils penned in an ancient script: *The mark of the mad dog—battle-rage and luck.*

"Luck. That's his power. They can't hit him!"

"What?" Kophas exclaims.

I do not reply. The mad markmaker, still howling, tackles his enemies bodily. Armor clangs as he bears another warrior down to the floor. His knives flash; he stabs the man in the throat. Then he springs up again, lashing out with both feet at a pair of assailants. The blows send them reeling backwards. Haza'ruux leaps on their chests with a guttural snarl.

In a matter of minutes, Haza'ruux is surrounded by half a dozen dead and wounded soldiers. The rest retreat, yelling and firing useless shots. "He's a deepcrafter. Back! *Get back!*"

"Who is that?" Kilmaya crawls up beside me.

"It's Haza'ruux." I tremble with both joy and terror. The eccentric artist who taught me the ancient sigils and this berserk, unnatural warrior—how can they be the same man?

"Haza'ruux?" Kilmaya's voice quavers. "I don't understand."

Kophas sputters, "Your clan has *deepcrafters*?"

"It's not deepcraft. It's the Arimaas. A mark of power."

"Great Ka," Kophas breathes. "You said that was a story."

"It is. A true story." I clutch his arm. "We should go. While he has them distracted."

"Hakk. Right, then." Kophas jerks his head in a nod. "I'll go first. I'll grab another weapon and cover you."

I help Kilmaya to her feet. I still hold the antique funeral-blade in one hand. I decide to keep it; I may still need a weapon. "Can you run?" I ask.

For a moment she clings to me, and then she finds her balance. "I will do what I must."

I glance out into the corridor again. Haza'ruux has driven most of the Ascendance troops down the street, back the way they came. They still take sporadic shots, but he does not appear to notice. Instead, he looses another rippling growl. The light lifts from his tattoos, hiding his body in a brilliant shroud. A shimmering, beastly outline engulfs his slender form.

"Go now!" I cry.

Kophas springs into the street, snatching up two fallen guns from the bodies on the ground. Still supporting Kilmaya, I follow him. The young warrior slings one weapon over his back, hefting the other in his arms. "Run," he orders. "Markmaker, what are you waiting for?"

I pause in the middle of the street. At the opposite end of the corridor, Haza'ruux faces the soldiers, his body a pulsing star in the dark hallway. Between us, a group of Serix civilians still huddles on the floor, their hands over their heads. There are perhaps fifteen or twenty of them—men and women, and a few children. Scattered around them lie the bodies of the dead.

I let go of Kilmaya. "Stay with Kophas."

"What are you doing?" She grabs my arm. Under the gauntlet, my injured wrist throbs with sudden pain, and I pull away.

"Go to Haza'ruux's house. You know the way. I'll catch up. Kophas, go!"

Kophas snatches her shoulder and pulls her, still protesting, away from me. I do not wait to watch them leave. Instead I dash towards the people on the floor. Still cowed and stunned, they only now begin to raise their heads. At the edge of the group, one man hugs a half-grown girl to his chest, shielding her with his body. When I reach them, I grasp the man by the shoulder. At the sight of my armor and sword, he rears back.

"Don't hurt us." His voice rattles in his throat. "Please."

"I am Serix. I'm here to help—"

The light from my headlamp falls on the man's face. For an instant I glimpse his tattoos—and then I recognize him. Starting violently, I step back.

It is Virik, the recordmaster. But his clan-mark is gone. On the side of his neck, a ragged cut seeps blood. The girl huddling in his arms—his daughter K'nima, Kilmaya's young apprentice—bears an identical wound.

My stomach turns; I cannot speak. The recordmaster, breathing heavily, looks up into my face. His eyelids flicker, and his features grow rigid. "You."

I remember Virik's anger when I gave myself up, the way he cursed me for bringing shame upon the clan. Now he kneels before me, bleeding, utterly degraded. He has renounced his ancestors. He has allowed himself to be cut off.

K'nima shudders with sobs. A middle-aged woman crouches beside Virik as well—his wife, Kandri. Her clan-mark has been stripped, too, and she stares up at me with a terror-glazed expression.

You are still Serix by blood. That will always be true, no matter what marks you have. Someone said that to me, a long time ago—or did I say it? I cannot remember. It does not matter.

"Recordmaster." I lower my blade and hold out my free hand. "I can get you all out of the sector, but you must come with me now. Do you understand?"

After a bewildered silence, he nods feebly. He grasps my arm, and I pull him upright. He sways, but then turns to his weeping daughter and lifts her up as well.

"Help your family. I'll tell the others."

I make my way through the rest of the group, repeating my message. One by one, the survivors stumble to their feet. Most of them I do not recognize—I am not sure they know who I am, either. It occurs to me how strange I must look with my bare feet, battered Ascendance armor, and antique funeral-blade. But they will have to trust me by my words and by the clan-mark on my neck.

When everyone has risen, I circle around to the front of the group. Behind us, another howl pierces the air. I risk a glance at Haza'ruux. He has taken on his full Arimaas form; as a savage, blazing war-hound, he charges the line of Ascendance soldiers. Without even trying to fire on him, they scatter.

I turn back to my clanmates and lower my visor to better see my path. Then I tap my helmet lamp. "Follow my light." I lift my blade and point up the street. "Now run!"

The group breaks into a clumsy, staggering jog. I lead them up the dark corridor, away from the soldiers. I have to restrain myself from sprinting. There are elders and children in the group, and nearly everyone is bleeding or in shock. If I dash ahead, they will not be able to keep up.

My stolen armor weighs on me heavily; the disguise is little use now. I struggle with the clasps on the breastplate, then tear it away and cast it to the ground. At once I can breathe more easily. Behind me, my clanmates gasp with effort, and someone whimpers.

Over the thudding of our own footsteps, another uncanny howl rises. I glance over my shoulder. Haza'ruux, in his Noxxiin form again but with his marks still shining, pursues us. Light sluices off his skin like water; he looks like something out of a nightmare. He runs not like an old man, but like a hunter in his prime.

"Haza'ruux!" I shout.

If he hears me, I cannot tell. As he nears, his face is a glowing mask of rage—and I wonder, for an instant, if he has truly gone insane. Virik stumbles, and K'nima shrieks.

"Haza'ruux. It's me. It's Flashing Blade."

The mad markmaker does not answer, but he slows, keeping his distance. Even so, people scream; some veer away, while others collapse to the floor, covering their heads.

"It's all right," I shout. "He's one of us. It's the mad markmaker."

I do not know if this allays their fears, but some people, at least, seem to grasp that he is here to protect us. While I rouse the group again, Haza'ruux stands guard—and when we resume our flight, we run by the ghostly violet light of his marks. Our shadows flare and dance against the pillars.

Street by decimated street, we hurry deeper into the sector. In the smoking darkness, I hardly recognize the corridors, but the ingrained memory of walking to Haza'ruux's house every day still guides my feet. Now and again I must sidestep corpses on the floor—some are Serix, but many are Ascendance. The mad markmaker has already been here.

This is the strength of the Arimaas. The sheer scale of the destruction overwhelms me. I wonder, for a fleeting instant, what Mekkalluthak would think if he could see it. But the guildmaster and his ambitions are gone, for good or ill.

As we run, we meet more Serix survivors. Some carry lamps and armfuls of belongings, trying to make their way to the sector gate—not realizing that the Ascendance has blocked that escape. Others dash frantically through the darkness, calling for lost family or friends, while still others huddle on the ground, paralyzed with shock and grief. In the most commanding voice I can muster, I urge these people to join us. Some do. But many shrink away, witless from the chaos and terrified by Haza'ruux's radiant marks. And I have to leave them behind—because if I wait, I will save no one.

Despite this, our group has more than doubled in size by the time we reach the narrower streets of Haza'ruux's neighborhood. I have not yet seen Kophas and Kilmaya. Did I miss them in the crowds? Or did Kilmaya lose her way? She does not come to this part of the sector often. But even as I begin to worry, I spot two figures up ahead, running towards us—a lean warrior in blood-spattered armor and my teacher.

At once I rush forward and take Kilmaya in my arms; she is wheezing hard. With a sob of relief, she embraces me.

"Markmaker," Kophas snaps. "We have to turn back."

"What?" I exclaim.

He points to the end of the hallway. "There are soldiers up there. And a deepcrafter."

Down the street, beyond the dark archway, lies the plaza adjacent to Haza'ruux's house. As I watch, a burst of silver lightning illuminates the plaza. I glimpse the silhouette of a broad-shouldered warrior in pale robes. Somewhere up ahead, a child screams.

My heart freezes. "The tunnel is back there. The one to the Underbelly. We have to get through."

"Are you insane?" Kophas grabs my shoulder. "We need to run, *now*—"

A blinding flash of light cuts him off. At first, I think the deepcrafter has fired on us; I drop my sword and fall to the ground, shielding Kilmaya. But then I hear the roar behind me.

The guttural sound shakes the floor, vibrating through my bare feet and into my bones. A searing violet glow fills the passage—and then a brilliant shape, four-legged and shaggy, careens past us towards the plaza. The silver-robed figure turns. White fire explodes from the deepcrafter's raised hands, surging through the archway. Open-jawed, burning like a sun, Haza'ruux springs into the inferno.

I shriek his name. But then a hot, blistering wind envelopes us, and I hide my face, pushing Kilmaya to the floor. Another explosion rocks the corridor—a barking of gunfire—a thunderous hiss, like rushing water or steam. Shrieks ring out, cut off by an unnatural, rippling snarl. Then even Haza'ruux's voice falls abruptly silent—and the only noise left in the plaza is the hysterical wail of a child.

I lift my head. The street stands black and still. In my arms, Kilmaya shivers uncontrollably. The rest of our clanmates crouch on the floor. Kophas clutches his gun, gazing rigidly at the dark archway.

"What is he?" The awe in his voice is plain.

"The Keeper. The Keeper of the Arimaas." With one hand I grope for my fallen blade. Then I rise and stumble forward into the plaza.

At the foot of the shattered fountain, Haza'ruux lies in a heap of debris: shards of tile, broken ceiling panels, twisted pipes still gushing water. Around him sprawl half a dozen corpses, including the mangled body of the deepcrafter. The mad markmaker's tattoos flicker dimly as he clasps a small and struggling figure—the crying child. The child's voice rings so raw and shrill that it takes me a moment to recognize him. Haza'ruux clutches Tyotik to his chest, curling around him protectively.

I sink to my knees beside them. The old man's eyes are closed. Under the beam of my headlamp, his chest and shoulders look blistered—yet his marks remain distinct, glowing like embers through the scorched skin. Tyotik, still shrieking, writhes in his arms.

I put down my blade. "Haza'ruux," I whisper. "Let go."

All at once Haza'ruux groans. His glimmering marks fade and go out, and he slumps against the ruin of the fountain. Tyotik scrambles out of his arms. I catch the terrified child, pulling him close, but he screams again and struggles violently.

I realize I am still wearing my Ascendance headgear—the boy must think I am another soldier. With one hand, I tug the helmet off and drop it in the rubble. "Kesh, now. It's Blade. It's all right."

For a moment longer, he fights my grip, but at last his eyes widen in recognition. His wailing chokes off, and he clings to my neck, shaking in silence. I cradle him against my shoulder. "Are you hurt? Where's your mother? Where's nakki?"

He doesn't answer. I glance around the wrecked plaza. In the darkness around me, I sense people shifting and groaning. There are civilians here; the soldiers must have dragged them out of their homes. Now, by the light of my discarded helmet, I see a cluster of people getting up, staring at the carnage in mute fear.

Kophas steps up beside me. In one hand he grasps his rifle, and with the other he supports Kilmaya. Wordlessly, they both look down at Haza'ruux. In a low voice, Kophas asks, "Is he dead?"

"No. But he's hurt."

Kilmaya does not speak. She stares at the mad markmaker, and then at me. Then Haza'ruux stirs. His breath rattles harshly in his throat, and his eyes flicker open. At once, Tyotik screams again, kicking and scrabbling. I turn to Kilmaya. "Can you take him?"

She fumbles but then bends down to lift the hysterical child from my arms.

"His name is Tyotik." Gesturing towards the people crouched at the edges of the plaza, I say, "Can you try to find his mother? Kana—her name is Kana. She lives nearby."

Kilmaya blinks, vacant, and I am afraid I have asked too much of her. But then she shifts, breathes, and embraces the boy more securely. "I will try."

A sigh escapes me. "Thank you."

I do not pause to watch her go. I return to Haza'ruux's side, where I find one of his limp hands and clasp it gently. His fingers are slick with blood—whether his own or someone else's, I cannot tell. "Haza'ruux. Teacher. Wake up."

He pants, his narrow chest heaving. Dark, blistered skin envelopes half his torso, and he quivers all over. For a minute his eyes wander, and at last he focuses on my face. "Flashing—Blade." He can barely speak. "Chieftain."

"I'm here." I do not deny the title this time. I wrap both my hands around his.

He blinks rapidly. "The clan. You must go. You must take them down— down into the dark."

"We're going to the Underbelly. We can hide there." Sick with dread, I gaze at his burns. "Can you walk?"

He does not seem to hear me. "Axdraa'dah," he mutters. With his free hand, he grips my wrist hard. "You must go—to Axdraa'dah."

He must be delirious with pain. I lean over him and whisper, "We're not going to the Deep Sleep today."

"Markmaker." Beside me, Kophas speaks abruptly. "We need to go. They're sending more troops this way—I just heard on the comms." He gestures at Haza'ruux. "And I think they're bringing more deepcrafters."

I bite back a curse. "How close are they?"

"I'm not sure. Where is this tunnel to the Underbelly?"

"Just down there." I point across the plaza towards the storage corridor.

He nods. "It's going to take time to get everyone in there. How many did you bring?"

"I—I don't know." I suddenly notice that the plaza is full of people. The rest of the survivors must have followed us. They stand wide-eyed, gaping in fear, waiting—the remnant of Clan Serix. Untangling my hand from Haza'ruux's grip, I stand up. I am no Mekkalluthak; I have never made a speech in my life. But I do not need to think about my words.

"Everyone," I call out. "Down that hall there's a shaft that leads to the Underbelly. I'm going to take you down it. I know the way."

Cries erupt from the crowd, despairing wails.

"The Underbelly?"

"We'll die down there!"

An accusing voice pierces the hubbub: "Aren't you the skin-changer?"

"Listen to me," I shout. "I have friends there—they will help us. You can come with me now, or you can turn back and give yourselves up to the Ascendance. You know how that will end." I pause, breathing heavily. "It is your own choice. But there isn't much time. There are more warriors com-ing—and deepcrafters."

Murmurs of terror ripple through the gathering. Then someone pushes to the front of the crowd. Virik still clutches his daughter's hand, and his wife clings to his other arm. His face is taut, and he glares at me. Then he says, "We'll come."

I shut my eyes in silent gratitude. My clanmates are loath to trust a skin-changer, but they will follow the recordmaster. "Kophas," I say.

"Here, markmaker."

I point towards the storage hall. "There's a door behind the crates. Can you open it for them? It's probably locked."

The young warrior obeys. Slowly, people shuffle after him. I bend down and return to Haza'ruux. He still pants, but to my surprise, he has propped himself up against the base of the fountain. Near his feet lies Kilmaya's funeral-blade. I grasp the hilt again—I feel safer with a weapon in my hand. Then I put an arm around Haza'ruux's wiry shoulders. "Can you stand?"

Hissing through his teeth, he nods. He leans against me, and staggering a little, I pull him up. Together we pick our way through the rubble, towards the maintenance shaft. The crowd parts swiftly when they see Haza'ruux—they seem afraid even to touch him. We reach the entrance of the shaft just as Kophas finishes prying it open. The door slides back with a clang; cool air and dim yellow light spill out.

Thank the ancestors. The tunnel lights are working; we will at least be able to see. I spot Kilmaya nearby. She still carries Tyotik.

"Teacher. Did you find…" But my voice fades at the grief in her face. She merely shakes her head.

An ache swells in my chest. Tyotik huddles in Kilmaya's arms, his face buried in her shoulder. His mother could be anywhere—likely even dead. And we do not have time to search.

"We'll have to take him with us. Can you hold on to him?"

Tight-lipped, she inclines her head. I glance at my clanmates. They stare at the open tunnel with dread; no one wants to be the first to venture in. I raise my voice again. "Recordmaster."

Virik steps forward, his family close behind. "Here," he says thickly.

"Can you lead them? Go to the left and keep walking until you reach the first intersection. I'll come in a moment. I want to make sure everyone gets inside."

"Very well." The wound on his neck still glistens with blood, but he does not complain. The recordmaster ducks under the doorway and steps into the tunnel. Kilmaya moves to follow him but then pauses, looking back at me. Her mouth half-opens, then shuts again. But I can read the unspoken question in her eyes.

Who are you?

I want to explain everything, to ask her forgiveness, but now is not the time. She will have to trust me a little longer. "Teacher, go."

Tyotik whimpers again in dazed, drawn-out sobs. Kilmaya shifts her hold, pressing him close. Then she turns away and vanishes into the shaft.

One by one, taut-faced and silent, the other survivors follow. I stand by the open door, watching and counting. Twenty—thirty—forty, and still coming. But all I can think is that it is too few.

Kophas has disappeared; he must have gone to guard the rear. Haza'ruux still leans against me. The skin of his back feels hot against my arm, but he breathes more steadily now. He has not spoken since I helped him up. His weakness frightens me. I remember, from our studies—how long ago they seem now—that the ancient warriors of the Arimaas were strictly trained not to overuse their power. Wielding the Arimaas too long or too recklessly could drive a man insane. If Haza'ruux reaches his limit, will he turn his savage strength against his own people? I have no idea. But leaving him behind is unthinkable.

"Out of the way! Let me through!"

Kophas shoves through the crowd towards me. "Markmaker, the reinforcements are closer than we thought. I was standing outside the plaza and could hear them coming."

People cry out in fear. "Go, go," I urge. The survivors surge forward into the tunnel.

"They're going to see us," Kophas hisses. "If they follow us down that shaft, it will be a slaughter."

"Kesh!" I do not want my clanmates to hear him. "Don't talk. Just get them inside."

All at once Haza'ruux shifts, shrugging off my arm. He supports himself against the wall. "Haza'ruux will stay," he rasps. "No one will pass this door."

"No. You're hurt."

"Haza'ruux is not hurt." He breaks into a manic grin. "Only a little tired."

"No!" I grab his arm. "I'm not leaving you here."

He snarls in reply. On his chest, the mark of the raving dog flashes and glows; light pulses through his skin.

I let go and back away. "They'll kill you!"

"Haza'ruux has more strength—than you know." He speaks through clenched teeth, as if restraining himself only by a terrible effort. "The Arimaas—protects—its Keeper."

The last knot of survivors struggles into the tunnel. Only the three of us are left standing at the door.

"I'll stay with him," says Kophas suddenly.

I turn, aghast. "What?"

"We can't let them find this tunnel. I can help distract the warriors—lead them away. The longer start you have, the better."

"Do you want to die? I didn't get you out of the Underbelly for this!"

"Markmaker." His voice is steely, with only the faintest hint of a tremor.

284

"I'm not going back there. And I do not think I will ever see the planets now."
His mouth twitches in a ghastly smile. "Let me repay you. Let me die as a
son of Tarriks ought to die—shedding my heart's blood for a worthy cause."

Without waiting for my response, he turns to Haza'ruux and drops to his
knees. "Keeper." He pushes back the visor of his helmet. "Honorable one. I
have heard stories of the marks of power. I did not know they were real until
now."

"Hakka." Haza'ruux's face, eerily lit with marks, creases into a crazed grin.
"You—Swift Heart. You are the hunter who has died and lived again. You
have come out of Axdraa'dah."

"Keeper, I beg you." Kophas trembles; his dark eyes glisten with reverence.
"Please let me fight beside you."

"Your fathers in the Dream—they have prepared a great mark for you."
Extending one bloodstained hand, the old man smears a sigil on the young
warrior's brow. "Stand with the Keeper, Swift Heart. Stand with Haza'ruux."
He cackles; his tattoos pulse even more brightly. "Only do not stand in front
of him!"

"No!" I almost weep with fury and helplessness. "I won't lose you both."

Kophas rises and turns to me. Under the soot-smeared visor, his face glows
with a strange ecstasy—and I know that my friend, this exile whom I labored
so long and hard to save, is beyond my reach. *Swift Heart.* Haza'ruux has
named him; he belongs to the Keeper now, body and spirit. Grief and hurt
and a bewildering resentment overwhelm me.

Kophas grips me by the shoulder. The fresh blood-mark glimmers on his
brow. "If we die, we die with honor. A Noxxiin can ask no more. You have
your clan to save."

Haza'ruux growls and draws his twin knives from his kilt. From the plaza
beyond, I hear the clatter of armored feet.

"Get out of here, markmaker!" Kophas shoves me bodily into the maintenance tunnel, then whirls around, lifting his rifle.

I stand at the entrance of the shaft, unable to move. Haza'ruux turns his
radiant eyes on me. His unreadable sigils twist and writhe like flames; his
body burns so bright I can barely look at him. An incongruous memory
springs to mind—the odd and harmless hermit sitting in his garden, drawing
in the dirt and singing to the children. I want to scream, *Don't go.* But I know
he would not listen.

He grasps the door of the shaft. In a beastlike snarl, he says, "Keep them
safe, Flashing Blade. The Mad Dog must go hunting."

He heaves the door shut in my face. From the plaza, I hear the shouts of
the Ascendance soldiers and the crack of their guns. I hear Kophas roaring,

"Kalimaa!" Haza'ruux's howl splits the air, a blood-freezing, otherworldly siren—the call of the Deep Sleep, if the Deep Sleep had a voice.

I reel about to follow my clan. And I run.

CHAPTER THIRTY-THREE

My clanmates have not gone far. They stand huddled at the shaft's first intersection, packing the narrow tunnel. A shuffle of feet and a drone of anxious talk echo off the metal walls. I can hear a child crying, inconsolable.

They're too loud. We'll be caught.

As I approach, still gripping my sword and panting from my sprint, I force Haza'ruux and Kophas from my mind. They made their choice. Now I must ensure they did not sacrifice themselves in vain. When I reach the back of the crowd, people turn and cry out.

"Markmaker!"

"Are the soldiers coming?"

"Where do we go?"

I raise one hand in a quieting gesture. "We need to keep moving," I say in the most level tone I can manage. "Please, let me through."

My clanmates press themselves against the walls to let me pass. But their eyes are fixed on me in a fervent expression that I know all too well.

Save us, markmaker.

A chill pricks my spine. As I push through the crowd, my gaze lingers on their clan-marks—or their wounds where their clan-marks should be. *We are all exiles now.*

At last, I emerge at the front of the crush. Virik stands in the tunnel intersection, talking with Kilmaya in a low, earnest voice. My teacher leans wearily against the wall, staring at the floor. Tyotik clings to her feet. Even before I have a chance to speak, the boy springs up and runs to me. I bend down and catch him.

"Kesh. You're all right."

He trembles in my embrace. Kilmaya looks up, startled. "Mariikel?"

"I'm here." I lift Tyotik in my arms and stand.

Virik peers past me, as if searching for someone. "Where is he?"

From the tension in his face, I assume he means the mad markmaker. "Haza'ruux stayed behind. And so did Kophas. They're distracting the troops—they told us not to wait."

The recordmaster grimaces and lowers his eyes.

"Mariikel." Kilmaya's voice cracks. She stares at me, her teeth half-bared in fear. "Is there no other place we can go?"

"I don't think so. If the High Council has outlawed the clan altogether, there is no public place that is safe. But as long as no one knows we escaped, I don't think they'll search the Underbelly."

She covers her mouth with one hand, muffling a groan. "How long? How long will we have to stay there?"

"I don't know, teacher. We can't worry about that right now."

Her eyes squeeze shut, and she sobs briefly.

"Listen to me." I step closer, aching to reach out and embrace her. But Tyotik still has his skinny arms wrapped around my neck, and I doubt he will let me put him down. "The Underbelly is not a death sentence. People live there. I've seen them."

"Exiles, you mean. The unclanned. Eating the ship's filth—"

"They make do with what they have." My voice rises. "The food they eat does not make them beasts."

Kilmaya's face grows rigid with despair. She turns her back on me.

Virik shifts, glaring uneasily. "I would like to hear more about these friends you have. How do you know they will help us?"

I hesitate. I am reluctant to tell them about all the outcasts I have marked. It would mean admitting to yet another lie, and I need them to trust me right now. "There are a few exiles that I've...helped in the past. I've brought them food. Medicine, sometimes. They may be able to find us shelter."

"That's it?" His mouth twitches. "We can't stay there. We need to get off the ship—"

"Recordmaster." Lowering my voice, I gesture at the frightened crowd behind us. "We don't have time for this. These are maintenance tunnels; a crew might come through and spot us at any moment."

Virik blinks rapidly, but then lowers his head in assent. I cannot help glancing at the congealed blood on his neck. It gleams an ugly dark purple.

Virik catches me staring. He flinches. "My family. They were going to kill them if I didn't—"

"Kesh. You don't have to explain." I, of all people, cannot condemn him for giving up his mark. "We need to move. Do you think you can take the back of the group? To make sure no one falls behind?"

"I can do that."

Without looking at me, he pushes past and disappears into the crowd.

Kilmaya still leans against the wall, her face hidden in her hands. An ache constricts my throat. "Teacher. If I knew of a safer place, I would take you there. You have to trust me." I shift my hold on Tyotik and reach out to her. "Please, teacher."

She brushes my hand away. "Don't call me that. I don't teach skin-changers."

The words stab me in the vitals. But I do not try to defend myself—instead I merely bow. Hugging Tyotik a little tighter, I turn to the people behind me. Then I strike the hilt of my sword against the tunnel wall to get their attention. At the clang of metal on metal, the buzz of anxious talk dies. "Everyone," I call. "We're going to start now. Stay close together, and stay quiet. We have a long way to go."

No one protests. As I stand before them, gripping the old funeral-blade, I am vividly aware of the cold floor under my bare feet and the creaking and hissing of the pipes behind the tunnel walls. My clanmates stare at me, mute and entreating.

Flashing Blade. Chieftain.

I close my eyes and banish Haza'ruux's rasping voice from my thoughts. Tyotik pulls on my tunic, nestling closer. His breath pulses hot and quick against my neck. Unbidden, the image of Hakham and Chervani, lying slain on their bedroom floor, rises to my mind. I clench my teeth until my jaw hurts.

By the blood of my ancestors, no more Serixan will die tonight.

Then I turn and step around the corner of the shaft. My clan follows.

When I used this route before, it took me the better part of an hour to reach the Underbelly. But then I was alone—I could walk quickly, and I could use the maintenance elevators without attracting unwanted notice. Now I have no disguise, and there is no way I can hide the fifty-some frightened people behind me. So I avoid transport hubs and elevators, and instead take the long way down: tunnel after descending tunnel, with trap doors and short ladders in between. I have no way to measure the time, but I know our progress is slow. Children cry, elders stumble, and all of us are drained. I carry Tyotik for as long as I can, but when my arms begin aching, I put him down and tell him to walk beside me. He obeys without a word, gripping the hem of my tunic in one hand.

Kilmaya also remains silent. She walks a short distance behind me and does not speak to me. I do not address her, either. But I cannot help noticing, as we descend further into the bowels of the ship, how her feet drag and her labored breath hisses through her teeth. Kilmaya has never seemed frail to me. But she is not young, either, and she has never made a journey like this before. For an instant, I imagine her clambering down a damp ladder in the darkness—slipping, falling, her body breaking on a platform far below... I lean one hand against the wall and halt.

The air of the tunnel chills my skin. That is a good sign—we have reached the lower levels of the maintenance shafts, which means the Underbelly is close. But then we will have seven or eight flights of ladders to climb down, and afterwards, once we reach the slums... I have not thought that far. We have no food or water. We will not even have shelters; we might have to sleep in the filth-strewn alleys. I will need to search for some of the exiles I know, to beg them for help—but will they even recognize me? They have never seen my true face.

I glance over my shoulder. My clanmates stand clustered in the narrow shaft, shivering, their faces drawn. Kilmaya wraps her arms around herself, her eyes dull with exhaustion. At my feet, Tyotik sinks to the floor. He whimpers.

They won't make it down the ladders, I realize. *Not like this.*

Again I peer into the dim shaft ahead. I don't want to stop. We have not yet met any maintenance crews—and I thank the ancestors for that. Perhaps some of Haza'ruux's battle-luck has rubbed off on us. Still, I do not expect our good fortune to hold out forever. Every moment we stay in these tunnels, we are in danger. But I am so tired that I cannot will myself to move any faster. My head pounds, and my right arm throbs with fierce pain. My throat feels dry and swollen—I cannot remember when I last ate or drank.

I face my clanmates once more. "Is something wrong?" Kilmaya rasps.

"No." I press my hands against my eyelids. My face burns, feverishly warm. "We're close to the Underbelly, but it will be harder, going forward. We should rest."

A groan of relief escapes the crowd.

"Only for a few minutes. We can't stay here. We're too exposed." I cough, and my own dizziness washes over me again. "Sit down. Everyone sit."

They obey, weary to the point of despondency. Some huddle against the passage walls, while others stretch out on the floor, heedless of the frigid metal. I want to join them, but I can't yet. I bend down and gently pry Tyotik's fingers away from my leg.

"Stay with Kilmaya." I point at her to make sure he understands. "I'll be right back."

He does not reply, but his eyes grow wide, dark with terror and accusation. I stand again and walk away. I am afraid he will follow me, but when I check over my shoulder, he is still where I left him, staring after me with his small teeth half-bared.

Carefully, I weave between the survivors crowded on the floor. I ask if anyone is injured. Some people have cuts and bruises from stumbling through rubble in their bare feet, and many have wounds where the soldiers stripped their clan-marks. Beyond that, no one seems seriously hurt—but everyone has been pushed beyond their limits. A few weep softly. Others ask for water. But I have nothing to give them.

At the far end of the group, I find Virik sitting against the wall with his family. Young K'nima leans against him, her knees curled to her chest, her eyes shut. Virik's wife, Kandri, tears a strip of cloth from her own tunic and wraps it around his neck, binding up the hideous wound. I hang back, reluctant to disturb them.

At last, the recordmaster glances up. "Hakka." His daughter stirs, too. Virik seems unsure how to address me. "Mariikel," he says finally. "Are we nearly there?"

I crouch down in front of him, resting the flat of my blade against my shoulder. My knees and hocks ache—it is a relief to stop moving, even for a minute. "We're close. But I thought we all needed a rest."

"Agreed." He grimaces, breathing deeply. Once again, I find his self-possession striking. He is clearly worn out and in pain, but he has done everything I asked of him without complaint. It is strange to think that only a few days ago, I knelt before him in his own hall, confessing my crimes. I remember, distantly, how terrified I was. But now I am glad of his steady presence.

I gesture at the length of empty tunnel behind us. "Keep an eye on the shaft. If you hear anyone coming, call me at once."

Virik nods but gives my sword a dubious glance. "What will you do?"

"I don't know yet." My upper eyes narrow, and I grip the hilt tighter. "Pray that we don't have to find out."

He grunts and rests his head against the wall. K'nima still huddles beside him, blinking at me with a peaked, hunted expression. "Markmaker," she whispers. "Are we all going to die?"

Virik pulls his daughter to him in a one-armed embrace. Kandri reaches out and grips her hand. "Kesh, Nima."

The girl buries her face in her father's chest. I watch her parents in silence as they murmur and console her. A fierce longing racks me, a wrenching grief. What would I give to have my own family with me now?

After a minute, Virik rouses himself and points at the bulky Ascendance cuffs that still encase my forearms. "Where did you get the armor? How did you even get out of the guild hall?"

I sense that he needs to talk, if only to focus on something besides his pain. I do not mind the distraction, either. In a low voice, I tell him of the Ascendance guards who broke into the holding cells, of their brief and deadly fight with Kophas, and of our escape into the chaos of Rixarii Street. The account seems to move Virik greatly.

"Kophas Tarriks. This was the same man who…?"

"Whose marks I changed?" I finish quietly.

The recordmaster looks away, as if ashamed. "He was a good friend to you."

"Yes." I swallow hard. I can still see Kophas's face glowing in the light of Haza'ruux's marks: hollow-cheeked, filthy with soot, yet radiant—transported with warrior's joy.

My brother.

We were brothers for a few hours, in arms if not in blood. I wonder, suddenly, what it would have been like to have Askko at my side tonight. Would he have fought for his clan against his faction? Would he have chosen to stay behind, as Kophas did? The thought is unexpectedly painful.

Virik remains silent for a while, discreetly ignoring my grief. Then he looks up again. "Did you see the guildmaster anywhere?"

"No. He told me before the attack that he had a plan to escape the ship. He was going to take me and Kophas with him, and that Tarriks commander, Jal'thor."

"He was?" The news appears to startle Virik. "What happened, then?"

"I don't know. The soldiers might have taken them by surprise—they may have been captured. Or they had to leave without us." I shift my sore legs. "He said he was going to come back when he had found allies. I don't think he knew… I don't think he knew the faction was going to dissolve the clan."

"If Mekkalluthak swore to return, he will find a way. I hope he escaped."

I do not reply. It is possible, I suppose, that Mekkalluthak and Jal'thor made it out of the sector before the Ascendance forces could find them. But even if the guildmaster is free, I cannot bring myself to place my hopes in him.

"Mariikel." Kandri speaks my name for the first time, low and hesitant. "Hakham and Chervani. I haven't seen them. Are they…not with you?"

A wave of heat tingles through my skin. When I close my eyes, I can still feel the frail weight of Chervani's body in my arms. "I didn't reach them in time."

A brief silence falls. "Kin's heart," Kandri gasps. "Oh, Mariikel."

"Kesh." The word comes out more harshly than I intended. But if I think about my aunt and uncle now, I will not have the strength to go on. I lever myself from the floor to stand. Then: "I am glad you have your family with you."

Virik lowers his head in anguish. He, too, was a friend to my adopted parents. Then he looks up at me again. "If there is anything I can do—"

"You are doing it already." I point my sword down the shaft. "Keep watch."

I stumble back through the crowded tunnel and return to Tyotik and Kilmaya. With a stifled groan, I sink to the ground and lay down my blade. I want to curl up on the floor, my head in my arms, and never move again. But my clanmates cannot see me like that. I have to be strong. They have no other hope left.

As soon as I sit down, Tyotik crawls into my lap. I do not mind—I feel chilled, and his little body is warm. I close my eyes and let him rest against me. In a few minutes, his shaky breathing steadies and deepens; I think he actually falls asleep. How desperately I wish I could join him.

The pain in my right arm intensifies; now that I have stopped moving, I can no longer ignore it. Slowly, so that I do not disturb Tyotik, I unbuckle the armored cuffs and slide them off. My wrist is even more swollen than before, and the skin surrounding the acid burn has turned a mottled dark gray. Even Haza'ruux's mark looks warped and distorted. I unwrap the soiled bandage around my wrist. The wound is sticky with a whitish, foul-smelling fluid—it is certainly infected now. It hurts to bend my wrist or flex my fingers. So far, my hand is still functional, but I am not sure how long that will last.

Axdraa'dah. Real healers are scarce in the Underbelly, and good medicine even more so. Why did I not ask my prison guards for medicine when I had the chance?

Because you thought you were going to be executed. You were waiting to die.

"What did they do to you?"

Startled, I glance up. Kilmaya sits against the opposite wall, watching me. Her clothes are disheveled and her eyes sunken. But there is a curtness in her tone, a hint of brusque concern that sounds more like the sharp-witted teacher that I know. And she has spoken to me. That fact alone floods me with relief.

"I did this to myself."

"What?"

"Haza'ruux's mark." I lower my voice. Our clanmates are not paying much attention, but I still do not want them to overhear. "I...tried to erase it."

Her eyes flick to the bandage on my arm, then back to my face. "Why?"

I grimace. I do not want to explain this now—I do not even know where to start. But Kilmaya, of all people, deserves an answer. "He was teaching me about the Arimaas—the marks of power," I say, barely louder than a breath. "I thought they were only stories. But when he showed me they were true...I was afraid. I didn't want anything to do with him anymore. So I tried to remove the mark." Cradling my swollen arm against my chest, I regard the sigil poem dully. "It didn't even work."

Kilmaya pauses, a glimmer of apprehension in her face. "Is it…a mark like his?"

"What? No. Not like his. There's no power in it." I turn my arm, studying the twining, calligraphic lines. *Not that he told me, at least.*

For a while we both fall quiet. In my mind, Haza'ruux's chilling howl echoes, and I can see him once more, springing and dodging between the Ascendance soldiers, a radiant phantom, dealing death. When I meet my teacher's haunted gaze, I wonder if she is thinking of the same thing. "Ancestors help me, Mariikel. I don't know you anymore."

I had almost forgotten—this is the first time we have spoken since before I turned myself in to the Serix authorities. I have not yet asked her forgiveness. I lower my head.

"I am sorry that I lied to you, teacher."

"Oh, kesh. What does it matter now?" She rests her head against the wall, glaring up at the tunnel ceiling. "I guess I should thank you. If you weren't a dirty skin-changer, I suppose I would be dead by now."

I accept the verbal blow without comment. She has the right to be angry, and I do not have the energy to defend myself.

"Great Ka, Mariikel." Her slender hands clench in spasms. "When they came to me—when they told me what you had done—" She gasps, her face twisted with bewildered grief. "If you had come to me, after Talorak's exile, I could have helped you. Why didn't you tell me?"

"I was afraid. I didn't want you to get into trouble."

"Hakk." She laughs bitterly. "And how much good has that done us, I ask you?"

We lapse into silence again, but I sense that Kilmaya is still angry. I yearn to reach out, to fall at her feet, to weep for every false word I have ever spoken to her. But I cannot take back what I have done. If I have lost her trust, it is no more than my due.

Wordless, I rebandage my wrist and buckle the armored cuffs back onto my forearms. To my left, in the length of empty tunnel, a distant clank echoes. I freeze, listening. I did not imagine it—there are footsteps coming towards us from beyond the next intersection. Behind me, a hiss of fear escapes my clanmates.

"No one move," I order. I lift Tyotik from my lap and give him to Kilmaya. He wakes and cries out as she clutches him in her arms. I snatch up my sword and rise. All at once I feel sharply alert; I stand with my legs braced and my heart pounding. I can feel the haze of bloodlust rising behind my eyes.

Touch them, and I will kill you.

Several yards away, two figures round the corner of the shaft and halt. Both wear hooded tunics and toolbelts, but at this distance, I cannot make out their marks. At the sight of the crowded tunnel, they stiffen visibly and draw back.

"Who's there?" A man's voice, alarmed, trying to sound authoritative. It is not the voice of a soldier hunting down outlaws. These people are maintenance workers; they did not expect to find us. But my body still tenses, ready to lash out.

"Who are you?" the laborer demands again. His stance widens defensively, and he puts a hand on his toolbelt. Both he and his companion gape at the people huddled behind me. "What—what in Ka's name—"

"Stay back." I thrust my blade out in front of me. But even as my limbs tremor with rage, I realize how pitiful I must look: a short, slight young man wearing a grimy tunic and bearing no marks of battle—my bluff is absurd.

Then the other laborer speaks—a woman's voice, quiet with astonishment. "They're Serix."

Silence drops between us. I breathe heavily, gripping my sword. Behind me, my clanmates shift and murmur, and a child whimpers.

"You're Clan Serix?" The man sounds hoarse.

"I don't want any trouble," I reply. "If you let us pass, I will not harm you."

But even as the words leave my mouth, I realize how foolish they are. Even if these people do not hinder us now, they can easily report our presence—to their superiors, at least, if not directly to the Ascendance. Either way, the High Council will hear of our escape. And then they will send troops to scour the Underbelly.

My fingers, locked around the hilt of the sword, grow numb. I cannot let these workers go. I cannot kill them, either—now that my initial terror has faded, I have neither the strength nor the willpower. I am not like Kophas or Haza'ruux; I have never shed blood in my life.

"You're not supposed to be down here." The male laborer grips something stashed in his belt—a knife, or perhaps a datscroll; I cannot tell. "What's going on?"

I hesitate, panic fogging my mind. I cannot see if these workers have faction-marks; I have no idea whether they sympathize with the Ascendance or not. But I have no lie prepared for them, either. I must risk the truth. "Ascendance troops invaded our sector. They are stripping our clan-marks. They are slaughtering us."

The woman gives a sharp cry. "Skin of the Deep Sleep." She clutches at her companion's arm.

The man, however, declares, "That's impossible. That can't be true."

"Look at us!" I spread my arms wide, baring my teeth in a snarl. "Do I look like I'm lying? Why else would we be here?"

The laborer stares. He does not answer.

"Axelikk." The woman tugs on his arm again. "The outage tonight, in the Serix sector..."

"That was a computer error," the man snaps. "Not a real outage. The tunnelmaster's message said so."

"That's what it *said*." Heat creeps into the woman's voice—an undercurrent of shock and anger. She gestures to the crowd huddled behind me. "Why don't we ask the Serixan? They were there." She turns away from her fellow laborer to address me. "Markmaker. Was there a power failure in your sector tonight?"

Something in her stance, her tone of indignation, stirs my hope. "Yes. Yes, there was."

"When did it start? What time did the lights first go out?"

I flounder for an instant. I realize I have no idea when the blackout began—I was asleep in my cell under the guild hall when it started. I do not even know what time it is now. But before I can stammer my ignorance, someone speaks up behind me.

"The fifteenth hour," says Kilmaya. "About half-past. I was awake for it."

The woman's eyes narrow in a look of vindication. She glares at her companion. "Is that the time the tunnelmasters said?"

"Ancestors." The man appears shaken. "Kin's blood. This is real, isn't it?" For a moment longer he gapes at us in dismay. "But—but where are you going?"

"To the Underbelly." My blade wavers in my grip. "If you'll let us. No one will look for us there."

Slowly the laborer's hand drops from his belt. The woman reaches out, grasping his fingers in her own. He turns to look at her. In the brief flash of their headlamps, I glimpse the backs of their hands. They wear matching marriage-marks.

Some expression, some silent understanding, passes between them. When the laborer turns back to me, his face is drawn. But his eyelids have stopped flickering in fear. In a gravelly tone, he says, "We did not see you, Serix. You were not here."

A great breath fills my lungs. "Do you mean it?"

"We swear it." The man steps forward, pushes back his hood, and places two fingers on his clan-mark. The woman imitates him. "By the blood of our ancestors, we will not tell anyone we met you."

A strange weakness overcomes me. When the laborers lower their hands, I see they are both Clan Tizzan.

"Thank you. Thank you. Honor with you both."

"And with you, markmaker." The woman's eyes glitter fiercely. "The nearest Underbelly hatch is down the passage to the left—a few minutes' walk. It needs a mastery-mark to open." Again she clasps her husband's hand. "We'll leave it unlocked for you."

I bow my head, overwhelmed. "Ancestors bless you."

"They should bless you." The man's voice has turned gruff again. "You should hurry, Serix. Spurs sharp. Be careful."

"We will."

When I raise my head, the Tizzan laborers are already retreating up the passage. And all I can think, as they round the corner and disappear back the way they came, is that they will never receive the tattoos they both merited tonight.

You have honor-marks no one can see.

The tap of their footsteps fades. The tunnel walls creak, and my clanmates whisper behind me. Dizzy, I return to Kilmaya. My teacher stands now, gripping Tyotik's hand as fiercely as if he were her own child. "What do you think?" she asks. "Will they keep their word?"

I lick my dry lips. "I think so."

Her eyelids flicker once. Then of a sudden she steps forward and embraces me. I hold her in silence as she quakes with great, shattering sobs.

CHAPTER THIRTY-FOUR

I rouse the clan, and we go on again. The rest did us some good; we travel a little faster and more steadily, until at last we reach the round, rusted hatch that marks the entrance to the Underbelly. Never did I think I would be so glad to see it.

On the wall nearby, the mark-scanner blinks steadily, indicating the door is already unlocked—just as the Tizzan workers promised. I send up another silent blessing on their behalf. I grip the handle with my one good hand, wrench it to the side, and tug open the heavy hatch. A cold and foul-smelling wind rushes through as it unseals. Behind me, Kilmaya grunts and covers her mouth. Others flinch at the odor, too, and a murmur of dismay ripples through the crowd.

The stench does not move me—I have been here too many times to notice it anymore. But the thought passes through my mind that this may be the last time I climb through this hatch. I have come to the Underbelly to stay.

This is no time for brooding; I have to keep my clanmates alive. Already, at the first whiff of the Underbelly, their strength is wavering. I stand up in front of the open hatch. "Everyone gather around."

With difficulty, they shuffle forward, surrounding the gap in the floor. Kilmaya, with Tyotik clinging to her, stands close by. She has said little since we met the shaft workers. But she does not take her eyes off me, as if she is afraid I might vanish if she so much as blinks.

When everyone has gathered near me, I point down at the black hole of the hatch. "We're almost safe. Once we reach the floor of the Underbelly, I can find people who will help us. But this last part is the most difficult." I pause, watching the haggard faces before me, the way they drink in my every word with voiceless desperation. "There are eight levels between us and the floor of the Underbelly. I would take you down by elevator, but it's too likely that we would run into more laborers. So we have to take the ladders." I grimace. "The footing is...not always good. We must be careful—I don't want anyone slipping. But we must also hurry." I swallow briefly, biting back my own rising fears.

"I will lead," I resume. "We'll rest on the platforms when we have to, but the less time we spend there, the better." I spot Virik standing beside his wife and daughter. K'nima still clings to his arm, staring at the open hatch in a trance of fear. "Recordmaster, will you take the back of the line? I need someone to close the hatch when everyone has gone through."

Virik inclines his head, his face gaunt but resolute. "Very well."

"Thank you. Make sure that people climb down one at a time. I don't want anyone crowding or pushing on the ladders." I pause again, my pulse pounding in my temples. My right wrist throbs even worse now, but I clench my fists and will the pain away.

Something jerks on the hem of my clothing. I startle and glance down to find Tyotik clutching a fistful of my tunic. The boy has hardly made a noise for hours, but he looks miserable. He is so young; it occurs to me that he is too small to reach the ladder rungs by himself. I will have to carry him, but I also need a way to carry the sword—I do not want to leave it behind, where it might be found. I turn the blade over in the dim light, letting my eyes linger on the name-sigils etched into the steel—Kilmaya's ancestors. This weapon bears the blessing of generations of Serix artists, and it is the only artifact I was able to rescue from our home sector. I owe it to the clan to bring this blade with us.

After a moment of thought, I crouch down and set my blade on the floor. "Come here, Tyotik. I need your help."

He stands before me, his gaze fixed on my face. Remorse washes over me. This child trusts me implicitly, believes that I will keep him safe from all the horrors he has seen tonight. What am I doing, bringing him to a place like the Underbelly? But I do not have a choice.

"Tyotik." I place a light hand on his shoulder. I can feel him trembling. "We have to go someplace...a little bit frightening. I'll carry you. But I need to bring my sword, too—to keep us safe." I touch the slender cord tied around his middle, which serves as a belt for his tunic. "Can I borrow this?"

He doesn't answer, but he does not protest, either, as I loosen the cord and pull it away. I unfasten the belt from around my waist and re-buckle it crosswise, over my chest. I take up my blade and wrap the cord around the hilt several times, then tie the sword securely to my belt. At last, I go to the boy again and draw him close.

"I need you to be very brave," I whisper. "Like a warrior. Like your nakko. Can you do that for me?"

His teeth chatter, and his narrow chest heaves, but he manages a tiny nod.

"That's it." I pull the boy to my chest and strap him into the makeshift harness. "I'm afraid it's not very comfortable. Just hold on to me, all right?"

Tyotik puts his arms around my neck and buries his face in my shoulder. I rise, widening my stance to bear the added weight more easily. The sword tied at my belt sways, bumping against my bare leg. I am glad that it is a ceremonial blade—if it were in battle condition, it could probably injure me.

There is nothing else to do; we are ready. As I stand at the edge of the hole with Tyotik clinging to my chest, Kilmaya eyes me anxiously. "Will you be all right?" she asks.

"I'll be fine. He's not heavy." The boy is so small and slender that he barely seems to weigh anything. Or perhaps I am stronger than I realized. "You come right after me, teacher."

She blinks without protest. I think I see a glimmer of relief in her face.

Exhaling deeply, I turn around and lower myself into the hatch, resting my feet on the first rung. Tyotik shudders at the draft and grasps my tunic more tightly. I stare into the dark and thrumming space below, and my head reels.

Ancestors, give us strength.

I think of Hakham and Chervani, and my long-dead parents, whom I barely knew, and all the slaughtered clanmates whom we left behind tonight. I think of Haza'ruux and Kophas. By now, probably, they have met the Deep Sleep, too. But they will have died well. They will have already crossed the chasm of Axdraa'dah, passing into the rest of the Long Dream.

Watch over us.

I step down, curling my toes around the frigid rungs. Then bearing my shivering little burden, I lower myself into the mouth of the Underbelly.

Tyotik is not much heavier than the markmaking satchel I used to carry down these ladders. I am not worried about him letting go, either. He grips my neck so fiercely that if he were a little stronger, he would choke me. When I have descended several rungs, I look back up at the hatch. For a moment, I am afraid Kilmaya will not follow. But then I see her lean over the hole. With awkward movements, she steps down. My heart throbs as I watch her.

There was a time, not so long ago, when I was determined never to tell Kilmaya of my journeys to the Underbelly. Not even in my nightmares did I imagine I would have to bring her here. To see her—my wise, lively, sharp-tongued teacher—reduced to groans of terror as she creeps down the ladder sends a terrible pang through me.

But I cannot climb for her; I can only watch. Around us, air currents tug at our clothes, and distant generators vibrate the metal under my feet. I wait until I see that other people are following Kilmaya. Then I pry my hands from the rung and continue descending.

Only the sharpness of my fear keeps me focused. I force myself not to look out into the vast windy chasm of the Underbelly, with its hulking beams and pipes. The rungs under my feet are slick with condensation. At my hip, the funeral-blade smacks against my leg and clangs on the rusted ladder. Tyotik pants rapidly, sobbing between breaths.

At last, I step down onto the echoing surface of the first platform. Kilmaya sways several feet above me, her shoulders hunched, her movements painfully slow. "You're almost there," I call as she lowers one unsteady foot. "A little farther—"

I am still speaking when a nearby vent roars to life with a blast of heated, stinking air. Kilmaya shudders, startled by the noise, and her sandal slips on one of the wet rungs. For an instant, she scrabbles in panic—then she loses her hold and falls.

"Teacher!"

By instinct, I hold out my arms. Her body collides with me, and we tumble to the platform in a heap. Tyotik, pinned between us, screams shrilly, and the hilt of the funeral-blade digs into my side. I struggle free and drag myself upright. "Teacher, are you all right?"

She curses repeatedly. I pull her to one side and let her lean against the platform railing. After pausing to make sure Tyotik is unhurt, I call up to the people still huddled on the ladder. "Don't stop. Keep coming. But careful! The ladders are wet."

With shaking hands, I unbuckle the belt on my chest and free Tyotik from his harness, then kneel in front of Kilmaya. Her eyes are thin slits, and through gritted teeth she chokes out, "I'm sorry—I'm sorry."

"Where are you hurt?"

"My foot." She points to her left leg. As gently as I can, I grasp her foot by the ankle. She sucks in a breath. "Don't touch it—"

I let go. The lighting here is poor, and I am no healer; I cannot tell how serious the injury is. The other survivors reach the platform one by one. They stand around nervously, staring at Kilmaya while she tries to muffle her cries.

"Teacher." I grip her hand. "We can't stop here. Can you stand? Can you put any weight on it at all?"

Vehemently, she shakes her head. But I put an arm around her, anyway, and pull her to her feet. With a scream, she stumbles against the railing. "Down. Put me down!"

I lower her to the platform again. "No use," she gasps. "I can't. Not like this." She lets her head fall back and shuts her eyes.

The platform is full of people now, and they have not finished coming down. I put my hands on Kilmaya's shoulders and shake her a little. "We need to keep moving."

"Can't climb with one foot. I'll fall again."

With a sick feeling rising in my belly, I glance around. Almost everyone has made it down now. This part of the Underbelly may be deserted, but the longer we stay in one place, the more likely we are to attract attention. And if Kilmaya cannot walk…I groan aloud. I could try to lead the group to an elevator, but I do not know where the nearest one is. Then, too, we would run the risk of being discovered.

Kilmaya grips my fingers. "Maybe…maybe it will feel better if I rest for a bit. Take the others down. You can come back for me."

I inhale sharply. To leave my teacher on a high platform of the Underbelly, alone and defenseless… If a taskmaster found her, or some hardened, brutal outcast…

"No! I am not leaving you here." I have already lost my family and two dear friends tonight—I refuse to risk my teacher as well. Looking around in desperation, I spot my discarded belt and sword on the platform. I face Kilmaya again and clasp her shoulders. "I'll carry you."

"Don't be ridiculous." Her lips curl back in exasperation. "You're carrying the boy already."

"He's not heavy. Someone else can take him."

Her eyes widen as she realizes that I am serious. "But you're not strong enough."

I offer her a tight little smile. "I've been training on these ladders for months. I can do it." I am not nearly as confident as I make myself sound. But I know that I have to try.

"No." Naked fear tinges her voice now. "I'll fall again. I will."

I ignore her. Nearby, Virik steps off the ladder, the last of the line. Swiftly I scan the rest of the crowd. Most of the people here are middle-aged or elderly, or they are children—not frail, but not fit to carry a heavy burden, either. They are already exhausted, and none of them are as surefooted on the ladders as I am. *No,* I decide. I cannot trust this task to anyone else.

I take Tyotik in my arms again. As I rise, I tell Kilmaya, "Take off your sash."

"What?"

"You won't fall if you're tied to me."

Her mouth opens, but no words come out. I turn and hurry over to Virik. "Kilmaya is hurt. I'm going to need to carry her. Can you find someone to take Tyotik for me?"

Virik hesitates, his eyes round with astonishment. Before he can reply, his wife Kandri steps forward, her lips set in a resolute line. "I can take the child. Give him here, Mariikel."

Without hesitation, I hand the boy into Kandri's arms. Tyotik struggles, wailing, clutching at my clothes. I extricate my tunic from his grasp only with difficulty. "Kesh now," I whisper as I back out of his reach. My heart aches. All he wants is to stay close to me, and I have to hand him off to strangers. "I'm sorry, Tyotik. It's only for a little while. I promise."

While Kandri hushes the hysterical child, I turn back to Virik. "Come with me. I'm going to need help."

He follows. After a few minutes mingling with the crowd, we collect a handful of belts and sashes. When we return to Kilmaya, she glares at us wildly. "Mariikel, this is madness."

"Leaving you here is madness." I bend down and take her sash from her hands. Lifting her injured leg, I wrap the cloth around her ankle and foot. It is not a proper splint, but the binding should provide a little stability. Kilmaya grits her teeth against the pain. Even as I tie off the bandage, I listen for the clank of approaching footsteps. "You have to stand up."

Ignoring her protests, Virik and I lift her up again. When she is standing, both hands gripping the railing, I move in front of her and turn my back. "Put your arms around me."

"No." Her voice shakes with anger. "I won't let you do this."

"I'll strike you senseless and carry you that way if I have to," I snarl. "Do you hear me? Hold on to me, now!"

The shock of my threat, I think, puts her past argument. Strangling a cry, she leans against my back and wraps her arms around my chest.

For a few minutes, the recordmaster and I fumble with the materials we collected, constructing a makeshift harness. Virik ties two sashes crosswise around both me and my teacher, then straps two belts on top of them. With the rest of the spare cloth, he binds us together at the waist. At every tug of the straps, Kilmaya groans—whether in pain or humiliation, I cannot tell.

At last, Virik steps back. "That's the best I can do." Then to Kilmaya: "You'll still need to hold on. But if you get tired, you won't fall."

My teacher does not answer. She leans most of her weight on me now, and I roll my shoulders, testing the harness. It seems secure—but if it fails mid-ladder, we could both die. That thought frightens me less than the thought of leaving her behind.

Virik regards me with his teeth half-bared. "Will you be all right?"

"I'll be fine." I give the harness another tug to reassure myself as well as Virik. "We'll go last. You take the lead; keep everyone moving. Simply follow the ladders straight down. And wait—here." I take up the funeral-blade from the platform. "Please carry this for me."

"Of course." He accepts the sword with a kind of wondering reverence and ties it to his own belt. Then his hand rises by reflex to touch his clan-mark.

When his fingers brush the bandage on his neck, he freezes. "I will see you at the bottom."

The recordmaster turns away and calls the clan together. One by one, they return to the ladder and resume their downward climb. Kandri descends after her husband with Tyotik secured to her chest; the boy still struggles and screams for me. They disappear into the gloom below the platform. K'nima comes next; the young apprentice stares at me and Kilmaya in open dismay. She is not the only one, either. I do not say anything to our clanmates as they pass us by. Instead I put one hand on my chest, clasping Kilmaya's arm.

I will not fail you, teacher.

After several minutes, the last survivors descend, and I hobble forward. I reach out and grasp the sides of the ladder. A stifled moan escapes Kilmaya. "Kesh," I whisper. Then, bracing myself, I step down onto the rungs.

As my teacher's weight leaves the platform, she grips me twice as hard as before. I grunt as the belt straps bite deep into my shoulders. Kilmaya pants against the back of my neck; I can feel the hammering of her heart in my own spine. I did not expect her to be so heavy. We are roughly the same height and build—and I have never carried my own weight before, not even on level ground. Now I am hanging off a ladder above a black and breathing chasm, and one false step—

There will be no false step.

I suck air into my lungs, and descend.

I can spare no thought for anything except the act of climbing—the burn of my arm muscles, the cold pressure of the rungs on my bare feet, the squeeze of the harness around my ribs, and above all, Kilmaya's limp weight, dragging my every movement off balance. She gasps at each jerking step, her arms locked around my chest. Her feet swing helplessly, knocking against my own legs or the ladder. I grit my teeth. Even though I tried to bind her injured foot, she still must be in intense pain.

Somehow, we reach the next platform. Immediately I collapse to the metal floor, and we both lie heaving for several minutes. The walkway is empty, but I can hear the echo of voices from below—Virik and the others have continued on.

I wish Kophas were here, or even Askko. Either of them could carry Kilmaya far more safely than I can. But Kophas is probably dead, and Askko is far away, fighting for the faction that destroyed his clan.

I haul myself upright. I pause for a minute to tear off a few strips of my tunic, with which I attempt to add more padding to the brutal harness. Then I crawl back to the ladder and grasp the rungs again.

Down and down we climb, between rattling pipes and whistling vents, through the buffeting air currents that blow hot or frigid by turns. I measure time in ladder rungs, and in the labored thudding of my own heart: *Grip and step. Grip and step.* I ignore the growing rawness of my hands and feet. Agony spasms through my shoulders. Whenever I put weight on my swollen right arm, I want to scream.

Every time we reach a platform, I grow more certain that I will not make it to the next one. But my body has become a slave to the taskmaster of my fear. At any moment, some guard or engineer might come clattering along the platform and spot us. So I drag myself onward. Kilmaya begs me to rest longer. I do not reply; I have no breath to waste on speaking.

We have descended several ladders when I find I cannot recall which level I am on, nor how many are left. An irrational terror takes hold of me. Perhaps they will never end. I have slipped into a nightmare Underbelly, which has no bottom at all—only an endless series of platforms, and between them, cold wind and empty space, yawning for me.

It would be so much easier to fall.

Where is the bottom?

Even the Deep Sleep's realm has a bottom—at least, Haza'ruux dreamed it did. The man in his vision only fell into the pit for a thousand days. *Grip and step. Grip and step.* Kilmaya has gone quiet, her arms hanging slack against my sides. Oh—but that man was me, wasn't he? Have I been on these ladders for a thousand days? I can't remember—can't recall much before this. Outside the bounds of my own racked body, the world has ceased to exist.

The harness strangles me; I cannot breathe anymore. Am I going to die? But maybe that will be all right. Haza'ruux will be there...and Kophas...and my family...

My foot hits something solid. It is not a rung, and it does not give the hollow rattle of a platform. My knees buckle, and my fingers release the ladder. I have just enough presence of mind to wrench myself sideways so that I do not land on Kilmaya. Then I crumple to the floor and lie there in a shuddering heap.

Kilmaya stirs. Her hands curl against my chest, and I feel her ribcage expand as she wheezes. I want to untie the harness, but my arms will not obey me.

Dimly, I become aware of people bending over me. Someone loosens the belts and gently pulls them away. I roll onto my stomach. Every part of my body throbs, or stings, or aches. Nausea sweeps over me; I convulse in a dry heave.

"Mariikel." Virik's whisper filters through my daze. "I think we've made it."

With an effort that dizzies me, I raise my head. Around us stand black alleys and dripping pillars. The rest of my clanmates are nearby. Many have simply collapsed on the floor, while others sit in a stupor of exhaustion. But they are alive. They are all alive.

"Where's Tyotik?" I rasp.

Almost before I finish speaking, the child appears at my side. Wordlessly, he curls up against me; he does not even whimper anymore. His slim little body feels cold.

For a moment I allow him to rest there, my mind blank except for an intoxicating sense of relief. With an agonized groan, I roll onto my side and push myself upright by sheer willpower. I cannot rest yet. Kilmaya is still injured; I need to see how badly. I do not want to stay in this open alley for long. Some of the outlaws here will prey on new exiles for clothing and supplies, and we are in no state to defend ourselves.

"Teacher…"

Kilmaya lies sprawled on the cold, filthy ground, heaving for breath. At my whisper, she turns her head a little. Our eyes meet. Her whole face contracts with a pained, almost wild expression, like a wounded animal.

"Don't move. You're hurt. Let me—"

I reach for her foot. But as I lean on my right arm, a queer, queasy feeling floods my body. My mind fogs, and my vision swarms with shadow, red deepening to black. My arm gives way; I lurch forward. I do not even feel myself hit the floor.

CHAPTER THIRTY-FIVE

I am lying on a massive table in a dim, low room. It is Haza'ruux's house, his studio, though the chamber seems cramped and dirty—not pristine like he always kept it—and the lights glow a dull red, like the lamps of the dreaming-room. On the ceiling, the sigil-paintings shift and rotate slowly, as if trying to resolve themselves into a single, sprawling, horrible sign. Watching it fills me with a visceral dread, but I cannot look away. My body aches all over. I am terribly thirsty.

I feel an agonizing certainty that something awful will happen when the symbols stop moving. Or perhaps the awful thing is happening already, and the sigils simply show the churning of fate. I have to get up—I need to warn my family. But I am too weak to even lift my head. And still the sigil-paintings shift, and spin, and melt into each other, until I feel ill watching.

There are people in the room with me. I recognize none of them; I cannot seem to focus on their faces. They mill and talk, oblivious to the spiraling horror overhead. Now and then, one approaches the table, picks up a tattooing pen, and writes something on my skin. I want to struggle, but I can neither move nor cry out. They are covering me with curses like the ones on the ceiling. Some of the faceless artists mark me in silence, while others laugh, talking to their companions in a gibberish I do not understand.

The low room presses in closer—the revolving sigils melt from the ceiling in thick, steaming drops. *Don't let it touch me. Out! Let me out!* But I am paralyzed on the table.

Now I drift into uneasy darkness, and now into another jumbled, nauseating dream. Sometimes I think I am in prison again, or lying on a cold, swaying platform, high above the Underbelly. But always, at the end, I find myself on the worktable in the mad markmaker's ruined house, watching the sigils spin. The dripping ink turns a deep violet color, flecked with gray globules. The walls look as if they are made of scorched muscle, fire-blasted flesh. I choke on the acrid stench.

Help me!

Then I notice another man in the room. He stands head and shoulders above the shadowy artists, and every mark on his body glimmers with light. He squints in irritation.

"What is this? What have you done to Haza'ruux's house now?"

I stare, open-mouthed. It is Haza'ruux himself. The room and the other people in it seem phantom-like in his presence. The walls morph back into ordinary panels, and the paintings on the ceiling stop moving.

Haza'ruux approaches the table. His chest is bare, gleaming with the great tattoo of the war-hound. But the radiance of his marks is gentler than I have seen it before: it ripples, not like fire, but like light playing through water. The old markmaker's face dances with awareness and humor. I have the strange sensation that he is too large for the room. He gazes down at me, shutting three eyes. "What are you doing here, Flashing Blade? There is work to do—much work, still."

They cursed me. Still I cannot speak. But he tilts his head, smiling.

"Curses? These marks?" With a callused hand, he touches my brow. His fingers feel rough and cool. "Poor ink, the lot of them. They will not set." He wipes his palm across my face. Ink comes off on his skin; he flicks it away as lightly as water.

At once I can breathe more easily. The ghost-artists have vanished, too; only Haza'ruux and I remain. We are still in his studio, but the room has changed again. It seems larger than I remember it, and airier—a fragrant breeze whispers against my face. The walls are translucent now, like windows; a swath of clear gold light streams in. At the edge of my awareness, I can hear water falling, far away. I sense, somehow, that beyond the walls of this room is a space larger and brighter and more open than any I have ever seen before. I gaze up at Haza'ruux, and a spark of memory flares in my mind.

"You're dead," I say slowly.

A crooked smile spreads across his face. "Says the man in Axdraa'dah. Have you marked the Deep Sleep yet, little skin-changer?" He laughs aloud, reveling in some joke that I cannot comprehend. "No, Haza'ruux is still running. He still smells the blood-trail—he must keep hunting." His marks flash briefly, and a manic light glitters in his eyes. "No rest, no rest for the Mad Dog. But the little chieftain, he may sleep for a while."

I breathe in the fresh, stirring aroma of the wind. "Can we stay here?"

"Here? Hakka. The Place of Dreams is only for Keepers. You would get lost." He strokes my forehead. "Haza'ruux must hide again—no safe place to dream on the old ships, now. He must go build a new house. Plant a new garden." Raising his head to the light spilling in through the walls, he fixes his gaze on some distant horizon. "Good soil on Kol'ihaz. Haza'ruux will go there. And you, Flashing Blade—" He peers down at me, grinning. "You will bring the children."

"I will?" I stare up into his face. All at once I feel like weeping. "Haza'ruux. Don't go."

He smiles again, draws a breath, and begins to sing a low, rhythmic tune. I feel I ought to understand the words, but they escape me, elusive half-memories. The room dissolves around us. His voice remains, rasping and distinct, even as the walls fade, breaking into a bright, cool mist that settles on my skin. Then the mad markmaker and his song are gone. Everything is gone. I drop into a soft surge of oblivion.

When I open my eyes, I am in a dark place, cramped and clammy. The close air smells foul, and I can hear something dripping. For a moment, I am afraid I have slipped back into my nightmare. "Haza'ruux?"

At my cry, someone stirs in the darkness beside me. A figure bends over me, blocking out the crooked sliver of light that filters through the low roof. A hand, a callused artist's hand, strokes my forehead. "Kesh, child," says Kilmaya.

Relief floods me, a palpable warmth in my body. Memory returns, too—wasn't Kilmaya injured? I carried her on my back. Down all those ladders… *Did I really do that?* I cannot imagine how. My limbs ache, especially my right arm. "Teacher?"

I cannot see her expression, but in the darkness she gives a gasp. "Oh, Ka." She grasps my face in both hands. "You're awake." Her tone is fervent—I wonder how long I have been asleep.

"Teacher. Where…?"

"How do you feel?" she demands.

I try to turn my head. I am lying on some kind of padding—a pile of rags, I think—beneath a heap of worn blankets. My tunic is gone; under the covers, my chest is bare. I can feel the faint tremor of the floor in my spine. Water drips nearby with a soft, metallic *plink*. Farther away, beyond the confines of the shelter, footsteps echo, and a baby wails.

I breathe the odor of the Underbelly deep into my lungs. Then I cough. "I'm…thirsty."

Kilmaya moves away for a moment. When she returns, she puts a hand under my head. "There isn't much. Someone went to get more."

My lips touch the edge of a flask, rough with rust. The water tastes bitter, full of grit. I can hardly swallow it. I break into another cough.

"I know," she says. "I'm sorry. I can't get it down, either."

She takes the flask away. I rest my head on the rags again. Even the small effort of drinking makes the darkness reel. "Where are we?"

"Mazatii's place." She finds my left hand and grasps it tightly. "Her people brought you here—after they found us."

Mazatii. Of course. The old healer used to bring people to me, when I came to give marks. A surge of gladness leaves me mute. We are among friends. I did not even have to seek them out—they rescued us instead. "Where are the others?"

"Kesh. They're all right. The exiles took them in."

"All of them?"

"All of them." Her voice catches slightly. "They are sharing their shelters and food...such as it is. Anything for the clan of Kaz'rethurax."

"Kaz...what?"

She laughs, but there is little mirth in the sound. "The honorable skin-changer. You didn't know? That's what they call you—your friends here." She says the word *friends* with a hint of acid. "How many, Mariikel? How many marks did you give down here?"

A dull pain seeps into my chest. "I don't know. I can't remember."

Her fingers loosen as if she means to pull her hand away. I hold onto her. "Teacher. It wasn't for money. I never took any."

"Oh, they told me *that*. One of your many virtues, it seems. I've been learning a lot about you, quiet one."

The name has a barb in it that I have never heard before. "You're angry."

"Angry? *Angry?* I am not even allowed to be angry. We're alive, aren't we?" But then she chokes off and bends over me, pressing her cheek to mine, crying. "You're alive," she says, over and over. "You're alive."

For a while neither of us speaks. When Kilmaya recovers, she sits up again and pulls the blankets closer around my neck. "Forgive me. You've done enough."

"Your foot," I murmur. "You fell."

"It's nothing. Well—it's broken. Mazatii put a splint on it."

The image of her face when I said I would carry her returns to me—her taut lips, bared teeth, and sunken eyes, smoldering with shame. We will never speak of it, that awful eternity of ladders and cold wind and swaying darkness—just as I will never tell her how I felt when I found her in her ruined home, alive. Some gratitude is too terrible for words.

"Have I been sick?"

"What do you think? You're not the only one. Anyone could take ill in this filthy place." She caresses my brow again. "But you didn't help matters, with your arm. It was all swollen up like a kharratyl bite. How in Ka's name did you manage to do that to yourself?"

I try to move my right arm. It lies by my side under the blankets and still throbs steadily. But the pain is duller than before—I can make a fist without a pang of agony.

"Mazatii wasn't sure she would be able to treat that wound. If her people hadn't gotten their hands on some proper injections…well." Her voice fails. "You were very sick, quiet one."

I wonder how many hours Kilmaya has spent at my side, nursing me in my delirium. And I wonder, too, how Mazatii managed to acquire an antiseptic strong enough to cure such a deep infection. I flex my fingers again and decide not to ask. Then a sudden worry seizes me. "Is the mark still there?"

"The mark?" She sounds surprised. "Oh—yes. It might look a bit mangled when it heals. But it's not coming off—not unless you take a knife to it."

I shiver weakly. "Good."

"Good? I thought you wanted it off."

"I thought I did, too. I didn't understand…what he was." A vision assails me—crystalline light, the smell of water, Haza'ruux bending over me, smiling. "I still don't understand."

A long silence falls. The floor rumbles, and far overhead a clatter of machinery echoes. Kilmaya sighs. "Ancestors help us. How many more of the old tales are true?" She strokes my hand again. "Virik told me about your family."

I am not prepared for the horrific onslaught of memories: the gaping bedroom door, the stillness, the reek of blood… *Nakki!*

I think I cry out because Kilmaya bends down, hushing me. "Kesh, now. Oh, my quiet one."

A wail rips from my throat. Kilmaya presses me to her chest, cradling me like a child. For a long time we hold each other in the darkness, until at last my sobs subside, and Kilmaya eases me back down on the blankets. "They are safe now," she murmurs. "They are at peace."

I do not answer. What does it mean for my loved ones to be at peace when their ashes will not rest with those of their ancestors? Our sector has been ransacked, our shrine most likely plundered and violated. We have no home now for either the living or the dead.

Clan Sko'larik fell, too. A soft voice speaks into the desolation of my mind. *And yet the Arimaas lives.*

I shiver under my blankets. Have our blood-kin in the Dream really granted our clan this terrifying gift? And if so, what are we meant to do about it? I have no idea. I only hope that there is a Long Dream, and that my family have passed into it—open and bright and warm, full of wind and running water.

Claim a home for us. I want to live by the ocean when I am old.

Kilmaya's fingers feel cold now. "How long will we have to stay here?"

"I don't know." As long as the Ascendance remains in power, we cannot return to the upper levels with our Serix marks. And I no longer have the materials I would need to create disguises or forge tattoos. We are stranded here.

From the opposite side of the shack, a faint whimper rises, then swells to a full-throated wail. Kilmaya shuffles across the low space. My eyes have adjusted enough to the darkness that I can just make out her shadow as she bends over another heap of rags. She picks up a small bundle, murmuring to it softly. At first, I think the child must be Tyotik. But the piercing screams belong to an infant no more than a few months old. After a minute, the baby quiets—not as if it has been soothed, but only as if it is too weak to cry for very long. Holding the tiny, fretting creature, Kilmaya limps back to me and sits down.

I blink, my mind still foggy. "There weren't any infants with us."

"He's the Penthar girl's child. I told her I'm useless with little ones, but I could hardly refuse to watch him. She needed the rest—she's been at your side almost as much as I have."

Something stirs in my memory, a wonder so strong it grips me like fear. "What girl?"

"The—oh. You wouldn't know, I suppose. She found us, after you collapsed. Kesh, now." She rocks the moaning infant. "She brought the healer, too."

Through the shelter's thin walls, footsteps and voices sound nearby. Part of the far wall, a curtain, folds back. A hunched figure steps in through the low door, carrying a lamp. The glow is feeble, but I still wince. Then a raspy female voice, like something out of a long-forgotten dream, says, "Hakka. Markmaker." And to Kilmaya, "Didn't I tell you the fever would break today?"

"So you did," says Kilmaya, subdued.

The old healer, Mazatii, crouches beside me and produces a small bottle. "Drink this. It's clean. Courtesy of the runners."

I drink. The water is cold, smooth, and tasteless. Vaguely I wonder what it took for her to acquire even a bottleful of properly filtered water. *The runners?* Does she have contacts among the clans to bring her supplies illegally? This water, and the medicine for my wound—how much have the exiles risked to nurse me back to health?

I turn my face away. "Let Kilmaya have some."

"You finish that," Kilmaya snaps.

Mazatii puts the bottle to my lips again, and I obey. When I finish, I exhale deeply. In the dim glow of the lamp, Mazatii smiles. "The boy is outside—the mute child. He has been very anxious to see you."

"The mute child?" I blink and struggle to push myself upright. "Tyotik?"

"Kesh." The healer puts a hand on my chest. But she turns her head towards the door and calls, "Let him in."

Tyotik enters, a slim dark streak. He has his arms around my neck before I can even speak. With my good arm, I cradle the back of his head. His breath pulses against my skin, moist and warm. Then all at once he sits up. With one slender finger, he touches my bare chest.

"Tyotik, what is it?"

He does not reply. Instead, he drags his finger in a jerking pattern on my skin—the same lines over and over, almost frantic. I close my fingers around the boy's hand. He trembles, pulls away, and traces the same pattern again, this time on my shoulder. And suddenly my mind makes sense of the lines. He is drawing the sigil for *sword*.

Or Blade.

"Tyotik." Something wrenches in my chest. "It's all right. You can speak to me. It's all right."

"I haven't heard him say anything since he came here." The healer glances over her shoulder towards the door. "Have you?"

"No, Mazatii."

A new voice—and yet familiar. Another woman stands in the entryway, watching me. I do not even have to see her marks to know her. Her eyes are enough—deep and burning and questioning, the same look she gave me when she held her sleeping son in her lap while I painted the fragile verity lines on his neck.

I move my lips. *Lakkia.* But I have no voice.

She bows her head. "Kaz'rethurax."

Don't call me that. But my tongue lies mute behind clenched teeth. I can remember the smoothness of her skin when I inked the child-mark on her shoulder, how she cursed me when I refused to take her son out of the Underbelly, how her eyes sparked with rage and shame—the same shame that burns my spirit now.

"There you are." Kilmaya gestures to Lakkia. "This is the girl you have to thank, Mariikel. She was the first to find us. And she knew you at once, too."

How? She never saw my face. Lakkia gazes at me, unblinking and unread-able. The thought of her bending over my fever-racked, naked body, washing my wounds, pierces me with humiliation. *I turned you away. Why are you here?*

Lakkia shifts warily and drops her eyes.

"Leave the food, Lakkia, and take the boy," says Mazatii. "Kaz'rethurax is hardly well yet."

Tyotik clings to me as the healer tries to pull him away. "He's all right. Let him stay." I say it partly for my own sake. His warm touch reminds me of the little plaza with the fountain, and Haza'ruux mumbling songs in his wild garden.

Mazatii relents without a word, then turns to Lakkia. The younger woman hands her a small bundle not much larger than her fist—the food that she worked or begged for, or perhaps even stole. I know I ought to thank her, but I cannot make myself speak. She steps over to Kilmaya. "I'll take him now," she says.

With visible relief, my teacher hands over the fretting baby. Lakkia settles the infant in the crook of one arm and turns to leave.

"What did you name him?" The words burst out of me.

Lakkia fixes her four eyes on me again. She cradles her son, and for an instant, a shy but luminous smile touches her face. "His name is Lironnak." Then she ducks out of the shelter and into the dim, thrumming alley.

Lironnak. Bright one.

Her face was so beautiful when she said her child's name.

CHAPTER THIRTY-SIX

Time passes strangely in the Underbelly. No change of lighting marks the days or nights—only an everlasting false twilight, filtering down through the soaring grid of pipes and walkways overhead. At all hours, vents roar and generators clatter, and one shift of exiles after another clambers up and down the spindly ladders. There is no distinction between these hours, as there is no distinction between the throbs of a heartbeat. More truly than any guild hall or council chamber, this place—this filthy, mired, unsleeping place—is the heart of our great ship.

This morning, or what counts as morning, I lie on the floor of our shelter, my thin blanket wrapped around my shoulders. Footsteps ring and shouts echo in the alleys outside. Far overheard, an alarm shrills, marking the end of the night shift.

Tyotik lies beside me, asleep, his rag of a blanket twisted around his lanky figure. The light through our curtained doorway just barely illuminates his slender features. His round, dark-skinned face is sharper now, and the hollows of his eyes have deepened. Two months of Underbelly rations have left him gaunt, even though I always give him at least half my share—sometimes more. Kilmaya chides me for that, though she does the same thing when she thinks I am not watching. She shares her food and water, too, with our clanmates who cannot work for their rations.

I reach out to pull a corner of the blanket over Tyotik's bony shoulder. The boy stirs, brow wrinkling in a fleeting frown. I hold my breath, not wanting to disturb him. Twice last night he woke in a terror, screaming in his dreams. He did not stop shrieking until I took him into my arms, where he clung to me for a long time while I traced invisible sigils of protection on his forehead. He has never told me what horrors stalk his nightmares, but I know the violence his child's eyes saw when Haza'ruux rescued him from the Ascendance soldiers. I only wish I could erase those images, as I once burned away tattoos. But removing memories—that is beyond my poor power.

315

I sit up and ease out from under my blanket. The dank, clammy air of the shelter envelops me. I shudder and pull on my hooded laborer's tunic. Then I crawl to the other end of the shelter to switch on our single lamp.

The dirty yellow glow illuminates a familiar space. Sheet metal walls, a slanted ceiling, a crooked shelf holding water flasks and meager bundles of rations: Kophas's old shelter. The space is cramped for three people—me, Tyotik, and Kilmaya—but I like to think Kophas would laugh, in his honest, impulsive way, if he knew he had given us not only his life but his home.

I kneel and push aside the pile of blankets that serves as Kilmaya's cot. Her shift at the infirmary starts a few hours earlier than mine, so she is always gone by the time I wake. Sometimes I wish she would not work such long and grueling hours—but I also treasure these moments of solitude before the day's labor. It is the only time I have now to pray.

From the lowest shelf, I pull out a long, slim object wrapped in rags. One by one I unbind the strips of cloth and let them fall to the floor, revealing Kilmaya's family funeral-blade. With my thumb I rub the cold steel, tracing the name-sigils etched in its gleaming surface. I balance the sword in my open palms like a fragile yet unbearable burden.

Flashing Blade.

My eyes drift to my own wrist, to the ornate tattoo peeking out from under my sleeve. The sigil poem has been marred a little, disfigured by the acid scar—a daily reminder of my own doubt and folly. Yet the mark's ancient beauty remains.

Haza'ruux. Mad Dog. Where are you now?

I have never told anyone of the radiant vision I had during my fever, nor have I seen Haza'ruux in my dreams since. But in my heart, I am convinced the mad markmaker truly spoke to me. I even cling to the hope that he escaped the ship. If he expects me to follow, to bring the clan to the planets—I have no idea where to start. But then, I did not believe him when he said I would be chieftain of Clan Serix.

A touch on my knee disturbs my brooding. Tyotik has crept up beside me, his blanket still draped around his shoulders. He presses his body against mine, huddling from the cold.

"Hakka." I set the sword back on the shelf and pull him close. "What are you doing, quiet one? Did I wake you?"

Tyotik reaches for my hand. With the tip of one finger, he sketches an invisible sigil in my open palm. *Blade.*

Tyotik has never spoken aloud since the massacre. I do not think his voice is injured—he still laughs and cries—but he refuses to communicate except through marks.

Serix. He traces another sigil in my hand. *Serix, hear.*

It is his term for the prayer that I say every morning, kneeling before the funeral-blade. "You want to say it with me?"

He blinks up into my face, eyes round and solemn. *For nakki.* He makes this request every day, but it still sends a pang through my body. I cannot bear to tell him that his mother might be dead. I prefer to hope, like Tyotik, that we will find her one day.

My fingers close around his slender hand. "Of course."

The boy snuggles against me, fingertip poised in my palm. I draw a long, shaky breath, and begin: "Serixan, ancestors, we call on you. By the bond of this clan-mark, hear us. Fill the blood of our hearts with strength..."

I speak each word with slow deliberation so that Tyotik can keep up. Every time he hears a word he knows how to write, he traces the sigil on my skin. We remember Tyotik's mother, and his warrior father, and my own parents, so many years deceased. We name Hakham and Chervani, asking for their peace in the Dream. And we entreat protection for all our Serix clanmates who did not escape with us, whose fate we do not know.

Askko's name always has a place in that last petition. What became of him when he learned of our clan's destruction? Did he remain a soldier of the Ascendance? Did he desert? Did the faction execute him simply for bearing the clan-mark? I may never know. But I pray that wherever he is, he has found an honorable path, fit for a true warrior.

At the usual close of the prayer, I take a breath to go on, adding a new ending to the invocation. "Sko'larikan, Keepers, we call on you. By the bond of our blood, hear us. Shield us with the strength of the Arimaas. Draw us out of the Place of No Dreams. Do not abandon us..."

I falter. In the quiet beyond the glow of our lamp, water drips and metal creaks in the shadows. I can hear the vast hiss and groan of the Underbelly far above us—like wind in the void, like the breath of the Deep Sleep.

"Do not abandon us," I whisper again. When I shut my eyes, I can recall Haza'ruux's marks radiating light, his face blazing with uncanny joy, with a terrible beauty.

Haza'ruux...I can't do this without you.

Tyotik stirs. He runs a hesitant finger across my palm. *Sad?*

"No." I smile softly and open my eyes. "Well—maybe a little."

The boy nestles under my arm. *Me too.*

We sit together in the quiet, watching the gleam of light on the funeral-blade, on the names of our kin.

After a breakfast of dried fruit and metallic-tasting water—the last of yesterday's rations—Tyotik and I make our way through the dim alleys to Virik's house.

The recordmaster and his wife and daughter live a few streets away, with a family of exiles who have fed and sheltered them since our escape. They watch Tyotik, too, when Kilmaya and I are both working at the infirmary. On the way there, the boy rides on my shoulders, clinging to my cloak with both hands. People smile as we pass, calling out to us from their low, shabby doorways.

"Greetings, Serix!"

"Hakka, Tyotik. How's the quiet one today?"

"Kaz'rethurax! Honor with you."

I return the well-wishes, though their title for me—honorable skin-changer—still mortifies me to no end. I have tried to explain that it is a meaningless word, a contradiction in terms. But I hear it so often that I have given up protesting.

At last, Tyotik and I reach a large, sprawling shelter with several connected rooms. The exile couple who own it have left already for their shifts at the recycling station. But I spot their two youngest children—a boy and a girl, a few years older than Tyotik—perched on the shelter's flat roof. Their ragged clothes hang loosely on their frames, and they survey the alley with a sharp and watchful air. But at the sight of me, both youngsters leap to their feet and clap their hands to their necks.

"Honor with you! Honor with you, markmaker!"

I smile. Unlike most people born in the Underbelly, these children have clan-marks: tattoos that I gave them back when I still served the outcasts with my pens and ink. They take unfeigned delight in the fact that they can greet me with a proper clan salute.

"Axiosan." I brush my fingers against my own neck and incline my head politely. "Honor with you both."

The children giggle, awed as usual at being addressed by a clan name. Then the boy recovers and waves a beckoning hand. "Hakka, Tyotik! Hurry up. We need another lookout."

I crouch and allow Tyotik to slide to the floor. The boy grasps my hand, signing a farewell sigil into my palm. Then, with an ease that still astonishes me, he scrambles up the slanting wall of the shelter to join his playmates on the rooftop.

A familiar ache settles in my chest. He looks like an exile's child now, with his grimy tunic and emaciated limbs. Would his poor Serix mother even recognize him? And yet he does not complain.

A shadow moves within the shelter doorway, and a ragged figure emerges into the alley. "Mariikel."

MARY JESSICA WOODS

"Virik." I dip my head. "Honor with you."

The recordmaster of Clan Serix leans against the rusting lintel, his hood pulled close for warmth. His face has changed, too, in the past months—it is not only gaunt with hunger, but also with exhaustion that leaves his gaze glassy and his dark skin sallow. Deep creases mar the corners of his eyes. "And with you." Briefly he raises a sleeve to his mouth to muffle a cough. Virik contracted a lung infection shortly after our escape to the Underbelly, and he has never fully recovered.

I glance past him into the empty shelter. "Where are Kandri and K'nima today?"

"Visiting clanmates." He wipes his mouth, grimacing. "Old Zirrok came down with sewer fever again. They went to share some of our water. Not that it will help much, but—" He breaks off as another deep, hacking cough shakes his chest. He turns away from me and wraps his arms around himself until the fit passes.

I place a steadying hand on his shoulder. "You don't sound so well yourself."

"It's no worse than yesterday."

"You've been saying that for weeks. I'll ask Mazatii if she has more medicine for you."

"Mazatii can't spare the supplies. You know that."

"I will ask," I repeat. "And if she has anything, you *will* accept it."

He leans against the doorframe, flicking a testy glance my way. "Is that an order?"

I smile faintly. "You may treat it as one."

"And I thought Mekkalluthak was a hard master to serve." Virik looses a bitter laugh. "He at least allowed a man to keep his pride."

"We're too poor for such luxuries now, I'm afraid." But I say it gently. The past two months have not been easy for him. Like most of our clanmates, he has not been able to work or earn rations since coming to the Underbelly. The combination of our Serix-made tattoos and our lack of exile-marks makes it too risky for us to join the labor crews, where the taskmasters might recognize us and turn us in to the Ascendance. Kilmaya and I were fortunate enough to take positions at Mazatii's infirmary, where the taskmasters hardly ever come. But Mazatii cannot employ everyone—so most of us, including Virik and his family, remain wholly dependent on the generosity of the exiles. It would be a difficult change for any man, but the recordmaster has taken it especially hard.

"Your family needs you well, Virik," I urge. "I need you well. And you will need your strength when you're able to start working."

"When." His eyelids droop. "Don't you mean *if?*"

319

I sigh through my nostrils. The only people nearby are the children play-ing on the shelter roof, but still, I lower my voice. "The runners will come through."

Virik grunts. "For medicines, maybe. But have these friends of Mazatii's ever smuggled markmaking supplies before? It's not so easy." He pauses and adds: "Though you'd know all about that, I suppose."

I curb another smile. "It's certainly easier when you're an artist. But I'm sure they will find a way."

He glowers as if the thought of anyone stealing from markmakers' studios, even for our own benefit, physically pains him. "Kin's heart. To think we have fallen so far that we *want* exile-marks. But if it means we can earn our own rations..." He meets my gaze, his face sunken with desperation. "This family... you know they are starving themselves to feed us."

"I know." It is the same for all the outcasts who have taken in my clan-mates. Their willing sacrifice of their hard-earned rations always takes my breath away.

"I can't bear doing nothing anymore." Virik's voice cracks. "I want to feed my own wife and child." He hides his face against the doorpost, and his whole body quivers with the fury of his grief. After a moment of hesitation, I steel myself and reach out. I place my palm on his neck, over the broad scar where his clan-mark used to be.

Virik stiffens. His eyes snap open, and he stares at me, teeth bared in a half-snarl. His pulse throbs under my hand.

"There's no shame in keeping your family alive."

His snarl gives way to a look of anguish. He bows his head, leaning into my hand. "Ancestors, Mariikel. How do you go on?"

Discreetly I release him and let my hand drop to my side. For a minute, as he recovers himself, I do not answer. Instead I tilt my head back and let my breath fog the air, inhaling the cold reek of machine oil and rust. From the rooftop, a giggling shriek rings out—Tyotik's laugh, the first noise he has made today.

"We have work to do yet, Virik." I smile in the dark, under the dripping beams. "That's all."

I quicken my steps towards the infirmary. My few minutes' conversation with the recordmaster has made me late for my shift. As I pass between the pillars that mark the entry to the sector, the shouts of harried workers, the clatter of equipment, and the hiss of steam from the washing station envelop me. Assistants hurry up and down the corridor, bearing armloads of rations or soiled bedding. The stench of disinfectant stings my nostrils, barely masking the pervading stink of refuse and blood.

I make my way towards the washing station. Lakkia is usually there; she has been training me as a healer's assistant. My days are full of ignominious tasks—cleaning filthy bandages, scrubbing floors, bringing food and water to patients too weak to feed themselves. Rixarii Street, with its embellished corridors and airy studios, has faded in my mind like a bright but distant dream. But I do not mind laboring beside these outcasts who used to come to me for marks—even Lakkia, with her critical eye and sharp words, quick to catch my clumsy mistakes. I am less lonely now, as an exile, than I ever was as a master artist.

Turning a corner, I spot another hooded worker staggering as she carries a heavy pail of water. I recognize the slim figure and limping gait at once. I rush to overtake her, then reach for the bucket handle and lift it out of her grasp.

"Let me take that, teacher."

"Great Ka!" Kilmaya starts away from me. In her surprise, she knocks the pail with her knee and sloshes hot water on the floor between us. Then she glares at me from under her ragged hood. "Don't scare me like that. You know I can't hear something as quiet as you in this deafening place."

"Forgive me." I smile and touch my brow in my old habit of apology. But I do not give her back the bucket. "What are you doing hauling water? You shouldn't be on your feet with this kind of load."

"Well, there were more rooms to clean than blankets to mend, that's all." Her nostrils flare in irritation, and she wipes her brow. A dark smear—muck or blood—sullies the artist's mastery-mark on her forehead. "They just finished a rather nasty amputation back here. Someone has to wash those floors."

I can see the fatigue in her eyes, under the veneer of annoyance. Even as she stands beside me, she eases her weight off her left foot. The broken bone has healed, but I know it still pains her sometimes, especially during her long shifts running errands throughout the infirmary.

"Let me help you, then."

"Oh, kesh." She steps around me, trying to reclaim the bucket. "You have your own work to do. Aren't you already late?"

I heft the water out of her reach. "Don't worry about that. It will be quicker with two of us, anyway. Lakkia will understand."

"I'm sure she will." Kilmaya squints in a cryptic expression. Without further protest, she turns and continues limping down the alley—but a little more easily, now that I am bearing her burden.

I remain by her side as we sluice down the frigid metal floor, scrubbing at the spatters of dirt and blood. Kilmaya does not speak much, but I notice the chapped skin of her hands, the exhausted flicker of her eyelids, the way her lips tighten in discomfort as she kneels… *She should not have to be here.*

My teacher loathes the infirmary work with every fiber of her artist's heart: the stench, the chaos, the unceasing sight of people wasting in pain and sickness. For my sake, I know, she tries not to complain. But the vacant misery in her eyes hurts me more than her nagging ever did.

We have nearly finished our chore when I hear footsteps drumming towards us. A shrill voice pierces the background clamor. "Kaz'rethurax!" A half-grown exile boy—a fellow infirmary assistant—skids to a halt in front of me, panting. "Thank the ancestors, you're here. A man's had a bad fall. You have to come."

I rise, still clutching a violet-stained rag. "Me?" I am not usually asked to assist with serious injuries. "What can I do?"

"He's paralyzed. Mazatii says he will die. And…" The young man gestures to his neck with a fearful grimace. "He has no marks."

A chill grips my spine. I knew this would happen—it was only a matter of time.

Beside me, Kilmaya climbs to her feet, then steps forward, as if to place herself between me and the distraught boy. "He has no pens or ink," she snaps. "Do you think he can conjure them up like a deepcrafter?"

"Teacher." I place a hand on her arm. "A blood-mark is permissible, in a case of life or death."

She bares her teeth. "Lecturing me on the law now, are you? It's a little late for that."

The words would have stung, once, but now I do not rise to the bait—instead I only press her wrist with gentle fingers. The young assistant glances between the two of us. "Please, markmaker."

"Tell them I'm coming."

The boy nods, gasps his gratitude, and dashes away. As he disappears down the alley, Kilmaya places both her hands on my shoulders. She bows her head, hiding her face against my chest. "Aren't you doing enough? What if the cut festers? You'll get sick again. This filthy place—" She chokes back a cry.

Oh, my teacher. How terrified she must have been, keeping vigil at my side for days while I lay in fever and delirium. I fold her in my arms, hold her quietly as she trembles. "If it were one of our own clanmates dying, would you tell me not to go?"

"No." Her fingers ball into fists, clutching my tunic. "Curse you. I don't know."

"Kesh." I exhale deeply, as though to calm her with my own breathing. "These are our people now, too."

She does not answer at first, but merely leans against me for a moment longer. Then at last, she steps back and lets her hands drop from my shoulders. "Hakk. Who am I fooling?" She offers a weary, bitter smile. "As if I have ever been able to keep *you* from doing what you've put your mind to. Go on, Kaz'rethurax."

I have no trouble finding the shack with the paralyzed man. I simply follow the sound of the screams.

I duck into one of the larger infirmary shelters—one that often serves as a surgery room—to find the space already crowded with people. Harsh lamplight glares down on the makeshift operating table, where a dark-skinned man lies on his back, stripped to the waist. I see with a pang that he is young still, a few years older than Askko, perhaps. He howls open-mouthed, like a stricken beast, so raw and shrill it makes my skin crawl.

Lakkia grasps the man's bandage-swathed head in both hands, holding it still. Mazatii leans over the table, feeding liquid into his mouth with a dropper. Behind them, half in shadow, two other exiles look on with agonized expressions. I guess they are the injured man's fellow laborers.

Mazatii glances up at my entrance. Relief floods the old healer's face. "Markmaker." She turns and hands the medicine bottle and dropper to one of the men behind her. "Give him the rest of this. It will help with the pain." Then she steps around the table and approaches me at the door. "Thank you for coming. He does not have much time left."

"What happened?" I murmur.

"He was repairing an elevator and his harness failed. He fell to the bottom of the shaft." Her lips curl in a snarl. "Deep Sleep take the equipment these poor men have to use. It is a wonder he lived long enough for them to bring him here."

My eyes linger on the wretched figure on the table. His screams subside to moans. Lakkia hushes him, coaxing him to keep his mouth open as his fellow laborer dribbles the painkiller onto his tongue. Lakkia's manner reminds me of the way she often soothes her own fretting child—gentle but unyielding, her voice both steely and tender.

Mazatti returns to the table. "Lakkia, bring clean water for the markmaker." She slips back into her usual blunt manner. "And a knife—something small, very sharp."

Lakkia dips her head in obedience and releases her hold on the injured man. Her gaze falls on me for an instant, and her smooth black brow wrinkles with a flicker of emotion—irritation? Concern? As usual, I cannot tell. Abruptly she hurries past me, out the shelter door.

I draw near the injured worker. As I place my hands on the edge of the table, an image flashes through my mind: another table, in another room, long ago. Talorak Tarriks, lying bound and sedated upon it. And me standing before him, paralyzed, about to give the mark of exile.

A groan from the dying laborer pulls me back to the present. When I glance down, I realize he is staring at me. "Are you..." His upper eyes flicker sporadically. He seems to have trouble forming words. "...a real markmaker?"

I shudder, banishing the darkness of memory, smiling through the old pain. "Yes. Yes, I am." I clasp the exile's limp, work-callused hand. "What is your name?"

He struggles for breath. "Brin—Brinnaro." Then he shuts his eyes again, exhausted.

I raise my head to address his two companions. "You know him?" I ask. "Do you know who either of his parents are? What their clans were?"

The two men share an uneasy glance. Finally, the older laborer sighs through his nostrils. "He's two generations unclanned, at least. Never knew his father. Says his mother never had a clan-mark, either." The man stares at the corner of the room, as if ashamed to be speaking these facts aloud, in my presence.

A pit opens in my belly. I bite back a curse of grief. *How many?* My hand tightens around Brinnaro's fingers. *How many have been born and died in this darkness?*

Lakkia reappears at my elbow. She holds a scalpel and a bucket of warm water that reeks of disinfectant. Wordless, she waits beside me for some signal. But I remain dazed, looking down at the markless exile who trembles in anguish before me.

What do I do?

I cannot give a true clan-mark if I do not know the man's ancestry. If I gain his consent, I can give him an adoption-mark instead, claiming him for Clan Serix—but while that might comfort his friends, it would not honor the life he has lived. He is a child of Underbelly. I do not want to pretend otherwise.

I glance round at the other people in the room. Everyone is waiting for me—I have to act. If only there were some other symbol I could use.

A clan-mark for the children of Axdraa'dah...

The younger of the two workers stirs and rubs the side of his neck. "Markmaker? Can you still help him?"

I stare at the worried laborer, transfixed. On his neck, just visible under the shadow of his hood, the exile-mark blooms like a bleak flower.

A strange, fierce wonder bubbles up in my chest. I could almost laugh.

I have been so blind.

"Yes." With shaking hands, I roll up the rough sleeves of my tunic. "I think I can."

Beside me, Lakkia holds out a rag soaked in steaming water and disinfectant. Does she resent standing here, like an apprentice, handing me tools? I do not know. She remains so reticent around me that I can never tell what she is thinking.

I squeeze water from the damp rag and wipe down both my forearms. As the grime lifts away, the sigil poem glimmers jewel-like on my skin, under the lamplight. One of the laborers mutters an exclamation of wonder.

I drop the rag back into the bucket. Still wordless, Lakkia offers me the scalpel. The tiny blade is about the same length and weight as a pen, but I cannot seem to handle it without fumbling. I lift my left arm and poise the knifetip against my own skin. On my right arm, the dense sigils of the mad markmaker's poem seem to shift and swirl before my eyes.

And he painted a sign in his own blood...

"Forgive me," I gasp to Lakkia. "My hands aren't very steady. Would you...?"

Her delicate nostrils flare. She stares at me, taken aback, the quiet pools of her eyes growing brighter and deeper. "Are you sure?" She sounds afraid.

"Yes." I slip the scalpel back into her grasp so that I cannot change my mind. "Please."

The tremor in her face stills into resolve. Silently, she grips the knife in one hand. With the other, she wraps her strong, slender fingers around my wrist. Her skin presses against my own, smooth and warm—like the night I first met her, when I traced a mark on her shoulder for her newborn child.

I shut my eyes and turn my face away. I barely feel the cut—a quick, razor thread of pain, and then the cool tickle of welling blood. Lakkia releases my wrist. I open my eyes. A glimmering streak of dark purple already trails down my arm.

Rich, burning violet running down the skin...

I swallow the urge to weep. But I feel light and whole now, suffused with a strange warmth. A hush falls over the room; even Brinnaro lies quiet, his battered chest rising and falling in uneven breaths. I dip my finger in the thin stream of blood.

"Brinnaro, son of the Underbelly." I touch my fingertip to his neck, tracing the first curving stroke. "You have been born into the keeping of the Deep Sleep. By this blood-mark, I break the bonds. I claim you..." My voice gives out for a moment. I tremble at the words leaving my own lips. "I claim you with the sign of the Keepers for the clan of the Arimaas."

Mazatii draws in a breath; the laborers stir and murmur, confused. Undaunted, I dab more blood on my finger and continue sketching the mark.

The pattern gleams, lurid and barely visible against Brinnaro's dark skin. It is not quite the exile-mark, nor the ancient symbol of the Keepers. It is something between the two, something new.

"Let this mark be for your pondering and striving." I linger over the old, familiar cadence, savoring the words. "Let it guide your thinking and your walking. Let it be your pride when you are strong, and your chiding when you waver..."

Under my touch, Brinnaro quivers. His mouth gapes wide, and a deep sob racks his broken body. One of his friends reaches out and takes his hand.

"This is a mark of truth." I finish the final flourish and let my arm drop to my side. "May you never dishonor it."

Brinnaro's cries fade to feeble gasps. But he smiles in his agony, trying to turn his head towards his two companions—his clanmates. The younger man bends over him, gripping his arm in a brotherly clasp. The older laborer sends me a look brimming with silent gratitude.

I blink in acknowledgement and stumble back from the table; I hardly know what I have just done. Mazatii stares at me as well. The old healer's brow furrows, but her lips turn upwards in a fierce, almost unsettling joy. And Lakkia—Lakkia takes my wrist, wiping away the blood that still drips unheeded down my arm.

For a minute, I stand mute, letting her bind up the scratch. I am keenly aware of her every touch—aware and afraid, as if her fingers might prick my skin more deeply than any blade. But I do not resist as she ties off the bandage—and, after an instant's hesitation, cradles my quaking palms in her own.

"Thank you, markmaker."

At her whisper, I dare to look up. She is smiling, too, her face alive with that rare, luminous expression I have seen only once before. And all her eyes are shining.

ACKNOWLEDGMENTS

This book owes its existence, first and foremost, to my friend and creative collaborator Donan Scholl. During our time as classmates at Wyoming Catholic College, Donan created a tabletop role-playing game called Watchpoint: a sci-fi/fantasy adventure full of space battles, ancient mysteries, and quirky, lovable characters. I was fortunate to be a player in this game, and I was so taken with the world that I began writing my own stories set in the Watchpoint universe. One of these stories—a strangely introspective tale about an alien tattoo artist—took on a life of its own and eventually became this book.

So thank you, Donan, for letting me build castles in your sandbox. Thank you for indulging my endless worldbuilding questions about everything from Noxxiin governmental structure to the effects of kharraktyl venom. Thank you for letting me borrow Haza'ruux "Mad Dog" Serix, who was just as weird and wonderful in your RPG as he is in this story. And thank you for bringing Mariikel so gorgeously to life in the cover art. This book owes you more than I can say. May it be only the first of many Watchpoint adventures.

My gratitude also goes to the numerous friends who read early drafts and cheered me along the way. To Emma Jermann and Brandon Seedorf, for the brainstorming sessions, camaraderie, and endless encouragement. To Anna Eby, Emily Felsheim, Audrey Patton, Anthony Isaac Reynolds, Olivia Seedorf, MaryAnne Spiess, and William Stivers, for your gracious feedback and enthusiasm. And to my college professors Dr. Jeremy Holmes and Dr. Glenn Arbery, who assured me that a classically educated liberal arts graduate need not be ashamed of writing about alien tattoo artists.

A special thanks to the Catholic Writers Guild Science Fiction and Fantasy Critique Group, especially to my beta readers Karina Fabian, Matthew P. Schmidt, Jackson Hayes, and Gail Finke. You all have made me a better writer and critique partner, and I'm eternally grateful.

My next shout-out belongs to the wildly talented team at Chrism Press. To my editor Karen Ullo, for seeing the potential in this story, and for working your editorial magic on every level of it, from worldbuilding to plot to prose. To Rhonda Ortiz, for your marketing advice and assistance, and for lending a listening ear when I was groping through the darkest and most agonizing stage of the revision process. To David and Roseanna White of WhiteFire Publishing: thank you for making it possible for Chrism to exist (and additional thanks to Roseanna for the stunning cover design). To my friend and copy editor, Rebecca Martin, for dealing with all my alien words—and for suggesting that I attend the 2019 Catholic Writers Guild conference where I first met Karen Ullo. This book might have stayed in the metaphorical desk drawer for a long time if not for the connections I made at that conference.

Finally, my unending gratitude to my parents, Timothy and Jennifer Woods, and to my siblings David, Christopher, Catherine, and Gregory. Thank you for being my first readers, brainstorming partners, and unabashed fans—and, frankly, for putting up with three years of writerly melodrama as I slaved over this project. You never let me give up on this story or on myself. I love you all. As the Noxxiin would say: Honor with you!

THE NOXXIIN CLANS

The Noxxiin Fleet is home to dozens of clans. The following list includes only the clan names that appear in the story of Markmaker. *The suffix -an or -in, when added to a clan name, indicates clan membership or the collective members or ancestors of that clan.*

Axios: Low-ranking manufacturers and construction workers.

Gabronik: High-ranking engineers and skilled technicians.

Penthar: Low-ranking farmers, livestock tenders, and food production workers.

Serix: High-ranking markmakers, inkmakers, and record-keepers.

Sko'larik: Ancient, legendary markmakers and warriors who bore the tattoos of the Arimaas.

Tarriks: High-ranking warriors, military commanders, and weapon manufacturers.

Tekkal: Mid-ranking pilots and navigators.

Tizzan: Low-ranking mechanics and maintenance workers.

Trechik: Mid-ranking warriors, security guards, and weapon manufacturers.

Trev'ban: Mid-ranking markmakers, inkmakers, and record-keepers.

T'sarek: High-ranking deepcrafters, warriors, engineers, and healers.

THE NOXXIIN LANGUAGE

Akk'aal: the eighth month of the Noxxiin calendar.

akkano: ancestor.

Akkano'dath: the flagship of the Noxxiin Fleet. The meaning of the name is debated; it translates to either "will of the ancestors" or "peril of the ancestors."

alkani: a potent spice used in many Noxxiin dishes.

ariik: courage.

Arik'nae: one of the three ancient alien races that once inhabited the Arovaan system and made war on the Noxxiin home planets. Little is known about them, and they are apparently extinct. (See also *Peshyakin, Syr*).

arimaa'rix: the legendary marks of the Arimaas, mystical animal tattoos that give the wearer supernatural powers in battle.

Arimaas: a legendary source of supernatural power guarded by an order of markmaker-warriors, the Keepers of Clan Sko'larik.

Arovaan: the ancestral planetary system of the Noxxiin race.

Arroqi: a small handgun commonly carried by Ascendance warriors.

axariix: coward

Axdraa'dah: the Place of No Dreams. In Noxxiin religious beliefs, this is the realm where the dishonorable dwell after death, cut off from their ancestors. It is ruled by the Deep Sleep, the Noxxiin personification of death.

axkolar: a battle or conflict in which the enemy was not a worthy opponent, according to the traditional tenets of the combat-code.

axnakk: a person born outside a lawful marriage; bastard.

burrik: a large carnivore with powerful taloned feet, four horns, four eyes, and brindled black-and-gray fur.

c'aani: a large herbivore with small limbs and broad, membranous wings. Native to the Arovaan system, but almost extinct on the Fleet.

chalka: a tough, leafy green vegetable.

chi'ar: first, rising, prominent.

Chi'arii: the Ascendance. The current dominant political faction of the Noxxiin Fleet, dedicated to retaking the ancestral planets by force.

dakali: daughter.

dako: son.

dalrikhani: a large dog bred to accompany warriors in hunts or battles.

dath: will, intention, purpose.

Dawravanii: the Noxxiin festival celebrating the new year.

dek'ar: second; the ordinal number two.

dethra: worthy weapon. One of the three tenets of the traditional combat-code, this rule states that the weapons and tactics used against an enemy must be fair, honorable, and not unnecessarily cruel or destructive. (See also *kolar, piitro*).

Devorak: a legendary cult of savage warriors who bore magical animal tattoos and ate the flesh of their fellow Noxxiin.

Draal'jian: the Long Dream. The Noxxiin concept of the afterlife, where the honorable dead go to dwell with their ancestors.

Draalyariik: a former ship of the Noxxiin Fleet, destroyed in the year 336 of the Wandering, famed for its extensive library of books and artifacts from the ancestral planets. The name translates to "dream of courage."

ech'taani: a small, ferret-like creature with pale fur.

grekyaa: a special oil used in the mark-erasing process, which breaks down the sealing-glaze that protects the tattoo.

hakk/hakka: an exclamation. Can indicate surprise, amusement, anger, and other emotions, depending on context.

harraktii: a lizard-like creature with six legs (archaic; see *kharraktyl*).

hazari-ruux: mad dog (archaic).

hvoss'ka: a rank in the Noxxiin military. Indicates an elite warrior who has acquired a high level of combat skill. Typically commands a small contingent of soldiers.

ji-nakki: grandmother.

ji-nakko: grandfather.

Ka: the creator deity in traditional Noxxiin religious belief. Also known as the All-Watcher.

Kaichilaal: the tenth month of the Noxxiin calendar.

kalimaa: a traditional Noxxiin war cry.

karu: a large tree with reddish-brown bark and broad leaves. The wood is used to make coins and other luxury items on the Fleet.

kazen: honor.

kaz'rethurax: honorable skin-changer.

kaz'valiim: honor with you. An expression of courtesy, used as both a greeting and a farewell.

kell-kantajiin: a type of sword (archaic).

kesh: hush; be quiet.

kharraktyl: a lizard-like creature with six legs and venomous teeth. The less dangerous species are sometimes kept as pets.

kiili: a fragrant cosmetic oil used by both male and female Noxxiin to burnish the skin and enhance the color of tattoos.

klasindi: a tea-like beverage made by steeping the seedpods of the klasindi plant in hot water.

kodath: danger, peril.

kolar: worthy opponent. One of the three tenets of the traditional combat-code, this rule states that the enemy must be of equal or greater military strength in order for the conflict to be considered honorable. (See also *dethra*, *piitro*).

kol-dawra: a traditional Noxxiin liquor.

Kol'ihaz: a planet in the Arovaan system. Has a warm, tropical climate and is covered mostly by ocean, with many large islands and archipelagoes.

kriar: a rare tree with fragrant white bark and pale leaves, the oil of which is said to have healing properties.

liir: light, brightness.

lirii'hir: sunlight (archaic).

mahak: to strike or hit (archaic).

Maha'lirii'kell: an archaic version of the name Mariikel. Translates roughly to "sunlight flashing on the warrior's blade."

nakki: mother.

nakko: father.

na'thalo: uncle.

Noxxiin Aurorii: Children of the Stars. The traditional full title of the Noxxiin race.

os'tekta: the main unit of Noxxiin currency.

Peshyakin: half-sighted. The Noxxiin term for the two-eyed alien race that inhabits the Arovaan system. One of the three races that made war on the Noxxiin home planets. (See also *Arik'nae*, *Syr*).

Peth'aal: the fifth month of the Noxxiin calendar.

piitro: worthy cause. One of the three tenets of the traditional combat-code, this rule states that a battle must be fought for a just and honorable reason. (See also *dethra*, *kolar*).

raith'aal: a traditional Noxxiin reed instrument with a harsh, piercing tone quality.

rethurax: skin-changer. A criminal tattoo artist who makes false marks or erases true ones.

rix: mark, tattoo.

rixar: markmaker, tattoo artist.

rixar'azahl: mad markmaker. A term for the order of hermit-artists protected by Clan Serix.

Syr: one of the three ancient alien races that once inhabited the Arovaan system and made war on the Noxxiin home planets. Known for their extremely advanced technology. Apparently extinct. (See also *Arik'nae*, *Peshyakin*).

tavla: a livestock animal raised for meat.

thuriiklesh: skin-eater. A special acid used to remove tattoos by burning away the top layers of skin.

trallak: a tree with black bark and violet-black, triple-lobed leaves. The bark and sap are used to make tattoo ink.

t'vanasyra: deepcraft (archaic; see *van'shorakk*).

tyal'shivii: arrowhawk; a large predatory bird (archaic).

val: to, with.

valk'taro: a high rank in the Noxxiin military. Commander of a warband.

valkya: battle-brother. A term of friendship used between warriors who have been through combat together.

van'shor (fem. van'shir): deepcrafter. A person who has a special technological implant, known as a bond, that allows the bearer to mentally manipulate matter and energy.

van'shorakk: deepcraft. A technology that allows the mental manipulation of matter and energy. Has a wide variety of applications in military, engineering, and medical fields. The deepcraft implant, or bond, requires the user to possess certain genetic traits in order to wield the power safely and effectively.

Van'shorii: the Noxxiin order of deepcrafters. Members may train as warriors, healers, or engineers, depending on their specialty. They also serve a quasi-religious role, especially at funerals; they are in charge of cremating the bodies of the dead.

Van'shorvanii: an important Noxxiin festival, commemorating the victory of the deepcrafters over the ancient, legendary cult of the Devorak.

yekri: a shrub bearing small, tart berries, which are eaten fresh or dried, or used to make a beverage.

CPSIA information can be obtained
at www.ICGtesting.com
Printed in the USA
LVHW092054210323
742163LV00004B/541

9 781941 720950